deal
with the
dead

also by

Les Standiford

Spill

Done Deal

Raw Deal

Deal to Die For

Deal on Ice

Presidential Deal

Black Mountain

Miami News December 4, 1960

Quicksilver Cay, October 12, 1952

The bastards got lucky

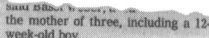

said Baker Thomas, who was the mother of three, including a 12-week-old boy.

deal
with the
dead

Les Standiford

G. P. Putnam's Sons   New York

G. P. Putnam's Sons
Publishers Since 1838
a member of
Penguin Putnam Inc.
375 Hudson Street
New York, NY 10014

Library of Congress Cataloging-in-Publication Data

Standiford, Les.
Deal with the dead : a novel / Les Standiford.
p.   cm.
ISBN 0-399-14704-7
1. Deal, John (Fictitious character)—Fiction.   2. Contractors—Fiction.
3. Florida—Fiction.   I. Title.
PS3569.T331528 D45   2001   00-055938
813'.54—dc21

Printed in the United States of America

1   3   5   7   9   10   8   6   4   2

This book is printed on acid-free paper. ∞

BOOK DESIGN BY LYNNE AMFT

Though I love South Florida just as it really and truly is,
this is a work of fiction and I have taken certain liberties
with geography and place names.
May they please the innocent and the guilty alike.

Deal and I would like to thank Captain Robin Smith,
Bill "Eagle Eye" Beesting, Rhoda Kurzweil, and Jimbo Hall for all
their help in the preparation of this book.

This book is dedicated to my father,
Ross Alan Standiford.
You go, Pee-Wee.

And let's not forget that first, wonderfully
generous Guernsey County librarian,
Ms. Helen Sunnafrank,
who opened the doors to adventure.

Reserving judgments is a matter of infinite hope.

—F. SCOTT FITZGERALD, *The Great Gatsby*

deal

with the

dead

prologue

DRACKEN LEANED ON HIS forearms, staring out over the rail of the *Polynesia* as a dark sedan approached on the dock below, its yellow headlights winding crazily through the maze of stacked cargo, crated machine parts, boats in dry dock, mounded lobster traps—all the who-knows-what of an aging, deserted boatyard jammed along the waterside beneath him. He liked this view, the sense of security it gave him—being the only Indian in the fort, as it were—watching Mr. High-and-Mighty Rhodes having to work his way through the mess to find Butch Dracken.

He smiled at the thought and reached to toss away the cigarette he'd been smoking. The butt twirled lazily down the wedge of cool night air separating Grant Rhodes's refitted gambling ship from the dockside where she'd been impounded by Dracken's boss—who happened, these days, to be the sheriff of Palm Beach County.

Dracken, of course, had lived other lives, as had the ship he now stood upon. He'd been a merchant sailor for a time, and while he had never served in that capacity on this vessel, the *Polynesia* herself had once had a German name and a tramp steamer's existence: loading coal in Norfolk, to be traded for Norwegian ore in Bergen, that given over for fish oil in Kobe, across to the States again, grain on the West Coast, through the Canal and back up for the coal on the East Coast, around and around we go, until the ship had gotten too small to be profitable.

Dracken knew about nautical matters, sure enough, and his familiarity led naturally to such assignments as this: "Go sit on that frigging boat, Dracken."

Though the truth was that Dracken had come to detest boats and everything about them. What had once seemed exotic and enticing in his youth now struck him as troublesome and doomed to disappoint. What he had set his sights on these days had a lot to do with staying in one place.

Just like Grant Rhodes had picked the *Polynesia* out of the scrap yard and given her a second life, that's what Dracken had in mind. A little horse farm up around Ocala, maybe, a place in the center of Florida that was as far from the water and the snowbirds as it was possible to get and still stay warm most of the year. He would like that, he nodded. All he needed was a stake, and his association with Grant Rhodes was about to provide him with that.

What was left of the cigarette struck the side of the canvas-sided companionway and burst in a shower of sparks above the oily water. Fireworks, Dracken thought, as the sedan pulled up to the dockside below. Fireworks was one bit of liveliness he could still abide.

"Mr. Dracken." Rhodes's voice rose through the cool air and up the gangplank toward him.

"I'd pipe you aboard, Lucky," Dracken called down, "but my pipin' whistle's broke."

Rhodes gave him a tolerant smile as he stepped onto the deck. Dracken knew Rhodes didn't especially favor the nickname, but circumstances being what they were, what did it matter?

"All the others are gone, then, are they?" Rhodes asked.

Dracken nodded. There'd been three of them assigned to the *Polynesia*: himself and two deputies who Dracken had known would be easy to get rid of. *Whyn't you boys take the rest of the evening off? You can return the favor another night.* Their heels had cleared dockside before he'd even finished his sentence.

"Just us chickens," Dracken said, waving toward the empty decks.

Rhodes gave a sign to the driver who'd accompanied him onto the ship, and the big man walked to the stern of the *Polynesia*. The big man—

some kind of Samoan, he looked like—produced a six-cell flashlight from under his coat and snapped it on. Dracken saw the powerful beam shoot out into the dark harbor. The light blinked a few times and then went out. Soon after, he heard the distant rumble of diesel engines start up.

The big Samoan moved away from the taffrail and came back toward them with his light tucked under his arm. "Go on, now, Julian," Rhodes said. The big man gave his boss a questioning glance, but Rhodes motioned him on toward the gangway. "I'll leave in the small boat along with the others," he said. The big man shrugged and went back down the steps.

Dracken walked to the opposite rail, where one of the *Polynesia's* searchlights was mounted, and snapped it on. He ran the bright spot over the surrounding waters until he found the approaching vessel, a medium-sized cabin cruiser that had already cut its engines and was swinging about parallel to his own. *Miss Miami Priss* was the name painted in gold and black across the stern. Dracken turned to Rhodes.

"Must be a comedown for you, riding a stinkpot like that," he said.

Rhodes regarded him neutrally. "It's Barton Deal's boat, in fact."

"Your builder friend?" Dracken glanced down at the idling cabin cruiser. "This ain't amateur night, for chrissakes—"

"Relax, Dracken," Rhodes said. "I borrowed the boat. It's just my men down there."

Dracken nodded, somewhat reassured. Finally, he snapped off the searchlight beam.

"How much time do we have?" Rhodes asked. The engines of the *Priss* had died away beneath them, leaving the slop of waves against the *Polynesia's* hull.

"Long as you need," Dracken said, glancing at his watch. "The Feds are supposed to take over tomorrow about nine, sheriff says."

"We'll be finished long before that," Rhodes assured him.

You bet your life you will, Dracken nearly said, but managed to hold his tongue.

It all took until just after midnight, as it turned out. First, there was the tying off of the *Miss Miami Priss* and the boarding of the two men of

Rhodes's who piloted her, along with their heavy equipment, a process made all the more difficult by the fact that it had been a while since the *Polynesia*'s cargo boom and winch had been pressed into service.

Then, after Dracken had discovered that they'd be working below-decks in the forepeak, there had been a bit of a problem starting the generator that fed power to that seldom-used section of the ship. Finally, they were in readiness though, the four of them moving down a stuffy passageway, Rhodes leading the way, followed by Dracken and the two uncommunicative assistants, dragging their welder's torches and tanks on dollies.

"In here," Rhodes said finally, stopping to gesture at a bulkhead door.

Dracken stopped and glanced at the watertight door, then at the water-streaked ceiling above. They were under the *Polynesia*'s forward decks, he calculated, right about where the forecastle hatch would be. All of his assumptions had proven right so far.

He leaned into the heavy wheel handle until it gave, then cranked it open, loosing an ancient smell of fish parts mixed with crushed coal and ocean damp into the narrow passage. He found the lights and switched them on, then stood aside as Rhodes joined him in a spacious, empty compartment.

Dracken glanced up at the hatchway set in the high ceiling above them, then around at the blank walls as the two helpers dragged their torches inside. "Who would ever know?" he said to Rhodes, by way of compliment. Not himself, that much was certain. He'd already combed the ship from stem to stern. No other way to find what he was after than this, not in the little bit of time there was left.

Rhodes gave him a nod of acknowledgment. He walked to the blank wall opposite and reached to a riveted strip that seemed to join two steel sections of bulkhead. The strip flipped up at Rhodes's touch, becoming a handle that he used to slide the hidden panel back.

There it was, Dracken saw, set solidly into the real wall of the bulkhead, the ship's safe, the thing he'd been searching for from the very moment that Rhodes had called about the job. Rhodes's treasure trove. The mother lode. Dracken's stake.

"Who would've thought?" Dracken repeated.

"Isn't that the point?" Rhodes said, and something in his tone dug at Dracken, though he could afford to disregard it now.

The two of them stepped aside as the cylinders were set up, the torches were arranged and popped into life. The assistants—one a cadaverous rail-thin man, the other a stocky sort who looked fresh off the farm—donned their heavy masks and set to work cutting the safe out of the wall.

"Couldn't you just open the damn thing right here?" Dracken said to Rhodes at one point.

"It doesn't suit my plans," Rhodes told him. That same you-don't-understand-shit tone in his voice. But Dracken simply nodded.

"You're the boss," he said.

Rhodes nodded and moved forward to say something to the tall man, who'd paused to flip up his mask and wipe sweat from his streaming face.

Now, thought Dracken. Who backed swiftly out the bulkhead door and slammed it closed behind him. He set the outer lock in place, then hurried off down the hallway and made his way through the twisting passageways to the midships cabin where he'd stashed what he needed.

He selected the department-issue Remington pump and his own Browning automatic, a weapon he favored for use in hunting deer. His friends liked to shoot deer and eat them. Dracken preferred to vaporize them. He'd even taken the BAR along on a fishing trip to the Keys once, had used it to bag—if that was the right word—a tarpon rolling a few feet off the end of a dock where they'd put up. Cornered deer and rolling tarpon, three men-fish in a bulkhead barrel, it was all the same to him.

Dracken draped a loaded belt of shells for the Remington over his shoulder—double-oh buckshot—then picked up two extra magazines for the Browning. He was moving quickly, but not carelessly. The three men he'd left behind might manage to cut their way through the bulkhead, given a few hours, but no way they'd be able to manage in the little time they had. He thought about taking along the .45 he usually carried in his duty belt, but decided against it. If he couldn't finish three trapped men with the two weapons he was carrying, then he ought to turn in his spurs.

He made his way up the crew ladder to the foredeck, his weapons cradled in one arm, stopping below the bridge to make sure all was quiet up top. Sure enough, the car that Rhodes had come in was gone, the boatyard back to its graveyard quiet, the surrounding backwaters empty. To the north, the distant lights of West Palm Beach sent a soft boreal glow into the sky, and to the east, a mile or so across the broad intracoastal channel, he saw a few winking lights from the place where the millionaires gathered.

Most of them were greedy, cutthroat robber barons, Dracken thought, and the realization gave him fresh resolve. He was not greedy—he aspired to no mansion nor to any exalted status in this life—and he was not so much a robber as a man who was about to relieve a true robber—gambling man Rhodes—of his burden.

Dracken smiled and moved quickly over the foredeck to the hatch cover he'd been looking up at just a few minutes before. No need to go to the trouble of moving the whole cumbersome thing. There were a couple of ventilation ports the size of bathroom windows he could open and use, and that would provide better cover anyway . . . just in case someone had been carrying a pistol he hadn't spotted.

He bent down and removed the pin from one of the covers and flipped it back, careful to stay out of the line of fire. But there was nothing but silence from down below, that and one thin beam of light arrowed up into the night above the tethered ship. He got on his knees and shouldered the BAR. He edged carefully toward the opening—just far enough to get a quick peek, now—then stopped.

Why would they be dumb enough to leave the lights on? he asked himself. He edged a little closer toward the open hatch and thrust his head up and back, quick as a mongoose strike, just enough time to see, just enough for a glance that chilled him. Two tanks, two idle torches, one closed door, and no men anywhere . . .

How could that be . . . , he was thinking, and was about to move forward for another quick glance, just to be sure . . .

. . . when the heavy flashlight barrel hooked under his chin at the same instant that something—a knee as heavy as a cypress trunk—struck him in the small of his back. Dracken arched up in reflex, a movement that only made the job in progress that much easier. He caught sight of the Samoan's face, heard the sharp snap echo off the bulwarks on either side of him. He realized, at the same instant that everything went numb: It was the sound of his own spine breaking that he'd heard.

Deal with the Dead

He willed himself to squeeze the trigger of the Browning, even though he had no idea where his aim might lie. The important thing was to go down fighting, he told himself. Die, but take the bastards with you.

He squeezed and squeezed again, or thought he had . . . but there was only silence in response. And soon there was the darkness, too.

one

"FLAMETHROWER—!"

The amplified voice, accentless, ahuman, rolled from the many banks of speakers stationed around the darkened open-air arena, washing over the crowd like a pronouncement of the gods.

The darkness, as well as the answering murmur from the crowd—noise enough to precede a rock star's entrance onto stage—made convenient cover for Halliday and his men. In such a melee as this, the three had approached the makeshift viewing stand without incident, had dealt efficiently with the guards at the bottom of the tucked-away steps, had made their way up before either of the men on the platform had noticed.

By now, Halliday and his companions sported all the proper passes, each in its little plastic pouch, each dangling from its own springy lanyard. The mustachioed Turk stationed near the top of the steps examined their credentials by the wavering glow of outdoor torches ringing the platform, then gave a respectful nod to what he had certified was a media entourage, stepping back to allow the three of them on board.

Ferol Babescu, a fabled international broker who had dealt in every illicit item to cross the black market since Mussolini came seeking arms, was sitting forward on the platform, ensconced by himself in a wicker sultan's chair that seemed to shudder under the man's great weight. Or perhaps it was just the growing roar of the crowd that vibrated the stand.

Halliday ignored the sounds behind him, the soft scuffing of the Turkish guard's sneakers as he left the platform. He stared out in the direction of Babescu's transfixed gaze—the fat man still unaware—and shook his head at the sight. Something significant seemed to have happened to the world during the time he'd been away, and Halliday was not sure if he understood quite all of it. He had come here for one simple reason, but there had been certain delays, hadn't there, and now Babescu's lunatic "festival"—some kind of Woodstock for the new millennium, if Halliday understood properly—was already under way.

Certain things would have to wait. And he *could* wait, Halliday thought as he surveyed the restless throng below. Waiting was one thing he had managed to learn in his time on the run.

"Quite the turnout, Babescu," Halliday said at last.

The big man started, his expression reflecting annoyance as he turned to see who had crashed the party. "We need quiet here—" he began, as his gaze traveled to Halliday's press credentials.

"Not much of a greeting for an old ward," Halliday said.

Babescu hesitated, then peered more intently through the flickering torchlight. There came a slight parting of his lips as the truth sank in. By the time he had maneuvered his bulk up and out of the chair, his astonishment had overtaken all.

"Halliday . . . ," Babescu said.

Halliday held a finger to his lips. "Halliday's no more."

"It *is* you, isn't it," the big man said, shaking his head in wonder. He paused, and a great smile spread across his features. "I knew it all along, of course. I knew you hadn't died . . ."

Halliday gave him something of a smile in return. He'd read many of the headlines himself. "Indicted Bond Trader Drowns in Mediterranean." "Thief Overboard." "Halliday Dies on Holiday." So clever, the international press.

Babescu was staring at him, his native conman's admiration slowly replacing his surprise. After a moment, he cut a glance toward the back of the stage. Wondering what had happened to his bodyguard, Halliday supposed. Wondering who Frank and Basil Wheatley were, moreover. Bulky, great-bellied Basil, and his chiseled bodybuilder brother; an unlikely pair of journalists if there ever were.

"Your man's gone off," Halliday explained.

Babescu peered down the steps, still clearly dazed. He shrugged.

"Turks," he said absently, as if that explained everything. He turned back to re-examine Halliday's altered features. "You look hardly anything the same," Babescu said, his voice still awed. "You look very good indeed."

Halliday nodded. "I'm making a fresh start, Babescu."

Babescu was eyeing him now. The crowd was stamping impatiently behind them, anxious for something to begin. Something flamethrower-like, thought Halliday.

"What's brought you *here*, then, Michael . . . ?" Babescu broke off. "Or is Michael gone as well?"

"Michael will do for now, Babescu," Halliday said. He glanced toward the field beneath them, where a great clanking of machinery had been set up.

"*Flamethrower!*" the announcer's voice intoned again, echoing all around them.

"Let's take up business later, shall we?" Halliday told the fat man. "For now, we'll enjoy the show."

There were many, many thousands out there beneath the dark Mediterranean sky, many of them young, many of them Americans. The first to arrive at the International Spectacle of Violent Self-Destruction had taken the choicest seats and were sitting shoulder to shoulder on the broad steps that had once led to one of the more noted temples of Artemis. Behind them, splintered Grecian columns rose up against the inky sky, and before them, on the gently sloping hillside, was spread the bulk of the crowd. Tickets bore a face value of $100 American, though none had been sold at that price for weeks. Scalpers in nearby Kuşadisi were said to have been receiving several times as much in recent days.

There came an earth-gargling rumble then, accompanied by a sudden blast of light, and the noise of the crowd rose. On the flat plain below, where Alexander's men had once camped and Hadrian's troops were said to have run mounted races, an odd machine had sprung to life, a tangle of gleaming silver pipes mounted on clanking half-track treads, belching fire from a stainless-steel nozzle the size of a tank cannon as it advanced slowly across the field.

A spotlight mounted on scaffolding erected on the temple site snapped on then, illuminating a wooden peasant's cottage standing in the path of the lumbering machine a few yards further along. What looked like a man stood in front of the cottage, a rifle upraised. The roar of the machine redoubled, and its fiery plume shot out like a frog's tongue. The unfurling flame smashed into the figure with the upraised weapon, obliterating it. In the next instant, the cottage itself was engulfed. The thatched roof exploded in a shower of sparks, and the walls seemed to waver in sheets of liquid flame. The crowd bellowed its approval.

"That is some righteous shit," Basil Wheatley said.

"Dead-on righteous," his brother, Frank, called back.

Halliday glanced at his men. He would not have characterized the two as spiritual in nature. But the expression on their faces, reflecting the flames that still leapt from the walls of the mocked-up cottage and from the smoldering straw stuffed image of a man down below, was unmistakably rapture's embodiment. Even those two caught up in this madness, Halliday thought. What did that suggest about himself?

"*Flamethrower*," repeated the toneless voice of the announcer, booming over the roar of the crowd. "By Andreas Volcansic."

A second spotlight sprang to life. A man in a black duster and drooping felt hat to match loped onto the field to stand before the now idling machine he had crafted, making a virtuoso's bow to the cheering crowd. When pasty-faced Volcansic rose, his hands held high above his head, the crowd's appreciation reached near ecstasy.

"What do you think?" Babescu asked.

Halliday shook his head. "I'm not sure *what* to think."

Babescu, who seemed to have recovered his composure, gave Halliday his Sydney Greenstreet, fat-man-in-the-know smile. "Just see what's coming next," he said.

Halliday had read about it in the international papers, of course. It was how he'd learned where Babescu was. The entire enterprise had been dreamed up by his former partner, this unlikely prophet with his finger on the drooping pulse of contemporary youth—or so he claimed—after having happened across some meager version of these proceedings during a visit to San Francisco a year or so before.

"The dark side of the technological universe," according to the fat man, who had watched two robots constructed of earthmoving machinery tear each other to pieces on an industrial site near the Mission District.

"Most of the bright ones go to work in Silicon Valley and make millions. But there are some—an entire sector of the technologically gifted, I tell you—who will have none of that," Babescu had been quoted. "Nothing virtual in *their* reality. I bring the best of them here at the beginning of the millennium and give them all they need to make their art."

And made a few quid in the process, Halliday supposed, gazing out over the assembled multitudes. Though Babescu was happy to profess an appreciation for things cultural, Halliday suspected that this was as about as close as such urges would get to actual manifestation. Even allowing for some slippage, it was a $5 million gate, and that just the beginning, according to their host. There was cable to think of, worldwide distribution, not to mention next year's event—anticipation of which would be frenzy-whipped by this year's audience—that might take place again at Ephesus, on the playing field of the gods . . . or perhaps in Albania, where Babescu had hinted that the officials were not so fastidious about what might be destroyed.

At the moment, on the field below, a man had stepped into a cylindrical steel cage, which itself was suspended from the boom of a smallish loading crane. The winch of the apparatus engaged with a whine and slowly drew the caged man a dozen feet or so off the ground. *"Fire Shower of the Apocalypse,"* intoned the announcer, as tongues of flame began to dance around the perimeter of the cage.

The crowd had quieted down during the preliminaries, but the sight of flames seemed to arouse them. A dozen yards from where Halliday stood, a young bare-chested man with half his head shaved bare, half covered with dangling blond locks, stood and began to shout, *"Cris-py—cris-py—cris-py!"* In moments, the whole crowd had taken up the chant.

The tongues of flame grew and then began to spin, becoming a solid revolving mass as the figure inside the cage was reduced to a motionless shadow.

"Cris-py—cris-py," the crowd chanted.

"Awesome," Basil Wheatley said.

"Burning-bush awesome," said his brother.

Deal with the Dead

Halliday glanced at Frank. He'd known there was something familiar about the younger, somewhat better-looking half of the Wheatley team, but now with the unexpected Biblical reference, with the flames and the anticipation of gruesome death animating the man's face, he could finally see it. Steve Reeves. Of course. All those Italian muscleman films. *Hercules. Goliath. Son of Spartacus.*

How had it eluded him all these weeks stalking Babescu? Halliday wondered. Whereas older brother Basil, who could easily lift a car end off the ground, was as round as his brother was sculpted and angular, and looked as if he might be more at home scratching his backside in some hillbilly situation comedy. So much for appearances, Halliday thought. Not only had he heard what these two were capable of, he had witnessed it; and for his money, the Wheatleys were the flesh-and-blood equal of the giant cannon they'd watched earlier on their way to Babescu's reviewing stand, a device that lobbed fifty-five-gallon drums of wet concrete the length of a football field onto the tops of junked-out Turkish delivery vans.

The steel cage, meantime, was flaming like a comet. Eerie shadows danced up the ruined columns, and the chanting of the crowd had transformed into an undifferentiated blood-drinker's roar. Perhaps slaves had fought with lions on the plain below, Halliday thought. Perhaps these young men and women had picked up ancient vibrations from the weary stones they sat upon. Babescu, his face gone scarlet in the reflected flames, seemed a reasonable representation of a bloated Roman emperor, after all.

There was a popping sound then, and the flames extinguished abruptly. Spotlights snapped on, illuminating the dangling, smoldering cage. The door swung open, and something toppled out. Instead of a charred figure tumbling to the ground, however, here was a person making an impossible, gliding descent, tracked by the beams of the spotlights, arms outstretched, a colorful cape billowing in its wake.

A man unscathed by flames, Halliday realized, tethered now to a cable that stretched over the top of the gaping crowd. The man whizzed past the makeshift reviewing stand with a grin, and moments later came to rest atop the temple steps, where he bowed to the roaring crowd.

"*Fire Shower of the Apocalypse,*" repeated the dispassionate voice of the announcer. "*Kaia Jesperson.*"

Not a man at all, Halliday realized as the caped figure snatched off the cap that had shielded her long dark hair from the flames. High cheek-bones, eyes dark and flashing as that great mane of hair. Halliday heard the cheering strengthen from the throng that covered the steps, and felt what the mob was feeling. They'll have her on the spot, he understood. Ravage her to pieces and howl above the scraps for more.

In the next moment, as if whoever was in charge of choreography knew exactly what thoughts might be afloat among the masses, the powerful spotlights were extinguished. When they came on again, Kaia Jesperson had vanished. Halliday glanced at Babescu: his fat imp's grin, his hands splayed atop his great, quivering gut in a parody of satisfaction.

"The stuff of life itself," Babescu said.

"Amen," said Frank Wheatley.

And the crowd roared on.

An hour or so later, the last of the crowd dispersed, the bizarre machinery hushed, Babescu sat in his wicker sultan's chair, staring over his brandy glass at Halliday, who leaned casually with his back to the railing of the stand. "You might have let me know, Michael . . ."

Halliday shrugged. "Discretion and all that."

"I'd have never let it slip—"

"Not intentionally, perhaps."

Babescu's expression was hurt. "I've known you since you were born. I've taken care of you like a father. No one could have gotten it out of me."

Halliday nodded, as if the line of discussion bored him. He glanced down at the darkened field below. Except for Frank and Basil Wheatley, who had gone off to inspect the now quiet mechanism of the Fire Shower of the Apocalypse, the grounds appeared deserted. Frank was poking about the controls of the converted front-end loader, while Basil had climbed into the cage itself. He stood with his hands grasping the bars in parody of the desperate inmate. The two were familiar with heavy equipment, being the sons of a New Jersey scrap-metal dealer, a man who'd made a comfortable living buying and selling surplus materials of dubious origin. Halliday turned his gaze back to Babescu, who might have seen some inquiry in his eyes.

"We have made history here tonight," Babescu said. "I have afforded these inventors opportunities they would never have found elsewhere."

"Babescu, the cultured thief," Halliday said. "You've watched *The Maltese Falcon* too many times, I think."

Babescu gave Halliday a glance, uncertain of his tone. An engine kicked to life in the distance and Halliday saw that Frank Wheatley had started the engine of the machine that maneuvered the Fire Shower of the Apocalypse.

"Those two had best be careful," Babescu observed. "It's a delicate apparatus. The owner is fastidious."

Halliday watched as the machine swiveled toward the platform, Basil grinning out at them from behind the bars of the swaying cage. "You couldn't have picked a more appropriate audience," Halliday said. "These men appreciate what heavy equipment can do."

Babescu glanced doubtfully at the growling machine, then turned back to Halliday. "You didn't come here just for the spectacle, Michael."

"True," Halliday said, watching the machine inch its way toward them.

"And this physical transformation," Babescu added. "Just what scheme have you cooked up now?"

"No more schemes, Babescu," Halliday said. "I'm coming back to life, that's all."

Babescu seemed to read something into his tone. He stared levelly back, ignoring the advancing machine. "You understand that I control everything in this part of Turkey, don't you?"

Halliday nodded. "Of course. Money talks, Babescu."

Babescu seemed mollified. He settled back in his chair. "Then why not get to the point," he said.

There was a grinding noise from the machine, and Babescu glanced away. "If they damage that device, they'll be required to pay."

Halliday stood and walked to the end of the platform, watching as Frank nudged at the controls of the machine, sending the cage into a wobbling arc. "Asswipe!" called Basil to his brother.

"Asswipe in a gilded cage," Frank called back. Their insults echoed off the nearby hillside.

"There are men who find themselves drawn to return to prison,"

Babescu said after a moment. "They find themselves uncomfortable, walking around free."

"I'm not one of them," Halliday said.

"And what is it you want from me?" Babescu put his brandy glass down on a nearby copper table and laced his fingers over his gut.

"Just what's due me, Babescu." Halliday gave him a meaningful look. "I want my money, now."

Babescu drew a breath that sounded something like a sigh. "There is no money, Michael. I sent word to you—"

Halliday dismissed the words with a wave of his hand. "Of course you did. Had the tables been turned, I might have done the same."

Babescu shook his head. "I assure you—"

"We'll forget about the trading accounts that you had access to—"

"What wasn't seized by the U.S. government was worthless," Babescu protested.

"I'll settle for the proceeds of my father's trust. If you passed along a quarter million a year to me, it probably paid twice as much. We'll figure the equity at ten million even, and let the interest go."

"The trust was seized as well." Babescu's eyes were glittering, perhaps from anger, perhaps from fear.

Halliday nodded as if he expected all this. He leaned forward, his hands braced on his knees. "Ten million dollars, Babescu. I want it now."

Babescu shook his head. "You're being unreasonable." The fat man glanced down the stairway behind him, perhaps looking for one of the mustachioed Turks Halliday had dealt with earlier: half a dozen dark-skinned men, all of them with stares that could shatter glass.

"You've spent every cent, the truth be told. Money I entrusted to you. Money my father entrusted to you . . ."

Babescu's eyes widened. "We're partners, Michael. As were your father and I before you. I've made investments on your behalf, that's all—"

Halliday shook his head. The fact that his father had trusted Babescu all those years had allowed Halliday to do the same. *Honor among thieves,* he thought, shaking his head bitterly. Stupidity seemed the true currency.

"I want my money, Babescu."

"And you'll have it back, ten times over . . . in time."

Halliday stared at him for a moment, forcing himself to calm. He sat back in his chair, noting that Frank had raised the dangling cage to its fullest height, was dropping it back down in a series of jerking movements while Basil shouted threats from between the bars.

Halliday glanced over at him. "I'm taking over," Halliday said evenly. "Everything you're invested in. I'm taking back what's mine."

Babescu glanced up sharply, and in that unguarded moment, Halliday saw the cruelty that lay behind the carefully crafted façade. In an instant, though, the saturnine smile was back, and Babescu was rising to his feet as if he simply needed to stretch his legs. An unusually graceful move for a man so bloated, Halliday was thinking.

Babescu's hand was going inside his coat. His other made a gesture toward the shadows, where earlier Halliday had seen the men stationed.

At the same moment, Frank Wheatley gave a yank on the controls of the Fire Shower of the Apocalypse, sending the steel cage hurtling toward the platform. The dangling cage, with Basil still inside, smashed through the flimsy railing like a wrecking ball, then drove itself into Babescu with a thud that vibrated the decking beneath Halliday's feet.

The fat man went down with a groan, the pistol he'd intended to draw skittering across the deck to Halliday's feet. Halliday glanced at the weapon, then kicked it over the side.

The fat man was struggling onto his hands and knees, his eyes glassy. Basil Wheatley had already jumped down from the dangling cage, steadying it with one meaty hand, while Frank played out cable until its floor rested solidly on the deck.

In an instant, Basil was across the reviewing stand to drive a fist into the fat man's broad back, just above the kidney. He drew back quickly and sent another to the base of Babescu's skull. There was a dull popping sound, and Babescu collapsed to the deck as if he'd been shot.

Basil snatched the fat man by the collar of his white coat and dragged him toward the cage. He jerked open the door of the cage with one hand, lifting Babescu inside as if he were stuffed with feathers.

Basil slammed the door to the cage, then gave his brother the thumbs-up. In moments the cage was dangling half a dozen feet in the air, Babescu's corpulent face pressed into furrows by the steel bars.

"You stole from me," Halliday said.

Babescu blinked down at him, then out into the darkness where he'd stationed his bodyguards. Bodyguards so recently retired. Indeed, Halliday thought, money did talk.

"For God's sake, Michael," Babescu managed.

"You took advantage when I was in a position of weakness," Halliday replied.

"I'll make calls," Babescu said. He struggled to pull himself upright, but his legs seemed unwilling to obey. "I'll see that you get everything that's yours, and interest besides."

"This isn't a banking transaction," Halliday said. He turned to Basil. "Give him the documents."

Basil motioned to Frank, who cranked the cage down a foot or two. Basil stepped forward, thrust a sheet of paper and a pen between the bars.

"What is this?" Babescu asked blearily.

"The item requires your signature," Halliday said.

"We could have reasoned out these matters, Michael," Babescu said, a plaintive note in his voice.

"Sign," said Basil Wheatley, rocking the cage with his hand.

Babescu scribbled his signature and handed the document out to Basil, who passed it along to Halliday. Halliday scanned the document, then folded it into his pocket.

"You want us to clean this mess up now?" Basil Wheatley said to Halliday, wrinkling his nose at a foul odor that had drifted over the stage.

Halliday nodded curtly, then started for the steps.

"Wait," Babescu called. "If it's money you want—"

Halliday kept moving.

"Your father's trust, Michael . . . for God's sake . . ."

Halliday paused, his hand on the railing that led down from the stage. The fat man reached out to grasp one of the blackened bars of the cage and was pulling himself forward. "It's gone, Babescu. You told me so yourself."

Babescu shook his head hastily. "More money than you've dreamed of," the man said. "I know where it is."

Frank and Basil exchanged glances, clearly impatient to get on with their business. Halliday froze the pair with a glance, then turned back to Babescu. "If there was cash to be had, you'd have spent it. I think we've learned that much."

18

Halliday signaled to Frank, who threw a lever on the control panel before him. The machine groaned with Babescu's weight, but the cable still began to coil, lifting the cage higher, inch by relentless inch.

"I couldn't get at it!" Babescu cried. "Damn it, man, listen to me!"

Halliday raised his hand and the rising cage creaked to a stop.

The fat man was slumped back against the bars like a hippo without a spine, his jowls gray and sagging, as if his flesh had begun to melt. "I can't move my legs," he said, as if he'd forgotten what he'd just been saying.

"The *trust,* Babescu," Halliday said, mimicking the fat man. "Or perhaps you're lying," he continued as Frank Wheatley gunned the engine of the heavy machine.

"I'm not," Babescu said quickly. "It's all there. I'm certain of it."

"You can produce all this?"

Babescu stared down at him. The whites of his eyes were yellowed now, and spidered with lacy red. "The trust resides in Miami," the fat man said. He thrust his hand into his jacket pocket and came out with a wallet. He fumbled with the wallet for a moment, then produced a key. "In a vault," he said, tossing the key toward Halliday.

Halliday snatched the key out of the air. He glanced at Basil Wheatley then back at Babescu, regarding him thoughtfully. "It wouldn't be there if you could have gotten at it. Tell me the story, Babescu. Quickly!"

The fat man's mouth opened and closed twice before the words began to issue. "Your father and I . . ." he managed, "we had something of a falling out just before he died." Babescu waved his hand as if it hardly mattered. "He revoked my right of trusteeship."

Halliday's nostrils flared. "Just a detail you'd neglected to pass along."

"The last time you and I met, we hardly had time for a heart to heart," Babescu said, his breathing ever more labored.

True enough, Halliday thought. He'd been tipped by informants within the Justice Department as to what was coming, but even so, he'd had less than a week to convert what assets he could and still make it out of the country. Eight years he'd been on the run, and no glittery residences for him, either. The glorious watering holes, those were the first places they came looking for you when they wanted their money back. Then the agonizing months of surgery, in and out of one clandestine clinic and another . . . And then the money had run out. And he'd had enough. He'd paid for what he'd done and more. He was going to live again, and nothing was going to keep him from it.

"Who has access to this vault?" Halliday said.

Babescu shook his head, staring down at the front of his trousers where a dark stain had spread. "I need medical attention, Michael. Immediate medical attention."

"You'll get it," Halliday said. "Who has access? A Miami law firm? One of your dubious CPAs?"

Babescu shook his head. "Your father wasn't one to trust organizations, Michael."

"Tell me, Babescu. Tell me, and I'll see that you're attended to."

Babescu stared back at him, the expression on the fat thief's face perhaps the most candid Halliday had ever seen. "I'd have never stolen from your father," he said, his voice a ruin.

"But you are willing to steal from me?" Halliday said. "Give me the name, Babescu. Let's get this over with."

Babescu hesitated, then turned away as he spoke. "Barton Deal," the fat man said, defeat evident in his tone. "DealCo Construction. Your father's old friend."

Halliday paused. "Barton Deal is dead, Babescu. He shot himself years ago."

Babescu turned back, defiant suddenly. "Barton Deal's the man Grant Rhodes gave his money to. And I haven't received a penny since he died. If you're interested, go to Miami and look for it. Now get me out of here."

Halliday stared at the fat man thoughtfully, then finally nodded. "That I will," he said. He put the key in his pocket, then turned to Frank Wheatley and gestured. Frank grinned and pressed a button on the console before him. There came a faint popping noise, and tiny blue tongues of flame began to dance about the perimeter of the cage, a lacework of flame that quickly grew to red and gold, and finally to a white hot storm.

"You want us to put it out?" Basil Wheatley asked.

Halliday, *né* Rhodes, stared up at the swaying fireball and past it, noting that the tips of the ruined temple once again glowed red in the reflection of the Fire Shower's flames. There had been no spinning cylinder of fire this time. Just the flames and the screaming and the eventual near-silence, as now.

"Let it take care of itself," he said.

Basil nodded and motioned his brother down from the control panel of the machine. "He says to let it go."

Frank nodded and clambered down from the seat of the machine. He glanced up at the glowing cage as he joined Halliday and his brother on the platform. "I'd have shot the fat fuck out of that cannon," he said. "See what happens to one of those trucks when a tub of guts like that hits it."

"Doubt we could have got him squeezed down the barrel," Basil observed.

Frank nodded, glancing up at the cage. "What's fat and burned to a crisp?" he asked of no one.

"You ought to learn better jokes," Basil said to his brother.

"What was that?" Halliday asked, pointing out over the platform steps, where he was sure he'd heard movement in the shadows.

In the next moment, Basil had knocked him off the side of the steps. He felt his breath go out of him as he hit the ground, realized that Basil was on top of him, shielding him with his thick body. Frank had already leaped down from the platform and was off into the darkness, his footsteps thudding rapidly away.

Halliday heard a cry, then a groan, the sound of bodies falling several yards distant. He struggled up, but Basil held him back.

"Sit tight," Basil said. Halliday saw the glint of a pistol in his bodyguard's hand.

In moments, Frank was back, a struggling form in a black cape tucked under his arm. "Look here, would you?" he said, jerking the cape back.

Halliday had pulled himself up by the railing of the steps. He blinked in the darkness, his eyes focusing on the captive Frank Wheatley held. The flashing eyes, the great mane of hair to match. As haughtily beautiful as he'd surmised. Perhaps more so, observed this close.

"You can let her go," he said to Frank.

Frank hesitated. Halliday glanced at Basil, who nodded at his brother.

The woman stood, shrugging her cape back into place around her shoulders. She looked at Halliday, then up at the cage. The flames, though still formidable, had begun to languish.

"That's *my* machine?" she said, her chin thrust forward. "Who do you think you are?"

"How long have you been here?" Halliday asked.

She stared back, gauging him. "Long enough," she said at last.

"Do you know who I am?" he asked.

She shrugged. "Someone else Babescu screwed." She glanced up at the cage. Something in that gaze, Halliday saw. "Too bad for him," she added.

Halliday hesitated. He glanced at Basil, who regarded the woman as he might a rock or a tree, or a bale of aluminum scrap.

Halliday was a man well used to making rapid calculations. There were risks worth taking and those that were not. He had another look at Kaia Jesperson, then turned to his bodyguards.

"Babescu left us a bit of brandy, didn't he?" he said to Basil.

It took Basil a moment to understand that Halliday was serious. "The bottle's on the platform," he answered finally.

Halliday nodded and turned to the woman at Frank Wheatley's side. It seemed the perfect time to reclaim the identity that had once been his. Just as it was time to reclaim the money that was his as well. Bond trader Michael Halliday was dead. Let him stay dead. He was Grant Rhodes's son. And he would get what was owed him.

"My name is Richard Rhodes, Miss Jesperson." His tone was firm but untroubled, as though they might have been standing in the lobby of the Ritz. "Perhaps you'd be willing to join me for a drink."

She stared back at him as if she'd expected the invitation all along. She flicked her gaze to Basil and to Frank, then to Rhodes, her expression neutral. "What do I have to lose?" she said. The way she lifted her chin made the words seem almost like a dare.

"Nothing," Rhodes said. "Nothing at all."

She shook her dark hair then and came on.

two

"SOMEBODY WANTS TO SEE you, *jefe.*"

John Deal glanced up from the set of blueprints he had laid out on a makeshift table: a sheet of three-quarter-inch plywood on a pair of sawhorses, a couple of bricks for paperweights keeping the plans from sailing off with the breeze into nearby Brickell Bay. All these years that DealCo had been his own to run, and he still found it odd to be referred to as "boss." As if Barton Deal, long since dead and buried, was still the *jefe,* and he was just the *jefe's* son. *How to explain that,* he thought, as he turned to make sure the blueprints were secure.

He was back at work for Terrence Terrell, one of the original personal-computer tycoons, and a longtime patron of sorts for what was left of DealCo Construction. A few years ago, with the company about to fold for good, Deal had supervised the renovation of the ten-bedroom, neo-Mediterranean main house that dominated the grounds behind him, one of the more attractive examples of the florid style that had been so popular among the elite building their winter "cottages" in 1920s Florida. Now, while Terrell was off with his family for a month in the south of France, Deal was back at the compound, hard at work on what Terrell referred to as a "gazebo" on a section of the property offering a stunning view of the Miami skyline just across the bay.

The first weather front of the season had passed through during the night like a giant squeegee, dragging a mass of hot, soggy air off the tip of the peninsula and south toward the islands. What the front left behind was a trailing breeze and the onset of what passed for fall in the American tropics—Deal, wearing a long-sleeved T-shirt for the first time since March, noted the Wedgwood blue sky arching down toward a cobalt sea, not a cloud in sight.

"Where is he?" Deal said to Gonzalez. He assumed the visitor was the county building inspector, a man who'd wanted to see Deal quite a bit lately, or so it seemed.

Gonzalez pointed vaguely toward the front of the Terrence Terrell compound. Gonzalez was as short, stocky, and bronzed as Lee Trevino, with a similar block-shaped head and a broad face that he kept as impassive as his Mayan genes prompted. This trait did not endear Gonzalez to some of the Hispanics with whom he worked, but the fact that he did not complain seemed to compensate. If they did not exactly trust a man not given to histrionics, still they tolerated him.

All that notwithstanding, Deal thought he could read something in Gonzalez's face, a set to those neutral features that was even more determined than he'd expect if it was the universally despised building inspector. Besides, the inspector wouldn't be waiting around front. He'd have been right there on Gonzalez's heels, waving a copy of the *South Florida Building Code* and spouting violations as he walked.

"Who is it?" Deal said.

Gonzalez shrugged. "*No se.*"

The kind of "I don't know" that meant he wasn't offering any opinions, either. Deal found a third brick on the ground beneath the table and set it on the breeze-rattled set of plans, then started off. He noted that Gonzalez was watching carefully, as if uncertain whether or not to follow.

Who could it be? Deal wondered. Terrell's next-door neighbor in this grand old stretch of Brickell Bay—the male-action-movie star—there to complain about the construction noise? Not likely. The star was on location, shooting *Death March VII*, the latest in a seemingly never-ending series—that's why Terrell had put Deal to work this month.

Or maybe it was Chief Jimmy Two Panther, the Native American spokesman who'd shown up last week when they were digging the footings for the gazebo. Chief Jimmy had been involved in the protest that halted work on a downtown high-rise when ancient Indian artifacts had been unearthed. Now he was turning up at any building project that commenced along the southern bay shore, a kind of ad hoc inspection force all his own. But Deal had given Chief Jimmy free rein to inspect the featureless contours of the footings his men had dug, and the old man had gone away content, even pausing to bless the site with a mumbled chant.

No, not the chief. And that left whom? Madonna? She'd once offered to buy the compound from Terrell, after all, just after the male action star had moved in. Maybe she hadn't given up. That would be okay, Deal thought. He could claim to be Terrell's property manager, which wasn't far from the truth, start off his Monday giving Ms. M. a tour of the palatial estate, see if he couldn't stretch it through Tuesday or Friday.

But it wasn't any of those, he saw as he rounded the corner of the wing of the estate, where Terrell maintained his home offices. There was a pickup truck parked in the broad gravel driveway on the distant side of the splashing central fountain, an old Chevy from the early fifties bearing a Georgia plate, its rounded fenders glowing cherry red even in the shade of the towering ficus trees that lined the circular courtyard.

Beside the truck stood a black man in white T-shirt and jeans, his shaved head glistening, his shoulders and thighs as rounded and bulky as the contours of his truck. He had his hands clasped in front of him, watching as Deal came crunching across the gravel, his lips set in a casual droop but his gaze unusually keen. No wonder he'd seen something in Gonzalez's face, Deal thought. The Mayan had met his African-American counterpart.

"You're John Deal?" the man asked, his hands still clasped.

Deal felt himself being measured. "That's right," he said.

There was something familiar in the man's face, but he couldn't place it. Close up now, he saw a smooth thin ribbon of scar tissue looping down from one corner of the man's mouth, accentuating the droll pooch of his lips. There was a knot at the bridge of his nose that made his eyes seem all the more deeply set, the gaze that much more intense. An athlete, Deal thought. Maybe the action hero's trainer, an advisor in kicking butt and taking names. Deal wondered briefly if he should have invited Gonzalez along.

"William Brown's my name," the man said. "Billy Brown's okay too." He stepped forward, put out his hand.

Deal felt a smooth dry palm, a surprisingly light grip. No macho gamesmanship there. Not yet, at least. "Gonzalez said you wanted to see me."

Billy Brown was still staring at him intently. "Yes," he said, something odd in his voice. "Yes, I did." Then something seemed to shift behind his eyes and he relaxed, turning to point across the courtyard.

"I heard you were looking to sell your truck."

Deal glanced at him, then across the expanse of gravel to where he'd parked the Hog. The vehicle had started off in life as a Cadillac Seville, but had long ago had its rooftop cut in half, its back seat and trunk removed and reconfigured. Rewelded, reglassed, and retrimmed by Cal Saltz, a man who, with Deal's father, had loomed large in the Miami landscape back in the salad days of DealCo Construction, the Hog now had the form of a gentrified pickup truck.

It sat in shadows, shadows later, shadows all day long. As much time as Deal spent in the vehicle, it was like a mobile office. And in the tropics, a little thing like keeping cool was important.

"Who told you I wanted to sell it?"

Billy Brown shrugged. "Couple of guys did some work on mine," he said, nodding at the cherry-red Chevy. "Named Emilio and Rodriguez."

Deal nodded. The two mechanics who'd taken a special shine to the Hog. They loved the vehicle, whereas Deal only tolerated it. He might have sold it long ago but for their intervention.

"Is something very special," Emilio would protest every time Deal suggested the two find him a buyer.

"Nobody else in Miami got one of these," Rodriguez would chime in. "We'll keep her fixed up, no reason to waste money on anything else."

And that much was true, Deal had to admit. The Hog did double-duty: comfortable as a luxury car in the cockpit, but set up as rugged as a pickup for hauling various materials around from job site to job site. If he made a score one of these days, though, managed to get just a couple of jumps ahead, the Hog was going to be history.

His wife, Janice, had nearly died in the vehicle, after all—run off a bridge and into Biscayne Bay by a hired killer who'd thought it was Deal doing the driving—and scarcely a day went by that Deal didn't glance at the Hog and think about that sorry time of his life when he had hardly anything and still it was enough for men to want to kill him for.

Deal with the Dead

Janice had nearly died and it had been his fault—crazy guilt, Deal knew, but real guilt, nonetheless. Guilt that never left him, looming always, along with the ghosts of Cal Saltz and Barton Deal, visages as formidable in his memory as the faces of presidents cut into a South Dakota mountainside.

"I've talked about it," Deal said to Billy Brown, "but I don't know that now's the time I'm going to sell."

Brown nodded, as if he'd expected this response. Probably Emilio and Rodriguez had prepared him. "You get attached to your history," Brown said.

Deal glanced at him. A philosophical turn he hadn't expected. Or maybe it was some kind of bargaining ploy.

"I'm just not ready," Deal said. Hardly about to get into the DealCo profit and loss statement with Billy Brown, was he? Explain how Terrence Terrell had thrown him another lifeline here while he waited for word on one of the half-dozen major project bids DealCo had floating about Miami? "Sorry you had to waste your time," Deal said.

But Brown shook his head. "No problem," he said. He moved his hand absently to one of his sizable biceps, scratching at still more scar tissue raised in gnarled welts there. Some kind of jailhouse tattoo, Deal realized, though he couldn't recognize any pattern in it.

"Truth is," Brown said, "I was wondering if you might have some work."

Deal hesitated. He glanced at the license plate on the Chevy. "You came all the way from Georgia looking for work?"

"Wasn't that way at all," said Brown, no edge in his voice. "But I'm here now—" He broke off, glancing around the spacious courtyard. They might have been standing before a Florentine palazzo, Deal thought, his eye roving the false bell tower, the red-tiled roof lines, the wrought-iron balconies hovering over them.

"Those two mechanics said you were always looking for a good man," Brown continued.

That much was true. Emilio and Rodriguez had referred Gonzalez to him, and a number of others over the years—the Hispañolé pipeline, as Cal Saltz had often called it. And Deal was a little short on help. Terrell's call had come in just as he was finishing up the shell on a strip center in far South Dade, and Deal had been shuttling crews back and forth trying to keep up the pace. He had less than a month to dry-in Terrell's gazebo, in truth a two-bedroom guest house and pool, and a penalty clause was ready to kick in if he didn't wrap up the shopping center by the end of next week.

"What kind of work can you do?" Deal said.

Brown shrugged. "You name it. I was on a framing crew last two years, until the work dried up. I can finish concrete, lay block, hang drywall, paint. I've done roofing work, but it isn't at the top of my list."

The last a mark in Brown's favor, Deal thought. His own father had put him on with a roofing crew the summer of his sixteenth birthday to teach him the construction business "from the ground up." The hottest, dirtiest, most exhausting work there was, most of the labor crew recruited from the ranks of the down-and-out and desperate. Deal had endured, but he still had flashes of the hell it had been.

Deal found himself smiling. "My father used to say he'd spent his whole life working just trying to stay off a roofing crew."

Brown made some kind of noise deep in his chest that might have been a chuckle. "Must've been a smart man."

"How long were you planning on staying down here?" Deal asked. He had no idea what had brought William Brown to South Florida and he doubted he was going to learn the real reasons any time soon. He did know that there was a high dropout rate among the new arrivals drawn here for the weather, the beauty of the place, the glitz.

After a few weeks in paradise, reality sets in. All these people speaking Spanish, the high cost of living, most of the available work in the low-paying service industry, not to mention the traffic, the heat, the confounding jumble of cultures: you could start at 79th Street, speaking Creole to a knot of Haitians standing on the street corner, drive the surface roads five or six miles south, by the time you got to Southwest 8th, you'd have passed though outposts of just about every Latin American and Caribbean civilization.

Deal, who'd grown up watching Miami change, loved what had become of it, but not everybody did. He wondered, for instance, how much William Brown knew of the fine distinctions some Hispanics could make among skin colors. Certain men who wanted to trace their lineage back to

Christopher Columbus, if not Queen Isabella herself, could outstrip a group of Klansmen when it came to matters of race.

"Stay as long as it takes," Brown was saying.

"Takes for what?"

"For whatever you got going," Brown said, waving his hand toward the whine of a power saw behind Terrell's imposing house. Brown rolled his big head on his shoulders. The gesture seemed apologetic. "Look, maybe you're paying your squat labor about fifteen dollars, plus you got insurance, workmen's comp and all that, gonna add up around twenty-one, twenty-two dollars an hour when it's all over."

Deal found himself amused. "Emilio and Rodriguez show you my books, did they?"

But Brown was going on. "What I say, give me a try. Pay me the fifteen, off the books. You don't like the way I work, just say. I go on my way, everybody's happy."

Deal shook his head. "If I gave you a try," he said, "it'd be on the books. Just like everybody else."

"Then let's go to it," Brown said.

"Is there someone I could call up in Georgia, a foreman on that framing crew, say?"

Brown met his eyes and nodded. "Where I'm staying, I got the man's card we worked for. He can tell you."

Deal nodded. "Bring it by, I'll make the call. If everything checks out, I'll put you to work. I'll also need your Social Security number and a copy of your driver's license."

Brown nodded, but the natural droop of his lips had deepened. "I could go to work today, bring all that back in the morning."

Deal hesitated, but *What the hell,* he thought, *what could happen in half a day?* "All right," he said, finally. "You can go to work, I'll pay you cash at the end of the day. Everything goes okay, you show up Monday morning, we'll take it from there. How does that sound?"

"Sounds good," Brown said, smoothing his palms down his heavy thighs. He seemed ready to follow Deal away.

"You might want to move your truck into the shade over there," Deal added.

Brown glanced up at the bright sky, then nodded his thanks and got in his truck, which started with a throaty burble. Deal watched him ease the vehicle in beside the Hog, thinking that he should ask just what work Emilio and Rodriguez had performed on the handsome Chevy, and whether their hefty rates for the general public might have contributed to Brown's financial plight, but by then Gonzalez was at his side to let him know that an auger had snapped on the boring machine, and the question slipped his mind.

three

As it turned out, Brown proved himself a more diligent worker than Deal could have hoped. Brown, for instance, was the one who chopped through the coral rock with a spud bar so that a chain could be looped around the top of the broken auger bit, his powerful arms driving the bar through the brittle limestone in a tireless, pistonlike rhythm.

What was locally referred to as "coral" was not that at all, Deal mused, watching Brown work. It was actually a form of limestone known as oolite, formed from layer upon layer of former marine life stacked up and pressured by the weight of eons. The formation, heaved up here and there throughout the Caribbean, in fact formed the bedrock under most habitable land south of Orlando and north of Venezuela. Furthermore, Miami not only rested *upon* this rock, many of its early homes and public buildings were constructed *of* it. As long as the stuff stayed in its damp, subterranean place, you could manage to chop through it, though the work was by no means easy. Once it was quarried, however, exposed to light and dried, it was as hard as marble.

The patch where the bit had lodged, for instance, was part of an outcropping that jutted up like a calcified dune from its gently sloping surroundings, and had been quietly baking in the tropical sun for the last few centuries. Even the powerful Brown was having a time. But as the bit was being drawn up, Deal got a grudging nod from Gonzalez, which meant that the new man had his foreman's approval as well.

About four o'clock, after giving Gonzalez an envelope containing a day's pay for Billy Brown, Deal left to check on the progress of the crew he'd hired to spray the textured ceilings on the units of the South Dade site. He'd left too late to avoid the rush out of downtown though, and it took him the better part of an hour to navigate the twists and turns of the slow, if scenic, coastal route.

The plasterers—cousins of the Nicaraguan outfit Deal normally used—were gone by the time he arrived, but a quick tour of the quiet units, still pungent with the doughy odor of plaster, convinced him that he'd had another stroke of good fortune. The popcornlike texture had been evenly and carefully applied, no slop on the walls, no major spills to scrape up before the floors could be finished, no callbacks necessary. Deal used his cellular phone to reach the painters, three Germans who'd come to Miami via Argentina, left a message that they could start on the walls the next day. He had no qualms about the Germans getting in and out on time, which left only the matter of the carpet as a concern.

Laying carpet for such a project normally entailed only snipping the right-sized swaths off a giant roll and gluing the pieces into place, but there'd been some delay getting the lot the developer had stipulated shipped down from the factory in Jacksonville. If the truck didn't arrive by Thursday, Deal would be faced with getting approval for a substitute, which would doubtless entail bringing in the architects, who in this case were notorious fussbudgets. He thought about trying Merit Flooring again, just to check, but he'd already spoken to Adam the expediter last Friday and again earlier that morning, and . . . well, he could only hope for the best.

He tossed the cell phone aside on the seat of the Hog and sat in the cool lee of the day, staring out his open window at the lonely façade of the shopping center. The site was off by itself, a few blocks inland from Old Cutler Road, where the homebound traffic sent up its distant hum. The place where Deal sat had been carved from an unbroken tangle of clawing Brazilian pepper trees and razor-edged sawgrass on the southernmost verge of the city's relentless sprawl. Soon there would be a bustle of traffic in and out of this deserted parking lot, customers desperate to get to Mailboxes U.S.A., Heavenly Ham, Eyewear Is Us.

It gave Deal no great pleasure to participate in the process of undifferentiated sprawl, and while he greatly preferred the renovation of grand examples of the architect's craft or picturesque bungalows perched at the water's edge, he did have a wife and a child to support, and a sense of duty toward the men whom he employed. There was even a certain wistful sense of obligation toward DealCo itself that motivated him, a kind of patrimony to maintain—today a strip mall, he could tell himself, tomorrow the world.

Once, of course, the firm had been preeminent among Miami's builders. DealCo had erected two of the great hotels of the fifties' heyday of Miami Beach, pleasure palaces built with teamster pension funds that had become the playground of Gleason, Sinatra, and the rest of the Rat Pack. In ensuing decades, his father had landed the construction of the Sea Trust Tower, soon to go spectacularly into receivership but still downtown Miami's tallest building, and after that, a number of the questionably funded condos and bank towers stitching the shores of Brickell Avenue and the adjoining bay, not far north of the Terrell estate. All of it attributable to the efforts of the legendary Barton Deal, who never met a developer he couldn't accommodate, and never mind the source of the cash.

But all that was past, the glory days of DealCo long gone, obliterated by the building glut of the eighties and its corresponding downturn of the local economy. Deal's father, his fabled bonhomie buried beneath the resulting landslide of debt and ill will, had cranked up his already prodigious drinking to newfound levels. In the end, he'd used a pistol to disperse his problems, painting the walls of his study with what was left of a self that had sometimes run roughshod over Deal's more idealistic notions of what a father should be, but which had never failed to amaze him—all that energy and drive and the capacity to take on any task.

So maybe that's what he was doing, Deal mused, trying to make up for his old man's shady practices and measure up at the same time, determined to bring DealCo out of the ashes but do it on the straight and narrow. The task would be a hell of a lot easier if he was able to use his old man's sliding morality scale, that much he knew. At the rate he was going, it was going to take somewhere into the next millennium just to get his head above water.

His cell phone began to chirp then, and he picked it up, glancing at the readout. He didn't recognize the number on the screen, but that didn't mean a whole lot. His subcontractors tended to call from whatever phone was handy.

"Deal here," he said.

"You sound more like your old man every day," the voice on the other end told him.

"That must be my curse, Eddie." Deal recognized the voice of Eddie Barrios. Eddie was a former fireman who had become a union rep, then parlayed that position into a lobbyist at city hall. He called every so often with a suggestion as to how Deal might land this or that job. The only problem was that most of the suggestions had the potential to land him a felony count or two as well.

"How can I help you, sir?"

"Jesus," Eddie said. "Another one of his lines. Know a guy forever, he still calls you 'sir.'"

"You're breaking up down here, Eddie," Deal said. "I'll have to call you back."

"Don't get testy, Johnny-boy. I just called to say congratulations."

Deal hesitated. "Congratulations for what?"

"I guess the connection straightened out," Barrios said. "Where are you, anyway?"

"A couple miles south of Black Point Marina," Deal said. "Why are you calling me?"

"The port job, my man. Your bid passed. You got the fucking job."

Deal felt a surge of hope rising wildly inside his chest, like an inflated ball someone had let loose way below the surface of a deep, dark lake. But he fought the feeling immediately. Everything in his nature told him that was the thing to do. The second you let your hopes up, then whack, it was off with your head.

"This is more of your bullshit, right, Eddie? You mean I *almost* got the job, all I have to do is pay somebody off."

There was a crash of static on the line and then Eddie was back, his voice full of impatience. ". . . right there on the dotted line, the minutes of the county commission. DealCo. I was *there*, for God's sake. As a friend of the family and all, I wanted to be the first to tell you."

And be first in line for whatever someone else's score might bring your way, Deal thought, still fighting the surge of hope that threatened to lodge somewhere high in his throat, snuff out his capacity for speech. He'd put in a bid on the principal terminal complex, a small part of a proposed international free trade center that would eventually triple commercial volume through the Port of Miami, making it the largest shipping hub on the East Coast. It was a huge project estimated to take several years to complete, bankrolled by a consortium of Swiss investment bankers and vaguely defined interests from the Middle East, but the county commissioners had held out for control of a slice of the pie: county government would control the awarding of contracts on a certain percentage of the dry land construction, or the Swiss and the sheiks could go find another city to woo.

After a fair amount of wrangling, the matter was settled, the commissioners firmly ensconced in the familiar position of patronage. Anything else, as the saying went, would have been unthinkable, at least in Miami.

The terminal complex, a glorified name for what would be essentially a dockside office building, was a relatively small blip on the project's huge screen. Deal's proposal totaled just over $20 million. But DealCo hadn't undertaken a project anywhere near that size since well before his old man's suicide. He'd put in the bid only at Barrios's insistence, and even then after warning Eddie that there would be no greasing of palms, no payment of lobbyists' fees for Barrios and Company, no funny business whatsoever. "Hey, Johnny," Barrios had said, "you get the job, you're going to need some help putting a subcontractor team together. We'll cross that one later on."

When Deal had discovered that the architects picked to design the building were a husband-and-wife team with whom he'd collaborated well on a couple of extensive home renovations in Coral Gables, he'd decided to go for it. Every night for nearly a month—two hours when his daughter, Isabel, was staying with him, four hours when she was back with Janice—poring over plans and working calculations that most firms would have had a dozen associates working on, Deal had painstakingly detailed his proposal, using everything his old man had taught him, every scrap of knowledge he'd picked up on his own.

The bid was cut to the bone, predicated on the contributions of competent subcontractors, the cooperation of suppliers, his own meticulous supervision, and a certain amount of good luck, but Deal knew it was workable, knew it was good. No one would be able to seriously undercut him, no one honest, that is—which left a rather wide crack in the door when it came to the awarding of public works contracts in South Florida.

Deal had delivered the thick packet of his proposal to the county offices on the morning of the deadline day, tapped it to his forehead for good luck, logged it in with the clerk, and then forced himself to put the matter out of his mind. And until now, he had been reasonably successful in managing to keep his hopes right where they belonged: tethered to a block of mental concrete about four hundred fathoms beneath the surface of possibility.

"You still there?" came Eddie Barrios's voice over the cell.

"I'm here," Deal said, something inside him still unwilling to accept the news.

"You don't sound real happy, *chico*. You still don't believe me or something?"

"I believe you," Deal said. Thinking, *I'll kill you if it isn't so.*

"I told you DealCo's time was coming around again. I told all my friends downtown, too."

Meaning, Don't forget you got a partner now, Deal thought. Maybe Eddie put in a good word for him, maybe not. He could be certain Ceci and Gene McLeod, the architects, would have spoken on his behalf. They were meticulous craftspersons themselves, had managed to get Deal pulled onto a couple of smaller jobs they'd designed when the original contractors had started taking things south. So Eddie and Ceci and Gene had done their part, and maybe for once the commissioners had said what the hell, let's go with the best bid for a change . . .

"Everybody told me, 'Yeah, we remember Barton Deal,'" Eddie was saying. "People want to see you doing good, Johnny."

"I'm glad to hear it." So add to the mix his old man's ghost, Deal thought.

"Gotta get out of here, my man, but you and I, we'll be talking, all right?"

Deal was silent.

"You know I can help, right?"

The *right* more of a demand than a question this time. "Sure, Eddie. We'll talk," Deal said. "And I appreciate the news, okay?"

He heard a sudden series of beeps, then pulled the phone away to see the "Discharging" legend on the tiny screen. In the excitement, he must have missed all the preliminary tones that would have let him know the battery was giving out.

He banged the phone against his palm, then brought it back to his ear. "Eddie?" Nothing but silence in response. What the hell. "I do appreciate it," Deal said, and tossed the dying phone on the seat beside him.

A pay phone kiosk had already been set in concrete at the edge of the strip center's lot, but there was no phone installed yet. Deal glanced in the direction of the principal landmark in this part of the county: Mount Trashmore, highest point in South Florida, where thousands of buzzards and gulls dotted the sky, cruising the updrafts over the enormous landfill where the waste of two million citizens was laid daily, inching steadily heavenward.

He knew he could make his way along the cross streets, past the landfill, and on to Black Point, the county-run marina and boat storage complex. He could find a pay phone there, but the thought of trying to talk to Janice in the shadow of a mountain of garbage, trying to make himself heard over the noise of boat traffic or mechanical hi-lifts hauling daysailor craft back and forth from the landing slips to their dry dock berths, just didn't appeal to him.

He knew, in fact, that he had no business calling her at all, not until he'd had official notification, seen with his own eyes everything signed and sealed, no Eddie Barrios bullshit factor to consider, but he couldn't help himself. That big ball of hope had burst loose from its full-fathom tether and exploded to the surface, and he was reeling in the seat of the Hog like a man with the bends.

He knew he would tell her. He had to. He would be cautious, of course, play the matter down, share his suspicions that Eddie had cooked it all up in his mind, put it on Deal for whatever unimaginable reason . . . but he *was* going to call. He had known Janice for twenty years now, and nothing of the slightest importance had taken place in his life that he had not shared with her.

Even now, the two of them living apart, sharing custody of Isabel, their daughter, Deal couldn't shake that connection. Didn't want to shake it, was what the truth was. "Come on, Deal, go out, meet somebody, get yourself a life," that's the sort of thing he was always hearing from his pal Vernon Driscoll, but who was Driscoll to talk? Divorced, half a dozen years out of harness as a Metro-Dade homicide cop, his idea of a big night was six bottles of Jamaican Red Stripe and watching whatever ball game was on the tube.

The fact was that, despite everything, Deal loved Janice. He had simply never met a woman who came close to commanding his interest the way she did. Sure, she was having difficulties, but who wouldn't? Twice, she'd nearly died at the hands of men who'd been intending to kill him. The first time she'd nearly drowned, the second time she'd been badly burned. And though time and surgery had erased the physical scars, the emotional damage had not gone away. Post-traumatic stress disorder, that's what the doctors had finally diagnosed, but giving the condition a name had not made it any easier to treat.

Time, Mr. Deal, that was the doctors' mantra. *Give her time, and give her love.* Sure, he thought, he could do that. After all, if it hadn't been for him, none of it would have happened in the first place.

He shook himself from his thoughts and turned over the ignition of the Hog, felt the powerful engine—bored, stroked, and turbocharged courtesy of Emilio and Rodriguez—set up its quiet rumble. Janice had almost died in this car, he reminded himself again as he pulled away from the vacant center. Maybe that was it: Every time he got in the thing, some of the bad karma rubbed off. He should get rid of the Hog, he told himself. He really should.

About halfway back to the city, he wheeled the vehicle off Old Cutler Road, down an overgrown lane that bored through a thick stand of mangroves and holly toward the water, then into the parking lot of what passed for the offices of DealCo these days. It was a sun-bleached, double-wide portable building set up on a stilt foundation fronted by a dusty expanse of crushed coral, and had once been intended as the sales office for a time-share resort that a major hotel corporation wanted to build on the surrounding 800-acre tract of bayside property. Federal regulators and environmental interests had intervened, however, and the project had been scrapped more than a decade ago, the area designated as a natural preserve and park that was still waiting to happen.

Deal's father, a minority partner in the venture, had managed to hang on to the ninety-nine-year lease for the lone acre upon which the sales office stood. He couldn't build anything new there—couldn't even erect signage—but he'd maintained the right to access the office that DealCo had installed for the hotel chain in the first place.

The place was hot and mosquito-plagued in the summer, isolated and hard to find in every season, but there was phone service, the price was right, and it actually suited Deal, whose business did not depend on a lot of drive-up traffic. He hadn't even employed a secretary for more than a year. On days when it appealed to him, he could hole up here like one of the original Miami settlers. He'd set up his desk chair on the wooden porch, drag the phone out to the limit of its cord, sit outside and conduct business, lord of a lonely domain.

Though it wasn't visible through the thick screen of mangroves, Deal was well aware that a narrow tendril of the bay snaked its way in to a point a dozen yards behind the office. He kept an aluminum canoe hung on the back wall of the place. When the weather was cool, he'd sometimes bring Isabel down and the two of them would paddle out to the bay. There were little patches of beach to find along the shoreline out there, places you could get to only by boat, where Isabel would skinny-dip and Deal would roll up his khakis and wade. He'd pack them a lunch, take along a couple of fishing poles, they'd tell themselves this was the day they'd catch the granddaddy snapper.

All that within eyesight of the Miami skyline, four million people surrounding them, and where Deal and Isabel played, they couldn't hear a one. The collapse of the project might have meant the dissolution of the last of his old man's many last Ozymandian dreams, but Deal was glad that it had happened that way. And no, as he told himself often, even the project working out would not have made a difference, would not have kept that pistol at bay.

About time for another one of those forays with Isabel, he thought as he got out of the Hog and held up his chin into the crisp evening air like a hound. What he could see of the sky was dusky pink. High up, far enough east to make it over the water, a lone osprey sawed its way along toward wherever home was, the hunt over for the day. Closer in, a squadron of parrots zigged and zagged noisily over the treetops, as uncertain and raucous as a car full of seniors searching out a spot for an early-bird dinner.

Maybe he'd move out of the fourplex in Little Havana, bring a hot plate and a cot down here, Deal mused. Change the name of DealCo to Mad Hermit Construction, let the world take care of itself. He smiled, trying to imagine what Janice would think of his fantasies, and reminded himself of why he was here at this moment, after all.

He crunched on across the gravel, made his way up the weathered plank incline to the little porch, and fished in his pocket for his door key. When he reached to insert it, however, he found the knob turning freely in his hand. He was going to have to get better about that, he thought. He didn't keep anything of much value in the office, but kids could make a hell of a mess . . .

That's what he was thinking as he stepped inside the office, his hand moving automatically toward the light switch. Then he saw the man sitting behind his desk, and all that warm bath of ease he'd managed to conjure up for himself slid away in the instant it took him to draw a breath.

four

"YOU'LL FORGIVE ME FOR startling you," the man said, his voice the practiced purr of a salesman. A band of dying sunlight fell through the opened door, cutting across the man's chest. Deal saw the lapels of a well-cut suit, a muted tie against a soft blue shirt. His face was still in shadow.

Deal stood, hesitant, in the doorway. Something told him to simply take one backward step, close the door, get back in his car and proceed, never mind the stop at "Go." Do it now, Deal.

He could see the man's hands clasped easily over his belt. Blunt, thick fingers, the nails carefully manicured. No weapon, no threat in the voice. It could have been his banker sitting there.

Close the door, Deal. Get out.

"Who are you?" Deal said.

"We'll get to that," the man said.

"You sure you're in the right place?"

"Quite certain, Mr. Deal."

Deal hesitated. He'd had a flash of a feeling he'd sometimes experienced as a child. He wouldn't have done anything to merit punishment, not really. Maybe swiped a candy bar from the Shores 5 & 10, maybe snuck a peek at some of his father's magazines. But that was all it took. As a kid, he'd been certain that sooner or later someone or something was going to show up when he least expected it, demanding restitution in full.

"I mean no harm, I assure you," the voice smooth, avuncular.

Deal reached to flip on the light switch, but nothing happened.

"It wouldn't work for me, either," said the man. One of the neatly manicured hands moved to the telephone set. He turned it around, facing the keypad so that Deal could see it. "The phone's out, as well."

Deal stared into the shadows at the vague silhouette before him. "It happens sometimes," he said. He glanced over his shoulder at the empty lot outside. "Where's your car?"

"It's out there," the man said.

"The hell it is," Deal said. "You want to tell me what you're doing here?" If the man had meant to rob him, assault him in some way, things would have already happened, he sensed that much.

"I came by to congratulate you, for one thing."

So that was it, Deal thought, a certain measure of relief washing over him. One of Eddie Barrios's cronies. The cross Deal was going to have to bear. But there was good news involved: Eddie must have been telling the truth if the sleazeballs were already rolling in.

The only thing was, Deal was not getting the right vibrations from this man. Most of Eddie's pals were the type that had to work at keeping their knuckles from dragging the floor. Whoever this was, making himself at home behind Deal's desk, he exuded a slightly more refined air.

Deal turned and pulled on the cord of the blinds that blanked the window by the door. Dim light filtered in from outside, enough to give him a look at the man who stared back placidly. A round, avuncular face to match his voice, thinning hair gray at the temples, dark circles under the eyes that gave him a weary, plaintive look. *A version of Tommy Lasorda in a business suit,* Deal thought. But he didn't imagine Tommy Lasorda would come creeping into someone's office while the occupant was out.

"Why don't you just leave me your card, I'll get back to you when I'm ready to start bidding out the subcontractor work," Deal said.

The man laughed, but there was no humor in it. "I'm no contractor," he said. "Not the way you mean it, anyway." He gave an airy wave of his hand. "Have a seat, Mr. Deal. I'd like to have a talk with you."

Deal gave him a smile of his own. "You break into my office, you don't want to tell me who you are—" He stopped, shaking his head. "We don't have anything to talk about."

"I'm a friend of your father's," the man said. "We go back a very long way."

Deal looked at the man's face more closely. "I've never seen you," he said.

"That's right," the man said. "You never have."

"You one of the wise guys he dealt with?" Deal said, though he didn't think that was it, either. "If the old man was into you in a big way, I'm afraid you're a little late to collect."

The man shook his head patiently. "If anything, I am indebted to your late father. Please, Mr. Deal, sit down."

"I don't have time," Deal said.

"Five minutes, I promise you," the man said. "What I have to say will interest you."

Something in the man's voice, the plaintive set of his features, tugged at Deal. He took a deep breath.

"We'll start with your name," Deal said. "You don't want to give it to me, get the hell out right now."

"Sams," the man said. "Talbot W. Sams." He nodded at a pair of battered file cabinets in a corner. "There's a file or two in there with my name on it."

Deal glanced at the cabinets. The name meant nothing to him. "You sure about that?"

Sams shrugged. "It was a boring wait. I took the liberty of checking."

"You've got nerve, I'll give you that much," Deal said. He pulled the battered side chair toward him, sat down on the edge of the seat. "We're down to four minutes."

The man gave him a nod, tenting his fingers before him. "Do you have any idea how you managed to secure that bid for the terminal complex building, Mr. Deal?"

Deal stared at Sams, ignoring the sudden surge of doubt he felt. "Because it was the best one submitted," Deal said, his voice even.

The man smiled, glancing around the spartan office. "It wasn't badly prepared, under the circumstances." He waved his hand in dismissal. "But that was hardly the reason."

Deal felt his anger building. "Look, you need to go on home now, call Eddie Barrios, tell him whatever it is the two of you had cooked up, it didn't work. You can also let him know he doesn't want to run into me anytime soon—"

"Eddie Barrios is a small-time grifter," Sams said. "I wouldn't send him to the store for a quart of milk."

"I'm out of here," Deal said, starting up from his chair.

He felt as much as heard the quick footsteps behind him, turned to find a hard-featured man in a suit moving out of the shadows in the far corner of the room. When the man withdrew his hand from his coat pocket, Deal saw the glint of steel.

"Why don't you just sit the fuck down," the thug said.

"Mind your manners, now, Tasker," Sams said mildly.

Deal turned back to the man behind his desk. "What is this?"

"*I* saw to it that your bid was accepted," Sams said. He checked his own watch, indicated the chair Deal had left. "Two minutes, Mr. Deal. Hear me out. Then you'll be free to go."

Deal glanced again at the hard-featured man who stood between him and the door. Tasker had apparently replaced his pistol and stood regarding Deal like an usher in a funeral home, his hands clasped in front of his crotch. Deal sat back in his chair.

"Who are you?" he said to Sams.

"Talbot Sams is where we'll leave it for now," the man said. He pointed toward the files in the opposite corner. "Your father and I made use of various other names, but that's hardly important. What's important is the opportunity I've come to present you with."

"Be still my heart," Deal said. "I don't know what you and my old man were into together, assuming you were, but that's not the way I work—"

"I know you're convinced your father was a criminal," Sams broke in, "that you think he shot himself out of shame—"

Deal was out of his chair and over the desk before Sams could react. He had the muted tie in one hand, was yanking Sams toward him, when he felt a stunning blow at his ear. The floor of the portable office seemed to tilt then, as if a giant tidal surge had swept in across the mangrove shallows.

Deal felt his feet fly from under him, his cheek bang off the top of the desk. He rolled onto the floor, his hands cradled over his head. He saw Tasker's legs moving toward him and, instead of trying to get away, rolled toward him, snapping a kick behind the thug's knee.

Tasker went down with a groan and Deal, his vision still sparkling, was about to roll on top of him when he felt the press of something cold at the flesh beneath his ear. "Let's all of us just calm down."

It was Sams's voice above him. Deal stared up out of the corner of his eye. He couldn't see the pistol gouging into the side of his neck, but he knew that's what it was.

"Are we calm?" Sams asked.

Deal nodded. After a moment, he felt the pressure below his ear ease slightly.

"Stand away, Tasker," Sams said.

Deal felt thick legs untangle themselves from his own, heard Tasker's muttered cursing as the man stood.

"You can get up now," Sams said.

Deal got to his hands and knees, steadying himself for a moment. There was a throbbing at the back of his skull where Tasker had hit him, but his vision seemed to have cleared. He got a hand on the edge of his desk and managed to lever himself up. The walls of the office seemed to bow inward, and he fell as much as sat in the battered chair behind him.

"Why don't you get Mr. Deal some water," Sams said, watching him closely.

"Let him get his own fucking water," Tasker said.

Sams swung his gaze to the man. *"Now,"* he said simply, and Tasker limped off to the cooler by the file cabinets.

Deal heard the familiar gurgle, felt the paper cup being urged into his hand. He drank the water, felt the cup tumble from his fingers to the floor. Could be a concussion, he thought, but then again, he'd taken harder shots. He stared up blearily at Sams, who had apparently put his pistol away.

"Better?" Sams asked.

Deal tried to shrug, felt a fresh jolt of pain at the base of his skull.

"I'm sorry if I offended you," Sams said. "I was simply trying to create the proper context for what I have to tell you."

"Yeah, I'm a big fan of context," Deal said. He brought his fingertips gingerly to the place where he'd been hit. A knot on his skull, some swelling of the tissue, but nothing wet to the touch.

"In fact, I meant to dispel certain misconceptions regarding your father's image," Sams said.

There was a sudden burst of light then, and Deal's eyes clenched in pain. He heard the hum of the little refrigerator he kept in the storage closet and realized that the electricity had kicked back on. He opened his eyes again, the pain at the back of his head beginning to subside.

Sams was staring placidly at him. Tasker stood off to the side, glowering at Deal as he rubbed the back of his knee. Deal turned back to Sams, whose resemblance to Tommy Lasorda had diminished considerably, the avuncular pose turned to steely composure.

"My old man was a pal of yours? That makes me feel a lot better."

Sams waved away Deal's irony. "Perhaps you'll change your mind when you've heard me out."

"Do I have a choice?"

"I'll tell you a few things," Sams said. "*Then* you'll have a choice."

Deal glanced at Tasker, who seemed ready to resume the old hand-to-hand. "Let's get it over with," Deal said.

"Good," Sams said. "You're going to find this interesting."

"I'll be the judge," Deal said.

"You're a chip off the old block," Sams said. And then he began to talk.

five

BARTON DEAL SAT IN a window-front booth at Wolfie's on Collins, staring out at the crazed traffic jamming the avenue. Carloads of Cubans waving banners, shouting slogans: *"Viva Fidel . . . Viva la revolución!"* They'd been at it for more than twenty-four hours now. Up and down Collins out here on the Beach, up and down Bayshore Drive and Brickell and Main Highway over on the mainland. Slogans, firecrackers, gunfire tracing the night skies. Kept him awake New Year's Eve, kept him awake New Year's Night. He rubbed the back of his neck, squeezed his tired eyes tight.

Crazy *cubanos* and their slogans and celebratory gunfire were bothersome enough, but that wasn't the only thing keeping him awake nights. He moved his hands to his eyes, dug in with his knuckles until stars and planets were whirling behind his lids. He sighed, opened his eyes, saw who was coming toward him, then sighed again.

"Señor Padilla," he said, mustering a smile. *"Con mucho gusto."* He half rose from his seat, but the bustling Latino man waved him back.

"Sí, sí, sí," Padilla said, sliding into the booth across from him. The little man was wearing a straw fedora and a pair of dark sunglasses. He glanced across the table with concern. "How are you, my friend?"

"I'm okay," Barton Deal said. "You look ridiculous."

Padilla touched his hat, the sunglasses, then gestured outside the window where a crowd of bare-chested men ran down the sidewalk holding a long banner of stitched-together sheets. Something had been hastily painted on the banner, but whatever it was exceeded Barton Deal's grasp of the language. "If they recognize me out there . . ." Padilla shrugged.

"I thought you'd be one of the good guys now," Deal said. The little man across from him was a former president of the neighboring island republic. He'd been deposed a decade before, had found refuge in Miami Beach, Star Island to be exact. A twenty-seven-room-mansion-on-the-water type of refuge. "Batista kicked your ass out, now his ass is out. Maybe they'll even ask you back."

"It is not as simple as that." Padilla gave him a tolerant smile.

"Politics rarely is," Deal said.

"One day I will explain it," Padilla said. "As for now, there is a bigger fish to fry, is that not how you say it?"

"More or less," Barton Deal said. He spread his palms on the table, glanced around the restaurant. "So, where are these friends of yours?"

"We are going to meet them now," Padilla said.

"Yeah, that's why I'm here," Barton Deal said.

Padilla stared at him from behind the dark glasses. "I mean you must come with me."

"Where?" Deal said, wary.

"They say to meet on the job site," Padilla said. "They feel it is more"— he broke off, searching for the word—"more *appropriate.*"

Deal sighed. What he wanted to do was snatch the little man out of the seat across from him, strip off the ludicrous sunglasses and hat, haul him outside, and hold him up by the neck for the inspection of the crowds outside, see what might happen. But he wouldn't, of course. Because his ass was in a crack that was more like a crevice on a California fault line, one that was widening by the minute.

Barton Deal had come back to Miami after he'd mustered out of the Army Air Corps in 1946, and started building bungalows for other servicemen who'd received their training on the silvery sands of South Florida and longed to return after the war. In a decade and a half, he had managed to turn a pissant contracting business into DealCo Construction, a burgeoning concern with half a dozen major building projects in various stages of completion around the county, a state of affairs most people would have considered a plus.

He was one of Miami's major employers, a member of the Chamber of Commerce, confidant of the mayor, member of the Bath Club and the Commodore's Club, a true man of substance. He was tall and lean and handsome, his tanned features bearing a certain resemblance to those of John Huston, or so he'd been told. He had a stunningly beautiful wife who'd been by his side all the way, first as his office manager and general factotum, and now his equal in working a room and a community, adept at making the movers and shakers—all potential clients—long to rub shoulders with the dashing builder and his glamorous wife.

There were parties at Casa Deal, the gracious South Bayshore home—legendary bashes that went on until dawn—raucous forays to the horse tracks and jai alai frontons and dog tracks, weekend expeditions to the casinos of Havana, where anything might happen and frequently did . . . even the birth of their son, John, hadn't slowed things down to any measurable degree.

But maintenance of such a lifestyle—important to the business as it was—required a fair outlay, and as Barbara began spending less and less time in the office and more and more time nursing the inevitable hangovers of her own, their financial affairs had managed to slip out of control. To make ends meet, Barton Deal had found it tempting to dip into the sizable draw he'd received from the corporation who'd hired him to build a series of Black Angus restaurants around Dade and Broward counties. To cover the inevitable shortfall that arose when the actual construction got under way, he was forced to borrow from the advance on the expansion of Dinner Key Marina, which he in turn made up from the draw on project C . . . and so on and so on, not to mention the fact that the drain had seemed to grow worse as time went on.

The crack had become a fissure, the fissure a crevasse, and with construction suddenly drying up in Dade, Barton Deal's little pyramid scheme was threatening to collapse altogether. He was facing the specter of bankruptcy at a minimum, and given the fact that certain of his unauthorized transactions involved public funds, he could imagine the possibility of criminal action as well.

All he needed, of course, was a ready infusion of cash, another project to borrow from, just until he could finish up with the restaurants, get his final draw, and use the profits—there would be profits, he was sure of it—to plug the original hole. Things would be tight for a while, of course, but they could adjust, get themselves back to a normal life, for God's sake. Barton Deal had a son now. He needed to unstrap the flak jacket from his liver, get back to the basics.

He'd been thinking such thoughts, making such resolutions, all the while that he had been waiting for Ugo Padilla, former president of the Republic of Cuba, who had promised to deliver him that necessary source of revenue—at a certain cost, of course. Now the man was here and the moment, it seemed, was at hand.

Deal rubbed his face with his hands and nodded to Padilla, who was staring at the napkins on the table between them. Deal glanced down. Columns and columns of figures he'd been adding, nothing balancing out, all of the negatives featuring way too many zeroes. He reached out, crumpled the napkins in his fist. "Why didn't we just meet at the job site to begin with?" he asked.

Padilla shrugged, already sliding out of the booth. "These are cautious men."

Deal laughed mirthlessly. "*There's* a new way to describe them." He slid a bill under the salt shaker and stood to follow Padilla away.

The traffic northward on Collins wasn't exactly light, but it was much better than Deal had expected. Padilla had suggested they take his car and Deal had not objected, though he was beginning to doubt his wisdom on that count. The little man had the wheel of the big Chrysler in a white-knuckled grasp that made it seem like he was trying to lift himself up for a decent glimpse of the road. He was a tailgater and a lane dancer, cursing in Spanish at the drivers around him, taking advantage of the slightest gaps in the traffic to veer left or right, gain a car-length's advantage.

"Are we in a big hurry?" Deal asked.

Padilla glanced at him. "No," he said, turning back to cut off a taxi on their right. A horn blared in their wake, but Padilla seemed not to notice. "I don't like to fool around, that's all."

Deal nodded. He glanced in the rearview mirror, saw that the driver of the taxi was shaking his fist. "You drive like this back in Cuba?"

"You think I drove myself in Cuba?" Padilla shook his head. "I never even had a license until I came over here."

Deal with the Dead

"Who would have guessed it?" Deal said. He clutched the armrest as the Chrysler cut back to the left, whisking past a Ford that had stopped for a red light. They plowed through the intersection, narrowly missing a delivery van that was trying to make a U-turn.

"*Pendejo!*" Padilla shouted at the driver of the van, which had stalled out in the intersection. He turned back to Deal, erasing the frown from his features. "I had a driver for a while, but my wife was always complaining that we needed to adjust, become more American, you know?"

Deal saw an elderly couple standing by the curb a hundred feet or so up ahead. It looked to him as if they might be contemplating crossing the road. "I guess," he said, hoping that the couple had enjoyed a long and happy life.

"It took me awhile, but now I enjoy this driving," Padilla said. He was staring at Deal, as if he wanted some kind of approval. The Chrysler had drifted to the right, dangerously close to the curb. The old man up ahead had noticed what was coming, had begun to urge his wife back across the sidewalk.

"Look out," Deal said, reaching toward the wheel.

"What's the matter with you?" Padilla said, pushing Deal's hand away. He jerked hard on the wheel, sending the Chrysler into a power slide off the boulevard, through a break in the curbing that looked like it had been gouged with a pick. They were bounding along an unpaved access road now, passing through a series of low-lying dunes that blocked the view of the Atlantic up ahead. "I could have had an accident."

Deal glanced back in the direction of the elderly couple, but the dust boiling up in their wake obscured everything. "I thought we were going to Bal Harbour," he said to Padilla.

Padilla nodded. "They are going to do that thing in Bal Harbour, too," he said. "But this is even better."

Deal stared at him suspiciously. They were nowhere near the site Padilla had been telling him about, a proposed office building just off Collins near the 125th Street Causeway. This was a relatively undeveloped area of the beach where street signs hadn't even been erected. A major chain had announced plans to build a resort complex along in here, but they were using their own people for the construction. Deal hadn't even bothered to put in a bid.

They were coming out the other side of the dunes now, the Atlantic in view, and Padilla slowed the Chrysler, which was beginning to wallow in the sand that grew softer near the water's edge. A moment later, Padilla hit his brakes and they stopped altogether. Padilla turned off the engine and turned to smile at him.

"So, what do you think?"

Deal stared back at him. The surf, kicked up by a norther that had passed through just before New Year's, was pounding a steady rhythm in the distance, hardly time for the crash of one wave to die away before the next thundered down. The breeze through the opened windows was stiff and steady, carrying with it the tang of seaweed and a hint of spray.

Over Padilla's shoulder, further northward along the beach where an old geezer with a nose protector was casting a line out into the surf, Deal could see great stacks of forming materials and rebar piled among the dunes. Up there, he realized, was where the great hotel complex would rise.

"I always liked the seashore," Deal said. "What else do you want to know?"

"I am talking about this site," Padilla said. "This land which is all around us."

"It'd be a great place to build a hotel," Deal said. "I suppose that's why Nicky Hilton is going to do it."

Padilla waved his hand, dismissing him. He reached to take off his sunglasses. "The Hilton is going up *there*," he said, using his dark glasses to point toward the great piles of material in the distance. "Down *here* is where our friends wish to build."

Deal stared at him. Without the dark glasses, Padilla's eyes took on a squinty, nearsighted look. Maybe that was part of the problem with his driving. "Build what?" Deal asked.

"Ask *him!*" Padilla said, smiling.

Deal turned around, saw that a limousine had pulled up on the sandy track behind them, the sound of its motor masked by the crashing surf. Doors had already opened. A couple of big guys whose expressions suggested they gargled carpet tacks for mouthwash stood in front of the limo with their hands folded in front of them. A chauffeur was helping someone else out of the back.

Deal with the Dead

A man in a black suit and a maroon tie, Deal saw. Full head of silver hair, not a strand disturbed by the breeze. Dark brows, a thick nose, eyes that bored in on anything that moved—in this case, boring in on Barton Deal, who had swung open the door of the Chrysler, getting out himself.

"Jesus Christ," Deal said to Padilla across the top of the Chrysler.

Padilla had put his dark glasses back on. He shook his head at Deal. "*This* man," Padilla said as the new arrivals came toward them, "he is much more powerful."

"You look at me like you know me, Mr. Deal," Anthony Gargano said.

"Who doesn't?" Deal said. Earlier that summer, the face before him had graced the front pages of most of the country's newspapers, as well as the covers of half a dozen major newsmagazines. "Crime Boss Calls Summit." "Feds Bust the Party." Et cetera.

Padilla winced, but Gargano seemed to find Deal's comment amusing. "Maybe it'd bother you, working for someone such as myself?"

Deal took a moment, watching a squadron of gulls whistle overhead, sail on toward the spot where the old guy was still working his fishing line in the dying light. Finally, he turned back to Gargano. "Do you pay your bills on time?"

The two bodyguards stared impassively, but Gargano laughed outright. "Padilla told me you were all right." He clapped Padilla on the shoulder and the little man had to shift his feet to keep his balance in the sand. "Ugo and I go back a ways, did he tell you?"

Deal shook his head. He was wondering how many times Padilla had been cuffed on the shoulder while hosting occasions of state in Cuba. Maybe Ernest Hemingway would have gotten away with it, he thought. He couldn't imagine anyone else.

"President Padilla told me that he represented an important client, that's all."

"Makes sense. Ugo is the soul of discretion." Sweeping his arm around their surroundings, Gargano continued, "So what do you think?"

That question again. "I thought I was going to meet some people, talk about an office building."

Gargano nodded. "Yeah, well, we got an office building or two in the pipeline, too. Right now this is what's on my mind. I want to build a hotel, right on this very spot. Place is perfect for it. Makes me sleepy just standing here."

Deal glanced up the beach. "Right next to the Hilton?"

"Right the fuck next to it," Gargano said. "Competition is good for business, don't you think?"

"I've heard it said," Deal told him.

"Thing is, we had intended to purchase the site north of here," Gargano continued, "but Mr. Hilton got wind of it somehow and managed to ace us out."

"The broker handling the acquisition," Padilla interjected, shaking his head. "People get greedy."

"Don't ask what else he got," Gargano said, giving Deal a meaningful look. "Anyway, I went to Mr. Hilton himself, explained how this project was a union undertaking, we're seeking to invest the pension contributions of thousands of little people all over the country. All they want is just to retire one day without going in the hole, et cetera. . . . You know what he told me?"

"I can guess."

"So many words, he said go shit in your hat."

Deal thought he heard honest disbelief in Gargano's voice. "So that's when you bought up this tract?"

Gargano nodded. "With Ugo's help. And we've already got a set of drawings." He nodded at one of the thugs, who went back to the limo, ducked inside, returned with a rolled-up sheet of blueprints.

"We managed to get a look at the plans for the Hilton," Gargano said. He smiled at Deal, tapping the fat roll against his palm as if he were holding a bat. "I had the architects work it out, angle of the sun, certain months of the year, all that." He smiled. "Where we're going to put our main tower, the shadow's gonna fall in that direction, cover up Mr. Hilton's entire swimming pool for about ninety-five percent of the tourist season."

"Like a permanent eclipse of the sun," Deal said.

Gargano stared at him for a minute, then his face lit up. "I like that," he said, beginning to laugh. "I like that a lot."

"So why me?"

Gargano's laugh had segued into a rasping cough, and he held up a hand to Deal until he could get his breath. "What kind of question is that?"

"Why bring this to me?" Deal persisted.

Gargano glanced at Padilla. "Because you're the best around," he said. "Ugo says so. He vouches for you one hundred per."

Padilla gave Deal a thin smile and nodded.

"I've never built a hotel," Deal said.

"So what?" Gargano said. "A hammer is a hammer, a nail's a nail. You saying you're not interested?"

Padilla was shifting from foot to foot, looking more nervous by the second, Barton Deal thought. "Of course I'm interested," he said. "As soon as you've got working plans, I'll go over them, work up a bid—"

"We don't have to bother with all that," Gargano said. "Ugo says you're right, then you're right. Whatever it comes out to, that's fine."

"You'd award a job this size without a bid?"

"Some jerkoff comes to me, pulls a figure out of the air, what's that supposed to mean?" Gargano waved his hand. "I do business on the basis of trust." He gave Padilla, who had stopped jittering about for the moment, a knowing smile. Then he turned back. "So tell me, Mr. Deal, can I trust you?"

"You can trust me," Deal said, "but what's the catch?"

"The catch?" Gargano lifted his brows and Padilla resumed his antsy two-step. After a moment Gargano shrugged. "The catch is, you agree to build a hotel the way it says here in the plans. You tell me how much it's gonna cost, what you want to make for your trouble, then you go to work. Hammer and nails, that's all you have to worry about from that point forward."

"Who keeps the books?" Deal asked.

"Now that's an item we take care of," Gargano said. "Frees you up to concentrate on what you do best."

"That's not exactly how I'm used to doing it," Deal said.

"People change," Gargano said.

"Do they?"

"I've seen it happen. Put a large sum of money in a person's hand, whole new emotions are born."

Deal had to laugh. "Say down the line, someone, a union trustee maybe, finds there's a problem with the books. Who would be liable?"

Gargano shook his head. "You are looking at the union trustee, my friend. The trustee, the trustor, and everybody in between. So there isn't going to be any problem down the line. The buck stops with me."

Deal nodded, but it didn't mean he was convinced. He had a flash of those long columns of numbers he'd been adding up back at Wolfie's, then glanced off to where the geezer had been casting. The old guy had his pole planted upright in the sand now, was sitting in a webbed lawn chair at the edge of the surf, staring out to sea. Sure, he could take this job, make those figures balance in a flash. But would he ever get the chance to finish his days like that old guy up there, farting around, watching the sun going down, trying to catch a fish? Maybe. Or maybe he'd just as easily end up swimming with them.

"It's something I'd have to think about," he said, turning back to Gargano.

Gargano glanced at his watch. "Sure," he said. "Take your time. I don't have to be at the airport for another half hour."

Deal stared at him. "You mean you want an answer *now*?"

Gargano put a hand on his shoulder. Maybe it was meant to be a friendly gesture, but Deal didn't feel anything tender in Gargano's touch. "You're a stand up guy, Mr. Deal. I didn't know that about you, we wouldn't be here talking. But you don't want this job, that's all you have to say. Goodbye, good luck, and we're done. I'll find somebody else. I don't have time to waste, that's all." He took his hand from Deal's shoulder and stood back, his hands clasped, evidently waiting for his answer.

Deal turned to Padilla, who held up his hands as if to ward him off. *Thees ees up to you, my fren'.*

Deal ran a hand through his hair. "I'm stretched pretty thin, right now. I'd have to hire a couple of people just to gear up . . ."

Gargano nodded at the second thug, who handed over a thin briefcase he'd been holding. Gargano hefted it, seemed satisfied, then extended the case to Deal. Deal stared at the case, uncertain.

"That's two hundred grand," Gargano said. "Form of a retainer. You can hire yourself a couple of guys, a couple of girls, whatever you like. Money is not going to be an issue here. All I care about is that we"—he paused and smiled again—"lay an *eclipse* on our friends over there. You make that happen, Mr. Deal, you and I will be friends for life."

Deal couldn't remember actually reaching for the briefcase, but he must have, for there was no mistaking its heft, its thick handle resting in his grip. Gargano and his entourage had already turned and were walking toward the limo.

He felt a moment of giddy panic—as if he were about to fall from a great height and could stop himself only by catching hold of a high-tension line. He glanced at Padilla, who stared back from behind his dark glasses like a Havana pimp. A voice in Barton Deal's head told him to rid himself of that briefcase—throw himself in front of Gargano's limousine, explain it was all a mistake. Another part of him was already gleefully adding and reading long columns of figures, every total accompanied by the satisfying *ka-chung* of a cash register.

Deal watched silently as the limo made its turn and began to purr through the dunes back toward Collins Avenue. He noticed that the sun was nearly gone and that the old geezer who'd been surf-fishing had packed it in. He had his webbed chair folded under his arm and was headed down the beach their way toting his tackle box and his poles.

"Why didn't you tell me who we were going to meet?" Deal asked Padilla.

"Would it have made a difference?"

"You're damned right it would have," Deal said. He brandished the briefcase between them. "Nobody does business this way." He stopped and glanced helplessly toward the dunes.

"It does not matter," Padilla said. "You have acquired the job."

"I haven't acquired anything," Deal protested. "No papers were signed. I give him his money back, the whole thing's off, simple as that."

"I do not think so," Padilla said.

"Bullshit," Deal said. The briefcase seemed to have grown much heavier, as if it were filled with concrete now. The breeze was whistling in off the water, and with the sun gone, it should have seemed cooler. But Deal felt feverish, felt a slick of sweat beneath his arms, on the back of his neck. He thrust the briefcase toward Padilla. "Take it back. Tell him it's too much for me to handle. Gargano's a businessman. He'll understand."

Padilla stared back at him. His mouth drooped as if he were sad, but with his eyes hidden behind the dark glasses, it was difficult to tell. "We have moved past that point now, my friend."

"Take the fucking thing," Barton Deal insisted.

"We have moved to a different plane, you and I," Padilla said.

"What the hell are you talking about?"

The old geezer had made a turn away from the line of the surf and was moving their way now. Even in the dying light, Barton Deal could see that he'd been wrong about the guy. He wasn't a geezer at all. All the trappings were there: floppy hat, white plastic nose protector, an untucked checkered shirt flapping over a mismatched pair of plaid Bermuda shorts. But the face was unlined, the eyes keen, the movements of the legs graceful and pistonlike as he came steadily up the slope of the beach toward them.

The man stopped a few feet away and nodded at Padilla, who returned the gesture. The man turned to Deal, removing the ridiculous nose beak and then the floppy hat. No, not a geezer at all. Burr-cut blond hair, pale brows, steely blue eyes, an athlete's body hidden behind the loose-fitting clothes.

"Looks like you got a lot of money there," the guy said, nodding at the briefcase in Deal's hand.

Deal gaped at him. He felt like he'd been rabbit-punched. After a moment, he turned to Padilla, feeling his mouth moving before the words would form. "Who is this?" he finally managed.

"Don't get your bowels in an uproar," the man said. "Padilla didn't have a choice in this."

If Deal had felt unease moments ago, he had moved toward full-fledged dread now. His mind was racing, trying to make sense of it all. They meant to kill him, take the money, flee to the Caribbean in a fishing boat? But where were the weapons?

The man dropped his chair in the sand, plopped his tackle box on the seat, stabbed his fishing rod into the soft sand at the edge of the packed roadway. He gave Deal something of a smile, flipped the lid of the tackle box open, and gestured at what was inside.

"We've got it all on tape, Mr. Deal," the man said. "A bit noisy with all the wind out here, but with the pictures and all, it'll make a convincing package."

"Pictures?" Deal was shaking his head. Instead of the innards of a tackle box, he was staring at what looked like a radio transmitter.

"There's more wire on Ugo than a Wyoming fence," the man said.

When Deal started toward Padilla, the blond man stepped forward. "I told you, he didn't have a choice."

Deal stared over the man's shoulder at Padilla, whose mouth had not lost its downward pooch. He spread his palms in front of him in a gesture of helplessness.

"I knew who he'd been doing business with," the blond man continued. "I made him a deal he couldn't refuse." He stopped and stared at Barton Deal for a moment. "Now it's your turn, I'm afraid . . . no pun intended, of course."

six

JOHN DEAL STARED HARD at the man seated behind his desk. He wasn't sure what expression was on his face, but he noted that Tasker had edged a bit closer to his chair.

"It was you, huh?"

Sams gave him a brief smile. "You're a quick study, Johnny-boy."

"You don't get to call me that," Deal said.

"Your father was fond of the phrase," Sams said.

Deal glanced at Tasker, the tendons in his neck and arms gone taut as stretched cable. He'd go one on one with either one of these men without a thought, take them both on, if no weapons were involved. But with both of them packing, he didn't stand a chance. He willed his hands to unclench from the rails of his chair and caught the hum of late homebound traffic out on Old Cutler when the breeze shifted.

"That's quite a story," Deal said. "Grifters usually have one."

Sams grunted, giving Tasker a look. "That's what you think I am, a grifter?"

Deal shrugged. "You tell me my old man was in bed with a mobster, you and some Cuban politician cut yourself in on the action. If it's true, I'm guessing that you crawled in here wanting to arrange something of the same with me."

"You're close," Sams said.

Deal studied the man's face. If things had happened the way he'd said, Sams would have to be in his sixties. Possible, he supposed, but the man in front of him still looked a decade away from geezerhood. "So what is it?" Deal said. "They don't have a retirement home for conmen? You want my help providing for the golden years?"

Sams gave his man Tasker a thin smile.

"I'm not a criminal, Mr. Deal." He reached into the pocket of his suit coat, withdrew a leather case. The case fell open and Deal found himself staring at a silver shield, along with an ID card that bore Sams's photograph.

Deal studied the ID. "Department of Justice?" He heard the skepticism in his voice.

"That's correct."

Deal glanced up at Tasker. Sams nodded. Tasker reached grudgingly into his pocket and produced his own shield. Deal glanced at it. "The picture makes you look almost human."

Tasker curled his lip. "You're lucky I'm on the clock, pal."

Deal turned back to Sams. "Is this the way you normally conduct your business?"

Sams shrugged. "It's a sensitive matter, Mr. Deal. It behooves us to be discreet."

"*Discreet?* I'm not sure that's the term I'd use."

"Write your congressman," Tasker said.

"Shut up," Sams said mildly. He turned back to Deal. "I'm here because I need your assistance."

"You've got to be kidding," Deal said.

"Haven't you figured it out yet, Mr. Deal? Your father was of great help to our efforts. It took awhile, but Anthony Gargano ended up in federal prison for tax evasion as a result of our collaboration. The government was happy, your father was happy. He could have gone to prison. Instead, DealCo fulfilled its contract with the various International Brotherhoods that Gargano represented. Your father's company not only built the Eden Parc, it grew and prospered far beyond that. Barton Deal redeemed himself, and he was handsomely rewarded for it. He continued to work hand in hand with this agency for many, many years, in fact."

Deal stared back at the man, a terrible worm of doubt having crept into his mind. "You kept him on the string?"

Sams pursed his lips by way of reply.

"You had your hooks in my father all his life?"

Sams looked down at the desk, shaking his head as if he were a schoolmaster dealing with a particularly recalcitrant student. "I've been trying to convince you that this is a matter of value for us both—"

Deal was out of his chair again without thinking. He was halfway across the desk when the heel of Tasker's hand shot toward his chest.

The man had meant to drive him straight back into his chair, but Deal's reach was even quicker. He caught Tasker's arm at the wrist before the blow could land, his fingers digging into the soft flesh and tendons there. Deal was no bodybuilder, hadn't been in the gym since his college days, but years of carrying steel, lifting partitions, driving nails with a twenty-ounce hammer, thousands of blows a day, thousands of days in a career as a hands-on contractor, had built a grip that the young guys at the fern-festooned Nautilus salons could only dream of.

Tasker groaned, his knees buckling. He sank to the floor, his face pale, and Deal would have backhanded him aside on his way around the desk if it hadn't been for the pistol that Talbot Sams had produced.

"Let him go," Sams said mildly. His expression made it clear that he would not be disobeyed.

Deal relaxed his grip, and Tasker pulled his hand away. He cradled it against his chest, still grimacing in pain as Sams waved the pistol at Deal.

"Sit down, Mr. Deal. We're all too old and civilized for this."

Deal hesitated, feeling the blood pulse at his temples. There was a roaring in his ears that made him want to block out Sams's words. Take his chance against that pistol, get in underneath the man's aim, take out a few decades' worth of anger. But something told him that there would be no getting under Talbot Sams's aim. He took a breath finally and sat back down.

"You're telling me you blackmailed my father all his life . . ."

"That's hardly the way to describe it," Sams said.

"I'll fucking bust your ass," Tasker hissed, coming up off his knees at last, his fist drawn back.

"Shut up or I'll put a bullet in you," Sams said.

Tasker hesitated, then saw the look in Sams's eyes. He backed off, still flexing the fingers in one hand.

"You fed him jobs, and in return, he was your snitch."

"Your father provided a valuable service to his community," Sams said. He made a motion with his free hand that indicated the world outside the flimsy building where they sat. "The fact is, there wouldn't be a Miami as we know it if it weren't for the business of money-laundering. Dirty money is the lifeblood of the economy, it always has been. Pirates lived here first, and then in the twenties and thirties came the binder boys selling worthless paper and underwater lots. In the fifties and sixties, it was the mob. In the seventies and eighties, it was the South American cartels. This is one of those special places where a tremendous amount of dirty money enters the system, Mr. Deal. It's where the sharks come to feed . . . and it's where I come to hunt."

"You killed him," Deal said.

"I don't know what you're talking about," Sams said.

"You killed my father," Deal said. "You killed him as surely as if you put that pistol to his head and pulled the trigger."

"Your father's health was failing, his business a ruin—"

"Sick and tired is what he was. No wonder, all those years, playing ball with scumbags so you could pick off the easy targets."

"I saved your father from prison," Sams said.

"You set him up!" Deal said. "You turned him into a snitch . . ."

Deal shook his head, still trying to come to terms with the enormity of it. His father living with such a burden all those years. Could his mother have known? But if she had, wouldn't she have told him before she followed her husband to the grave? There'd been none of that, however, no tender last words about his noble father. Instead, she had sighed, "We hoped for better, didn't we, John," and breathed her last.

"Give us five minutes," Tasker was saying to Sams. "I get finished with him, he'll tell you he's sorry out the other side of his head."

Sams stared at him dryly. "Give it a rest, Tasker. Someday you'll thank me." He turned back to Deal. "I think I've held you up long enough, Mr. Deal . . . it's about time we concluded our business."

"You're here because you want to do the same thing to me that you did to my father?" Deal shook his head. "You can forget it. I was doing fine before you came along. Take your rigged bid and your office terminal and cram it up the Justice Department's ass."

Sams held up a hand as if to staunch Deal's outrage. "Your father could hardly have shared the details of our arrangements for any number of reasons, not the least being your own protection," Sams said. "He collected plenty from the clients we steered his way and no one ever asked for a penny of it back. I can tell you that your father was comfortable with our agreement. He came to enjoy it, in fact—taking the money of a criminal, then seeing him brought to justice in the end. Mobsters and the leaders of drug cartels are not men to whom the concept of betrayal applies, Mr. Deal. Murderers lose their rights to loyalty, it's as simple as that."

"If my father was proud of what he'd done, I would have heard about it," Deal said. "Somehow, some way, he would have let me know."

"He was very proud of you," Sams said. "He wanted only the best for you. He was confident that you'd succeed."

Deal shook his head, stunned at the man's effrontery. "What made you think I'd listen to this? How could you possibly imagine that I'd work for you?"

"Because you're the man I need," Sams said.

"You've been too long in the harness," Deal said.

Sams managed a patient smile. "Do you know who's behind the international free trade project?"

Deal stared at him. "Swiss investment bankers. Oil sheiks."

"It's a convenient story," Sams said, dismissing the notion.

"You've got all the answers," Deal said. "You tell me."

"The principal investor was a man named Ferol Babescu. He had a number of interests in the Middle East, including a significant trade in Egyptian cotton. He made the lion's share of his fortune in hashish and opium, however."

"Sounds like a DEA matter to me," Deal said.

"They've been involved," Sams said. "That's how certain information came to me. Babescu died in August, murdered by a man who subsequently assumed a role in the development of the Miami Free Trade Zone."

"And I'm supposed to care about this?"

Sams shrugged. "A few hours ago, you were delighted to learn you'd be profiting handsomely from your part in the project, Mr. Deal. Does it mean anything to you that the entire undertaking is the work of criminals?"

Deal paused, trying to remember that euphoria he'd allowed himself to flirt with when Eddie Barrios's call had come. It seemed a lifetime ago. Now he was being told that the bid had been rigged, that the job was dirty. "I haven't done anything wrong," he said. "If what you say is true, then my part in this is history. Go find someone else to play games with."

Sams lifted an eyebrow. "So *you* say, Mr. Deal." He lifted a manila folder from the desk and showed it to Deal. "We've compiled a substantial body of evidence that suggests otherwise, including an affidavit signed by one Edwin Barrios—"

"Eddie Barrios?"

"—admitting his complicity in a kickback scheme involving the former director of the Port of Miami and two members of the county commission." Sams dropped the folder on the desk between them. "Mr. Barrios names you as his co-conspirator."

Deal stared back, his disbelief quickly being replaced with outrage. And some other feeling creeping in there as well. Something he recognized as helplessness. He saw there was a grin on Tasker's face.

"This is total bullshit."

"We have taped telephone conversations between you and Mr. Barrios, in which you offer certain inducements in return for his influence—"

"I never offered Eddie Barrios anything."

Sams nodded to Tasker, who had produced a pocket recorder. Tasker pressed a button and Deal heard first Eddie's voice—*"You know I can help, right?"*—then his own, *"Sure, Eddie, I appreciate it. We'll talk."*

"That's out of context," Deal said. "You've pieced things together—"

"Juries love to hear a tape," Sams said. "They hear the voice of the accused, all the doubts just disappear."

"Fuck you," Deal said. "File charges. Play your tapes. We'll see what goes down in the end."

"Ah, the lone and noble warrior," Sams said, lifting another file. "But in this case, the warrior is not so lonely." Sams moistened a finger, flipped a page inside the folder. "He has a wife who requires a rather costly regimen of medical and psychiatric treatment. He has a young daughter enrolled in a private school where her own anxieties can be more closely monitored—"

"You sonofabitch," Deal said. He'd meant to convey loathing but his voice sounded defeated, even to himself.

Sams laid the folder back on the desk. "It doesn't have to be this way, John. We can work together."

There was silence in the room for several moments. Deal stared at the pistol that Sams had placed on a corner of the desk, willing the weapon to reconstitute itself in his hand. He'd killed before, in defense of his own life and that of Janice. In many ways, this seemed to him a similar circumstance.

And yet he knew that even if he could manage the feat, it would lead nowhere. These were the "good guys" staring him down. The defenders of honor and decency. Upholders of the law.

"Who is this person?" Deal asked. "The one who killed Babescu. Why does he matter so much?"

Sams gave Tasker a look that betrayed satisfaction. The quarry weakening at last. Sams took a glossy photograph from the stack of papers on the desk and slid it toward Deal.

Deal picked it up, saw a close-up image of a tall man with slicked-back hair and an engaging smile stepping off a cabin cruiser onto a dock somewhere—it was a telephoto shot, which rendered the background vague, but the man's tanned face seemed somehow familiar—maybe a minor film star, or a PBS talk-show host.

"He uses the name of Rhodes," Sams said. "He claims to be a Canadian citizen and to have made a fortune in Great Lakes shipping."

"But that's not true?" Deal glanced up from the photograph.

"I don't think so." Sams seemed to be watching him closely, as if he were wondering if the name rang any bells.

Deal shrugged. "Then who is he?"

"Someone I want," Sams said. "That's all you need to know."

Deal stared at him. "If you want this guy so badly, then why not go pick him up?"

Sams smiled. "It's not as simple as that," he said. "There are certain laws."

"That hasn't stopped you so far," Deal said.

It brought a dry laugh from Sams. "I need to be absolutely sure, Mr. Deal. That's where you come in."

"Why not plant one of your own men somewhere in his organization?" Deal said. "I'm no cop."

"Precisely," Sams said. "You are exactly who you appear to be. That is your strength in the matter. I can use you—" He broke off and began again, his tone softer this time. "You will be able to ingratiate yourself with Rhodes," he said. "From that position, you will have access to certain information, which will tell us what we need to know."

"Ingratiate myself *how*? If this guy is really who you think he is, he's not going to come anywhere close to Miami."

Sams shrugged. "One thing at a time, Mr. Deal. All I need from you at this juncture is your assurance that you're willing to cooperate."

Deal stared at the folders spread across the desk before him. His father a government informant, himself about to be conscripted into the same service?

A part of him wanted to deny everything he'd heard, dismiss it all as nonsense, part of some scheme of Eddie Barrios's meant to somehow pry a few dollars loose from a fat contract. But he couldn't make it wash. Eddie Barrios was a flea next to the man who sat across the desk from him.

"Why is this so important to you, Sams? You need another big score to get your retirement pay up a notch?"

Sams gave him a neutral look. "I have my reasons and they don't concern you. All I'm interested in is your cooperation."

"Cooperation," Deal repeated, shaking his head wearily. He took another look at the files lying on the desk. "What choice do I have?"

Sams smiled then, and for a moment the gesture seemed genuine. "I'm pleased to have you on the team," he said. He stood up from behind the desk, gathering his papers. He picked up his pistol and replaced it under his coat.

"That's it?" Deal asked.

"Oh, that's hardly it," Sams said, "but that's enough for now."

He stepped from behind the desk and moved briskly toward the door. "You'll be hearing from me, Mr. Deal. In the meantime, enjoy your good fortune." He flashed his self-satisfied smile. "You have a brand-new life ahead."

Then he was gone, followed closely by Tasker, who held Deal's eye briefly before following out the door. After a moment, Deal stood from the chair and walked out onto the porch.

It was dark now, the moon not yet risen above the screen of the surrounding mangroves. He scanned the dim roadway that led out through the trees, but saw no sign of movement. He leaned with his hands on the rough wooden railing, listening for the sounds of receding footsteps, for a motor starting up, but there was only the distant hum of traffic out on the highway and the screech of tree frogs in the mangroves, a sound much diminished at this time of year.

Maybe they were ghosts, Deal told himself. Maybe he'd dreamed it all. But how to explain the lingering ache at the base of his skull, and the knot of rage that lingered in his gut?

He thought he heard something then, the far-distant sound of a car's engine grinding to life, the spurt of sand as wheels chewed away in the night. But he couldn't be sure. He turned from the railing and walked back into the office. He picked up the telephone. He wasn't surprised to hear the purr of the dial tone restored. He tapped out the only number that mattered to him and stood wondering what he was going to say to Janice.

seven

"This is *the* tunnel, isn't it?" Kaia Jesperson said, glancing out her window as the speeding Mercedes ducked down beneath Parisian street level. "The Alma tunnel?"

Richard Rhodes gave her a look. She looked no less lovely to him than the moment he'd first laid eyes on her weeks before in Turkey. He thought of his father suddenly, and knew it was because of her. Yes, how he wished Grant Rhodes were still alive to meet this woman.

"We made love in the same bed, ate at the same table," he said, turning back to Kaia. ". . . now we're taking the same route to the airport."

"Made love," said Kaia. "Is that what you'd call it?"

"I would," said Rhodes.

"Hmmm." She was turned away, seemed to be studying the tunnel walls, where graffitists proclaimed their undying devotion to the victims of the famous crash.

He glanced toward the front of the limousine, but Frank and Basil Wheatley sat stoically in the front seat, the glass partition raised.

"Did you have this thing for the princess?" she asked.

Rhodes looked over. "Don't be ridiculous."

She turned to face him. "I bear a certain resemblance, you know. People say this sometimes."

"Is that so?"

She twisted her hair in her hand, pulled it back on her head, gave him a smile meant to be winsome. "I thought perhaps you had a fetish of some sort."

He watched her skeptically. "I don't think the princess ever appeared quite so salacious."

She lifted her brows and let her long hair tumble free. "Salacious," she repeated. "Now there is a word."

"It suits," Rhodes said, and thought to himself that it did. Not only did flames surround Kaia Jesperson, he had discovered, they boiled up within. There had been times when he'd had sex as frequently in the past, but never had it been a single person who'd ignited those desires. Flames, he thought. Acrobatics. Spectacles of violence.

"Can we stop?" she said, bringing Rhodes back.

"Here?"

"I want to see," she said, shaking her head. "I missed the place where it happened."

It took Rhodes a moment to get his mind off the sex. When he'd finally understood, he glanced at his watch. "We're a bit late," he said.

"For what?" she insisted. "You own the plane."

He sighed and nodded. He pressed a button on the armrest console. "We need to turn around," he said.

Basil glanced back at the still-closed partition. It was reflective glass. The big man would be staring at his own reflection. His lips moved, but the sound came from speakers hidden somewhere in the plush upholstery. "What'd you forget?"

"Miss Jesperson would like to see the spot where the accident took place."

Basil digested this, nodding without comment. He turned and said something to Frank, who raised one hand from the wheel in response. Basil turned back to the partition. "Okay. We'll swing around just the other side—"

The words were hardly out of his mouth when something slammed into the side of the Mercedes, sending it veering toward the tunnel wall. Kaia gave a nearly inaudible cry, jerking away from the window as the heavy car rode up over the curbing. There was a grinding sound that shook Rhodes in his seat, and a shower of sparks as metal sheared on stone.

Deal with the Dead

The rear of the Mercedes caught something and rebounded back into the traffic lane. Rhodes felt another thud, then hurtled forward off his seat. As he went down, sprawling across the carpeted floor, he caught sight of a pale blue van beside them, its side door sliding back.

"Look out," Kaia cried in his ear as she flung herself on top of him.

A man in a fatigue jacket and a wool cap jammed on his head appeared in the open doorway of the careening van beside them. The man had an automatic rifle in one hand and was trying to hold himself upright with the other.

But the Mercedes had steadied itself now. Rhodes felt the surge of the big engine as Frank Wheatley jammed the pedal down.

"Tell me you staged this," Kaia cried. "Say it's for my benefit."

Rhodes heard chuffing noises beside them, felt a lurch as the tires of the Mercedes blew. The car sagged to one side, but kept going.

The van flashed past, then hit them again, this time near the front. The two vehicles were locked together now, engines at redline, each straining to drive the other to oblivion. In the end, it was the Mercedes that lost the battle, its tires chewed down to the rims, furrowing the pavement, costing them too much speed. The right fender crunched into the wall and the two vehicles swung about, broadsiding to a halt across the traffic lanes.

And where *was* the other traffic, Rhodes thought as he slid forward, his back and shoulders driving against the rear-facing seats. The moment the Mercedes ground to a halt, he scrambled to his hands and knees. Outside, he saw the rear doors of the van fly open. Two more men in watch caps and camouflage jackets jumped down, automatic weapons braced.

"Dear God," said Kaia Jesperson. She reached for the handle of the opposite door, ready to run for it.

Rhodes lunged, caught her around the waist, pulled her down. "You don't want to do that," he said. He rolled on top of her, thinking oddly, *Smoked black windows, they'll be shooting blind . . .* and then the roar of gunfire began.

To the men dressed in the yellow fatigues of a Paris roadworking crew stationed at either end of the tunnel, it might have sounded like a choreographed eruption of jackhammer work. To the four men who had

71

leaped from the van, fingers held tightly to the triggers of their weapons, it seemed like they had created the roaring at the end of the world.

Bullets slammed into the windshield, the hood, the side windows of the targeted Mercedes in a deadly, seemingly endless hail. Sixty seconds it might have taken to empty the clips and the reloads, perhaps a few more. Every square foot of the expensive, gleaming sheet metal erupted into tight-stitched pustules, pristine window glass transformed into frost-etched sheets.

One of the assassins, the man who'd been in the side door of the van, strode forward toward the Mercedes, his weapon chattering bullets, spewing fire now at near point-blank range. Abruptly he paused, bringing his hand up, slapping at his cheek as if something had stung him there.

He tottered for a moment, then spun sideways. His left ear was gone, along with a section of his scalp, where a pale, fleshy tulip seemed to have bloomed. He was dead before he hit the ground, his weapon silent, his bloody palm thrust upward in a permanent gesture for help.

The three who were left, their own clips spent, stared in amazement at their fallen colleague and also at the steaming, blasted hulk of the Mercedes: the glass shattered, turned white by a million spidery fault lines, the once glossy skin of the hood and doors peppered with hundreds of bullet holes. It was eerily quiet in the tunnel now, though their ears were numb with the residue of gunfire.

"Ricochet," said one of the men finally, in a language only they understood. He pointed at the fallen one and shook his head, and his two comrades nodded grudging understanding.

The three stood stunned by this freak occurrence, by the roaring that still lingered in their heads. It must have registered in the mind of one man—all that glass shattered, yes, but still intact; as well as the question of what might have caused that ricochet—but by the time an explanation had occurred to him, it was too late. He had opened his mouth to point at the blasted car, was about to pass on his suspicions . . .

. . . when the front passenger door of the limo flew open and Basil Wheatley appeared with a stubby-barreled shotgun in his hands. The first blast from the streetsweeper hit the two men closest to the van. One, who had taken the brunt of the tight pattern, flew backward through the still-open side doors. The other threw his hands to his face, where stray buckshot had tattooed his forehead and cheeks. This man was in the midst of a curse of pain when the second blast from Basil's shotgun blew his hands, and the head behind them, into a hot pink froth.

The fourth man, who had finally understood that he and his colleagues had been firing their weapons at an armored limousine, did not wait to see what happened to his colleagues. He turned and stepped quickly behind the sheltering rear door of the van, jacking a fresh clip into the magazine of his weapon. There was another boom from Basil's streetsweeper, but the buckshot was deflected by the van's door. Another boom, another harmless clatter on the steel at the assassin's back. One more round, the assassin calculated, then he'd have the chance to take his shot.

He steadied himself, waiting, about to swing around the sheltering door, blow away that hulking man and his shotgun . . .

. . . he heard the racking mechanism of Basil's weapon engage, the roar of the shotgun echoing through the tunnel, and knew it was time to make his move.

But there was something wrong. He felt a strange weightless feeling, a numbness where his legs should have been. Instead of stepping forward, he realized he was moving back, toward the flapping opposite door of the van, which itself seemed to have tilted strangely.

His hands felt cold and useless, his fingers turned to stone. His head had jerked backward, affording him a momentary glimpse of the tunnel's soot-stained vaulting. Then his chin was on his chest, which seemed warm, and dark, and wet. His cheek bounced off the opposite door frame, then struck the gritty pavement below, but he felt no pain.

He lay motionless, his unblinking eyes focused steadily on the back of the door where he'd been hiding. He saw the great rupture in the steel sheathing there, just where he'd been leaning, saw the tendrils of metal reaching inward at what might have been belt level. He felt the slightest tingling at the base of his spine, or where that part of him had been at least, and in the next moment, before he could even try to look down, he felt nothing at all.

By the time the blue van emerged from the other end of the tunnel, the blockades had already been cleared, the yellow-clad men posing as roadworkers vanished. Angry motorists, incensed at the delay, eager to make their own way along, paid no attention to what vehicle might have passed them by. It was nearly dark. Who would have noticed a few pellet holes, or paid attention to the driver of some service vehicle after all?

"A scattergun is good," Basil Wheatley was saying, "but you always want to keep you a deer slug packed." He was in the passenger's seat, Frank was behind the wheel. "That's your ace in the hole, little brother."

"Pack a deer slug, drive a bulletproof car," answered Frank, who kept his eyes on the road ahead. "That's what Daddy always said."

"Don't get smart," Basil said, but there wasn't any malice in his voice. He glanced into the back of the van and waved his hand to his passengers as if to suggest that what was going on between him and his brother was of little consequence.

One of the passengers was Kaia Jesperson, who sat haggard-faced on a wooden crate in the cargo area. She turned to Rhodes, who sat on the corrugated metal floor opposite her, his back against the rattling side door. "Why didn't you tell me the car was armored?" she asked.

Rhodes shrugged. "There wasn't much time for discussion," he said. "I didn't want you running outside, that's all."

She nodded, watching him in the strobelike effect of the passing streetlights. "Does this sort of thing happen to you often?"

"Babescu had friends," Rhodes said, his tone philosophical. He gestured dismissively. "We'll be leaving them behind, now."

She lifted one of her expressive eyebrows. "They seemed quite determined to me. How do you leave men like that behind?"

He shrugged. "They made a gesture, it didn't work out. Sometimes that's the end of it."

"And if it isn't?"

The van rumbled across a rough stretch of pavement, making speech impossible for a bit. He stared across the dim interior at her until the rumble had subsided. "You don't have to get involved," he said.

"I'm already involved," she said.

"I'm serious," he said. "You're free to go your own way."

"You would trust me?" There was the slightest tone of mockery in her voice.

"Implicitly," he said. And it was true. If he knew anything, he knew that he had nothing to fear from this woman.

"You think I'm as soulless as you are," she said.

Rhodes glanced at the front of the van. What did the Wheatleys make of such conversation? he wondered. Where did it fit in the world of deer slugs and car crushers and down-home aphorisms?

"You enjoy cheating death, that much I know," he said.

It brought dismissive laughter from her. "I was too frightened to breathe back there. My pants are wet."

"Even so," he said.

Rhodes felt a hesitation in the vehicle's momentum. He glanced forward.

Frank Wheatley spoke over his shoulder. "The turn's coming up. We still going to the airfield?"

"I'm not certain yet," Rhodes said.

He turned back to her. "What do you say, Kaia?"

"I like the way you say my name," she said. "I wish you'd use it more often."

Rhodes nodded, waiting. The hum of the tires beneath him was muted now.

"Where will you go?" she asked.

"Home," he told her, as if he had not shared his intentions with her already.

"Home," she repeated. "An interesting concept for the soulless."

"I'm going home," he said. "What would you like to do?"

She smiled at him. The look in her eyes seemed somehow patronizing. Yet her lips were full of promise. "I'll go with you," she told him.

Rhodes nodded again. He took no sharp intake of breath, nor any marked release. No variation in his pulse, no dilation or constriction of his pupils, no detectable change in the pressure of his blood. And still . . . and still . . . he felt himself a different man.

He glanced at Frank. "You can turn here," he called.

And, of course, they did.

eight

"WHY DON'T YOU GO to the police?" Janice said.

Deal pursed his lips, glancing across the corner of the L-shaped bar at Two Chefs, where a sleekly dressed couple sat toying with pale pink drinks in stemmed glasses. The woman—jet black hair, dark eyes, bright lipstick—wore a plum-colored silk dress with a plunging neckline and pressed herself to the man's arm as she whispered in his ear. No danger of being overheard—nothing short of gunfire was likely to attract the attention of those two.

"And tell the police what, exactly?" He took a swig of Red Stripe from a squat brown bottle. "That I had a conversation with a guy?"

"He tried to blackmail you."

"Yeah?" He glanced at her. "Where's the evidence?"

She thought about it. "Well, if you got the contract fair and square, they could look into it, see exactly how it happened . . ."

Her voice trailed off and he knew she'd realized as soon as she said it.

"There are only two possibilities," he said. "Sams actually rigged it somehow, some way that I'd take the heat for if anyone investigated—" He broke off, shaking his head. "Or it's all bullshit. Either way, it stalls the project and gives everybody else who wanted it the opportunity to climb back in."

He gave her a bleak look. "It's the biggest piece of work we've had since my old man died, Janice. If I get the county oversight board on the case, it could queer the whole deal before it gets off the drawing board."

"Well," she said, sounding petulant. "He did break into your office."

"Maybe I left the door unlocked," he said, feeling exhausted. A couple of hours ago, he'd been ready to celebrate the revival of his fortunes. Now it took an effort to lift his beer.

"You *do* things like that," she agreed. He could tell by her expression that she was trying to stay calm. She raised her own glass, sipped her martini, closed her eyes tight, as if she were trying to will trouble away herself.

"This is good," she said after a moment. "I haven't had a martini in a long time."

Two weeks ago, he wanted to tell her. Sitting here, on these stools, at this same bar. But he didn't. It had been one of the not-so-good nights, when the "other" Janice had shown up. Not the beautiful, self-possessed woman he'd known for so many years there beside him, but the distracted, hesitant stranger who glanced over her shoulder every half-minute while she talked, as if she were waiting for the arrival of someone or something that had been about to swoop down for a long, long time.

Deal felt a pang going to the very core of him. If he insisted, if he tried to remind her of that last encounter, he would only wound her. She didn't mean to drift away, to erect that self-referential shield about her very being. She simply did. It is just what happened sometimes, and just as troubling was the fact that it often seemed apropos of nothing.

The doctors could not say why, beyond positing that it was another of the seemingly endless manifestations of post-traumatic stress reaction, a disorder so protean that the best practitioners were prone to throw up their hands: "Nothing you can do about it, Mr. Deal. Nothing for you to do but be supportive, and loving, and patient."

Easy for them to say. But Deal knew this: Men who had meant to kill him had nearly killed his wife, and ever since that time, he had lived with the possibility that the person he loved most in all the world would, without warning, simply drift away from him—for a day, a week, a month. Worst was the fear that one day it would be forever. And no amount of reasoning could ever convince him that it was not, at bedrock, his own damned fault.

He forced himself from his gloomy thoughts, determined not to let this time with her go sour. He smiled at her. "You look terrific," he said. He poured some of the beer in the frosty glass that Cyrus, the bartender, had brought with his Red Stripe, then touched the glass to hers.

She smiled. "Thanks," she said. "I got a haircut." She fluffed the short hair at the back of her neck.

"I noticed," he said.

"You must not like it, then," she said, "if you didn't say anything."

"I *do* like it," he insisted. He was about to say that it made her look younger, but he wasn't sure if that would sound right. "I'm just a little distracted, that's all."

She smiled brightly, gave her head a toss. "It's okay," she said. "Hair grows."

He stared at her. How anyone so lovely could have doubts about her appearance was beyond him. That was another lingering effect of the attacks. She'd been badly burned, all right, but what scars remained were virtually invisible, a fine line here and there, most of it hidden under even that short haircut. But that didn't matter, did it? *Be supportive, Mr. Deal. Be patient and understanding.* In this case, leave well enough alone.

"Did you say something?" she said, glancing up from the menu Cyrus had left.

"No," he said. "Unless I was thinking out loud."

She shrugged and lay the menu down. Her gaze traveled over his shoulder at the couple opposite them. "I think that woman intends to have sex with that man," she said.

Deal glanced over his shoulder, then back at her. "People do that," he said.

She gave him a look that didn't discount the possibility. "Do they?" She bent to her drink and sipped, so that Deal couldn't tell if she was hiding a smile. Living apart hadn't put an end to their sex life, but it had certainly had an effect. Sex with the "other" Janice was out of the question, so that every one of their "dates"—weekly, more or less—loomed for him with all the charged uncertainty of a college boy's blind date.

"Stop thinking about it," she said, putting her drink down.

"Thinking about what?"

"You are *so* obvious," she said. "We haven't even had an appetizer."

"Neither have those two," he said, nodding over his shoulder.

She rolled her eyes. "Would you like me to behave that way?"

He shrugged. "Not *here*, maybe."

She shook her head, and he could tell by the new set of her features that she was back to business. It was like watching weather sweep across a plain from a great distance, he thought. No trouble reading Janice's moods.

"So how much of this do you really believe?" she said. She was leaning toward him on her elbows, staring at him over her drink.

He shrugged. "I'm going to talk to Vernon Driscoll. He can find out if the guy's for real."

"And if he is?"

Deal gave her a bleak look. "That's all I've been thinking about since I called you."

"Say it's all true," Janice said. "About your father, about everything. Would you do what this man Sams wants?"

Deal took a deep breath. "That's just it. I don't know what he really wants. If it just means keeping my eyes open, picking up some dirt on a major scumbag, I don't know. Maybe I can justify that much."

He broke off as Cyrus the bartender approached and slid a plate of something between them. "Did I order this?" Deal asked.

Cyrus shrugged. He was in his fifties and had once tended bar on a yacht owned by Aristotle Onassis. He had perpetually squinted eyes and a bushy mustache that sometimes made it difficult to read his facial expression. "It's an artichoke and lobster thingy," he said. "Franco's experimenting," he added, referring to one of the chefs. "He wants to know what his favorite diners think."

"I already know it's good," Janice said. She had leaned to cut a piece of the dish with her fork. "Anything Franco does is good."

"Where's the lobster?" Deal asked, peering at the arrangement on the plate. Carved rosettes of what he presumed were artichoke hearts drizzled with a mustardy lacework of sauce . . . it seemed too attractive to eat.

"Tell Franco it's an awesome thingy," Janice said. There was a tiny yellow dot of sauce on her upper lip. Deal reached for it with his finger, but she beat him to it with her tongue.

"I'll leave you two alone," Cyrus said.

"Bring more food when it's ready," Janice told him.

"Did you want to order?" Cyrus said.

"Just take care of us," Janice said.

Cyrus smiled and nodded. *You're smitten by her too, pal,* Deal thought, watching the man walk away.

"You were saying?"

"It's never as simple as what they make it seem, that's all," Deal said. He noticed his beer was empty and wished he'd asked Cyrus for another. Then he saw the man coming back their way, squat brown bottle and fresh frosty glass in hand.

"The guy's not just saying he'll pull the job away," Deal continued as Cyrus glided away, "he's threatening to ruin me if I don't cooperate, have me sent to prison for bribery." He stared at her, feeling fresh anger at Sams's references to the medical bills, a part of the encounter he'd left out. "He wouldn't go to those lengths unless there was more to it than what he was telling me."

"You want to call his bluff, don't you?"

He gave her a look. "If things get really tough, we could set you up in business: Madame Janice, sees all, tells all."

She smiled, but her heart wasn't in it. "I want to tell you to do it, just blow him off and see what happens, but—" She broke off, shaking her head. "It all seems so crazy. I think we need to wait and see. Maybe it's some crazy con job, like you say. Maybe this will all just go away."

Deal nodded. "I'm hoping," he said. He didn't think he sounded very convincing.

"You'll talk to Vernon, then?"

Deal nodded. "He gets back tomorrow."

She looked at him. "He's working out of town?"

"Orlando," he said. "He hired out to Disney, doing background checks for the seasonal Santas."

"Come on," she said, her face a mask of disbelief.

"Seriously," Deal said. "The company has to be very careful about who runs around their parks dressed up like that."

"God," she said, shaking her head. "What a world."

"You can say that again," he said. And then Cyrus was back with more food.

. . .

"Okay now," Janice whispered, her breath hot at his ear. "Just lean back all the way. Try to get your hands flat on the bed."

"I liked my hands where they were," Deal said.

"So did I," she said, "but I want you to try this."

He leaned back, then dutifully pressed his palms into the mattress beside his ears. "There," she said, adjusting herself atop him. "Doesn't that feel good?"

"It was feeling pretty good already," Deal said. If she moved again, he thought, if she so much as breathed too deeply . . .

"It's the stretching part," she said. "It makes everything feel better."

"Have you been doing this with other people, Janice?" *Best to ask, to hear about it straight out,* he thought. At a moment when he felt good enough to absorb almost anything.

"Of course not," she said, bending to kiss his chest. "Exercise sex. It's not a secret, Deal. I read about it in a magazine at the doctor's office."

"I've got to try your doctor," he said.

"She's a gynecologist," Janice said. He felt her breath at the hollow of his throat, her tongue teasing his breastbone, her teeth nibbling the prong of one nipple. "Just stay where you are now," she said.

"I'm not going anywhere," he managed. She sat up, then leaned backward, her hands locked beneath him, pulling at the small of his back.

"Good," she breathed. "That's so good."

"I take it back," Deal said. "I *am* going somewhere." He felt, in fact, like he was heading for a different universe.

"Oh yes," she said, moving, twisting, and then he knew that she had joined him and they were flying through the spangled dark together.

Hours later? Days later? Another lifetime altogether?

"Mommy?" It was Isabel's voice, sounding meek in the early morning light.

He felt Janice tug the sheet higher over their shoulders. "Yes, sweetheart?"

He'd been lying in that dazed pre-awake state, stupid with contentment, all his concerns banished, far too greedy to let himself simply back into sleep. Not without the guarantee that he could relive it all in his dreams, at least.

"Is Daddy here?" she asked. The door was halfway open now—he could tell by the sound of her voice.

"Daddy who?" Janice said softly.

"*Mommy!*"

"Who's that knocking at my door?" Deal said.

"I *thought* you were here," she said, giggling. She came quickly across the carpeted floor and sat down on the edge of the bed.

Deal sat up now, and she eyed his T-shirt speculatively. "You slept over," she said.

"I did," he agreed.

"That means we get pancakes," she said.

"Of course," Deal said.

"Give us a few minutes, Isabel." It was Janice's voice, muffled beneath the covers.

"Okay," said Isabel, smiling at him. Janice's eyes, his cheekbones and chin. She would be a handsome woman, he thought. Maybe not delicate, but beautiful just the same.

"Pancakes it is," Deal repeated.

"Go take your shower," Janice said.

"Okay, Mommy," Isabel said. She leaned to kiss Deal on the cheek and then scampered out. "Daddy's here!" she announced as she closed the door after her.

Deal felt Janice's hand find his and squeeze. "Pancakes," she said. "You spoil her." She raised herself up on one elbow and stared at him sleepily.

"Everyone needs spoiling once in a while," he told her.

She gave him a speculative look. "Since you put it that way," she said. "Why not?" And came his way.

nine

"So, how'd the Santas check out?" Deal said, his thoughts still drifting over the events of the night before.

Saturday evening now, he and Vernon Driscoll were sitting in the breezeway on the second floor of the fourplex Deal had built in Little Havana, taking a moment away from the matter of Talbot Sams. As they had arranged earlier in the week, Deal had picked Driscoll up at Miami International and filled him in on what had happened on the twenty-minute drive back to the building where they both lived.

Deal kept one of the apartments for himself and rented out the others. Driscoll, an ex–Metro–Dade homicide cop and now a private investigator, was one of his steady tenants. Another was Mrs. Suarez, a Cuban lady of indeterminate age who had come to function as Isabel's grandmother in absentia. The fourth apartment had been occupied by a revolving cast of characters over the last few years: the last tenant, and far and away the most attractive, had been a dancer at the Copa Club on Southwest 8th Street, which featured a forties-style review said to be reminiscent of the grand old days in Havana. The dancer had recently married one of the club's owners, however, and one of the downstairs units was currently vacant.

"Every one of them clean as a whistle," Driscoll said. He rummaged in the cooler beside his chair and brought out a beer. "You want one?"

"I'm fine," Deal said. It was after five on a Saturday—he could open a beer if he wanted, but the prospect didn't appeal to him. He felt weary, his early-morning euphoria having gradually waned over the course of the day, in direct proportion to the length of time he'd been away from Janice and Isabel. Next weekend, he'd have his daughter with him, but it seemed a distant prospect . . . and while his time with Janice had gone far beyond what he might have expected, he knew better than to call so soon. They hadn't spent consecutive nights together for more than a year. *Your frustration is natural, Mr. Deal. But the last thing she needs is to feel pressured . . .*

"The problem is," Driscoll was saying, having downed half his beer at a gulp, "you can't find anything on a guy, you have to figure he's dirty, you know what I mean?"

Deal looked at him. "So if you find something on a person, he or she is a dirtbag. If you don't, they're dirtbags for sure."

Driscoll nodded, wiping his mouth on the back of his hand. "Almost invariably."

Deal rubbed his face, trying to bring some energy back. "They teach this at the academy, I guess. Cop Logic one-oh-one."

Driscoll grunted. "You pick it up on your own, my friend. The real world is not a pretty place."

"Give me a beer, Vernon. I fear a claiming contest coming on."

"I'm just telling you what you already know." Driscoll pulled out a beer for Deal, flicked its cap away with his thick thumb. He turned the bottle around so he could read the label, then glanced at Deal. "Hatuey? What the hell is that?"

"They were out of Red Stripe up at the market," Deal said. "This was on special. It's an old Cuban brand. Made in the U.S. now."

"Are we referring to our corner market?" Driscoll pointed in the vague direction of the neighborhood *grocería* that sat a block or so away, a dusty, out-of-time operation run by a Cuban couple in their sixties.

"Where else?" Deal felt a fierce loyalty to Rogelio, the old man who ran the place. Rogelio had spent seven years in one of Castro's prisons, had escaped and come to the United States in a cargo container via Mexico.

Driscoll grunted again. "I bet they ran out on purpose. I went in there the other day for a loaf of bread, all they had was Cuban. Sure, we have *pan,* the guy is telling me. I told him never mind the *pan,* I want a nice soft loaf of Wonder Bread, the kind I can squeeze up and put it in my back pocket if I want to. He looked at me like I was crazy."

"Maybe you need to move away, Vernon. You could find a nice retirement home in West Virginia, rediscover your roots."

"I like it here," Driscoll said. "It's interesting. All I'm saying is keep some Red Stripe beer and Wonder Bread on the shelf. Is that too much to ask?"

Deal sighed. "Sounds like the Bruce Jenner diet to me," he said.

"You can forget the scare tactics," Driscoll said. "Remember what happened to that Fixx guy, the one who started everybody jogging?"

"He had a heart condition to begin with. Jogging prolonged his life."

Driscoll glanced at his watch. "That's what you say. The way I figure it, all the rest of the joggers are about to start dropping like flies." He held up his beer between them. "What your heart really needs," he said, " is a nice little cushion of fat wrapped around it. Keeps it insulated from the extremes of hot and cold."

They could go on like this forever, Deal knew, at least as long as the beer held out. "Maybe you should write a book, Vernon."

"I have contemplated that very thing, Johnny-boy. Don't think I haven't."

That nickname again. Okay coming from Driscoll, of course. Vernon Driscoll had known his father, from back in the glory days. But it spun him right out of the dull-edged torpor he'd let himself fall into, forced him right back to contemplation of the specter of Talbot Sams leering out from behind his own desk.

He leaned forward himself then. "So what do you think, Vernon? Can you find out about this guy Sams?"

Driscoll nodded. "If he's on the screen."

"Meaning?"

"Some of those guys are spooks," Driscoll said. "Whatever name he gives you, that doesn't have to be *him*." He shrugged.

Deal nodded, remembering something. "He said I'd find his name in the DealCo files."

"It's worth checking," Driscoll said, "but even so, it could still be an alias."

"I suppose," Deal said.

"You tell anybody else about this?"

"Janice."

Driscoll glanced at him. "You tell her to keep it to herself?"

"She knows that much," Deal said.

Driscoll nodded his head slowly. "It's a hell of a note, isn't it? Just the thought of your old man under the thumb of the Feds all that time."

"You think it was possible, then?"

Driscoll stared at him. "Anything's possible, that much I've learned." He straightened in his chair. "But whatever else he was, your old man was stand-up. He wouldn't have screwed anybody that didn't deserve a screwing. Matter of fact, it makes me feel better thinking it could have been him, sending some of the scumbags away."

Deal thought about that for a moment. Maybe there was some solace there, but it couldn't make up for all the rest.

"This Sams would have to be pretty good at what he does," Deal said finally. "I mean, to have used my father all that time and never blow his cover."

"Yes," Driscoll agreed. "He would have to be very good indeed."

"Does that make him good enough to hide from you?"

"Possibly," Driscoll said. "But I've dug people up from the witness protection program before. Finding anyone's usually just a matter of time." He cut another glance at Deal. "Meanwhile, how bad can it be? You just won yourself a nice little piece of a great big pie."

"If it's true," Deal said. "I'll find out Monday for sure. I called Jack Tate at the business desk of the *Herald,* but they hadn't heard anything. So far, all I have is the word of a conman and a spook."

"Well, I don't know about this guy Sams," Driscoll said. "But you can trust Eddie Barrios to smell a buck at a hundred paces."

Deal sipped his beer. The light was fading and he saw a lamp go on in Mrs. Suarez's apartment across the way. Music was playing somewhere in the distance, a plaintive ballad in Spanish, more Mexican than Spanish by the mellow sound of it. "I keep telling myself, Assume it's all true, then what's the worst part? I take the job, and along the way I help bring down one of the bad guys."

"There's a point," Driscoll said.

"And just about that time, I think of my old man putting that pistol in his mouth." He stared at Driscoll, his jaw rigid.

"You don't know why that happened," Driscoll said softly.

"That's what I used to think," Deal said. "Now all of a sudden, I'm not so sure."

Driscoll sighed and stood to put his hand on Deal's shoulder. "I'll make a couple calls in the morning," he said, "but it'll probably be Monday before I can get much accomplished. Meantime, why don't I buy you dinner down at Fox's? Uncle Walt was so happy his Santa Clauses were clean, he gave me a fat bonus."

Deal shook his head. "Uncle Walt's dead."

"I'll buy you dinner anyway," Driscoll said.

"I appreciate it," Deal said. "But I'm not so hungry right now."

Driscoll lifted an eyebrow. "Whatever you say, Johnny-boy." He clapped Deal on the shoulder and headed toward the stairwell. "Meantime, I wouldn't worry too much. All you've heard so far is a bunch of talk."

Deal managed a smile, lifting his beer in salute as Driscoll descended the stairs. "You're right, Vernon," Deal said. "So far it's all just talk."

He remembered then that he'd wanted to tell Driscoll that he'd hired a new man himself, that perhaps the ex-cop could exercise his background-checking skills on a Mr. William Brown of south Georgia, but the matter hardly seemed pressing.

Something that could wait for another day, he thought, listening to the echo of Driscoll's receding footsteps. The sound seemed to blend perfectly with the beat of that plaintive Spanish song and the thought that was looping through his mind, that he realized bothered him more than anything else:

Bad enough that you shot yourself, old man. But why couldn't you at least have left me a note?

ten

DEAL HAD INTENDED TO drive back to the trailer office off Old Cutler and begin his search through the company files for any sign of Talbot Sams. After Driscoll left, he'd gone into his own apartment and showered, trying to muster up something resembling energy. He put on a T-shirt and jeans, suitable attire for digging through musty papers, he thought as he slipped into a pair of Top-Siders and made his way out, past Mrs. Suarez's glowing windows and down the staircase to the street, where he'd parked the Hog earlier.

He made a U-turn in front of the building and piloted the Hog north a couple of blocks to Southwest 8th Street then turned, cruising eastward past the long line of *mercados* and *ferreterías*, dressmakers and storefront cigar factories, cafés and *farmacias*. Many of the shops were shuttered by this time on a Saturday night, but the street was still lively with foot traffic, far more so than most urban streets these days, he reflected. An anachronism, perhaps, to find a citizenry afoot on a weekend night, but just one more mark in Miami's favor, at least so far as Deal was concerned.

He moved along out of the brightly lit commercial district and underneath the elevated roadways of I-95 and Metrorail, the barrier that effectively divided Little Havana from downtown Miami. Here, shabby apartment buildings, low-rent offices, and once-impressive homes, most of them converted into rooms for rent, lay in the eternal shadow of the elevated roadbeds. If there were people afoot in this area, they were being cautious about it.

A couple more blocks, however, and everything changed again. He brought the Hog to a stop at a traffic light on Brickell at the southernmost end of the banking district that trailed down from Miami's central city in a parade of high-rise steel-and-glass monoliths. Most of the buildings on his left were fronted with broad plazas, splashing fountains, and impressive plantings, and many of them bore signage in a welter of languages far beyond Deal's capability to translate. No foot traffic here, of course— none for hours now. He was staring across the broad boulevard at the imposing façade of the Bank of Brunei, fourteen stories of gleaming glass and marble, and one of the last great gasps of DealCo, when he heard the tap of a horn behind him.

He noticed that the light had turned green and gave an apologetic wave of his hand as he swung south onto Brickell, where the banks gave way to even grander condominiums and where, sixteen stories up a thirty-two-story residence tower, the salad days of DealCo had come to an end. They'd had to default on the construction loan and lay off two hundred men less than a month before Christmas. His father had emptied his personal bank accounts to provide some form of severance pay. A week after that, Barton Deal had emptied his brains onto the walls of his study.

Deal glanced at the building as he went by. Long since finished by whomever the trustees had engaged, the building was now a showpiece, glimmering against the night sky. Floor-to-ceiling windows, broad balconies, penthouses that promised a view all the way to Paradise itself. Full of happy people, Deal thought, though he knew that was hardly true.

He realized he had edged over into the left lane, looking by instinct for the break in the median that would take him down a lane to the Terrell estate, six acres of prime bayfront property eagerly sought after by real estate speculators. It was where he'd been going every day for the last couple of weeks, after all, no surprise that he'd nearly made the turn without thinking.

What did surprise him was his failure to turn back out into the traffic lane and continue southward to his intended destination. Instead, he waited for a couple of oncoming cars to pass, then made his turn across the double lanes and onto the crushed coral path that led to the big double gates. He reached above the visor, where he kept the remote that Terrell had provided for him, found the unit, and pressed the "Entry" button. The gates began their ponderous inward swing and Deal nudged the accelerator of the Hog, edging forward in synch with the doors.

He told himself he was simply going to check on the job, make sure everything had been wrapped up as he and Gonzalez had discussed before he'd left on Friday, but he knew that wasn't really it. What he was looking for was something far more important, though God knows why he expected to find it on the estate of computer guru Terrence Terrell.

He shook his head at himself, easing the Hog along the tunnel-like driveway through the oaks and palmetto and sea grape. The thick vegetation was not only a barrier between the main house and the busy road, but a reminder of the previous state of affairs in the area. Not a hundred years before, the whole near coastline of South Florida had consisted of such an unbroken tangle—until the late 1890s, Miami was virtually uninhabited, nothing more than a couple of muddy streets hacked through the undergrowth. Now Terrell had one of the few pieces of the original wilderness left, and the hounds were baying, waiting for him to tire of life in the tropics and sell out so that another tower or two might rise on the site.

Deal broke out of the dense vegetation then, catching sight of the impressive main house up ahead, its barrel-tiled roofline silhouetted against the glow from downtown. Maybe not so strange that he found himself drawn here, he thought as he pulled to a stop in front of the ever-splashing fountain.

He got out, glancing up at the empty house. Lights in random rooms, each of which would change over the course of an evening, simulating the activity within an occupied house, all of that controlled by Terrell-designed devices, and what else would you expect from a man who had once controlled the biggest part of the non-IBM personal computer market? Competition had eaten into Terrell's once fabled position, of course, but discussing the decline of his fortunes was a little bit like feeling sorry for General Motors.

Deal rounded the side of the house by his usual route, his eyes adjusting to the dark now that he was out of the car. He sidestepped a piece of sculpture—a woman folded serenely into herself—and caught sight of the outline of his gazebo on the broad lawn that sloped down to the water. Not "his" gazebo at all, of course, though until the day he finished the work, it would be.

He stepped over a pile of two-by-twos stacked near the steps to the porch of the structure and pulled himself up onto the deck that would someday hold a set of chairs and a table, and perhaps a couple of chaise longues, where guests would sit and gaze out at the untroubled waters of Biscayne Bay and, if they chose, turn their attention further northward to the dramatic skyline of modern Miami. Now it was just himself, an unfinished railing, and a couple of piles of sawdust, Deal thought, at the same time realizing that this was where he'd been heading all along. Some force drawing him to this very spot where he could hold fast to an unfinished spar of pine and stare across half a mile's expanse of inky water toward a breathtaking skyline that his father—and, yes, he himself—had helped create.

He wasn't sure what he expected to find there in the sight before him, but there was some measure of comfort in the very thought that he'd had a hand, however small, in creating that cityscape out there, reflecting against the bay. Nor did it matter really that such a concept would, along with a couple of dollars, get him a cup of coffee in any snappy restaurant that was a part of all that glitter. *You have done things that matter, Deal. As did your father before you. Never lose sight of that much . . .*

"Something to look at, ain't it?" the voice came from behind him.

Deal turned, startled, then felt something strike him above the ear. He went down on his hands and knees, then felt a foot drive into his ribs. His breath left him as his chin bounced off the wooden deck.

"Sure as hell don't see much of this in Georgia," came the voice at his ear. He felt a hand on his head, felt his hair twist tight, realized he was being hauled upward like a rag doll. "Not the part I come from anyway."

A fist struck his cheek and Deal went over backward, crashing through a temporary brace he'd toe-nailed himself, to hold the railing in place. He hit the railing with his shoulder, heard a sick wrenching of wood as his two hundred pounds torqued against it.

In the next moment, the railing gave way and Deal was over the side in a mass of splintering wood. There was an instant of weightlessness, then a pile-driving blow as his back and shoulders slammed into the damp ground below. He glanced up, but this part of the house was in deep shadow. He sensed more than saw the silhouette of a big man diving after him, and though he was still out of breath, without the strength to offer any defense, he managed to twist aside, evading the man's grasp.

He struggled to get his feet under him, to push himself up, then felt a hand clamp onto one ankle. He clawed at the grass, trying to keep himself from being pulled backward. He felt his hand brush a broken chunk of porch railing, snatched it up, and swung weakly, desperately, behind him.

There was a cry and Deal felt the grip on his ankle weaken. Still gasping for breath, he jerked his ankle free and rolled under the shelter of the deck, scuttling now like a wounded animal. By the time he had rolled around the shelter of a support post, the man was under the porch after him, but Deal was finally sucking air into his lungs. He braced himself against the post and lashed out with a solid backhand blow of the two-by-two.

There was another cry, but the man managed to get hold of his club before Deal could draw it back. The two of them struggled for control of the club for a moment, and Deal felt the power there. Not anyone he'd have picked a struggle with, he thought, then abruptly let go of his makeshift club. He hooked his arm around the support post and pistoned his heel forward, only guessing his aim in the inky darkness. He felt a satisfying snap, like a wet rag slapping against concrete, and there came a matching groan.

Deal pushed away from the post and rolled back toward the lawn. There were plenty of two-by-twos there. Concrete blocks. A spud bar you could drive through the heart of an ox.

As his hands roamed blindly over the debris in the grass, he grabbed another length of railing and rolled back on the deck as a vague shape came out from under the structure beneath him. *Ought to be getting onto his hands and knees about now,* Deal thought, lunging forward with the length of wood in both hands. He leaned off the deck and onto his assailant's back, dropping his hands over the man's head. Then he pulled backward violently, wedging the broken spar tight against the man's throat. The man struggled wildly, pulling Deal off the porch as if he weighed nothing, but still Deal held tight to the length of wood, one hand a fulcrum at the base, the other a lever at the back of the man's head.

Deal heard gagging noises, felt the power going out of the man's struggles. In moments the man had collapsed into the grass, Deal on top of him still holding tight to the broken chunk of railing as if he were trying to strangle an ox with its own yoke.

The strangling sounds were weaker in the man's throat now, and the movements of his legs had changed from kicks to something more like galvanic twitches. "I can kill you," Deal gasped. He gave a nudge at the base of the man's skull to be sure he had his attention. "You know that, don't you?"

There was a gargling sound by way of answer and Deal released the pressure on the back of the man's head by an infinitesimal degree. "One move, I'll crush your throat, you understand?"

Another gargling sound. Deal backed the pressure off another notch. "Who are you?"

A coughing sound this time. Deal kept his arms poised, ready to increase the pressure in an instant.

"Bown," the man gasped. "Bil-bown."

It took Deal a moment to understand the man's strangled speech. "Billy Brown?" Deal repeated, hearing the disbelief in his own voice. "What the hell are you doing? This is Deal, goddammit."

He had started to relax his grip at Brown's throat when he felt an elbow smash into his ribs. "I know who you are, motherfucker," Brown said, trying to buck him off.

Deal, his mind a welter of confusing signals, felt himself slammed back against the edge of the deck. There was an electrifying pain in his back, and he felt his grip on the two-by-two beginning to give way. *And that'll be the end of you, Johnny-boy,* came the voice from somewhere, willing him to hold fast.

He ignored the pain at his kidneys and locked his legs tightly around Brown's ribcage, squeezing for all he was worth. Brown growled beneath him, a sound that rattled through Deal's own ribs, then bucked once more, trying to drive Deal against the projecting timbers of the deck.

Deal twisted as they fell back again, managing to get his hand locked at the base of Brown's neck. He levered his hand forward, jerking backward at the end of the broken spar, and felt Brown's legs buckle. When the two of them went down this time, Deal did not let up.

He dug in against Brown's frantic struggles, pulling on one side, shoving on the other, until finally the man went limp. Deal hesitated one more instant, then released his hold on the club. He pressed his fingertips to Brown's neck, felt the throb of a pulse still working there.

The stack of two-by-twos had been tied with baling twine, he knew. He'd cut it open earlier that morning himself. He scrambled quickly to the tumbled stack and pawed through the wood until he found the cord. He hurried back to Brown's inert form, pulled his thick arms behind him and bound him at the wrists. He pulled the end of the cord down to Brown's sneaker-clad feet and was finishing the hasty job of hog-tying when he felt the man begin to stir.

"I'll kill you," Brown coughed, and thrashed about, trying to free his hands.

Deal dropped down, pinning a knee on the man's chest as he flopped onto his back. "You won't kill anybody," he said. "Calm down. Tell me what this is about."

"Fuck you," Brown growled.

Deal stared down, trying to get a look at the man's face in the darkness. Was he high on some drug? Deal wondered. Or just indulging in some normal psychosis? Docile job-seeker by day, deranged killer by night. Welcome to Miami—now draw your weapons.

"You sure you know where you are?"

"Know exactly," Brown said, his voice raspy, almost a hiss.

Deal glanced about the darkness, wondering briefly if Brown were alone. "Somebody sent you after me? Is that what this is?"

"Know who you are, what you did."

Deal stared down, puzzled by the remark. The psychosis theory was starting to seem more and more convincing.

"What are you talking about, 'what I did'?" He patted his pockets but knew it was a futile gesture. His cell phone was still in the Hog, un-charged, where he'd left it the day before.

"Don't matter now," Brown said, his voice more somber.

"Well, you don't have to talk to me," Deal said. "You can explain it all to the police." Of course, the words seemed something of an idle threat to Deal. He doubted the twine would keep Brown immobilized for very long, once he'd gone for help. And it seemed out of the question to try to carry the solidly built man back to the Hog. What was he going to do, then? Choke the man back into senselessness? He was trying to remember if there was something more substantial in the Hog that he might use to beef up his job of hog-tying, when Brown broke the silence.

"Ought to be you talking to the police," the man muttered. Not exactly the tone of a psycho, nor of a hard-bitten killer, Deal thought. He leaned aside, trying for a confusing look at the expression on Brown's face.

"What are you talking about?" Deal said. "What is it that you think I've done to you?"

"Not me," Brown said. Deal heard an unfathomable bitterness there. Then Brown added, "What you did was to my brother."

eleven

DEAL STARED DOWN THROUGH the darkness at the man he had pinned to the ground, wondering if he had heard correctly. "Your brother?" He shook his head, searching the roster of men whom he had fired, refused to hire, had beaten out for jobs, but there was simply nothing there. "I don't know anybody named Brown."

"Ain't my name," Brown said. "Wasn't *his*, either."

Deal sighed. So that explained the reluctance to come up with an ID during their "job interview" of the day before. Another jailbird pinned under his knee, then, trying to hide a past in order to get a decent job. But that didn't exactly explain everything, now, did it?

"You want to tell me your real name, then?" he asked the man beneath him. "Or just wait and talk to the cops?"

"Russell's my name," Brown said. "Russell Straight. My brother, name of Leon."

"Leon Straight . . . ?" Deal was repeating the words even as it all swept over him like a storm-driven tide off the bay. Whatever was in his voice must have satisfied the man he'd pinned to the earth with his knee.

"That's right," Russell Straight was saying. "What you did to my brother, I come down to pay the favor back."

Deal stared off into the starlit heavens, scarcely believing what he had heard. Leon Straight. A former Dolphin defensive end from a small college in Georgia, a big man with bad knees and an attitude that would make a steroid abuser seem like a model citizen. He'd played half a dozen games healthy, a few more on painkillers, had left the team before the season was over. There had been a rancorous dispute over contract terms—a grievous oversight attributed to Leon's since deceased agent.

More cogent was Leon Straight's post-football career: a stint as an enforcer for Hialeah racketeer Raoul Alcazar. In the course of which he'd crossed Deal's path. And more importantly, that of his wife. He'd kidnapped her, held her captive in a Stiltsville fishing cabin, nearly killed her and Isabel, then their unborn child.

"You're Leon Straight's brother?"

"Am," said Russell. The defiance had not left his voice.

Deal glanced around their deserted surroundings, still trying to come to terms with it all. "You've been following me?"

Russell stared up at him, unfazed. "The man that owns this place could use a faster-closing gate. There's some more work for you, Mr. DealCo, you still alive to do it."

"Maybe we *ought* to leave the police out of it," Deal said. He glanced at one of the scattered two-by-twos nearby. It wouldn't take long to finish Straight, and it wouldn't be hard to hide the body. By morning he could be part of an enlarged footing for the deck, and an archeologist could wonder at the remains a few hundred centuries from now.

"Never thought otherwise," Russell said. "You or me. I messed my chance. You might as well get it over with."

Deal stared down at Russell Straight. "I didn't kill your brother, Russell."

"Doesn't matter what you say now. Tell me you're Puff Daddy come down to see Madonna, it's all the same to me."

"I saw him die," Deal said. "But that's not the same thing."

He felt something move inside Russell Straight's chest. Or maybe it was just his knee shifting on the man's flesh. "Leon wrote to me," the man said. "Told me you took what was his, he was going to take it back. He told me who to look for if things didn't work out."

Deal considered this. "It took you long enough to get here."

Straight made a sound that could have been meant as a derisive laugh. "I had myself otherwise indisposed."

"You were in prison."

"No shit, Sherlock."

"He told you about the man he worked for, Raoul Alcazar?"

"About both you two. He knew what he was up against. Up against the man all his life."

Deal shook his head. "You think Raoul Alcazar and I teamed up against your brother?"

There was silence beneath him. "Raoul Alcazar wanted me dead," Deal said finally. "He sent your brother after me. Then your brother decided he'd had enough of being Alcazar's goon. Leon tried to turn the tables, which would have been fine with me, except that he kidnapped my wife as part of his scheme. I found out where she was and came to get her. It's as simple as that."

"I thought you said you didn't kill him," Russell Straight said. There was something resembling uncertainty in his voice.

"I didn't," Deal said, reliving the terrible night in his head. He'd had to pilot a cabin cruiser through the approaching bands of a hurricane all the way out to Stiltsville, that bizarre clutch of weekend homes and fishing camps built on pilings half a dozen miles out into the bay from where he knelt right now. He'd found Janice where Leon Straight had stashed her inside one of the homes, and had been about to chance their return to the mainland when all hell broke loose.

First, Leon had blasted through the door and they'd begun their brutal struggle. Deal could still remember the strength in that big man's body. If Raoul Alcazar and his men hadn't turned up, he might not have been here to tell his side of the story. His good fortune, Leon's loss.

"Your brother and I were fighting when Alcazar showed up and stopped it."

There was no reaction from Russell, but Deal paused, a small distinction having occurred to him. "Your brother hated Alcazar. I was just a guy in the way. But things got ugly between the two of them. Leon realized Alcazar was going to kill everybody, leave your brother to take the blame."

"Just like I told you," Russell Straight muttered. "Leon lived his whole life being ripped off by the man."

"One thing Leon wasn't was stupid," Deal said. "I'm not so sure about you."

"Stupid would be listening to you," Russell Straight said. "Go on. Do what you gonna do. Get it over with."

Deal with the Dead

"Leon finally figured it out," Deal said. He could still see it, Raoul Alcazar standing over him, about to pull the trigger of a pistol and send Deal to oblivion. Alcazar would have done it without a thought and stepped back to climb aboard the helicopter that hovered just above the deck of the storm-tossed Stiltsville house, leave all the mess for someone else . . .

. . . when Leon Straight came out of nowhere—the fiercest rush he'd ever put on in a career full of indifferent achievement—and snatched the helicopter by one rail, sending it into a deadly spin, the literal sack of a lifetime. A chunk of helicopter blade cut Alcazar in half before he could pull that trigger. The ensuing explosion took Leon with it. And Deal, and Janice, and Isabel had survived. Not without scars, of course, the emotional ones perhaps even worse than the physical. But they had survived just the same. Hadn't they?

"Your brother died taking Alcazar out," Deal said. He drew a breath and stared out over the bay. There were pinpoints of light in the distance. The lights of fishing boats bobbing behind the reef's protection, that's all they were, most likely. But Deal could imagine the lights came from that far-off, impossible collection of homes rising up on their pilings like ghostly structures from a dream. "I don't know as I've ever said this to anyone," he said, "and I'd be hard put to prove it was his intention, but the fact is, Leon Straight saved my life."

"Maybe you should tell somebody who cares about that, mister," Russell Straight said. "Come on, now. Do it!"

"You think I'm going to tell you your brother saved my life, then turn around and kill you? That makes sense to you?"

"I don't know what makes sense to white people," Russell Straight said. "I know you could say anything about my brother, because he's dead now. Dead because of you . . ."

Deal was shaking his head again. "I think you know better, Russell. And I think if you'd meant to kill me to begin with, then we wouldn't even be having this conversation. If you'd had your mind made up, you wouldn't have let it happen this way."

"Who elected you inside my head?" Russell Straight said. "You sound like one of those jailhouse doctors, try to tell me how I think, what I feel."

"I'm telling you what *I* think, that's all."

There was another pause. Finally, Russell Straight spoke. "You calling the police, then?"

"Should I?" Deal said.

"What kind of question is that?"

"A simple one," Deal said. "If I stand up and turn you loose, do I have to worry we're going to start this all over again?"

"My brother said you were crazy. Now I know why."

"You came down here with an idea in your head, Russell. Then you met the real person behind that idea. I'm thinking that now, after we've talked, it's possible you've changed your thinking."

Deal could tell that he was thinking it over. "Leon said you were like that rabbit in the battery commercial. Boom-boom-boom on that drum, straight ahead, no matter what."

"The Energizer bunny?"

"Was a compliment, coming from Leon."

"I see. So what about it? You ready to get up now?"

"This is some kind of trick, right?"

"It's not a trick, Russell."

"Leon did like you said, why would you let me go?"

"That was Leon."

"I already told you what I came here for."

"Yes, we've had that conversation."

Deal felt the man's inhalation of breath. "Man, you are something else."

"You give me your word," Deal told him, "I'll let you go."

Another pause. "Okay, it's over."

Deal stood up, feeling his knees pop as he did. "Roll on your side."

Straight did as he was told. Deal fished his Swiss Army knife out of his pocket, flicked it open, eased the blade between Straight's wrists. The edge slipped through the twine like cutting butter. He eased back from Straight, his grip still ready on the length of two-by-two.

Straight got to his feet and rolled his shoulders, staring through the darkness at him. "I'd like to have a smoke," he said.

"It's a free country," Deal said. "Kill yourself if you want to."

It brought a laugh from Straight. Deal sensed him going for something in his pocket and tensed, then relaxed when he heard the ping of a

Zippo opening. There was a flash of flame and he saw that a cigarette had appeared in Straight's lips. The lighter flame blinked out, replaced by the glowing tip of the cigarette.

"I picked it up in the yard," Straight said. "You got to have something to do."

"Looks like you pumped some iron, too," Deal offered.

"I did my share," Straight said. He took another deep drag off his cigarette, regarding Deal over the glowing tip. "I think back on what Leon said about that straight-ahead rabbit, now. But in my mind, I was seeing this fat-cat contractor, some blubbery kind of guy I'd have to dump in a wheelbarrow to get him moved around, you know?"

Deal shrugged. "I don't blame you for being upset about your brother."

Straight glanced out toward the bay. "Leon wasn't no choir boy," he said. "But he took care of me when we were growing up. Send money home to our mama after he left. He was plenty mad, he found out I was going to jail."

"What did you do?" Deal asked.

There was a pause. "I stole a car. Me and another kid. We were just fooling. But it was Georgia, you know?"

Deal nodded. "How about your father?"

"We don't talk about him," Straight said.

"All right," Deal said. It was quiet enough that he could hear the cigarette hiss. "What do you intend to do now?"

Straight looked at him. "I hadn't thought much about it."

"You got a parole officer back home?"

Straight shrugged. "I'm all right on that."

Deal thought for a moment. "The last I recall, we were talking about your experience in construction."

Straight laughed again, flicking his cigarette in a long arc toward the water. "You'd still offer me a job?"

"Only if you wanted one."

"Whoo-ee," Straight said.

"Maybe you made that part up, about working construction?" Deal said.

"No," Straight said. "That's my trade. Like I told you."

"Well, then," Deal said.

Straight hesitated. "You serious, right?"

"Think about it," Deal said. "The offer's open."

"You are something else," Straight said.

"So I have been told," Deal said.

Straight stood staring at him through the darkness for a few more moments. Russell Straight still seemed to be shaking his head when he moved away.

twelve

"DOES THIS RESEMBLE THE guest in question?" Talbot Sams asked as he handed the artist's rendering across the gleaming conference table to the desk clerk who'd handled Rhodes's arrival at the hotel he'd used in Paris.

There were four of them in the offices the hotel's manager had turned over for their use—Sams, Tasker, a representative of the national police, and the clerk. They'd had to wait while the clerk was located and then brought in, giving Sams plenty of time to take in the surroundings: a suite of rooms opulent enough to suggest Louis XIV would have been comfortable there. There was a painting of the fabled king on one of the paneled walls, in fact—rouged cheeks, marcelled hair, nancy-boy getup—and Sams suspected the value of the portrait alone would have underwritten a year's worth of his activities.

He listened as his languid French counterpart repeated the question to the clerk in their mutual tongue, but it was a waste of time. Sams had taken Latin as his foreign language requirement in high school and college. Truly a practical choice. Once Rome became a world power again, he'd have a terrific edge.

The desk clerk, a banty little man, glanced at Sams as though he'd been asked to handle soiled underwear. He gave the rendering a cursory once-over, then shook his head. *"Non,"* he added, in a way that suggested it had been a preposterous question. At least Sams didn't need a translation.

He took the rendering back and glanced at it again himself. A typical police artist's sketch, he thought. About as distinctive as the pictures conjured up by alien abductees. *It was the eyes,* he thought. *They could never get the eyes.* But under the circumstances, it was as good as he could do.

He'd been given a lead by sources at Interpol, but Sams had arrived in Lucerne to find the Swiss plastic surgeon's clinic—an eighteenth-century manor house overlooking the city's namesake lake—a charred wreck, the files obliterated, the doctor who'd performed the surgery missing. An assistant had provided the information upon which the sketch of Rhodes was based, but Sams counted the woman as reluctant as the hotel clerk before him. As if she'd been guarding the details of a numbered bank account, Sams thought.

He'd been on his way to the airport, ready to return to the States, when word came of the incident in Paris, the bloody shoot-out at what was clearly a star-crossed section of public roadway. The bodies of four unidentified Turks recovered, associates of Ferol Babescu, Sams was certain.

"Have a look at this," Sams said, handing the clerk a photograph of Rhodes in another guise.

The hotel clerk studied the photograph more closely. After a moment he looked up at Sams. "I know this man," the clerk said, in perfect English.

Sams glanced at the detective beside him, but if the man had heard, he showed no signs of it. Sams wanted to ask why they'd been speaking through an interpreter for the last five minutes, of course, but he knew it would get him nowhere. "You know him?" he asked the clerk.

"Of course," the clerk said. "He is a famous American criminal. A financier." He spoke as though the two were synonymous.

"And how do you know him?" Sams asked, glancing at his French counterpart, who was busy picking invisible specks of lint from his immaculately tailored suit. Probably holding up the man's lunch, Sams thought. Or an assignation with his mistress. Tiresome Americans, always obsessing about guilt and punishment.

"His picture on the television, of course," the hotel clerk said, as if Sams were a dimwit. "He drowned off the coast of Saint-Tropez."

"He didn't drown," Sams said, more to himself than the clerk. He pointed at the photograph in the hotel clerk's hand. "Does the man in the photograph look like the person who called himself Richard Rhodes?"

The clerk looked at Sams with evident distrust. He glanced back at the photo, then at the detective beside Sams, speaking in rapid-fire French. Sams didn't get a word, but he could catch the drift all right. "*Non, non, non!*"

After a bit, the French detective held a hand up to stop the flood of words and turned to Sams. "He reminds us that it was late when Rhodes checked in and that the young woman attended to the details. He does not think that either the drawing or the photograph resemble the man who called himself Rhodes, though now that he has seen the photograph, he feels that the drawing shows some resemblance."

Sams drew a deep breath and glanced at Tasker. He could read Tasker's inclinations in the set of his jaw and thought that his assistant's restraint was noteworthy. Finally, Sams turned back to the detective, handing over the artist's rendering. "Ask him to have another look, why don't you?"

The detective took the rendering and handed it over to the clerk once again. After a moment, the clerk put the rendering on the table and spoke briefly to the French detective. The detective said something sharply back, and the clerk elaborated. Finally, the detective turned to Sams.

"He says it is a crime."

"A crime," Sams repeated patiently. He had worked at the business of criminal investigation for many, many years. His experience included diverse encounters with a great range of suspects, witnesses, informants, victims, perpetrators, and other representatives of the human species. He had not spent a great deal of time in France, but he had spent enough. Under other circumstances, and were this interview being conducted on more familiar turf, there were other methods to which he might turn with the man across the table from him. But no matter. He had developed a patience that would outdo even this.

"The eyes," the detective said, waving his hand at the drawing in explanation. "He says that the man who called himself Rhodes had very expressive eyes and that this portrait does not nearly do him justice."

"I see," said Sams, his hand traveling to the drawing. He picked it up by one corner and held it before the eyes of the desk clerk. No matter what the urges that flitted through his mind, he was confident that his blood pressure had not risen an iota.

"Does that mean that he does, in fact, believe this resembles the man who calls himself Rhodes?" Sams said, speaking to the detective.

The clerk said something to the French detective. "Except for the eyes," the detective said.

Sams folded the drawing and put it inside his coat. "We'll get an artist over to work on the eyes," he said to the detective. "Tell this person he can go."

The detective dismissed the clerk with another rapid burst of French. Whatever he said did not seem to make the clerk happy. The detective waited until the door had closed behind the clerk, then checked his watch.

"You wish to speak to the manager, yes?"

"Do I?" Sams asked.

"He's anxious to assist," the Frenchman said.

"He's anxious to get his money from the bastard who stiffed him for a twenty-grand tab," Sams said. He stared back at the impassive detective for a moment, then sighed inwardly. "All right, have the man come in."

The detective nodded, then reached for a phone that sat on the table nearby. In a moment, the door the clerk had left by opened again, and a tall man in a vested suit and a three-penny resemblance to Charles de Gaulle entered the room. To Sam's surprise, he hesitated at the doorway, waiting for an attractive young woman wearing a chambermaid's outfit to join him.

"This is Mademoiselle Dechartres," the manager said.

Sams glanced at the detective, who shrugged.

"Perhaps she has information that will be helpful," the manager said, meaning that he was certain she did.

Sams stood and indicated a chair. The young woman looked ready to bolt from the room. Perhaps one too many floggings from the management, Sams thought.

"Go ahead, Giselle," the manager said. "This man is an American detective. Tell him what you told me."

Sams thought about correcting the manager, but it hardly seemed worth the effort. "You know something about the Rhodes couple," Sams said, expecting one of the others to translate.

"Rhodes was not her name," Giselle Dechartres said in a soft voice.

Sams stared at her. "How do you know that?" He noted her full, dark lips, found himself thinking of plums.

The young woman glanced at her boss, who gestured with his formidable chin. The woman turned back to Sams, then dropped her gaze as she began to speak. Sams found himself thinking about her costume. Snug-fitting black dress, starched white apron. Ridiculously trite. And still he fantasized having the room cleared, watching her shed those garments bit by bit.

"The woman told me," Giselle said. She glanced up, apparently finding approval in her boss's gaze.

Probably the same licentious thoughts flitting through de Gaulle's mind, Sams thought. The old bastard.

"I'd attended to the room throughout the week the couple were here. One day I was called to replenish the towels. The woman was in the room by herself. She engaged me in a conversation."

Sams lifted an eyebrow. "Concerning?"

"Various things," Giselle said. "She asked me if I liked my work, if I were from Paris. She told me her name was Kaia, that she was not married to the man with whom she was staying."

"Did you wonder why she was talking with you about these things?" Sams asked.

Giselle shrugged and glanced at her employer. De Gaulle gave a meaningful nod. Giselle turned back to Sams. "It is not unheard of for guests to suggest certain improprieties," she said.

Not in the case of certain chambermaids, Sams thought. "She wanted to have sex with you?"

Giselle shrugged again. *Insouciance*, Sams thought. The greatest aphrodisiac of them all. "She suggested I might like to travel with them," Giselle said finally.

And all the sights you'll see, Sams thought, staring at those plumlike lips. "Did she say where they were going?"

"Somewhere warm," Giselle said. "She showed me the many swimming suits she'd purchased."

As in modeled them? Sams wanted to ask, but he was forcing himself back to business already. "What else?" he asked.

The woman cocked her head, her expression asking if he really wanted to delve into certain realms. "That's all that matters," she said.

"Kaia," he repeated. "That's the only name she gave you."

"The only one," Giselle Dechartres replied. Sams thought he detected a note of wistfulness there. "There was a phone call," the chambermaid added. "She told me she would have to hurry. I never saw her again."

"It was the same day that they left," the manager cut in at this point. Sams heard the emphasis on *left*. "Skipped out" was what he meant.

Sams nodded and made a note on a pad he always carried. He'd already examined the phone records. The call had come from a stolen cellular phone, its owner a British businessman who'd reported his loss during a watch-buying trip to Switzerland. Whoever had helped Rhodes cover his tracks had also suggested it was time to move along.

"Thank you, Ms. Dechartres," Sam said, standing. He willed himself not to watch her departure from the room.

"We're finished here," he said to the detective who was his escort. The hotel manager was making what sounded like plaintive inquiries to his countryman in their native tongue, but Sams was already on his way toward the door, Tasker at his side.

"Where to?" Tasker grumbled.

Sams barely glanced at him. Still several steps behind, but compared to where he'd been the last several years, the trail was fairly glowing. He was onto his man again, of that much he was certain. "Didn't you hear?" he said, still envisioning the droop of Giselle Dechartres's disappointed plumlike lips. "We're headed someplace warm."

thirteen

"So let me make sure I got it right," Vernon Driscoll was saying. "A guy jumps you, tries to kill you, it ends up with you offering him a job."

Deal nodded and reached to pick up his coffee. It was Sunday morning and the two of them were sitting at a tiny Formica-topped table inside the cafeteria at Parrot Jungle, one of the holdover attractions from the tamer days of Florida tourism. It was a junglelike place on the far south end of Coral Gables, once a far-flung destination for area citizenry. Now it was an anomaly for the neighborhood, an out-of-time aviary *cum* arboretum surrounded by million-dollar estates. But inside the old coral walls, you could still buy a breakfast for less than an hour's wage, sit in the other-era cafeteria, and watch out the big glass windows as the staff groomed and readied the various species of birds for another arduous day of being looked at by visitors.

Deal had been bringing Isabel here since she'd been old enough to walk. She'd taken to the big birds immediately, drawn, or so Deal thought, by the similarity in their raucous modes of speech: a couple of words, a squawk or two, then another non sequitur—why wouldn't a toddler feel at home?

Of course, Isabel was no toddler anymore. Eight years old, getting tall, rail-thin, looking more and more like her mother every day.

Right now, she was out in the petting area watching raptly as one of the trainers held a large black cockatoo her way. After a moment, Isabel extended her hand: in it a soda cracker. The bird cocked its head, seeming to check with the trainer for permission. The trainer, a young woman with bronze skin and a close-cropped haircut, nodded. The bird turned and used one of his claws to take the cracker delicately from Isabel's fingers. The thing held the cracker to its formidable hooked beak and began to nibble: first one corner, then the next, until the last speck was gone. The smile on his daughter's face as she watched it all made Deal's eyes water.

He turned back to Driscoll, who stared at him as if he were one of the zoo attractions. "What?" Deal said. "Were you waiting for an answer?"

"No, I was just practicing for the parrots," Driscoll said. "Polly's a fucking idiot, like that."

"This is a family place, Driscoll," Deal said.

"Yeah, but there's nobody else in here," Driscoll said.

True enough, Deal thought, glancing around the empty room. Almost eleven, the morning grooming just about at an end, the breakfast eaters dispersed, the lunch crowd yet to form. Deal sighed and leaned across the table toward Driscoll. "Russell Straight is a kid, Vernon. He made some mistakes—"

"Two plus two equals five, that's a mistake," Driscoll said. "Grand theft auto is a felony. So's assault with intent." The ex-cop tasted his coffee, stared down at it like he could see Straight's reflection there. "If you were somebody else, the guy might have accomplished just what he set out to do."

Deal turned his palms up in a placating gesture. "Look at it this way, Vernon. If the guy were to come to work for me, then at least I could keep an eye on him."

Driscoll snorted. "If you'd have called the cops last night, you'd know exactly where he was right now."

Deal rolled his eyes. They could continue like this right on through the arrival and departure of the lunch clientele, and probably the late-afternoon snack contingent as well.

"I wonder what it was like being partnered up with you on a long stakeout, Vernon." Deal glanced out the window, noting that the big cockatoo was sitting on Isabel's shoulder now.

"In what way?"

"I wonder, did the other guy ever get the last word?"

Driscoll was staring out the window now, too. "All the time," he said. "What's to argue about? Cops tend to think a lot alike."

Deal nodded, watching idly as the big bird ducked its head toward Isabel's ear. The thick glass dampened the sound, but it looked as if the thing might be offering his daughter advice. The expression on Isabel's face suggested she was seriously considering it. "Can you remember being eight years old?" he asked, glancing over at Driscoll.

"I was never eight years old," Driscoll said. "I was promoted straight to adulthood."

"Seriously," Deal said.

"I am serious," Driscoll said. "My old man walked out when I was four. I had three paper routes by the time I was eight—after school I carried *The Daily Jeffersonian, Grit,* and *TV Guide.* Saturday mornings I sold donuts to the same people. Saturday afternoons, I cut yards. I got a real job when I was twelve."

Deal turned from the idyllic sight outside the window. "What'd you do for fun?"

"I didn't have any fun."

Deal stared at him—the big man's face was neutral. "How about Sundays?"

"Sundays, my old lady took me to church."

"All day?"

Instead of answering, Driscoll made a pistol out of his hand, cocked his thumb, winked, and fired.

"What kind of church?"

"The kind that comes out of a Cracker Jack box," Driscoll said. "A lot of praise-the-Lords and turning yourself in to be saved a couple times a month. There was talking in tongues, too, as I remember."

Deal shook his head. "You never mentioned any of this stuff before."

Driscoll shrugged. "I don't recall you asking."

Deal glanced back outside. The trainer had the cockatoo back on her arm. She and Isabel were chatting animatedly. It was the kind of scene that could come out of a dream of childhood. Thank God for small favors, he thought. Given all that his daughter had gone through, she deserved it. The thought of Talbot Sams and his veiled threats rekindled a steadfast rage inside him, but he pushed it back. He was not going to have this morning with his daughter spoiled.

He turned back to Driscoll. "So you worked hard, Vernon. You stayed out of trouble, therefore everybody else should be just as capable as you."

Driscoll's eyes widened slightly. "Doesn't matter what I did or didn't do. Just because you grow up hard, that doesn't mean you get a free pass."

"Agreed," Deal said. "But I'm thinking maybe Russell Straight got something out of his system last night."

"You better hope," Driscoll said. "Meantime, I'd lock my door if I was you."

"You think a lock is going to stop a bad guy?"

Driscoll stared at him. "It's a figure of speech, that's all. You're getting to be as bad as me."

"Daddy!" It was Isabel, running breathlessly into the cafeteria. "I got to hold the bird. Did you see, Uncle Vernon?"

"I sure did, sweetheart," he said. Whatever Driscoll had missed in his own childhood hadn't kept him from appreciating Isabel's, Deal thought.

"The bird said I was pretty, Daddy." She turned to him, her eyes shining.

"Smart bird," Deal said, gathering her in his arms for a hug. She smelled like the shredded eucalyptus that covered much of the grounds outside. Eucalyptus and fresh little girl.

"Are we going to see the show? Oscar's going to ride a bike on a wire stretched all the way across the stage, Gaby says . . ."

Deal gave her a wistful smile. There was a small amphitheater inside the grounds of the attraction, where they'd seen a dozen versions of the act: birds riding bikes on the high wire, birds soaring through flaming hoops, birds adding and subtracting, birds reciting the Pledge of Allegiance. "Not today, sweetheart. I've got to get you back to Mommy."

"Please?" She gave him her most plaintive look.

"Next week," Deal said. "We've got the whole weekend together then, remember?"

"Daddy!" she said, in a tone somewhere between complaint and resignation.

"I had a bird like that once," Driscoll said.

Isabel turned. "You didn't."

"Sure I did," Driscoll said. He turned to Deal. "You remember *Baretta*, right? I had a snitch who lived over on South Beach before it got fashionable, liked to think of himself as Robert Blake. The guy got whacked, his landlady was going to put this bird out in the trash, I kid you not. I took the thing home with me."

Deal glanced at Isabel, who seemed to have missed most of Driscoll's implications. "Where is it, Uncle Vernon?"

It was the kind of setup that Driscoll lived for, Deal knew, but the burly ex-cop simply smiled and rubbed Isabel's dark curls. "He lives with Marie, now, sweetie."

"Marie and Vernon used to be married, Isabel," Deal said.

She nodded. "Like you and Mommy."

Deal felt a pang. "Right."

"Anyways, Marie decided she liked the bird's company better than mine," Driscoll added.

"She did not," Isabel said.

Driscoll shrugged. "Ask her."

"He's kidding," Isabel said to Deal.

"He does that," Deal said. He stood and lifted her up in his arms. "Time for us to go now, kiddo."

"Can we go to Marie's and see your bird sometime, Uncle Vernon?"

"Sure, if we can get a SWAT team to cover us," Driscoll said.

"What's that?"

"He's kidding again," Deal said. "He means that he and Marie don't get along very well anymore."

"Oh," Isabel said. Her eyes clouded, and Deal felt another pang, one that he felt all the way to the back of his knees. He and Janice had been doing their best, trying to maintain some sense of family despite everything, but as time wore on, it became more and more difficult to convince Isabel that they were any kind of a unit. He tried to imagine Vernon Driscoll, slogging along the slushy streets of a West Virginia winter, three different paper bags slung over his eight-year-old shoulder, but somehow the image simply would not come into focus. It wasn't the kind of difficulty Isabel had had to face, granted, but tough times came in many guises, that's what he decided.

He gave his daughter another hug and set her back on the floor. "You ready?" Deal said, turning to Driscoll.

Driscoll glanced up at him. "I'm always ready," he said, pushing his bulk up out of the spindly looking chair. He leaned toward Deal as the three of them moved to the doors, where a teenaged kid in a hair net was polishing the glass, readying for the afternoon crowd. The ex-cop put his hand on Deal's shoulder and squeezed. "That's the point I was trying to make there a little earlier. You should always be ready, too, my friend."

Deal thought about an answer, but by that time, they were outside the heavy glass doors and the shrieks of the parrots had taken command.

fourteen

"Château Margaux," the sommelier intoned in an appropriately reverential way. "Nineteen sixty-four."

Rhodes barely glanced at the bottle and nodded his head at the proffered cork. The sommelier nodded and handed the bottle carefully to an assistant, who transferred it to a pouring cradle as carefully as if it were formed of sugar glass.

"It looks like blood," Kaia Jesperson observed as the assistant turned a smoothly working crank and the crystal decanter began to fill.

"Far more valuable than that," Rhodes said, staring across the candlelit linens at her. She wore a black cocktail dress with a plunging neckline, had her auburn hair knotted tightly atop her head. Every man in the elegant room had been stealing glances at her. He'd spotted one couple with their heads bent close, their eyes darting her way. Obviously they were trying to agree on just who she was, Rhodes thought. What movie star, what society prominence, had graced their presence tonight?

The sommelier himself set out their glasses, first for Rhodes and then Kaia. "For the lady," he said with a bow, then disappeared like smoke.

She was about to say something to him then stopped, turning back to the goblet at her place. She registered it then and glanced up at him, a smile teasing her lips. "Rubies," she said, taking hold of the necklace that trailed up over the rim of the glass. "At least they *look* like rubies."

She had the necklace uncoiled from the goblet by now and had draped it around her neck. The couple who'd been watching them were agog.

"That was quite a trick," she said.

He shrugged. "A high compliment, coming from you."

She glanced him. "Meaning?"

"That stunt you managed in Kuşadisi, of course. I've been wanting to ask how you did it."

She stared at him levelly now. "I wouldn't call it a stunt."

"I don't mean to—"

"It's not a trick, Richard. To try to explain it to someone who hasn't been there . . ."

"Been where, exactly?"

She paused and looked away momentarily. "Even if I explained it to you, you wouldn't understand. It would be like trying to teach a person to swim who's never been in the water."

"Try me," he said.

She sighed then. "All right. This much, no more."

She closed her eyes, drawing a breath that lifted her shoulders a fraction— *Summoning energy,* Rhodes found himself thinking. After a moment, she opened her eyes and lifted her hand from her lap and brought her palm above the candle that burned in an ornate silver holder between them.

When Rhodes realized what she was doing, he started for her wrist, but she stopped him with a sharp nod of her head. Her eyes had not left his. He felt like a rabbit caught in a snake's crosshairs.

She held her palm to the tip of the flame for what seemed an eternity. Rhodes saw what was happening, but still found it difficult to believe. He'd played childish games with fire himself: pinching out candle flames with his fingers, slashing his hand karate-fashion through the flames of a campfire until the fuzz on his arms had been singed away. But this was altogether different, her hand unmoving, the tip of the flame blossoming against her skin . . .

Reason told him that Kaia's hand should be burning, the flesh blistering, her skin crisping . . .

. . . but she stared back at him steadily, her gaze unwavering, not the least flicker of pain on her features. Finally, she withdrew her hand from the tip of the flame and held it across the table to him, palm up. Where he might have expected charred flesh was nothing but an indistinct smudge, the slightest dot of soot.

He glanced up at her, dumbfounded. He noticed that the woman who'd been stealing glances their way was gaping at them, her mouth open, a forkful of dessert frozen above her plate.

"Take my hand, Richard," Kaia commanded.

He did as he was told, cradling it gently in his own.

"Go ahead," she told him, "feel my palm."

He looked at her uncertainly, then pressed his palm to hers. *Cool to the touch,* he thought. And dry. As if nothing out of the ordinary had happened.

"It's impossible," he said. "How—"

"No," she said. "That's it. We can talk about other things now."

He released her hand. The couple who'd been eavesdropping were whispering busily to each other.

He opened his mouth as he turned back to her, then saw the look in her eyes and reconsidered. He had determined that this would be the perfect evening. He glanced at the necklace that she had donned and lifted his glass in submission.

"It becomes you," he said.

She allowed her smile to blossom for him at last. He felt the blood beating at his temples, an ache at the back of his throat. He wanted whole pitchers of rubies to pour for her. A tub of diamonds for her bath.

"I'll take your word for it," she said, glancing down at the snowy plane of her chest. *King Solomon's mines,* he was thinking, they were nothing compared to what he was staring at.

"And thank you," she added, bringing her gaze to his. "That *was* very clever."

The sommelier was back with another glass, his face as impassive as ever. Rhodes felt a moment's giddiness. He wanted to clap the man on the shoulder, assure him it would be perfectly acceptable to demonstrate pleasure.

The sommelier, meantime, had poured half an inch of wine into Rhodes's glass and stood offering it to him in his massive black hand. Rhodes tasted and nodded. "Yes," he said. "Quite good."

Quite good? His own words echoed inside his head. The wine was magnificent. The enigmatic woman across the table from him was beyond that, a woman who could, it seemed, walk through fire—and never mind just how she managed it.

He had spent a lifetime making and spending money, more money than he'd ever dreamed of, none of that had ever pleasured him as he was pleasured now. Suddenly there was a *reason* for what he did. Approval to be sought. Admiration to be gained. For the first time in years, he found himself yearning for The Lucky One's presence. The one man in all the world who could appreciate his find as Rhodes himself could.

"I was wrong," she was saying, holding her glass aloft toward him. Her lips glistened in the candlelight. "Not blood at all. It's like drinking rubies."

Rhodes nodded. He brought his own glass up and toasted her. "To rubies," he said. "And to you." He waved his hand to indicate the wine and the necklace she wore. "All these things have been waiting for you to give them life."

"That's a charming thing to say," she said. She tossed her head and glanced at the whispering couple across the room. The two immediately averted their eyes. She turned back to him, taking another sip of her wine.

"Everything is charming here."

"I'm glad you like it."

"Why on earth wouldn't I?"

He shrugged, glancing around their surroundings. *Stresa,* it was called these days: the cuisine northern Italian; the décor, French. The staff all local Bahamians. Broad plate-glass windows looking out upon a forested glade a stone's throw from a gaudy resort, but most of the tourists kept to the tiki bars and the Americanized restaurants closer to the water's edge. Rhodes felt comfortable here, more comfortable than he'd felt in years.

"My father had this place built, you know."

She shook her head, bemused. Her gaze swept around the room once again. "When was that?"

"A long time ago," he said. "It was different back then. More 'New York night spot.'"

She nodded. "Is that why we stopped in Nassau? Auld lang syne?"

He shook his head.

"Then why?"

"This is home," he told her.

She stared at him. "I thought we were going to the States . . ." She trailed off, her glass tilted slightly in her hand.

"You don't want to spill any of that," Rhodes said with a nod. A waiter had materialized at their table to set down gilt-edged plates bearing what looked like pâté dotted with caviar. He couldn't be sure. Beyond the wine, Rhodes had left the menu to the captain.

When the waiter was gone, he turned back to her. "My father was born in New York. He moved to Florida early on. He did well there. But things eventually took a turn."

"They always do," she agreed.

"Yes," Rhodes said, nodding to her. "It was required of him to leave rather suddenly."

"When was this?"

"In the fifties," Rhodes said. "About the time that everyone else in the Caribbean started going the other way."

"And this is the place he came to?"

"My father found gracious haven in the islands," Rhodes said.

"And you grew up here?"

"Off and on," he said. "I went to school in the States, got my start in business there."

She nodded thoughtfully. "Your father was a criminal?"

He looked at her gravely. "Who isn't?"

"What exactly did he do?"

"He gambled."

She nodded. "Who doesn't?"

He tipped his glass to her. "He had clubs on the mainland and a party ship that anchored just off Palm Beach for many years. This was in the forties and fifties, before Las Vegas, before gambling became tawdry. He was a charming host and very good at what he did. The Lucky One, that's what the Hispanics called him."

"An interesting name," she said. She nibbled at her pâté, made an approving sound somewhere in her throat. "That project in Florida you talked about with Babescu," she said after a moment, a question in her voice. He nodded, noting that her gaze did not waver when she mentioned the name. "I thought that's where you were going, that's all."

"I may yet," he said. "But there's something I need to find first."

"You don't strike me as the sort of man who lacks for anything," she said mildly.

He had a bite of the pâté himself. The flavor seemed to have been designed with the explosive wine in mind. "I wish my father were here to meet you," he said.

"So do I," she said. "What is it you need to find?"

He dabbed at the corner of his mouth and signaled with his nearly empty wineglass. In seconds, the assistant was back to pour them more.

"The fact is, I'm nearly broke," he told her.

She glanced at their surroundings then touched the rubies at her neck, hardly convinced. "Are these on loan, then?"

"Wealth is a relative thing," he told her. "Babescu, the bastard, robbed me blind. You happened in on the end of our discussion."

When she didn't flinch, he went on. "What he didn't squander on preposterous ideas like that spectacle in Kuşadisi, he sank into this colossus in Miami." He shook his head. "Shipping, ports, international trade. The man fancied himself the next Onassis."

"Why not just sell out?" she asked. She turned her gaze discreetly. "It's all yours now, after all."

He shrugged. "It's hardly the time," he said. "Once the project gets off the ground, then maybe I'll be able to unload . . . ," he trailed off, shaking his head. "As the old saying goes, it takes money to make money. I need cash quickly, and I can't make myself visible in certain quarters."

"You're wanted in the United States," she said. It was not a question.

He put his wineglass down and stared at her. "Kaia, I'm wanted everywhere." He paused and waved his hand at the room. "Everywhere but *here,* that is."

She glanced toward the entrance of the place uncertainly, as if she expected a squadron of police to burst in. "And you have money in Nassau?"

"Nearby," he said.

"What does that mean?"

"It means there's someone in Miami I need to speak to."

She had more wine, a full swallow this time. "You meant it when you say you have to *find* it, don't you?"

He leaned forward. "Kaia, you *are* beautiful, you can walk through fire, but that's the least part of it." He reached to take her hand. "You understand me. You're a kindred spirit."

She was looking at him, but her mind was elsewhere, still calculating all he'd told her over the past weeks. "It's your father's money, isn't it?"

He smiled. "Amazing. Simply amazing. If I'd had you with me all this time . . ."

She sat back in the brocaded chair. "You've brought me all the way to Nassau to go on a treasure hunt."

He smiled. "To take possession of what's rightfully mine, that's all."

"Who is this person you have to speak to?"

Rhodes shrugged. "He's a building contractor, the son of an old friend of my father's."

"He has your money?"

He gave her a speculative look. "I believe he can point me in the right direction."

"Assuming he would want to."

He smiled. "Frank and Basil can be persuasive."

She chose to ignore the implication. "Why now, Richard? Why didn't you come here a long time ago?"

"For one thing, I didn't need the money, or so I thought. I made a big mistake, trusting Babescu," he said, shrugging. "And I was undergoing some extensive medical procedures that made travel impractical."

"You're sick?"

He thought he saw concern in her eyes. The thought only enhanced the bittersweet ache he felt every time he looked at her. "Nothing like that," he said. "Just a bit of cosmetic rearrangement."

She looked at him carefully. "Whatever it was," she said, "they did it well. Make sure to give me the name of your doctor."

"What on earth for?" he said. "You're perfect."

"Time catches up with everyone, Richard." She bent to her plate and finished the pâté in a bite.

Even the way she chewed her food seemed attractive, he marveled. He knew he was in trouble now.

She put her fork down and smiled. "How old are you?" she asked.

"Does it matter?"

"Not really," she said. "Have you ever been married?"

He raised his eyes in reply. "We're getting to the basic questions a bit late, aren't we?"

"Maybe it's the wine," she said. "Have you been married?"

He paused, gazing up at the ceiling momentarily. "'Were a woman possible as I am possible, then marriage would be possible,'" he said.

"That's rather lofty," she said.

"It's the work of an American poet," he said. "The speaker fancies himself too eccentric ever to find a mate."

"How does it turn out?"

"It's a poem," he told her. "Poems don't turn out."

She nodded as if she'd accept that authority.

"How about you?" he asked. "How is it you're still all alone?"

She gave him a tolerant smile. "There's plenty of time. I was with a man when I got into the spectacle thing, you know."

He didn't know, and didn't really want to know, but he nodded sagely anyway. "So all that was *his* game to begin with?"

"He was a Swede," she said, as if it explained a number of things. "We met in an ashram, in India."

He lifted his head in recognition. "So *that's* where you learned to walk on coals."

She glanced at him sharply. "I thought we were finished with that," she said.

He held up his hands in surrender. "I'm sorry," he said.

She nodded, then glanced away for a moment. When she began to speak again, her voice had a wistful tone, he thought. "Karl was a genius, but a troubled one. I followed him from India to London. We lived together. He was on the web before there was a web. All-night chats over the ether with other disembodied spirits." She shook her head wearily and took another sip of wine.

"That's how he learned about SRL." She gave him a practiced smile. "The next thing, we were off to San Francisco."

"SRL?"

"Survival Research Laboratories," she said. "More angry geniuses. There are a number of them, loosely knit groups with similar names: Peoplehaters, Cybernasia. It's a countercultural thing. They'd fry all of Silicon Valley if they could."

"And from that came the spectacles?"

"Even a genius needs an audience," she said.

"Whatever happened to Karl?" *Mangled by some giant slice-and-dice machine?* he mused. Roasted by a first-generation firecage?

She shrugged. "Karl found out what kind of money the American geniuses had turned their backs on. He went to work for the enemy. The last I heard, he was working on military applications for the Pentagon."

He nodded. "So Karl's found his niche."

"He's still angry," she said. "But now he's destroying things and being well paid for it."

"What happened to the two of you?"

"If he hadn't gotten his rocks off sufficiently during the day," she said, "he took it out on me at night. I got tired of it."

Rhodes felt an unreasoning anger rise within him. "He hurt you?"

She shrugged. "Nothing serious. I like it on the edge, in case you haven't noticed. But on top of everything, he'd gotten so gloomy, and there we were in *California*." She smiled and finished her wine. In an instant, the assistant was there to pour the last of the bottle into her glass. The man gave an inquiring glance at Rhodes, who sent him scurrying off to the cellars with a nod. "Besides," Kaia said as the man disappeared, "I'd gotten interested in the spectacle of the thing, you know."

"The magician's assistant becomes the magician herself?"

"I suppose that's it," she said. "There is this thrill, standing there, a few inches away from certain death. And knowing that I choose to be there."

Rhodes rested his chin on his interlaced fingers. "I'm only speculating here . . ." he began.

"Speculate away," she said.

"Karl started off an outlaw, then was co-opted by the system."

She shrugged. "So what?"

"So now you find yourself in the company of a true fugitive from justice. What does that tell you?"

"Whatever you're implying," she said, looking at him in amusement, "I'm here because you invited me."

"So you are," he said. "It was just a thought, that's all."

"Analyze it anyway you like," she said. "The wine is wonderful. It's even better, wondering just how you're going to pay for it."

He smiled back. "It excites you, does it?"

She leaned closer. "It's almost like being inside that firecage."

He nodded. "I can feel the heat myself."

The couple who'd been gawking at them over dessert had scttlcd up and were walking past their table now, with no pretense at hiding their inquisitive stares. The sommelier was headed their way bearing another bottle of Chateaux Margaux, his expression coming dangerously close to a smile.

Ah yes, Rhodes thought, turning his gaze back to her: How his life had finally coalesced. Beneath the snowily draped table, he felt her bare foot graze the inside of his thigh. *Ah yes.*

Somehow the rest of dinner passed.

fifteen

MONDAY MORNING, DEAL WAS sitting behind his desk in the portable office, stacks of files strewn on its surface before him. He'd put in a call to City-County first thing, had to leave a message on voice mail. Then he had set about combing through old DealCo records, searching for some trace of Talbot Sams. He'd had no luck, but then again, he'd only made it about halfway through the first drawer, cursing the haphazard nature of the system, or lack thereof, when the phone rang, echoing in the otherwise silent office.

"John Deal," he said into the receiver.

"It's Gladys Collum," a woman's voice came back. "In Mr. Martinez's office. You called about your bid."

"I did," Deal agreed. He was ready for anything.

"What was your question?" The voice abrupt, annoyed at having to waste time on actually being of service.

"I'm wondering about the status."

"Excuse me?"

"The status of the port office building bid," he said. "I was told the matter had been decided."

There was a pause on the other end. Deal heard the rustling of papers, then a muffled voice calling something to a co-worker. In a moment, she was back. "Where did you get that information?" she asked.

Deal hesitated, but he didn't hesitate long. "Eddie Barrios called me Friday afternoon," he said. If he was blowing Eddie's cover, too bad.

He heard Gladys sigh audibly. "Just a moment," she said into the phone, and then he heard another muffled voice.

In the next moment, there came a click, and another voice cut in on the line. "This is Rafael Martinez. How can I help you?"

Deal closed his eyes, took a deep breath. Martinez was the new oversight manager for the project, installed by a mayor who had run on a promise of "strict accountability in public works" to voters long accustomed to anything but. Deal knew little about the man—he'd had a brief handshake the day he turned in his bid.

"This is John Deal," he said. "I'm calling about the port offices bid."

"Eddie Barrios called you?" The tone of Martinez's voice left little doubt as to his opinion of the man.

"That's right," Deal said.

Another pause. Deal could have sworn he heard the drumming of fingertips on a desk top. "I'd like to know how these things get out," Martinez fumed.

"Look—" Deal began, but Martinez was already going on.

"There's a process, you understand. Put in place for very good reasons."

"How about Talbot Sams?" Deal interjected. "He called, too."

"I don't know anyone by that name," Martinez said. Deal thought he said it a little too quickly.

"Couldn't you just give me the word, Mr. Martinez?"

Another pause, but not as long this time. When he spoke again, Martinez's voice had lost some of its edge. "I don't suppose there's much point in *my* toeing the line," the man said. "No one else seems to pay attention to protocol."

"Are we moving up on a 'yes'?"

"Your bid was chosen, Mr. Deal," Martinez said. "The notifications went out by messenger this morning."

Deal felt a surge of conflicting feelings well up inside him. Relief, pleasure, satisfaction, validation of his efforts: those he was grateful for, were all to be expected. But just as quickly came suspicion and anger trailing in the wake. Compared to the distaste he'd felt when Eddie Barrios called to tip him to the news, the specter of Talbot Sams, sitting in this very chair, claiming he'd arranged it all . . .

"Was there something else I could help you with?" Martinez's voice cut into his thoughts.

"No," Deal said, staring across the room at the waiting file cabinets. There was no point in irritating Martinez further, he thought. "I guess not. If something comes to me, I'll bring it up the next time I'm in. I guess we'll be seeing quite a bit of each other, now."

"Not on this job," Martinez answered quickly.

"What do you mean?" Deal asked. DealCo hadn't had a government contract since the early eighties, but he could still remember his father's grumblings about the time it took to process paperwork through the downtown bureaucracy.

"The way it's set up, you'll coordinate through the general contractor. The only way you'll be in here is if there's some kind of a problem."

Deal paused. "So where do I go next?"

"All that's in the paperwork on its way to you," Martinez said.

Deal raised his eyebrows. "Well, I guess that's it, then. Thanks for your help, Mr. Martinez."

"My pleasure," Martinez said as he hung up, his tone conveying any number of emotions, none of them pleasurable.

Deal stared at the receiver for a moment, then replaced it in the cradle. *Good old Eddie Barrios,* he thought. What did it say about a guy who likes to give good news, and everybody despises him anyway?

He heard the sounds of a motor outside then, someone winding down the lane toward the offices. The messenger, he thought, a man bearing the envelope from city hall, Deal's ticket back to a serious business life. He stood and went to the door, unable to keep from thinking about how differently the moment might have been configured: no Eddie Barrios, no Talbot Sams, no separation from Janice or his daughter . . . Why couldn't there be one simple, unalloyed moment of joy, no strings, no conditions, he asked himself . . .

. . . and then opened the outer door of the office to find Russell Straight's cherry-red pickup nosing to a stop in the parking area beside the Hog. Deal hesitated as the throbbing engine shut down, and Russell Straight, clad in jeans and a T-shirt that seemed painted on his sculpted body, stepped from the cab of the truck. No handy chunks of two-by-two anywhere around, Deal realized. No spud bars, no hammers, no tiger net, no Magnum .44s. Just himself and a pair of hands.

Straight rounded the front of his pickup and stopped, folding his arms across his chest as he stared up at Deal. Veins bulged from his forearms and biceps like those on the arms of impossible bodybuilders. How had he managed to get the best of the man? Deal asked himself.

Something in Russell Straight's countenance suggested he was wondering the same thing. "I went by the job," the man said finally. "They told me I might find you over here."

"So you have," Deal said.

Straight nodded, glancing around the deserted surroundings. "You seem to like it close to the water," he said.

Deal shrugged. "A person lives in Florida, he ought to."

Straight pursed his lips, considering the wisdom of Deal's remark. "I been thinking about those things you told me," he said after a moment.

"Is that right?" Deal answered, his tone as neutral as Straight's.

"What you said about Leon," Straight said.

"What about it?" Deal said. He drew a breath. If this was heading toward something, then it would happen any moment now.

"Didn't come here to *ask* you about anything," Straight said. "Just wanted you to know I decided you were telling the truth." He cut his gaze out over the mangroves momentarily. "The way you see it, anyway."

"I'm glad to hear that," Deal said.

Straight turned back. "The other thing's the job." The man was squinting a bit in the early sun.

"What about the job?"

"I'd like to stay on and work," Straight said. He rolled his head atop his broad shoulders as if his neck was stiff. "If that's all right."

Deal nodded. "The offer's still good."

Straight stepped forward then and extended his hand up toward the railing. Deal took it, felt the calluses, felt the power in the man's grip. It wouldn't take much for Russell Straight to jerk him clean off the porch where he stood, that much he knew.

"One thing, though," Straight said, releasing his grip.

"What's that?"

Straight looked off again. "I'd need you to—like I said—pay me off the books. Just for a while, at least."

Deal hesitated. There were thousands of undocumented workers in South Florida, to be sure, most of them illegals from the islands, as well as Central and South America. Maids, nannies, gardeners, fieldworkers, mechanics, assembly-line workers. Chase them out tomorrow, half the restaurants in the city would have to close. The INS would stage periodic raids every now and then, haul off most of the personnel from some hapless garment shop while the TV cameras rolled, but everyone knew the economy of the area depended upon the practice.

His old man had considered the use of undocumented workers a form of exploitation, though, and Deal had carried on in the same fashion. A man who worked hard deserved the same pay, the same benefits, the same status as everyone else. Russell Straight's case seemed a bit different, though.

"I just want a little time on my own," Straight was saying. "Earn enough for my keep. Then maybe go on back home, we'll see." He shook his head. "I go on the books, there'll be the man on me before you know it."

Deal nodded. He stared out over the mangroves himself, looking for whatever it was that Straight might have been focused on. Vernon Driscoll would be beside himself if he were here. His old man, too, most likely.

"All right," Deal said finally. He turned back to the man. "For a while, anyway," he added.

Straight stopped short of a smile, but his nod seemed a reasonable substitute. "I'm ready to start when you say."

"I'm going back over to the Terrell site in a bit," Deal said. "We'll get you started then."

Straight nodded. "I'll wait in the truck," he said.

Deal glanced at the Chevy, fairly gleaming against the dark green tangle of the mangroves. The breeze had shifted back in from the ocean, signaling an end to the cool weather. "I'm going to be a few minutes. It might get hot out here."

Straight looked around. "I *been* hot," he said.

"Suit yourself," Deal said.

He started inside, then stopped and turned back to Straight. "We'll keep our arrangement between you and me," Deal said. "If you don't mind."

"That's fine," Straight said. "I appreciate you taking care of me."

Deal gave him a wave then and went back inside the office. He gathered the loose files littering his desk and was moving toward the yawning file drawer for another sheaf when the phone rang again. He dumped the files in the drawer and picked up.

"John Deal," he said.

"Congratulations, John," the voice on the other end came. There was a hiss of static in the background, as if the call were coming from a great distance.

Deal felt the muscles in his jaw tighten. "Is this you, Sams?"

"I take it you've received the official word by now?" The voice cheery, unconcerned.

Deal pulled the receiver away from his ear and checked the readout on the caller ID. *Unknown caller.* "Of course," he muttered.

"I didn't catch that."

Deal sat on the edge of his desk, pondering things for a moment. "Are you tapping my phone, Sams?"

"What kind of a question is that?" Sams said. "I simply assumed you'd have ascertained the facts—"

"Bullshit," Deal said.

"I assure you—"

"Never mind," Deal said. He'd have Driscoll check the lines later. But he had no doubt that, one way or another, Sams knew every detail of his earlier conversation. "Martinez told me the county was out of the loop on the job I landed," he continued. "But you must have known that yourself."

"I believe I conveyed that you were an invaluable part of the team, Johnny-boy." The connection had cleared a bit, though Deal thought he could hear another conversation crossing theirs in the background.

"I told you not to call me that," Deal said.

"You did," Sams said. "Forgive me."

"And I'm not part of anybody's team," Deal said.

"Unfortunate terminology, that's all," said Sams. "I trust you haven't changed your mind."

He hadn't made up his mind in the first place, Deal thought. But until he knew a few more things about Talbot Sams, it would be prudent to keep the man pacified. "Where did you learn how to talk, Sams? What do you do when your batteries run out?"

"There's no need for that sort of thing," Sams said. "We're going to be working together for some time."

"So what happens next, Sams? I'd like to hear your notion of that."

"Nothing happens," Sams said. "Nothing unusual, anyway. You'll meet with the officials of Aramcor Development, arrange to coordinate your own activities within the greater scheme of the project, and then you will go about your business."

"That's all?" The background conversation was clearer now. Two women speaking a foreign language, chatting animatedly about something that seemed to delight them both.

"For now," Sams said.

"I take a meeting, then I go to work."

"Was there something else you had in mind?"

"There's something else *you've* got in mind," Deal said.

"You're simply going to establish yourself as a trustworthy and competent building contractor, John. That shouldn't be a stretch."

Deal thought for a moment. There was a distant peal of laughter from one of the women in the crossed conversation. Sams seemed unaware. "You're convinced this guy Rhodes—whoever he is—is calling the shots at Aramcor?" Deal asked.

"I'm certain of it," Sams said.

"I'm still not clear on what you expect me to do," Deal said. "I never went to spy school."

"I want you to learn everything you can about the present functioning of the company, including just how closely Rhodes is tied to its day-to-day operations. I want to know where he is based. I want to find out what banks he uses to channel the project funds—"

"Why don't you just call Dun and Bradstreet?"

"There's the information that's part of the public record, and then there is the true gen, as one of our more accomplished men of letters liked to say," Sams replied. "You're going to get the true gen. And if there should be any unusual requests, you'll pass that information along as well, of course."

"Unusual in what way?"

"I think that's self-explanatory," Sams said. "We'll consider such matters as they arise."

"Suppose they figure out what I'm up to? What then? Do you and Tasker burst in, guns blazing?" There was a brief pause. Deal noticed that the women and their cheery conversation were gone.

"There's little chance of that," Sams said mildly. "Your father managed his role for quite some time without ever being compromised. We'll have an eye on things, rest assured."

"So you say," Deal countered. "I'm just supposed to waltz into an office somewhere, tell them I'd like a look at this Rhodes's cooked set of books?"

"Hardly," Sams said. "You're going to ingratiate yourself, become a fellow traveler."

"How's that going to happen?" Deal protested. "I'm the token local builder here. My little building doesn't amount to much in the larger scheme of things."

"The dollars aren't the point," Sams said. The connection had cleared considerably. It sounded as if the man might be in the next room. "You're tied in locally. You're a valuable resource for an outfit like Aramcor. You know how things get done down here."

Deal thought he heard something in Sams's voice and felt the anger building inside him again. "You put the word out about DealCo, didn't you?"

Sams sighed. "The word's always been out, John."

"You sonofabitch."

"Criminals gravitate toward criminals, John. It's the way of the world."

"I've spent the last six years of my life trying to build my company into something decent, now you want to turn it to shit?"

"Let's not be melodramatic. It's not like we've taken out an ad in the papers."

"You don't have to, goddammit—"

"Goodness is as goodness does, John. Let's keep our eyes on the goal, shall we?"

"Fuck you, Sams," Deal said, and slammed the phone back into its cradle.

sixteen

DEAL ROSE FROM HIS desk, every nerve ending on fire. He glanced around the office, looking for something to take his anger out on. He caught sight of the battered file cabinet, its top drawer still yawning. He strode forward, about to send his fist into its side, then caught himself at the last second and slammed his forearm against it instead. The flimsy metal caved inward with a groan and the open drawer, already leaning precariously, tumbled out of its frame. Deal had to jump backward to keep his foot from being smashed. The corner of the heavy drawer dug into the floor, gouging out a chunk of vinyl tile and dumping file folders everywhere.

Deal stood surveying the mess, rubbing his forearm absently. The side of the cabinet looked as if a cannonball had caromed off it. He could have easily broken his hand, he thought, shaking his head.

He bent down and began to gather the tumbled folders together when the door of the office swung inward. "Everything all right?" It was Russell Straight standing in the doorway, staring down at him.

"Everything's fine," Deal said, still feeling contrite. He waved his hand at the file cabinet. "I just pulled the drawer out too far."

Straight's eyes traveled to the battered file. "Uh-huh," he said, not sounding convinced.

"Let me pick this stuff up, then we'll go."

"Need some help?" Straight offered.

"I'll be right there," Deal said, his voice rising.

"Just asking," Straight said. He backed out onto the porch with his palm held up and closed the door behind him.

Deal righted the fallen drawer, then stood to try to slide the thing back into the cabinet, but it was hopeless. He sighed, dropped the drawer down on the floor again, and began dumping files haphazardly back on the hangers. With the new contract, he would need a secretary once again anyway. Let her put things back in order.

He had managed to replace about half of the strewn folders, was trying to wrestle another batch into place, when he realized there was something wrong with the file on the bottom of the stack, as if a bunch of papers had gotten wadded up in it during the fall. He set the other folders aside and checked inside the last, seeing nothing but a single slip of paper, a pink copy of an invoice from a California supplier of wire molding: one neat, flat sheet.

The folder itself was thick in his hand, however, and far too heavy for what was in it. Puzzled, he turned the thing over in his hands, realizing then that there was a second piece of manila glued to the back of the original folder. Maybe something inside there, he thought, something hidden inside? He stood and took the folder back to his desk, switched on the gooseneck lamp, and held the folder up for a closer look. Sure enough, a seam was visible, little specks of dried glue bulging here and there where the two pieces had been pressed together.

He withdrew the Swiss Army knife he always carried, flipped open the smaller blade, and worked the edge between the two pieces of heavy paper, then carefully sawed one side of the packet open. He turned the folder on its end and shook it gently, watching as a folded packet of heavy, gray-flecked stationery and a key dropped onto the desk top. His glance traveled to the key: flat, the size of a house key, with a rounded top and two square teeth. *No house key,* he thought. *Maybe for a safety deposit box.* He picked up the packet of papers then, and unfolded them.

The top sheet, stiff as sail canvas, was a piece of Barton Deal's letterhead bearing the address of the family home on South Bayside Avenue. Nothing typed, but there was a yellowed clipping of an article from the defunct *Miami News* taped to its face: "Mob Boss Sentenced." It was dated December 4, 1960, and carried the byline of Howard Kleinman, a reporter who still posted an occasional column on Miami history in the *Herald*. Deal scanned the piece quickly, but found nothing there of note: Anthony "Ducks" Gargano convicted on multiple counts of embezzlement, bank fraud, and tax evasion. A hefty prison sentence from Carlton Cope, legendary ball-busting judge for the Miami district. No mention of Deal's father, of course. Nor of anyone named Talbot Sams.

Between the first and second sheets was a faded photograph of Deal's father and mother on a dock somewhere in the Caribbean, along with a tall, distinguished man in boater's whites whom Deal did not recognize. Deal's father's Bayliner, the *Miss Miami Priss,* was tethered to a piling in the background. The view was toward the shoreline, where a broad lawn sloped upward toward an imposing Bahamian-styled mansion.

His mother wore a loose-fitting one-piece bathing suit and was turned in profile to show off her obviously pregnant belly. Deal's father—his barrel chest bare and bronzed, his arm draped over his mother's shoulders—seemed the very image of a contented man. Deal had seen any number of such snapshots before, for his parents had loved cruising the islands, especially before he was born.

As for his parents' Gatsbyesque host, Barton Deal had a way of befriending total strangers inside of half an hour at any hotel bar in the world. This man was undoubtedly another of the pack. He turned the photo over and saw his mother's handwriting: "Quicksilver Cay, October 12, 1952," went the legend, in flowing script. Beneath it he saw that his father had added something in darker ink: "The bastards got lucky." Deal shook his head, puzzled. Who were the "bastards," and what good fortune had they enjoyed? He shook his head at the nonsensical quality of the scrawl—who could ever hope to understand the jumbled thoughts going through his father's mind? He glanced again at the snapshot, then set it aside and turned to the rest.

The second sheet carried a clip from the *Herald*—no dateline included, but Deal didn't need one. This clip, though equally yellowed, had come from the 1970s, the year of Deal's graduation from high school. "All

Prep Football," the caption read. A smudged photo of long-haired and afro'ed high school boys in team jerseys and street pants, Deal among them, the only representative from a Miami Central team only so-so that year. He'd played both ways: tight end on offense, linebacker on defense, had made the all-star team (and earned a scholarship to Tallahassee) as the latter, more a result of tenacity than talent. His father had circled Deal's visage, his nose still taped from one of an endless series of smashings. He had added his own inscription in what looked like the same ink he'd used on the back of the photograph: "My son," he'd written. As if anybody needed to know, Deal thought.

Deal felt his throat constrict, realized his balance was wavering. He sat down in his office chair, forcing himself to take deep breaths until he felt steady again. He had another glance at the clippings, then set them aside, turning his attention back to the key. He picked it up, turned it over, found a three-digit number chiseled into the opposite face, but no other identifying markings.

His father had banked at a downtown branch of Coral Gables Federal; after his mother's death, Deal had cleared out what little was left in boxes belonging to both his parents. It was possible this was simply a duplicate key—he certainly couldn't remember the numbers of the boxes he'd opened. And while Gables Federal had long ago been gobbled up by one of the out-of-state behemoths, the branch office was still in place and conducting business. If it was a box key, the matter should be easy enough to check out, he thought, rubbing the smooth metal between his thumb and forefinger as if it were some kind of talisman.

Some secret treasure trove, he thought. A key, one photo, and two news clippings: his father's hidden legacy.

He folded the clippings back into the packet, then stuck the papers into the pocket of his shirt. Deal glanced at the key again, hefted it in his hand. After a moment, he leaned back in his office chair and stared up at the creaking ceiling of the portable building, wondering just what he had done to earn this present place in the cosmos: His wife gone away from him to live, treading the narrow path between normalcy and god-knows-what each day, his earnest-to-a-fault daughter torn by confusion, a killer's brother come to town intending to end his life, a shadowy CIA type apparently bent on blackmailing him, and now his suicide father sending messages from the grave.

What to do about it all? he wondered, and could hear his father's voice in answer: "You've got your health, boy. Soldier on."

Sure, Deal thought. What other alternative was there? He took another deep breath then, stood, and went toward the door to do just that.

seventeen

"Too bad we didn't bring a fishing pole," Frank Wheatley called to his brother. He braced one hand on the console of the roaring Cigarette, the other locked on a windshield brace. His hair flew straight back in the slipstream like it had been frozen into place.

Basil, who was at the wheel of the big boat, gave him a withering look. "Yeah, you could be trolling for something at forty knots."

Frank shrugged. "Sailfish can do that. They can hit fifty or sixty in short bursts."

Basil looked at him again. "Sailfish? How would you know?"

"It was on TV this morning," Frank said. "The Caribbean Sports Channel."

Basil turned back to the undifferentiated waterscape in front of him. Seas three to four feet, a slight tailwind, nothing but clear skies ahead. "You see any sailfish out there, Einstein?"

"Not right now," Frank said. "That's why we need bait."

Basil didn't bother to respond. Any kind of answer would only encourage his brother. As far as he knew, Frank had been fishing exactly once—if "fishing" was the right term. The two of them had gone out to Dishman's Lake one afternoon, in search of a hundred-pound catfish said to lurk in the murky depths of the long-abandoned quarry waters. They'd climbed to the top of one of the surrounding cliffs, and Frank had lobbed a chunk of concrete block, with a burning stick of dynamite attached, down into the deep waters. The concussion had sent about a thousand goggle-eyed perch, carp, and suckers floating to the surface, along with a few catfish, but nothing remotely close to the hundred-pound range. Basil had thought the incident proved the story about the catfish was bullcrap. Frank had argued that they simply needed to come back with more dynamite.

"Wouldn't you like to have one of these babies back on Ramapo?"

Basil glanced at Frank out of the corner of his eye. "Are you talking about this boat?"

"I'm not talking about sailfish," Frank said.

Basil snorted. "George Washington could throw a dollar across Lake Ramapo. You couldn't get this thing out of idle before you'd have to turn it right around."

"Yeah," Frank said. "But women like a fast boat."

"What if they do?" Basil asked.

"It doesn't have to *go* fast, it just has to *look* fast. Something like this, you'd just park it at the dock, sit back, and wait for 'em to flock on board."

"There's a plan, all right." Basil's voice was getting sore from all the shouting. He wondered why nothing ever seemed to stop his brother.

"The guy back at the dock on Paradise told me they had twin 'Vette engines in this thing."

"Is that right?" Basil said.

"You imagine how fast a Corvette could go if it had two engines in it?"

"Pretty fast," Basil said.

There was silence for a few moments. Basil knew that his brother was staring at him, but he was not going to give him so much as a glance in return.

"How come you're trying to be agreeable?" Frank asked.

Basil glanced up at the sky, so blue it hurt to look at it. "Because it's a nice day," he said. "Perfect day for a boat ride."

"A *long* boat ride," Frank said. "I don't see why we couldn't just fly where we're going."

"You know why," Basil said.

"We could have used different names. It's not like we haven't done that before."

Basil finally turned on him. "Are you getting tired of this line of work, little brother?"

"I'm just saying—"

"Because if you are, the old man's still holding a place for you back at the scrap yard in Jersey."

Frank gave him a petulant look. "You know what I'm saying."

"And you know what *I'm* saying. The minute you start trying to cut corners, try to make it easier on yourself, that's when everything goes to shit. The boss has a plan, we have to follow the plan."

"I was just thinking—"

"Thinking?" Basil said. *"Thinking?"*

"Oh, forget it," Frank said. "If that's the way you're going to be."

"Somebody's got to keep a hand on the controls."

"That's what we count on you for," Frank said.

"See, the way you look at it, we're going to waltz up there to Miami, everything's going to go just the way we want it to, we'll get in, see who we have to see, do what we have to do, in and out—no muss, no fuss."

"Why shouldn't I?" Frank said defensively. "That's the way the Zen do it."

"The Zen?"

"They're a kind of monk," Frank said. "They want to shoot an arrow, they think about it hitting the bull's-eye before they pull the string. They want to hit a tennis ball to a particular spot, they see a picture in their minds before they even swing. The point is, you want something to happen a certain way, then that's the way you picture it beforehand."

"This is something else you saw on TV? Monks playing tennis?"

"Guys who'd studied with the monks. A couple weeks ago. One of those British channels."

Basil stared at his brother. "A little knowledge is a dangerous thing," he said finally.

"You're just jealous," Frank said, "because I keep an open mind. I'm willing to grow. You, on the other hand, you think you already know everything. That makes you an old man, Basil. Old before your time."

Basil nodded. He thought about just reaching out, giving Frank a three-inch punch to the breastbone, send him right over the rail, let him swim with the sailfish. But exasperating as he could be, Frank *was* his baby brother. He might have been blessed with the body and the looks of a movie hunk, but somebody had wrapped up the package before all the parts had been installed. Hardly Frank's fault.

"You're right, little brother," he said. "You are the creative side of this team."

Frank stared back at him, suspicious, but Basil knew the flattery had already begun to do its work. "But these Zen you were talking about," he continued, "they're Chinamen of a sort, aren't they?"

Frank nodded. "I think so."

"Well, that's something else about Miami."

"What is?"

"There's no Chinese there," Basil said. "Lots of just about everything else, but very few Chinese."

"So?"

"So, you go into a new place, you want to be tuned into the operative vibrations, if you know what I mean. You seen what happens when one of those karate guys puts a bunch of moves on Clint Eastwood, right?"

"He pulls out his Colt and shoots them in the nuts."

"Bingo, little brother," Basil said. "So we want to end up like Clint, not like the guy with the hole in his balls."

"So over the side with the Zen," Frank said. "That's what you're trying to tell me."

"All I'm saying is, stick with the plan."

"Get in and get out quick, but be ready, just in case."

"That's it," Basil said.

"No going through customs, coming in or going out."

"Carry whatever you damn well please along with you."

"Like guns and stuff."

Basil smiled. "And stuff."

"Makes sense, I guess."

"We're on the same page now," Basil said, pointing at the horizon where tiny nubbins that were really seaside skyscrapers had come into view. "Miami, here we come," he said. From out of the corner of his eye, he saw his little brother draw back the string of an imaginary bow and let an arrow fly.

eighteen

"You'd need a court order, identifying yourself as the executor of the estate," the young woman behind the marble-topped desk was saying. "Along with a death certificate, of course."

Deal stared across the cool stone surface that separated the two of them. "Carla Acevedo," her nameplate read. She was clad in a conservatively cut black suit that failed to hide the lush figure beneath. She wore a bright red shade of lipstick that contrasted with her sleek dark hair and matched her polished nails. He suspected that in some other context, and shorn of the need to conduct a megabank's business, she might seem attractive. Assuming she owned a human personality, that is.

"I don't know what your assistant told you," Deal said, glancing toward the outer office where Russell Straight sat in a chair that looked too small to contain him, leafing through a magazine under the eye of the equally no-nonsense receptionist. Deal had suggested to the man that he make his own way along to the Terrell job site, explain to Gonzalez that he'd been hired on, but Russell had demurred, citing Gonzalez's dubious attitude. In the end, Deal had given up and brought Straight along to the bank. It was only a few minutes out of the way, after all.

"I'm not interested in accessing anything at the moment," he said to Carla Acevedo. "I'd just like to know if my father kept another safety deposit box here."

The look she gave him wasn't entirely unsympathetic. "I'm sorry," she said. "I can't give out that information. Not without authorization. If it were your privacy involved, I'm sure you'd want us to do the same."

"If I were dead," Deal said, "I don't know that I'd care a whole hell of a lot."

Carla Acevedo stared back at him. "Nonetheless . . ." she said, in her careful, unaccented speech.

Deal couldn't remember the last time he'd heard the word spoken aloud. How were you supposed to argue with *nonetheless*?

He put the key down on the marble desk top. It made a little clinking sound in the plush quietness that surrounded them.

"Maybe you could just tell me if this *looks* like one of your keys. I mean, there wouldn't be much point in me coming back here with a bunch of paperwork if this is the wrong bank."

The woman glanced down at the key, then back at Deal. "Our policy—" she began, but Deal cut her off.

"I could stand over there by the entrance to the vault," Deal said, pointing outside. "Ask everybody who goes by, 'Does this look like yours?' We're not talking state secrets, for God's sakes."

The woman gave him a speculative look. Maybe she'd already pressed the security button under her desk, he thought. Get this lunatic out of here. He mustered a good-natured smile to show that he was harmless. "I'm just trying to save us all some time," he said.

After a moment, she dropped her glance to the key, as if she were noticing it for the first time. "How old is that?" she asked.

"I don't know," Deal said. "My father's been dead for almost ten years."

She glanced up at him. "The bank was entirely remodeled after the consolidation," she said at last. "The vault as well, the boxes, all the keys changed out. That was before my time, I'm afraid . . ."

"Isn't there anybody around who would remember?"

She stared at him for a moment, then glanced at her watch. Maybe she had a lunch date, he thought. If that was the case, he knew he'd be out of luck. Finally, she sighed and picked up the key. "Do you mind if I take this?"

He held up his hands in surrender. "Please."

"I'll just be a minute," she said. She stood and came around her desk, nylons whisking, a discreet floral scent washing over him in her wake. She was through the swinging glass door, into the outer office, and past Russell in a few long strides.

Russell also turned to watch her go, Deal noted. When he turned back, his gaze met Deal's through the glass. Deal smiled but Russell went back to his magazine without an acknowledgment. *At least we know you're human,* Deal thought, settling back in his chair.

He sat for a few moments, contemplating the list of all the things he had to do yet in this day, things he'd put off in order to butt heads with officers of banks. He'd managed to reach six on his list, knowing he'd never get half that much accomplished, and how about placing that ad for a secretary, when he heard the suck of air at the swinging door again. In the next moment, Carla Acevedo was back, trailed by a stoop-shouldered man who looked like he'd passed retirement age long before. "This is Mr. Nieman," she said. "He's been with the bank for a while."

And then some, Deal thought.

"I owned too much stock in Gables Federal for them to show me the gate," Nieman said. "Otherwise I'd be in mothballs."

"He likes to joke," Carla Acevedo said, her smile strained.

"Nothing funny about it," Nieman said, though he didn't seem particularly upset. Deal had also noticed Nieman was holding the key in his hand.

"My name's John Deal," he began, starting out of his seat.

Nieman waved him back down. "I know who you are," he said. "Your father was a customer from the days Hector was a pup. I'm sorry he's gone."

"Thanks," Deal said. "It's been a while, in fact."

"Has it?" Nieman said. "Time tends to get away from you when you're older." He blinked pale blue eyes behind a pair of wire-rimmed glasses as Carla Acevedo shifted impatiently beside him, from one foot to the other. Nieman gave her a look then turned back to Deal, unhurried.

"Your father used to bring you in here in short pants," Nieman said. "He was a fine man. He's greatly missed."

Deal nodded. "I appreciate it, Mr. Nieman."

Nieman seemed lost in thought for a moment. Carla Acevedo had her lovely lips pressed tightly together. Finally, the old man seemed to remember the key he held in his hand. He glanced down at it, then back up at Deal.

"The young lady here says you wanted to know if this key belonged to one of our boxes."

"That's right," Deal said.

"I'm sorry to disappoint you," Nieman said. "Our original keys were brass. We never used silver. Ever. For another thing, we kept the numbers consistent, even after the remodeling." He paused after that word, as if it had caused something to stick in his throat.

"Three-twelve was never registered to your father," he continued. "It belongs to the widow of a dairy farmer from Miami Lakes. She's had it for fifty years—"

"Mr. Nieman—" Carla Acevedo tried to interrupt.

"The old biddy used to call *me* down every time she wanted to open 'her war chest.' I won't go into the reasons for that."

"We're really not authorized—"

"Never mind," Nieman said, waving her concern away. "We're not naming names. And Mr. Deal isn't going to tell anyone anyway, are you?" Neiman glanced at him mildly.

Deal shook his head, trying to keep a straight face. "Well," Deal said. "I appreciate all your trouble . . ."

"It's no trouble at all. Got me away from wool-gathering. That's about all I do around here anymore."

Carla Acevedo mustered a smile. "Actually, Mr. Nieman's vice president in charge of special projects for the bank."

"Oh, yes," Nieman said. "I dream special projects up, and if they cost anything, the fellows at headquarters shoot them down." He dug into his pocket for a card and handed it over to Deal. "Once upon a time, we sponsored the Orange Bowl parade, all by ourselves. Give me a call if you come up a spare million or two to underwrite something charitable, Mr. Deal."

"I'll be sure to," Deal said, grinning now.

"I'm sorry I couldn't help," Nieman said, handing over the key as well.

"I'll keep checking around," Deal said, slipping the key back into his pocket, visions creeping into his head of himself trooping through an endless series of banks, an endless succession of Carla Acevedos to en-counter. "It was a pleasure to meet you, Mr. Nieman," Deal said. He extended his hand to Nieman's. The old man's palm was parchment-skinned and nearly fleshless, but his grip was surprisingly strong.

"Try a couple of the foreign banks down Brickell," Nieman said. "The Brits favor silver in everything."

"Do they?" Deal was glancing at his watch, wondering if he'd be able to make it to the job site before everyone broke for lunch.

"I started my career in banking with a branch of the Bank of London," Nieman said. "With our own private dining facility. Sterling on the tables there, of course, sterling safe box keys, sterling everywhere you looked."

Deal didn't have to ask what the man thought of the ultramodern de-cor all about them. "I appreciate your words about my father."

"I meant every one of them," Nieman said. He held up his wavering hand in farewell. Deal gave Carla Acevedo a nod and then went out to col-lect Russell Straight.

nineteen

"I GOT THE DISTINCT feeling this Sams is a spook, all right," Vernon Driscoll was saying over the thwacks of hammering coming from inside the Terrell guest house.

He and Deal were standing on one of the decks outside, staring out at the bay as they talked. The warm winter easterly had calmed, and the flat water had begun its transformation from crystal blue to pewter as the sun drained out of the sky. It seemed very peaceful out there, Deal thought, watching a solitary pelican lumber through the balmy air toward shore. Of course, just below that deceptively lovely surface, a big fish had his sights on a little fish, and there was a bigger one yet, just waiting in the wings. Why was tragedy so much more poignant in the tropics? he wondered.

"I went through the standard bureaucratic inquiries, but nobody in the system is owning up to Talbot Sams being an employee of the Justice Department." Deal cut Driscoll a glance, but the big man held up his hand. "That don't mean much, of course, because there's a lot of outfits who keep guys in key positions out of the public eye. I could be some kind of headhunter who wants to steal Mr. Terrific Employee Sams away for a competing firm."

"Sure," Deal said. "The KGB, MI5, there are lots of them out there."

"More importantly," Driscoll continued, "I ran him on the computer six ways from Sunday, every national and state public record database, couldn't get anything that matches up." He brandished an inch-thick stack of paper at Deal and shook his head. "I did come across an ex-government employee named Talbot Sams in Beaufort, South Carolina. The guy's retired from the IRS—now he's a minister. And he's eighty-two. That seem like a fit?"

Deal laughed mirthlessly. "How about Tasker?"

Driscoll shrugged. "There's not really much to go on, there. Low-level guy, no first name, or maybe Tasker *is* a first name. Hanging around with somebody goes by Talbot, after all."

Deal glanced at the stack of papers. "So that's how you do it these days, spend a couple of hours on the internet, you get everything there is to get?"

Driscoll gave him an apologetic look. "I used to watch Marie fool around on her computer, I'd think to myself what a hell of a time-sink *that* is. Now I do half my business on the 'net . . . or Osvaldo does, that is. I still couldn't tell you the difference between a hard drive and a soft."

Deal nodded. Osvaldo Regalado was a computer geek, one of a long line of contacts Driscoll had carried over from a twenty-five-year career in law enforcement. A few years back, Osvaldo had turned state's evidence against a couple of his employers—major white-collar criminals from Boca Raton who'd concocted a phony mortgage scam—and had found himself tossed in front of a Metrorail train for his trouble. He'd survived, but lost both legs as a result. Driscoll had gone to great lengths to see the man through rehab, as well as an ensuing alcoholic nosedive, and now employed him as a researcher in D & D Investigative Services, the company that Driscoll had convinced Deal to invest in.

"There's other ways, of course," Driscoll was saying. "But now we know the easy way isn't going to work. This is a guy who's made a point of burying himself. It'll take some time, that's all." Driscoll gave Deal his what's-a-guy-to-do look, then glanced through the open patio doors to where Russell Straight was bent over, apparently beating a wooden partition into submission.

"How's your new help working out, by the way?"

Deal followed Driscoll's gaze, watching Russell. The man set one sixteen-penny nail with a tap of his hammer, then drove it all the way home with a single blow. "He's a human nail gun," Deal said. "Watch him go."

Russell sent another nail to the bone—the last one he needed, apparently—then stood back and levered the skeleton of the partition to a standing position as easily as if it were constructed of balsa wood. He grasped the ten-foot section of wall by one of its central members and swung it into position, then bent and slammed another nail through the cleat and into the plywood subflooring in one fluid motion. In seconds, he had moved catlike to the opposite end of the partition, where it butted up against another wall, and nailed it firmly into place with a couple more strokes.

"So what'd you do, fire everybody else?" Driscoll asked.

Deal glanced at his watch. Gonzalez and his men had been gone nearly an hour. "What can I tell you, Driscoll, he's eager."

"Once, I heard about a guy that could pound nails like that," Driscoll said. "Turned out he kept a bar of soap in his nail pouch. Shortly after the house was built, the nails started working loose, the damn thing almost fell down."

"I told you that story," Deal said. "It was a guy who used to work for my old man."

"Is that right?" Driscoll said. "I guess I forgot. Anyways, I don't see any soap in Russell's hand."

"Nor do I," Deal said. The sky was leaden now, the water's surface dark, the pelican safe at roost, or so he hoped. He turned back to Driscoll. "What's next with finding Sams?"

Driscoll gave him his patented shrug. "Lots of things. We could let Osvaldo set up a tap on your phones, wait for him to call again. Of course, if he does work for Big Brother, he'll be sweeping the lines himself. Or he'll have his phone hooked to a rerouter, we'll be running him back to the switchboard of some VA hospital in Santa Monica. It'll be like 'Spy Versus Spy.'"

"What are you trying to tell me, Driscoll? That it's hopeless?"

"Not at all. It's just not like on TV, that's all. You want me to bring in a couple of guys, have 'em stake you out, we could do that. The guy shows up again, we just follow him."

"Which would be expensive."

Driscoll rolled his thick shoulders. "It wouldn't be cheap. I got a couple of guys owe me favors, though."

"I don't know," Deal said.

"If it was me," Driscoll said, "I'd wait. See what develops. Meantime, you got yourself a nice piece of work, who cares if this joker says he set it up?"

"I told you what he said about Janice and Isabel."

"Yeah, and it could be a bunch of smoke he's blowing, too," Driscoll said. He glanced out over the nearly dark waters. "I vote we start with Osvaldo, let him hook into your phones, what do you say?"

"All right by me, I guess," Deal said. He massaged the back of his neck, working against a headache he felt coming on.

"Pretty out there, isn't it?" Driscoll asked, nodding at the glittering Miami skyline that was flickering now on the opposite crescent of the bay.

Deal was about to agree when he heard footsteps at the doorway behind them. Russell Straight was coming out onto the porch, untying a canvas nail bag from around his waist. "About out of light inside," he said to Deal.

"That's all right," Deal said. "You've done more than a day's work. It's time to go home."

Straight was about to turn away when Deal spoke again. "Meet my friend Driscoll," he said. "Vernon Driscoll, say hello to Russell Straight."

Driscoll turned from the railing and nodded. Russell Straight regarded him for a moment, then nodded back. "You the cop," he said.

"I was a cop," Driscoll said evenly. After a moment, he added, "Your brother was Leon Straight."

"He was," Straight said.

The way the two stared at each other was as if they'd created an energy beam between them that could fry anything that tried to cross through it. "Your brother could have been a good ballplayer," Driscoll said finally.

"*Was* a good ballplayer," Russell said, his tone neutral.

Driscoll nodded. "How about you? You a ballplayer?"

"I box some," Russell said, shrugging.

"You any good?"

"I did all right."

"You don't box anymore?"

"Not for a while."

Driscoll nodded. "It's a tough sport."

"That it is," Russell agreed. He glanced out at the nearby bay as if something had caught his attention there, and indeed something had, though it was only Russell who could see it, a vision he'd be condemned to for the rest of his days.

Ten years ago, himself seventeen, the same person, but a different life—or where his life had turned, more like it . . .

. . . not a gym at all, but a rinky-dink all-purpose auditorium in Cordele, Georgia, a building three quarters of a century old, the air stale, the lighting dim, the padding of the rickety row seats thin and tattered. There was a gray-looking movie screen hanging lopsided high in the flies above, and a set of wood-backed basketball goals set up on either end of the creaking stage, which, presuming basketball had actually been played there, would make for a court little more than half the size of regulation.

The ring, scaled down by a foot in each direction by a promoter eager to encourage more close-quarters action, had been erected squarely between the goals and was set out close to the edge of the stage, above a boarded-over orchestra pit. Folding chairs had been set up to create some semblance of a ringside. Anyone sitting too long in the front rows was sure to develop a monumental neckache, staring practically straight up at the fights, but the seats were full there, as were most of the others in the auditorium, and no one had complained.

There had been half a dozen bouts before this main event, moving up steadily through the weight classes, if not in level of talent. The last fight had ended when an eager light heavyweight, a farm boy from Damascus, had lost his mouthpiece, then stepped into a head-butt from his opponent. There were still teeth scattered across the blood-streaked canvas out there. From the corner where he sat, Russell Straight could see them glinting yellow as corn kernels.

"This is when it happens," came the voice at Russell's ear. "Don't forget yourself."

Russell nodded as if he were getting good advice. His so-called trainer, an ancient black man—he'd had to have been old when this place had been built, Russell thought. "Why they wasting money on that fool?" Russell said, staring across the ring at his opponent. A white man from Atlanta, supposed to have been a kick-boxing champ, had all the moves and reflexes of a heavy bag.

"Don't matter," said the old man at his ear. He sponged tepid water from a plastic bucket onto Russell's brow. "Do what you supposed to do."

The old man was gone then, the pail withdrawn, the stool slipped away beneath him as the bell rang. Scheduled for ten rounds, it would go four. Russell knew why, of course, but it had made him feel better to ask.

He danced out to the center of the ring, feinted, jabbed, stepped back, feeling a fallen tooth grind beneath the sole of his shoe. Just fooling around, waiting for his lumbering opponent to come on, get things over with.

"You ain't Cassius Clay," someone yelled from the predominately white audience. Russell smiled. His opponent had finally made it to the center of the ring and pawed a jab his way.

Russell dodged it easily, circled to his left, and fired a jab of his own that snapped the white man's head back. His opponent lunged forward, clamping his arms over Russell's and pulling him close. "Get cute, nigger, I'll bust your ass."

"Uh-huh," Russell said. "Gotta make it look good." He could hear the rasp of the man's breathing, the guy winded just from getting off his stool. Russell leaned in hard, shoved him forcefully away. The crowd booed as the man staggered back.

"Head-butt," screamed the same heckler from ringside. "Come on, ref."

The referee, a florid-faced man who looked like he'd be at home on the seat of a tractor, shook his head at Russell reprovingly and motioned the two to resume. Russell's opponent stepped forward, unleashing a combination: a left hook that glanced off Russell's shoulder and a right that missed altogether. Russell, sidestepping, sent a left high on the man's cheekbone. The man staggered into his own corner, his head bouncing off the frayed turnbuckle.

When the man's head snapped back, a spray of blood flew from a cut that had opened on his forehead. Russell turned away, but it was like trying to duck a bucket of water tossed his way. His eyes were burning suddenly, his vision blurred. He felt a solid blow—bone against bone at his forehead—and though he was stunned, instinct sent him backpedaling away. There was a blow at his midsection, then a third that struck him in the groin. He felt some fragile thing burst inside himself and doubled over, staggering back, out of control now.

His back drove against the tightly strung top rope and sent him hurtling again toward the center of the ring. He blinked, seeing two white men coming toward him, both with faces masked by blood. The crowd, rowdy enough all evening, was in a frenzy now.

"Kill him," shrieked the man at ringside. "Kill that nigger sonofabitch!"

Russell, his legs gone rubbery with the last low blow, saw the white man's fist draw back in a blurry mirrored action, saw two gloves blossoming huge his way. He ducked and fell as much as stepped on forward, driving a desperate right of his own toward what he hoped was the actual man. Miss, and his momentum would be enough to send him out of the ring, a dozen rows up.

He felt his fist strike flesh solidly, though, and knew that he'd guessed right. As hard a punch as he'd ever landed, coming off the ropes like that, and never mind that luck was what had guided him. He spun on a step or two, thrown aside by the force of his own blow, then turned to find the white man tottering upright, one hand clutched to his throat, the other pawing blindly at the air.

The crowd was beyond reason now, the noise an unrelenting din. Russell saw one moon-faced bald man—surely the one who wanted a nigger killed—clawing at the edge of the canvas as if to drag himself into the ring. But he didn't care about that one now. He cared only about the man who had butted heads with him, then sent the blow that had broken something deep inside, none of that necessary, Russell scheduled to lie down all the while.

There was still a red film that shrouded his sight, but whether it was blood or rage, Russell could not tell, nor did he care. He ignored the pain that had ignited in his bowels and strode forward—a left to the white man's chin that sent him to the ropes, another flush to the face as he rebounded back . . . and then fell down.

Russell didn't know how to account for what happened next, might never be able to find the words, in fact. He was intelligent enough to know that the manner of his upbringing figured in, as he also realized the deep hatreds fostered in the place he'd grown up had encouraged it as well. And he was honest enough to admit that some part of what had always been inside himself had surely figured in. But still, he could not truly explain it, not to judge nor jury, not to psychiatrist nor prison counselor, not even to himself.

All he knew was that he had done it, had found himself on top of the fallen white man in a makeshift boxing ring in a pissant south Georgia town, shrugging off the referee who tried in vain to stop him. Ignoring— if not inspired by—that frenzied crowd of white men, to strike again and again at the motionless form beneath him . . .

. . . fist after falling fist . . .

. . . until there was a moment of blessed darkness, followed by light as bright as truth, and he was standing on the unfinished porch of a rich man's guest house somewhere in the tropics of Florida, shivering as if with fever and as if it all had happened only moments before.

"I said, it's a tough sport," Vernon Driscoll repeated. "But then again you look like a tough guy."

Russell regarded Driscoll calmly. "You don't know the half of it."

Driscoll lifted an eyebrow then turned to Deal. "I'll give Osvaldo a call when I get home," he said. "I'll see things get handled."

"I appreciate it," Deal said. He noticed Driscoll seemed to be waiting for something. "I have to close up here, Vernon. You don't have to wait."

"You sure?"

"I'm sure," Deal said.

Driscoll nodded then and started down from the deck.

"Nice to meet you, Russell," Driscoll added as he started toward the front of the main house.

"You too," Russell Straight replied, his face an equally neutral mask.

Two big dogs, Deal found himself thinking. They'd done everything but hike their legs on the corners of the porch. He sighed and turned to Russell. "You got everything picked up in there?"

Russell held out the hammer he'd been using. "This belongs to Gonzalez. He said give it to you when I'm done."

Deal stared at the hammer. He heard the sound of Driscoll's car starting, the sound of gravel crunching as the ex-cop drove off. "Go ahead and keep it. Soon as you pick one up, you can give it back to Gonzalez your-self."

"You're the boss," Russell said doubtfully.

"That I am," Deal said. "Go on, Russell. I'll see you tomorrow."

Russell saluted him with the handle of the instrument, then stepped down and traced Driscoll's path toward the front of the house.

twenty

"You can't dock that boat here." The voice came out of the shadows, startling Frank Wheatley so that he almost went backward over the rail of the Cigarette.

That was the down side of a tropical lifestyle, he thought. All these plants and trees and underbrush, a zillion birds squawking, bunch of creepy nocturnal animals on the prowl, how were you supposed to see if somebody was sneaking up on you?

"Yeah?" Frank said, peering up through the evening shadows toward the top of the seawall where Basil had tied them off. His voice was steady, but he was sure the guy had seen him nearly go overboard. He hated that, feeling the least bit vulnerable, but what could he do now but make the best of it? "Why's that?" he added.

"Because I say so," the guy responded. He moved a step or two out of the shadows to loom over the boat, his silhouette about as thick as one of the concrete pilings that rose at the edge of the seawall. "This is private property."

Frank nodded. He knew that there was a snazzy condo hidden back there behind all the foliage, but he wasn't really agreeing with anything. He was nodding because he saw that the guy had a stubby-barreled pump-action shotgun tucked under his arm. He also noted that the guy carried the weapon in a decidedly casual way, which suggested that he knew very well how to use it.

"You some kind of security guard?" Frank asked, though he knew better. He might have left school midway through the ninth grade, but it wasn't because he was stupid. His shop teacher had gone to smack Frank alongside the head for fooling around with a band saw for the *third* time in a day, and Frank had snatched the man's hand in midair and turned to sling him right on out a second-story window of West Trenton Vocational Tech. The teacher had suffered some cuts from the glass, along with a fractured collarbone and a fair ration of bumps and bruises, but Frank had known the fall wasn't going to kill him. Throwing him out a third-story window, now *that* would have been stupid . . .

. . . as would thinking that a condo security man had been issued a weapon modified in a way that violated several federal firearms statutes. The fact was that the guy up there stood surely on the same side of the law as did Frank and his lamentably absent brother, Basil.

"That's right," the guy on the seawall said. "For your security, I'm telling you to get your ass out of here."

"I can't," Frank said. There was a mosquito on the back of his neck inserting what felt like a hot icepick deep into his flesh, but he held off slapping at it, not wanting to do anything to alarm the man with the shotgun.

He was also wondering what was taking Basil so long. On their way down the channel that led to this dockage, they'd spotted the market where his brother had gone off for something to drink. Distances on land were a little deceptive when judged from the perspective of a boat, but surely there'd been plenty of time to walk there and back.

"This isn't multiple choice, asshole. Get going." The man had turned so that the shotgun pointed straight down into the Cigarette. He didn't have his finger on the trigger, but still it was unnerving. Frank had seen what his own brother could do with a weapon just like it, after all.

Very slowly, Frank lifted his hand to point at one of the pilings. "I'm tied off," he said. "How'm I supposed to go anywhere?"

"We'll take care of that," the guy with the shotgun said. He backed carefully toward the piling where the stern line was looped and, keeping the shotgun on Frank, undid the rope with his free hand. Frank heard the soft thump of the rope as it fell onto the deck behind him.

Frank watched carefully as the man moved along the seawall to where the second line was tethered. There was another insect digging into the back of his hand and a third boring a hole in his cheek. "Aren't the mosquitoes biting you?" he called to the man on the seawall.

The guy undid the forward line and tossed it onto the Cigarette's prow. "You come back here again, you're dead meat," the guy said.

"Sorry to have disturbed you," Frank said. He was about to reach for the ignition when he saw the dark shape rise up suddenly behind the guy with the shotgun.

"Hey—" the guy said, but the word was quickly cut off, replaced by weird sucking noises that sounded like a pool vacuum with something jammed in its line. The man's feet were lifted off the ground now, kicking wildly.

Frank saw the shotgun tumble from the man's hands. He lunged for it, but the thing went into the water with a splash and disappeared. A few moments more, and all was quiet on the seawall again.

"Why do you figure he wanted us out of here so bad?" Frank asked, following his brother over the thickly landscaped grounds. In the distance sat the place they were headed for, an interesting-looking building with lots of wood and jutting angles and plenty of smoked glass. Balconies and patios were everywhere, though no one seemed to be outside. All the windows were closed, lights burning golden and cozy behind them, everybody safely tucked away for the night, or so it might seem.

Basil glanced back at the Cigarette where they'd stowed the body, then shrugged. "This'd be a good place to bring in some contraband, don't you think? Maybe we interrupted us a drug deal."

"You think?" Frank asked, glancing around.

"Who knows?" Basil shrugged again.

"Maybe we ought to wait around, take it off ourselves."

Basil stopped then and turned to him, his hands on his hips. "Didn't we just have this conversation earlier? Keep your eye on the plan, and all that?"

"Like the Zen?"

Basil sighed. "You going to start that again?"

"I was just thinking, that's all."

"I told you . . ."

"Forget it," Frank said. "I'm focusing as we speak. I am seeing this operation going down exactly as we planned."

"That's my little brother," Basil said, and then they were off again.

twenty-one

"YOU ARE SOMETHING ELSE, Osvaldo," Driscoll said to the powerfully built man in the wheelchair.

"The computer does the work," Osvaldo said in his soft-spoken way, no false modesty in his voice. He wore a full beard neatly trimmed, his jet black hair pulled back tight into a ponytail. His arms were those of a bodybuilder, his chest swelling the fabric of a sleeveless T-shirt. Though his trouser legs were empty, neatly pressed and pinned just above the knees, he radiated enough energy to make Driscoll feel tired just looking at him.

At the moment, Osvaldo's gaze was still fixed intently on the glowing screen before him. They'd been tracing through the various reports together, Osvaldo navigating around and over the various computer fire walls constructed by one state agency after another like an eel whisking through a drift fisherman's nets.

Driscoll turned away to rub at his burning eyes and glanced at the humming printer that was churning out hard copy of the facts they'd so far unearthed. "You're not surprised he's a con, are you," Osvaldo said over his shoulder.

Driscoll shook his head, waiting for a growling eighteen-wheeler to crest the overpass that coursed only a few yards away from Osvaldo's third-story apartment door. "I didn't figure him for a killer, though."

"Maybe he's not," Osvaldo said, pushing back from the Formica-clad door that served as his desk.

"You beat a man to death with your bare hands, what does that make you?" Driscoll asked.

Osvaldo shrugged. "An avenger, perhaps . . . sometimes a martyr."

Driscoll shook his head. "The law is not a philosopher, Osvaldo."

"I hear the law is a ass," Osvaldo countered.

Driscoll glanced at Osvaldo's empty trouser legs. The law had hardly done this man any favors, now, had it? He turned, gesturing toward the tiny kitchen. "You got any beer?"

Osvaldo nodded. "I keep it just for you."

Driscoll walked to the refrigerator as another eighteen-wheeler cranked its way up the overpass, then began a spine-rattling series of shifts back down. Six bottles of Jamaican Red Stripe on the bottom shelf, squat brown soldiers, each with a red-and-white label glistening out at him. Osvaldo hadn't been kidding about who the beer was for, Driscoll thought. The man hadn't had a drink in better than three years now. Three years and counting.

"Why don't you find yourself a quieter place, Osvaldo?" Driscoll asked, coming back into the room with an open beer in hand.

"I like it here," Osvaldo said. "You should come by at rush hour. You open the windows and close your eyes, it sounds just like the surf pounding at the shore."

"The surf, huh?" Driscoll snorted, as the echo of the eighteen-wheeler died away.

"Besides, they have a good workout room. You ought to see it."

"I was going to get into exercise once," Driscoll said. "Then I took a nap and the urge just disappeared."

"Some nice-looking women come in there," Osvaldo said.

Driscoll glanced at Osvaldo. He suspected some of the women weren't visiting the place just to work on their abs. "I guess there's an up side to everything," Driscoll said.

"You could start out slow, build up to where you'd like to be," Osvaldo said.

Driscoll put a hand on his formidable gut. *No six-pack there,* he thought. *More like a case, a case and a half.* "I'm where I like to be already," Driscoll said. "A high wind comes along, I'm not going anywhere."

"Suit yourself," Osvaldo said, raising an eyebrow.

Driscoll had a slug of Red Stripe, thinking briefly about how life would be without beer. What he felt were probably the same emotions as the French philosophers contemplating the abyss. "You remember Leon Straight?" he asked, waving the beer at the growing mound of paper in the printer tray.

"Who doesn't?" Osvaldo said. "A real bad actor. The Dolphins could use a guy like him these days."

"Quite a family history," Driscoll said. "I'm sorry I didn't meet the old man."

"You're not as tough as you like to sound," Osvaldo said.

"No?" Driscoll raised an eyebrow of his own.

"Deep down, you like to think the best of everybody."

"Yeah, I'm going to nominate Russell Straight as a teen mentor," Driscoll said.

"You could have turned your back on me, Driscoll."

Driscoll made a noise in his throat. "That's different."

"No, it's not," Osvaldo said.

"You didn't kill anybody just because they pissed you off. In fact, I believe it was the other way around."

"Maybe I haven't so far," Osvaldo said, staring at him levelly. "But there's hardly a day that goes by when something happens and I don't think about it."

Driscoll waved his beer again. "That's different, too," he said.

Osvaldo shook his head. "You sit in this chair all the time, you'd be surprised the thoughts that go through your head."

"You going to get a rifle, climb up in a tower somewhere?"

"If I could climb, I wouldn't care about the rifle," Osvaldo said.

Driscoll felt it like a punch to his formidable gut. "I didn't mean anything, Osvaldo. You know that."

"I'm just trying to make a point," Osvaldo said.

"Point's made," Driscoll said.

Osvaldo nodded. "So what are you going to do about Leon Straight's little brother? Call his parole officer up in Georgia, arrange a pickup?"

Driscoll glanced at him. "First thing, I'll let Deal know what we found out. The guy's already assaulted him, for chrissake. Wouldn't it make you nervous having him around?"

Osvaldo shrugged. "Maybe Deal was right. If Russell Straight meant business, he would have finished the job in the first place."

"Bleeding hearts are everywhere," Driscoll said, finishing the Red Stripe. He noted that the printer had finally stopped chunking out the pages. "I'll tell Deal, then we'll see. The more important question has to do with this Sams character."

Osvaldo nodded, but his expression was anything but positive. "The guy is nowhere," he said. "The name's a phony. It has to be." He gave Driscoll a bleak look. "I'm not sure there's anything else I can do, unless you can come up with more on the guy."

Driscoll nodded and glanced at the empty in his hand. He could have another, he thought, let the heavy thinking go until morning. Have six or eight more, in fact, see if he couldn't stretch his already straining belt to a notch in the course of a night. He dropped the empty in the trash basket by Osvaldo's door-top desk and patted his stomach. "I gotta go, Osvaldo." He reached for the stack of papers in the printer tray and held them up in thanks. "I appreciate the trouble."

Osvaldo gave him a look. "I get paid these days, remember?"

"That's right," Driscoll said, reaching automatically for his wallet. "How do we stand, anyway?"

Osvaldo held up a hand to stop him. "We have an accounting program now. It cuts checks automatically."

"No kidding," Driscoll said. "When did that happen?"

"I told you about it," Osvaldo said. "Last month."

Driscoll nodded. "You said something, I guess. This means you control my finances, huh?"

Osvaldo smiled. "Be nice to me, Driscoll."

Driscoll waved on his way out the door. "It's a brave new world," he said.

"Welcome to it," Osvaldo called back. And Driscoll was out into the night.

twenty-two

"I understand you've been asking after me," came the voice over Driscoll's shoulder. He had just slid behind the wheel of the Ford where he'd parked it in a corner of the always crammed and poorly lit parking lot of Osvaldo's building, had his seat belt pulled halfway toward the catch.

Fucking A, he thought as a pair of arms encircled him. He'd been as careless as a schmuck civilian. Which, though he *was* a schmuck civilian these days, hardly qualified as an excuse. *Too many days running credit checks and following adulterous businessmen around,* he thought, feeling the fabric of the seat belt wrapping his arms, then coiling up under his chin. No real danger, no threat to keep him trim and on his toes. He was pinned back against the headrest of his seat now, choking, gasping for breath. Plenty of danger here. Threat potential plenty high, thank you very much.

"Careful, Tasker," he heard the voice behind him say. "We don't want to give the Department a bad name."

"He's got a gun."

Driscoll heard what he assumed was Tasker's voice, felt a hand sliding beneath the lapels of his coat, sensed his .38 sliding free.

"I'm going to assume you have a permit to carry this," the purring voice behind him said. "Possession of an unlicensed firearm is a serious matter, you know."

An armed citizenry is a polite citizenry, Driscoll wanted to tell the man.

Something he'd read somewhere recently. But his voice wasn't working at the moment. Strangled by his own seat belt, he found himself thinking, *What a way to go.* Maybe they'd chisel it on his headstone.

"Let him breathe, Tasker," the voice came.

Driscoll felt the pressure at his throat lessen. The sensation was accompanied by the press of something cold and steely under his ear. Shot with his own gun, he was thinking. The very worst fate of all.

"Is that you, Sams?"

"We can use that name if it suits you," the voice came. "By now I'm sure you realize that it refers to no one, truly."

"There's an eighty-two-year-old minister who'd puke if he knew you were using it," Driscoll said.

"Do tell," the voice said. "I'd like to know why you were so interested in finding me."

"I'm a private investigator," Driscoll said. "That's privileged information."

"Are you charging your friend and business partner, then?" Sams said, his voice as mellifluous as a radio announcer's. "Has John Deal put you up to this?"

When Driscoll didn't respond, the seat belt at his throat coiled tighter. "If you know everything, why bother asking?" Driscoll managed.

"There are also significant penalties for interfering with a government investigation," Sams continued. "You could find yourself in very serious trouble."

"That means I'm doing fine right now?"

"I don't need your interference," Sams said. Driscoll thought that a certain hiss of anger had crept into the man's voice. "Now tell me what you're after."

"That's pretty obvious, isn't it? You break into a guy's office, threaten to blackmail him unless he engages in some industrial espionage on your behalf, why wouldn't he want to find out who you really are?"

"I identified myself, I assure you," Sams said.

"Maybe it didn't seem too convincing, the way you conduct your business and all," Driscoll said.

"I'm trying to apprehend one of the more elusive fugitives from justice," Sams said. "It's hardly the sort of thing that's handled under the sunshine laws."

"So it would seem," Driscoll said, struggling to swallow. "But I don't think the Justice Department would condone blackmail."

Sams laughed dryly. "I'm certain you never did anything of the kind when you were trying to gain the cooperation of an informant, *Detective*."

"I leaned on scumbags, if that's what you mean," Driscoll told him. "Deal's no scumbag. Just the opposite, in fact. He'd do a hell of a lot better for himself if he wasn't so honest."

"It's a wonderful cover story, that much I'll grant you," Sams said.

"What are you talking about?" Driscoll asked.

"It's my experience that the apple rarely falls far from the tree," Sams replied. "Or to put it another way, like father, like son."

Driscoll found himself struggling against the restraints at his arms. "If you think John Deal is crooked, you're crazy," he said. "And if you think he's just going to roll over and do what you tell him, you're crazier still."

"Oh, I think he will," Sams said. "Particularly if he's made of the stuff you seem to think he is. He'd never want to see harm befall those he cares about—"

"You're no government agent," Driscoll said, still struggling at his bonds.

"Such a naïve man," Sams said. "But this has been a useful conversation after all. I do believe you're motivated by your fervent belief in Mr. Deal. Perhaps he's sold you a bill of goods, or perhaps your vision of the man is an accurate one. Either way, I'm going to get what I'm after."

"And what's that, Sams?" Driscoll demanded.

"It doesn't matter," Sams replied calmly. "You've served your purpose, I'm afraid. We're only wasting time."

Driscoll felt the chill the words conveyed and tried to struggle free. But suddenly the pressure at his throat was tremendous. And then the lights went out.

twenty-three

"Come on, Janice," Deal said, speaking to himself.

He gave up on the doorbell and moved to pound on the door of the condo she rented on the edge of Coconut Grove. It was a lively place, a smoked-glass-and-redwood holdover from the sixties, close to the water and still populated largely by a set that at least considered themselves younger—and so it was impossible to tell whether the throbbing of bass notes he felt through the deck at his feet came from inside Janice's apartment or one of those above, below, or on either side. He'd also noted that Janice often cranked her stereo high these days, something she'd never done when they were living together.

No such throbbing of music back at the fourplex, he reflected. Mrs. Suarez might turn up the Neil Rogers talk show midmorning, especially when the sardonic host played one of his satirical musical spoofs, and Driscoll sometimes overdid the TV volume during a 'Canes or Dolphins game, but that was about the extent of it. Maybe he ought to loosen up, Deal thought, soup up the volume when he delved into his Coltrane tapes, never mind if he annoyed his neighbors. He was the landlord after all.

And it wasn't that the entire array of Janice's new behaviors unsettled or annoyed Deal. In fact, he welcomed, sometimes applauded certain of these changes. Her newly aroused tastes in music, in exotic foods, an awareness in the subtleties of wine, had drawn Deal out as well. But there were troubling inconsistencies, signs of a lingering fragility, suggestions that no matter how much patience he expended, no matter how great the reserves of tender memory, respect, and longing, that the bond that they'd once shared would never mend again.

On a given day, he might find his hand brushing hers, their shoulders touching as they walked, and he would look into her eyes and see that everything that he still felt for her was mirrored precisely in her gaze. They even continued to have sex, though on a basis so random, so unpredictable, that chaos theorists would be disarmed. Teeth-rattling, eyeball-aching sex of a sort that left Deal exhausted and stupidly satisfied as a bludgeoned ox . . . and Janice up and out of bed as though she'd finished a workout at the gym and was now ready to pick out a new set of drapes.

Far more worrisome was the sense he sometimes had that he'd unaccountably become a stranger to her. In passing conversation, he'd recall some outing, some encounter with a casual acquaintance, only to be met with a blank stare or sometimes an outright denial that she knew the person in question or that such and such had ever happened. Worse yet were the times when he saw the distrust creeping into her gaze. They might be discussing the time that Deal promised to bring Isabel home from an outing, or his assurances that he understood her need for "space," or for time . . . and despite anything that he might say, Deal would see the doubt in her eyes and—worst of all—at times, the fear.

He checked his watch then, saw that he was a few minutes late, but didn't think much of that. He gave the door a solid pounding this time. He'd picked up Isabel's call on his answering machine at home. "All A's, Daddy. You know what that means."

And he did indeed. "All A's" meant a double-scoop cone at Whip 'n' Dip, Isabel's favorite purveyor of ice cream. It was an arrangement conjured up by Deal, a somewhat shameless ploy to garner an additional bit of time with his daughter, and one that even Janice countenanced, given her concern with the status of their daughter's schoolwork.

There'd been times during the past couple of years that something—most likely the strain of her parents' separation, according to the family therapist—seemed to have overwhelmed Isabel. Her effort would suddenly drop unaccountably, her attention span in class and study would dip to near nothing, her interest in school become nonexistent. Bad enough that it should happen, Deal thought. Even more galling to have someone like Talbot Sams use his daughter's difficulties as a lever.

But he was not going to think about such things tonight, he thought. He was going to take his daughter out for a treat. He'd spoken to his wife about it earlier, received her blessing, and now he and Isabel were going to go and have a good time together, nothing else to consider. If he could ever get his wife to answer the door.

He knocked again, hard enough to rattle the door in its frame. He stopped, realizing that something was odd. He reached for the door handle itself and shook. That heavy wood rattling loose in its frame. No way it could do that if the heavy bolts were shot, Deal thought, and bolting her doors was something else that Janice never failed to do these days. She'd grown up in rural northern Ohio and had displayed a tendency—alarming to Deal, a Miami native—to leave car and house doors blithely open. The first thing she'd installed in the Grove apartment, however, had been a hardened steel deadbolt to supplement the one already there, a purchase she'd even consulted Vernon Driscoll about.

He turned the knob then, felt the latch give. He pushed, and the door swung slowly inward.

"Janice," Deal called. He thought the music was louder now. A good sign? Or was it bad?

In any case, there was no response to his call, and Deal glanced over his shoulder before stepping inside. Sandalwood hung in the air, a stick of incense still smoldering on a table in the entry—another proclivity of the new Janice. To Deal, incense was no accouterment of a New Age life, but something you burned to cover the smell of the pot you smoked. Of course, that may have been why she was burning the incense, Deal told himself. That would be something he could understand, at least.

"Janice," he called again as he moved on down the hallway. The music *was* more intense inside, some concoction of sitar, chimes, gongs, and bass designed to make a listener mellow. *Sure. A couple of joints, an hour of this music, your head would turn to cheese,* he thought.

He moved quickly down the hallway toward the living room, telling himself there was nothing unusual. Janice and Isabel were in one of the bedrooms in the back of the unit, the music too loud for them to hear the bell, or his knock.

He came out of the hallway into the main living area of the condo, a spacious combination of living room and dining room that looked out onto the jungly outdoors, separated from an open kitchen only by a serving bar, above which shelving dangled from the open-beamed ceiling. There was a light on above the serving counter and another reading lamp burning near the fireplace in the corner of the living room. Enough light to see that there was no one there.

He was moving more quickly now, across the tiled floor of the living area and down the back hallway toward the bedrooms: one doorway dark, the other a square of light. Isabel's room, Deal registered, the two of them in there figuring out what his daughter ought to wear.

"Janice," he called again. They'd been married all these years, but just strolling into her new "space" was an act not to be taken lightly, unlocked entry door or not.

He tapped on the half-open door to his daughter's room before poking his head inside, then stopped short. Sure enough, what looked like half a dozen discarded outfits were tossed haphazardly across his daughter's bed, and several pairs of shoes and sneakers were scattered on the nearby floor as well. But no Isabel and no Janice inside the room.

Deal checked his watch again, then turned back to the hallway, puzzled. The bathroom door ajar, the lights dark. He glanced inside Janice's room, saw in the reflected light a neatly made bed, the doorway to the master bath dark as well. Had he gotten the time wrong? He was sure he'd said eight-thirty, a little late for a school night maybe, but it was still short of nine.

He went back down the hallway, trying to remember Janice's cell-phone number, but was drawing a blank. He'd had to memorize three of them in the last year. First she'd changed her service, then she'd lost her new phone. The old Janice had never misplaced so much as a matchbook. She'd kept old magazines stacked up by month of issue, had meticulously labeled and organized video tapes of birthday parties and family outings. Now, she might keep things neat on the surface—witness that tidy bedroom—but open an underwear drawer or a closet door and whole new intimations might spring up.

He was back in the kitchen now, forcing aside his thoughts and flipping open cabinet doors to find the list that was always taped to the back of one, all the necessary phone numbers. He could just go jump in the Hog, he thought, try to catch up with them at Whip 'n' Dip, but what if they'd gone somewhere else? One thing was certain: As surely as he made any assumptions about what Janice might have in mind these days, he could count on being absolutely wrong.

He had opened up all the cabinets now, but still found no such sheet. He was about to give up, when he saw the notepad lying on the counter near the kitchen phone. He picked the pad up and checked Janice's scribble: "D. out of town thru Sat. Switch weekend with I. to next?"

It took a moment for things to sink in. Someone had called Janice? Said he'd be called away, wanted to change his days with Isabel? What the hell was going on?

He tossed the notepad down, his mind racing. *Talbot Sams,* he thought. Something the sonofabitch had cooked up. But what could the man intend? And why would Janice just take the word of whoever might have called? She ought to know he'd never entrust such a call to someone else. Again, he cursed whatever fates had changed his happy and contented life. What had he done to deserve it, after all? He'd never asked for much, never even aspired to the kingpin status his old man had always seemed to chase. A family. A decent life. Work he enjoyed, and which he felt mattered. *Such presumption,* he thought bitterly.

He reached for the phone then, his first thought to call Driscoll. He'd managed to get the first three digits dialed when he saw the unmistakable shape of a man stepping out of the shadows toward him.

twenty-four

"You okay?"

Driscoll heard the words coming to him as if he were lying far below the surface of the earth—at the bottom of a pit, maybe. The place they toss your carcass when you're too old, too slow to run with the herd any longer.

"Come on, now. Talk to me, man."

Driscoll realized his cheeks were being slapped. Whoever was doing it was trying to be gentle, but it was like Driscoll trying to whisper, or dance the minuet.

"I'm okay," he managed. "Cut it out, already." He blinked his eyes, saw that he wasn't at the bottom of a pit at all. There was the shadow of a burnt-out light stanchion looming over him, outlined like a curious Martian against the dim glow of the night sky. The distant reaches of the parking lot of Osvaldo's building, he realized. There was someone with him, too. Somebody with one hand propping him up, another hand still batting his cheeks.

"Cut the crap," he said. He got a handful of the guy's shirt front, was trying to pull him down.

"Take it easy," the guy said, brushing Driscoll's groping hand away as if it were a child's. "It's me. It's Russell Straight."

Driscoll lay still a minute, doing his best to gather his thoughts. "What happened?" he managed finally. "Where the hell'd you come from?"

"You're lucky I was here, my man. Those guys saw me coming and took off. Elsewise, you might be dead."

Driscoll glanced around. Sure enough, there was his Ford a few feet away, the driver's door still gaping open. Like the damned thing was embarrassed for him, he thought.

He got a hand beneath himself, pushed against the gritty pavement. He managed a sitting position and felt at his throat, raw from where the goon had choked him. At least the dizziness had evaporated. He glanced through the darkness at Straight, who still squatted beside him. "You been following me, Russell?"

Straight shrugged. "I came over to Deal's place. I needed to talk to him. But I don't see his car. Then you show up and go inside his place. When you take off again, I figure I'll follow you, see what the hell you're up to."

Driscoll pinched the bridge of his nose. "You saw me go into my own apartment, dumb-ass."

"I'd watch my mouth, I was you," Russell said evenly.

"I live there," Driscoll continued. "Deal's my landlord."

There was a moment. Driscoll saw Straight's shoulders go up in a shrug. "I guess that makes you *really* lucky, then," he said.

Driscoll rose to one knee, then felt Straight's hand under his arm. "I can manage," Driscoll grumbled.

"Sure you can," Straight said. "I just happen to be here, that's all."

Driscoll was standing now. He felt his head teeter for a moment, then settle back between his shoulders where it belonged. "You get a look at these two guys?" he said to Straight.

"More or less," Straight said. "It's pretty dark back here."

"How about the car they were driving?"

"Other side of that wall," Straight said, pointing.

Driscoll saw a vine-covered cinder-block wall running along the border of the parking lot. There was another apartment complex over there, with its own exits and entrances to a different set of streets.

"I heard tires squeal, a big engine cranking," Russell continued. "I was more interested in what happened to you."

Driscoll nodded. "I appreciate it," he said.

"What was it I interrupted, anyway?" Russell asked.

Driscoll looked at him. "Couple of asswipes wanted my wallet," he said.

"Uh-huh," Straight said. "How come you still got it, then?"

Driscoll felt in his pocket. "Just lucky, I guess."

"Whatever you say," Straight told him.

"What was so important to tell Deal, you couldn't wait till tomorrow?" Driscoll asked.

"Tell you what," Straight said. "You want to be up-front with me, maybe I'll be up-front with you. Elsewise, we're at squares."

Driscoll hesitated. By all appearances, Russell Straight might have just saved his life. On the other hand, Driscoll hardly knew the man, had no idea what his true agenda might be.

"I was on my way to get a beer," he said finally, his hand rubbing at his raw throat. "Maybe we could sit and talk."

"Beer sounds good," Straight said, his voice neutral.

"Then follow me," Driscoll said, and moved as steadily as he could manage toward the Ford.

twenty-five

"You're John Deal?" the big man asked, moving into the glow cast by the countertop light.

"Who the hell are you?" Deal asked, gauging his options. He'd been expecting Sams or, more likely, Tasker. And while Tasker was no pipsqueak, the man before him was huge, Wrestlemania huge, his bulk filling the passage between the end of the counter and the facing cabinetry.

The big man, who must have come through the opened balcony doors, held up his hands in a pacifying gesture. "Don't get yourself worked up," he said. "Everything's okay." Under other circumstances, the guy might have looked benign, a round-bellied appliance repairman called out on a late-night gig.

"Everything's okay?" Deal said, edging toward the other end of the counter. The guy was big, but he couldn't be that fast. "Maybe you're in the wrong apartment."

"Not unless you are, pal." A new voice, from behind him.

Deal spun around, found a second man—bearded, taller, thinner, but only in relation to the other one—approaching from the hallway. No escape in either direction, then. What to do now—go for one of the frying pans that dangled down from a set of ceiling hooks?

"You two work for Sams?" he managed. He knew there had to be a knife drawer somewhere in the cabinets behind him, but there was no telling which of them Janice had decided it would be.

"*Uncle* Sam?" the taller man asked, an odd lilt to his voice.

"Shut up, Frank," the big man said. He pointed at Deal. "You can take your hand out of that drawer. Right now."

Deal stared back at the man, feeling his hand close around what felt like a balled-up pair of socks. *Jesus Christ, Janice.*

"Where're my wife and daughter?" he said, as though he hadn't heard the man. He'd let go of the socks, had found what felt like a smallish pair of pliers. How every modern kitchen should be equipped.

"I saw two ladies headin' out of the parking lot just before you got here," the big man said. "Get your hand out of that drawer."

"Sure," Deal said. He'd found what was surely a spice bottle, had spun the cap off with his finger. The smell of curry had already risen up from behind him, but it blossomed huge as he snapped his hand upward and out, flinging the contents of the bottle toward the big man's face.

"Goddamn!" the big man cried in pain, flinging his hands to his eyes.

The other man, the bearded one, was coming toward Deal, but he'd expected that move. Instead of ducking away, Deal strode forward, maybe a surprise for a man accustomed to having his quarry flee. Deal brought his forearm up under the onrushing man's chin, always an option for a shorter, smaller blocker facing a too-eager pass rusher, and no one to call a penalty on this play.

The bearded guy caught the blow full force and careened into the side-by-side refrigerator, snapping off one pull handle and sending the freezer door open as he fell. A ceramic bowl full of fruit fell from the counter to the floor and smashed. Deal tried to step over the fallen man, but felt a big hand clamp on the back of his shirt.

He lunged up, caught hold of one of the dangling cooking pots, and jerked, bringing the entire rack crashing down from the ceiling. He ducked as the rack swung past him, metal clanging off steel and glass and tile like a bus going through a storefront. He heard a groan from the big guy behind him, but the grip on his shirt held fast.

Nothing had hit Deal—or if it had, he hadn't felt it. He now had the saucepan he'd snatched by its handle and glanced down to find the thinner guy he'd put on the ground sliding around in the mess on the floor, trying to get to his feet.

Deal swung down mightily and the guy looked up just in time to catch the bottom of the pot across his cheek. There was a dull *clonging* sound that reverberated all the way to Deal's shoulder. The pot itself cracked cleanly off its thin aluminum handle, rebounding crazily somewhere into the living room.

The thinner guy was down again, but the one behind him still had him by the shirt. If the big guy ever got both arms around him, he'd be finished, Deal thought, tossing the useless pot handle aside.

He fell forward, catching hold of a shelf on the open freezer door, but his feet were slipping in crushed orange pulp and pottery scraps, and he felt the flimsy plastic of the door shelving ready to give way in an instant. Whatever was inside the freezer had to be hard, he thought, his other hand groping the frigid interior. He just prayed he wouldn't find celery, or lamp shades.

Nothing but frost-covered shelving as far as he could tell, however, and besides, he was going backward now, drawn inexorably by the hand of the big guy, who was still sputtering and cursing, the smell of curry everywhere. Deal caught hold of the lip of a steel freezer bin, but the thing whizzed straight out on its track, hesitating only a moment before it shot free. Something solid struck him in the chest as the shelf fell, though, and he threw up his hand reflexively to catch it.

A sufficiently rocklike handful it was, with a couple of knurls making for a firm handhold. Cornish game hen, he thought. Something he'd always hated, to Janice's dismay. But at the moment it seemed a terrific argument for living the separate life. He raised his hand high and twisted about, bringing the frozen ball down on the crown of the big man's head. The guy didn't even groan as he fell.

Deal felt the grip on his shirt go slack and he spun away, heading for the hall. He hadn't gotten past the end of the counter, though, when he felt a pair of arms around his legs. A good sure tackle, he was thinking, as he went over, his head clipping the edge of the counter.

Boil up the socks and add the curry, went the crazy thoughts through his star-pinging head. *You always make a mess when you cook, Johnny Deal.* He could hardly say he was sorry. *Employ pliers to pull socks from steaming water.* Emeril Lagasse had nothing on him or Janice. What a recipe.

Serve with well-bludgeoned game hen. Season with crushed peel of thug. He loved Janice. He loved Isabel. *What a mess.* And then his thoughts winked out.

twenty-six

"You're going to eat that thing?" Russell Straight asked, pointing at the plate the bartender had put in front of Driscoll.

"You think I was going to hatch it?" Driscoll asked him. He picked up the peeled, pickled-pink egg and bit down. The cool texture felt soothing against his scratchy throat. He washed the egg down with a swallow of beer, then had another bite, and a third, which completed the process.

"You are a tough guy," Straight said, sipping at his own beer.

"That cholesterol business," Driscoll said, "it never bothered me. I figure if you don't challenge your heart a little, how's it going to stay strong?"

Straight lifted his beer in response. "Let's hope it works out for you."

Driscoll nodded. He had another swallow of his draft, then glanced around the horseshoe-shaped bar, making sure no one was paying attention. He needn't have bothered. This was Flaherty's, after all. The bartender was standing at the opposite end, idly polishing a glass and watching a Heat game unfold. A couple other patrons sat down there—one guy wearing a bowling shirt, the other a Miami Heat warm-up, all of three of them cheering a Hardaway assist, a thunderous Mourning jam. Three guys who looked like they couldn't manage a push-up among them were high-fiving like it was them who'd just scored.

There was a white-haired guy sitting closer, but he was staring at his palm through smeared glasses like Moses had chiseled the tablets there, his lips moving soundlessly—maybe he was trying to find a commandment he was still capable of breaking, Driscoll thought.

He turned back to Straight then. "You know what I was doing just before those guys jumped me?" he asked.

"Looking for a new apartment," Straight said, not meaning it. He'd been staring at the old guy, too.

"A buddy of mine who lives in that building has a certain facility with computers. I was in his place reviewing your accomplishments as a prize fighter," Driscoll said.

"Is that so?"

Driscoll nodded, waiting.

"Cops like to pull stuff like this, you know," Russell Straight said, staring ahead. It looked like he saw something coming his way. He didn't seem worried about the prospect.

"Do what?"

"Say some shit, hope a man will just jump salty, say some things he doesn't mean to."

Driscoll shrugged. "If you have things to talk about, then go ahead."

"What do I have to say? If you did your business like you claim, you already know all you need to know."

Driscoll glanced over at the old guy. He'd switched hands, seemed to be counting something off on his fingers. Driscoll turned back to Straight. "You were in the joint for killing a man, and that's when your bad-news brother got his ticket punched. You get sprung, the first thing you do is come to Miami looking to take out your grief on John Deal, but that doesn't go according to plan. Now you're still hanging around. It only makes sense that I'd like to know why."

"You Deal's keeper, are you?"

"I'm more than that. I'm his friend."

"Leon was my friend."

"He did a lot for you, huh? Wrote you long letters while you were in the slam? Sent cookies?"

"I was you, I wouldn't run my mouth about something I didn't know."

Something in Russell Straight's tone caught Driscoll off guard. He paused, noticing a time-out had been called on the TV game. He signaled the bartender for another round, then turned back to Straight.

"You have no idea how I grew up," Straight said. "Leon wasn't there, I might not have made it."

Driscoll nodded.

"I'll let it go, what you said about my brother," Russell continued. He glanced over. "This once."

Driscoll nodded again. Say what you want about any felon, the person is always somebody's son, somebody's lover, somebody's big brother. He didn't know the particulars of the brothers Straight's upbringing, and he didn't want to know. Given the outcomes, he could guess. The point Russell Straight was making, Driscoll could let himself concede.

"I want to thank you again for getting me out of a jam back there," Driscoll said at last.

Straight nodded. "We were going to talk about that."

"Yeah," Driscoll said. "You were going to tell me why you went to Deal's place."

Russell looked at him. "You like to play poker?"

Driscoll shook his head. "I work too hard for my money."

"That's a shame," Straight said. "You'd be good at it."

"What's your fascination with John Deal?" Driscoll said.

Russell Straight took a breath, clasping his hands together. The bartender had brought them another round, but Driscoll noted Russell wasn't halfway through his first. He seemed to be making up his mind about something. It seemed to take a while.

When he turned to face Driscoll again, his expression had cleared. "I was on my way out of town," Straight said. "I thought I owed it to the man to tell him I was leaving town . . . and to thank him for what he did."

Yeah, for not having your ass arrested, is what Driscoll thought. But he kept it to himself. "You went over there to quit, huh?"

"However you want to put it."

"And then you decided to follow me?"

"We already went over that."

"Uh-huh," Driscoll said. "But something's not adding up. You don't work for me, Russell. You leave town, I'm supposed to care?"

"Here's something to add on," Russell said. "You're not a cop anymore and we're not sitting in the station house. But you want to know the truth, I thought you might be messing with the man, in which case I'd tell him about it. The other thing, maybe he sent you to his place to pick up something, you're going to take it to him. In which case, I'd let it go. Walk up and shake his hand, say goodbye."

"Just acting in his best interest, huh?"

"Same as you," Straight said.

"A guy you were ready to take out a couple days ago."

Straight shrugged. "He could have dumped a world of trouble on me. I owe the man for that."

"You bet your life you do," Driscoll said.

"Are we finished with that part now?" Straight asked.

Driscoll opened his hands in a gesture of surrender. "I guess we are."

"You never told me why those guys jumped you," Straight said.

"Yeah, I did," Driscoll said.

"You said they wanted your jack, which is a bunch of shit."

"A man is entitled to his own opinion," Driscoll said.

"This is bullshit, man. I told you the truth. Now it's your turn."

"I had a need to know, my friend. I don't think that applies in your case."

"Maybe it does," Straight said. "You been nosing into my business, maybe those guys were, too."

"Did they look like parole officers to you?"

"I don't know what they looked like. That's something else we've been over."

"They didn't give a rat's ass about you, Russell, that's all the information you need."

"So you say, Mr. Egg-Sucking Cop."

Driscoll felt the muscles in his neck and shoulders knotting. "Just how good a fighter were you, Russell?"

"That what you want to find out?" Russell asked, his face impassive. Neither one of them had raised their voices by so much as a decibel. "We're supposed to go outside, I'll show you Thursday morning coming out your ass?"

"Dream on, my friend." Like the poor old guy a few stools down, Driscoll had his own palm upraised now. But he wasn't seeing commandments there. Just the calluses, and all the scars.

Russell shook his head as if the matter had lost interest for him. "You say the thing don't have to do with me, I'll take your word." He glanced at Driscoll mildly. "Just do me one favor."

Driscoll lifted an eyebrow in response.

"Someplace else John Deal could be?"

"His wife's, maybe," Driscoll said.

"Yeah? They split up?"

Driscoll gave him a look.

"Whatever," Straight said. "How about you give him a call, say I wanted to get in touch, that's all. I'll say my goodbyes, head on out of your way, Mr. Driscoll."

Driscoll hesitated. Russell Straight slid some coins across the bar toward him. Driscoll glanced down at them as if a toad had plopped them there. Not that he was at all sure about the man, but if all it was going to take was a phone call to get rid of him, it was a small price to pay.

"Keep your money, Russell," Driscoll said. And moved off to the phone to call Janice.

twenty-seven

"RED . . . RIGHT . . . RETURNING," DEAL'S toneless voice called out. The Cigarette's motors were a soft rumbling backdrop as Basil Wheatley guided them at near-idle through the shallow Bahamian waters toward shore.

"What's he talking about?" Frank Wheatley said, glancing down at Deal's tightly bound form.

"That's nautical talk, Frank," his brother said. "Sort of like 'full fathom five,' or 'I'll keelhaul ye landlubbers,' stuff like that."

Frank nodded dubiously. He pointed at one of the red buoy markers materializing out of the darkness ahead of them. "That red one's on the left."

"Uh-huh," Basil said. "Who you going to trust, little brother? Me, or some guy who's talking in his sleep?"

A contemplative look came to Frank Wheatley's features. "I guess I don't have much choice," he said finally. He glanced down at Deal again. He was blinking, licking his lips, the picture of a man unaware. "He's awake, by the way."

Basil nodded, his eyes fixed on the gathering shoreline ahead. "Just in time," the big man said. He'd spotted the lights at the end of the jutting dock and was making toward landing. "See how he's doing. Maybe he's thirsty."

"My brother wants to know if you're thirsty," Frank said, staring down at Deal.

Deal with the Dead

Deal stared upward, trying to blink his eyes into focus. The side of his head ached, pulsing with every chugging beat of his heart. He watched as the image of the bearded man above him—his face softly illumined by the lights of the Cigarette's console—shimmered into two, then coalesced again. He tried to move his arms, to lift himself into a sitting position, and thought that maybe he had been paralyzed by the blow to his head. Then he realized he'd been tied.

"What's going on?" he managed. His tongue felt thick and cottony. He *was* thirsty, he realized. Extremely thirsty.

"Here," the bearded man said, extending a plastic water bottle his way. Deal stared at him.

"Oh, yeah," the bearded man said. He reached for the snap top of the bottle, pulled its built-in spout open so that Deal might drink.

"Why don't you untie me?" Deal said after he'd managed a few swallows.

"You think I'm stupid?" the bearded man said.

Deal decided not to answer.

"We'll untie you," the big man behind the wheel of the boat said. "Just as soon as we get on shore."

Deal tried to get a look over the side of the cockpit, but it was hopeless. "Where are we?" he managed.

"Quicksilver Cay," the man behind the wheel said.

"As in . . . ?" Deal said, still groggy.

"As in the Bahamas," the big man said.

"I've never heard of it," Deal said, though some distant bell seemed to be ringing in his head.

"It's private," the big man said. "There's different names on some of the maps. That's what it's called now."

Deal sank back, resting his aching head against the still-thrumming sideboards of the cockpit. "Do you mind telling me why I've been kidnapped?"

"Kidnapped?" the bearded man who towered above him said. "Who's kidnapped?"

"Shut up, Frank," the big man said as the boat nudged up alongside the dock. "Jump up there and secure that aft line."

"Fore and aft," Frank said, hopping up onto the dock. "I always get those two mixed up."

"Back there," the big man said, pointing. Then he glanced down at Deal. "You got any brothers?"

Deal shook his head.

"You're lucky," the big man said, gesturing at Frank, who was busy tying off the rear of the craft.

"If I'm not kidnapped, what am I?" Deal asked.

"We tied you up so you wouldn't come at us again," the big man said.

"It was self-defense," Frank called down from the dock.

"This is fore," the big man said, tossing up another rope to his brother. He turned back to Deal. "He's right, you know. I got a knot on my head the size of a hen's egg. My eyes are still burning from whatever you threw at me. Frank's ear is going to need stitches from where you hit him with that pan. All in all, I'd call you a pretty violent individual."

Deal stared up at him, not sure he'd heard correctly. It was the blow to his head, he thought. He wasn't really tied up in a boat somewhere in the Bahamas. It was all a lunatic dream. It would have been easier to believe his story if his head didn't hurt so much.

In the next moment, the big man had cut the engines. He turned and grabbed Deal under the arms, lifting him as easily as if he were a child. "Coming up," the big man called to his brother.

Deal felt another strong pair of hands underneath his arms, and then he was on the dock. "Don't try anything funny," Frank was saying, propping him against one of the thick wooden pilings. "You fall in the water, you're gonna drown."

"Don't worry," Deal said. In the greenish glow cast from the pale dock lamp, Deal got a look at his tightly bound hands and feet. Plastic grocery bags, he realized. They'd tied him up with knotted-together bags from Publix—an item Janice had never saved a single one of in all the time they'd been together.

In another minute, the big man had vaulted onto the dock as well—a graceful movement for a man of that size, Deal thought. "You're all calmed down now, right?" he said to Deal.

Deal nodded. Even if he were somehow to overcome the two of them, what would he do next? Commandeer that Cigarette, rocket out across a set of unfamiliar shoals in the middle of the night? *No,* he thought, breathing in the odors of beached seaweed and sulphur that rose from the tidal shallows surrounding them. Right now he was willing to settle for getting his hands untied, working out the kinks in his stiff arms and shoulders, see if the pounding in his head might then subside.

"Call up to the house," the big man said to Frank, "let them know we're here."

Frank nodded and moved off toward a phone mounted on a stanchion nearby. There was a stainless-steel-topped cleaning table there, a hose neatly coiled underneath, but something in its pristine aspect told Deal there hadn't been a fish filleted there in a long time. As if he were attuned to such thoughts, the big man pulled what looked like a boning knife from a scabbard on his belt and bent down at Deal's feet. He glanced up—a last warning there, Deal thought—then flicked out with the knife, severing the bonds at Deal's ankles as if they were spider's threads.

Deal allowed his feet to work apart in tiny sidelong steps. For a moment, he felt himself teetering, ready to go over backward, but he gritted his teeth and forced himself to steady.

"Hold out your hands," the big man said, eyeing him.

Deal did as he was told. He felt the cool brush of the knife blade as it slid between his wrists, and then his hands were free. "Don't forget," the big man said, tapping the slender point of the knife at Deal's chest. "It's nothing personal, but I'll gut you as soon as look at you."

Deal nodded, unwrapping the knotted plastic from his wrists. He noticed that Frank had finished his mumbled conversation on the phone. "He says to come on up, Basil."

"Now there's a surprise," Basil said dryly.

Basil, Deal thought. Never had a name seemed more apt. Bass drum. Bass fiddle. Base element. One giant load of Basil.

Basil stared at him. "That way, my friend," he said, pointing over Deal's shoulder.

Deal had the last of the plastic off his wrists now. He turned, realizing he was looking for a place to dispose of the scraps. Kidnapped by Man Mountain Basil and his bodybuilding brother Frank, and here *he* was, worried about despoiling the environment, Deal thought. He was almost distracted enough to miss the sight before him, might have walked along the pier too far, gotten too close to shore, where he quite possibly would have lacked the right perspective to put it all together.

But he hadn't. He'd glanced up at the right time, had seen it, and the realization that swept over him was enough to start his head pounding like the steel drummer's part in an island street-corner band.

It was dark, sure. So there was no way of seeing the sparkling green sweep of lawn that lay up ahead. And even though most of the house lay in shadow and all that he really registered was its shape and its commanding presence at the top of the rise, Deal knew.

Quicksilver Cay. The legend scrawled on the back of a faded snapshot. No ghost of his father standing there on the dock, smiling back at the camera, of course. And no shimmering presence of his mother tucked against that imposing, hail-fellow form. But still Deal saw it all, the snapshot he'd discovered in his father's secret cache conjured in his mind as if he were a human camera and time had no meaning at all. The image, Deal realized for one fleeting instant, would be forever burned into his mind: the enduring touchstone for everything he quietly aspired to, and—how could it be?—all things in life to avoid.

The only person missing in the tableau seemed to be that simulacrum of Gatsby, who'd been caught in that long-ago photograph—whoever he was. And as Deal stumbled on, prodded by the very real hand of Basil at his back, he wondered if that might be the person he was going to meet.

twenty-eight

"THE COPS TOLD YOU *what?*" Driscoll asked Janice. He saw her lower lip trembling and reminded himself to keep his voice on an even keel. Contending with the Russell Straights of the world was one thing. Janice Deal was a far different matter.

"The officer in charge said all this was no proof of anything other than a break-in." Her eyes flashed as she swept her arm around the devastated kitchen of her condo. "He didn't even seem too convinced of that."

"You get his name?"

She nodded, biting her lip, and handed him a card.

Driscoll glanced at it but didn't recognize the name. He nodded, staring at the spatters of blood across the otherwise pristine face of the refrigerator. "Maybe this is the way they cook at his house," Driscoll said.

"Cops . . ." Russell Straight said, shaking his head. Driscoll had introduced the two of them at the door. To his credit, Straight had offered to wait outside, but Janice had insisted he come in.

Driscoll shot him a look, but Straight paid no attention. Worse yet, the look Janice gave Straight made Driscoll realize she couldn't agree more.

"What's *happened,* Vernon? I've called Deal's apartment, his office, his cell phone . . ." She stared at him, her eyes pained.

"Now, we don't know for sure that this has anything to do with Deal," he cautioned.

"Not you, too, Vernon," she cried. "I don't think I could take it. I didn't want to argue with the police in front of Isabel, but I'm scared to death—"

Driscoll stepped forward then, wrapping her in his arms. Lending aid came naturally to Driscoll, but comfort was another matter. He felt awkward, patting her back like some kid playing Joseph in the school play, supposed to know just how Mary felt.

"Come on now," he said. "We'll sort this out. Whatever it adds up to."

After a moment, Janice's sobs had subsided. "I'll be okay," she said, stepping back from him, managing something of a smile. She tore a paper towel off a tumbled roll, inspected it for blood, then raised it to give her nose a hearty blow.

Driscoll noted that even in the red-eyed, glowing-nosed shape she was in, Janice was an extremely attractive woman. Maybe even more lovely when she was distraught, he thought. And given Deal's recent history, there'd been plenty of distress. Things ever got on an even keel with them, it could be she'd look ordinary enough for Deal to get over her. Sure, Driscoll.

"Isabel's asleep?" he asked, cutting his glance toward the back of the place.

"Thank God," Janice said, blotting her eyes with the back of her hand. She stopped, looking at him more closely. "What's the matter with your chin?"

Driscoll realized he'd been massaging the aching muscles in his throat. "Got tangled up in my seat belt," he said, shrugging it off. That's all they needed to get into right now. Send her shrieking right off the planet.

"How about this message you picked up from Deal?" he said, forcing his hand away from his rubbed-raw throat. "When did that come in?"

She shook her head. "It wasn't Deal himself," she said. "It was a call from someone's office. A secretary, I assumed. She said that Deal had asked her to call."

"Let's listen to it," Driscoll said, pointing toward the answering machine that sat undisturbed on a nearby counter. It was one of the few items that hadn't been knocked askew.

Janice shook her head again. "I erased it before we went out." She turned toward the machine. "Unless you do, you have to listen to everything all over again. I hate that thing. I've been meaning to get a new one . . ."

Driscoll nodded. "You don't remember any names?"

She looked at him helplessly. "She must have said the name of the firm, but I wasn't paying too much attention at first. I thought it was somebody who wanted to sell me something. When I realized what it was really about, I jotted down what's there."

She gestured at the pad that Driscoll held in his hand. "Out of town," he said, glancing up at her. "This woman didn't say where?"

"No," Janice said. "It was stupid not to keep the message, I know—"

"Hey—" Driscoll tried to stop her.

"—but I was so upset that he'd do something like that, on such short notice. It's a little thing, I know, but Isabel always looks forward so much—"

"Janice—" Driscoll said.

She broke off and stared at him. "I'm sorry, Vernon. I don't mean to babble."

"Don't worry," he said. "You didn't do anything wrong. I ask all these questions, it doesn't mean anything. I'm just thinking out loud, okay?"

She managed a nod, but Driscoll wasn't sure he'd eased her burden. She sighed and turned away to right a fallen vase on the counter. "The police said I couldn't file a missing-person's report, it was too soon," she said. Her voice was softer, barely above a whisper.

"Yeah," Driscoll said. "It's a little too early for that." He glanced at Russell Straight, who stared back at him with that look that seemed to question Driscoll's every word.

He glared back at Straight, then turned to Janice. "Here's what we're going to do," he said. "I'm going to swing by the DealCo offices, see if our boy might be working late."

She opened her mouth to say something, but Driscoll held up a hand to stop her. "You know that phone's always going on the blink. He could be over there crunching numbers on this new contract, all the worry's for nothing—"

"But—"

"Then I'll check at Terrell's place, and that strip center he's finishing up down south, just to be sure. It wouldn't be the first time he went back to work at midnight." She stared back at him, maybe calmed a bit by the reassurance in his voice. "You left a message on his phone at the apartment, right?"

"Of course."

"Then he'll call if we cross paths somehow." He paused, glancing around the wrecked kitchen. "You need some help with all this?"

She shook her head. "It'll give me something to do." She glanced up at him. "You'll call me?"

He saw it in her gaze then, the bedrock anguish, the unmistakable connection she still felt. He wanted to take her by the shoulders, tell her then and there, *Cut the shit, Janice. Take Deal back. Get your life under way again* . . . but it was hardly the time, and that wasn't his job anyway, now, was it?

Instead, he simply nodded. "I'll keep you posted, every step of the way."

She managed a smile then and bent down to retrieve something from the floor. "I'm throwing everything away," she said. "All of it."

He got a look at what she was holding when she stood. It looked like a miniature turkey, but he realized that it was actually a Cornish game hen. He'd seen them in grocery stores all his life, but he'd never seen anybody actually buy, or eat, one. It crossed his mind to say something of the sort to Janice, but she'd already pitched the thing into the trash can with a thud.

What the hell did it matter anyway, Driscoll asked himself, his thoughts on Cornish game hens or anything else? All that really mattered was the task at hand. He was headed for the door, turning his attention to that. He noted that Russell Straight was right behind him.

twenty-nine

"In here," Basil said. He put his meaty hand on Deal's shoulder and guided him off the darkened main hall of the house into a dimly lit study.

The room had the same vaguely musty smell that characterized the rest of the house, only stronger: old plaster, wood, and aging fabric, cured by half a century's worth of humid tropical breezes and unleavened by the antiseptic sweep of air conditioning. Other odors as well in these close quarters, Deal noted: leather, bindery glue, the lingering odor of cigar.

As his eyes adjusted, he took in the furnishings: a massive, other-era teak desk with a tufted cordovan-leather chair, dark as the tiled floor beneath his feet. A matching wooden captain's chest that took up most of the wall behind the desk. Bookshelves lining the room, a fair portion of the volumes leatherbound, and others with dust jackets chipped and yellowed. *Kon-Tiki,* he read on one spine. *Lost Weekend* on another.

Opposite the desk was a well-worn leather couch, its cushions as puffed and rippling as if they'd been covered in cotton. Beside the couch was a portable bar: liter-sized bottles of British gin, arcanely named Scotch, island rum. An old-fashioned seltzer siphon. An ice bucket and a set of crystal glasses.

"Make yourself comfortable," Basil said from the doorway. "The boss'll be here in a minute."

In the next moment, the big man was gone, closing the carved panel door behind him. Deal didn't hear a lock click, but what did it matter? He could start rifling the drawers, he supposed, see if he couldn't find a weapon, but knew that would be wasted effort as well. He could see no phone in the room.

He walked to the portable bar, lifted the top of the ice bucket. Sure enough, half full of cubes, these looking like they'd come from a commercial icemaker. Somewhere was a big, placidly humming machine lodged in a kitchen that could service the fleet, or an ambassador's dinner, he supposed. He worked his aching neck muscles, noting that the throbbing in his head had subsided. He reached into the bucket, helped himself to a handful of ice, dropped it into a glass that seemed to have the density of Jupiter.

He picked up the soda siphon, pressed what looked like the feeder, and shot his glass nearly full. *What the hell,* he thought, and added a splash of Scotch from a bottle that looked like it had been aged in a peat bog. He sipped at the drink, then sipped again. Had Gatsby been a Scotch drinker? he wondered. If he had been, this was surely his brand.

"My father favored that one," a voice behind him came.

Deal turned and looked at the man who stood there. He hadn't heard the door open. He realized he still had the bottle of Scotch in his hand.

"I'm not surprised," Deal said, putting the bottle back among its pals.

"I owe you an apology," the man said, stepping into the room. He left the door open. Deal wondered if Basil and Frank were out there, lurking in the shadows.

He'd been expecting somebody in a smoking jacket, Deal thought. The guy before him was wearing rumpled khakis and a denim shirt, his sandy, shortish hair mussed as if he'd just got out of bed. He extended his hand, an earnest expression on his refined features. "I'm truly sorry for the way this turned out."

Far too young, Deal was thinking. No visible resemblance to the man who'd stood on the dock out there with his own parents a third of a century ago. This guy clearly just the latest in a series of dubious types to have occupied such digs as these. There was a lot of that kind of movement through the off-islands.

He ignored the offer of a handshake as the guy moved in, noticing he was a little off in his initial estimation. He'd taken him for much younger at a distance, but up close he saw the tiny lines at the eyes, at the throat, telltale indicators that even good surgery couldn't erase. Guy his own age, Deal thought, possibly older. The guy stared back at him in a wide-eyed, TV celebrity's manner that might have reflected enthusiasm. Or maybe it was just a by-product of the face lift.

Deal had another sip of the drink, his initial light-headedness progressing toward a full-fledged buzz. *What the hell,* he thought. *What the hell.*

"Basil and Frank told me something of what happened." He gave Deal what passed for a sympathetic look. "That was hardly my intention."

"Well, that fixes everything," Deal said.

The guy cocked his head, as if he were measuring Deal for a new suit. "I wouldn't pick you for a man who could hold his own against those two, if you want to know."

Deal stared at him. "You mind if I ask what your intention was?"

The guy was shaking his head, apparently in brain-lock. "I've seen Frank bend a car bumper in half. Basil could probably fold it over again."

"Is there a lot of call for that kind of talent?" Deal asked.

"Actually . . . ," his host began, then let himself trail off. Deal wondered if the guy might be on some drug.

"Tell Frank I'm sorry about his ear," Deal said. He put his glass down on the silver tray where he'd found it. "Are we going to talk about what I'm doing here?"

"Of course," the guy said. "You'll forgive me." He gestured at the couch. "You might want to sit down."

Deal shrugged but kept his feet.

"The fact is, the two of us are business partners," the man said.

"Business partners," Deal repeated.

"I'm Richard Rhodes," the man said. "Aramcor Development."

There was silence as Deal stared at him, trying to digest it. But it had to be. He was looking at the man Talbot Sams had wanted him to get close to. Well, that little matter had been taken care of then, hadn't it?

"As in the International-Free-Trade-Zone Aramcor?" Deal said, finally.

"That's correct," Rhodes said. He didn't seem particularly proud of the fact, which was something of a plus.

"I don't recall seeing your name on any of the original paperwork."

Rhodes shrugged. "There've been a few changes." He waved his hand as if the "changes" were of little consequence. "The fact remains, you've been awarded a significant portion of the undertaking."

Deal shook his head in disbelief, the vision of Talbot Sams sitting at his own desk clear in his mind. "They didn't tell me being kidnapped was going to be part of the contract," he said to Rhodes. "Maybe we need to renegotiate."

"I can understand your feelings." Rhodes gave Deal what might have been meant as an apologetic expression, holding a hand up to forestall him. "But circumstances make it difficult for me to travel as freely as I might like. I sent Basil and Frank along to explain matters to you, in hopes that you'd agree to a discreet meeting here."

"Maybe they should have just asked," Deal said.

"They intended to, I assure you . . ."

Deal glanced at a framed print on the wall behind Rhodes. The old customs house in downtown Nassau. It was a staple of cruise-ship tourist art, though this was better than most.

"Just why is it you didn't want to come talk to me yourself?" Deal asked. He doubted it was a question Talbot Sams would have approved, but he was past caring.

"Is that important to you?"

"Under the circumstances, there's quite a bit that seems important," Deal said. He had another sip of his drink. "But I'm guessing that either someone in the States wants to kill you or someone else wants to put you in jail. That's why you're holed up over here. You don't want to talk about it, it's okay by me, but at least let's not bullshit each other."

It got an outright smile from Rhodes. Added to the wide-eyed gaze, it made him look like a slightly surprised jackal. He seemed to be contemplating how to respond when another voice issued from the doorway.

"Is there going to be a fight?"

Deal glanced over Rhodes's shoulder, saw her leaning with a hand pressed languidly at the door jamb as if she'd been there a while. Her expression suggested that she might not mind a fight.

Rhodes turned around, apparently as surprised by the woman's appearance as Deal was. "Kaia," Rhodes said. "I thought you were asleep . . ."

Kaia, Deal thought. The right name to go with the accent. European, it seemed. One of the northern countries.

If she heard the note of uncertainty or disapproval in Rhodes's voice, she didn't register it. She had her eyes on Deal as she pushed easily away from the door frame and moved on into the room. She was wearing a pair of oversized black pajamas—Rhodes's, Deal guessed—the belt cinched tight at her waist, the pant legs rolled at her slender ankles. The effect might have been clownish had the woman been any less attractive. In this case, it only made her all the more alluring: plenty of rustling silk and all the body parts responsible, Deal thought. He wondered if he should have had the drink.

She put a hand on Rhodes's arm as she approached. "You didn't mention we'd be entertaining," she said. It didn't sound like a complaint.

When she moved past Deal toward the bar table, he caught the scent of her: shampoo, the faintest hint of jasmine mixed with citrus, along with the muskiness of flesh that had been wrapped up awhile in bedclothes. She splashed Scotch—the same bottle he'd gone for—into a glass and turned, sipping at it neat. The look she gave Deal suggested she knew every thought in his head.

"This is Mr. Deal," Rhodes told her, as if it explained all things.

She tilted her glass Deal's way. "Charmed," she said, her voice tinged with a huskiness that the Scotch could have only enhanced.

"So am I," Deal heard himself reply. He'd never heard anyone use the term in conversation.

He felt light-headed, literal as a dunce, as if Rhodes might have slipped something into his glass. Her eyes were a striking shade of green, her tousled hair reflecting shades of auburn from the parchment-shaded lamp on the desk. There seemed to Deal no good enough reason on earth to have left this woman's bed. Certainly not to come talk to the likes of himself. *Throw the prisoner in the dungeon, Basil. There'll be plenty of time in the morning.*

"I saw what he did to those men of yours, Richard. I wouldn't antagonize Mr. Deal if I were you."

She spoke to Rhodes, but her eyes were on Deal, waiting to see what he made of her little joke. Deal didn't know what he made of it. All he could be sure of was his gaze, locked stupidly on her.

"We were just having a conversation," Rhodes assured her.

She glanced aside, as if she'd forgotten Rhodes was there. She tossed her thick hair and raised her glass to finish her drink. Deal saw a flash of pale skin beneath her tilted chin, another deeper down the plane of her chest when she bent to place the glass on the bar table. *Oh my,* he found himself thinking, though he wasn't quite sure what the trouble was.

thirty

THE WOMAN IN THE flowing pajamas moved to the couch and perched herself on one of its pillowy arms, her legs crossed, her hands clasped at one knee. "Well, don't let me stop you two from talking," she said, pursing her dark lips together. An expression that would bring a man wading through a lake of hot lava, Deal thought, willing his gaze back to Rhodes. How must it feel? he wondered. How many men had she seen stare back at her as he was?

"Kaia can be trusted," Rhodes said. His voice was calm, but Deal suspected that Rhodes was simply trying to maintain his cool.

"I don't doubt it," Deal said. *If you'd sent her instead of Basil and Frank, it would have saved us all a lot of trouble,* is what he thought. He had to look to be sure he was still holding his glass. "I think we were just getting to the good part."

"Are you sure you won't sit down?"

Deal glanced at the chair behind him. Sitting suddenly seemed a reasonable prospect. He placed his glass beside Kaia's and let himself sink.

Rhodes, meantime, had settled himself against the edge of his desk. He stared intently at Deal, his already wide-eyed gaze switched to overeager mode. Beyond energized. Positively electric.

"You don't recognize me, then."

Deal shook his head, not certain he'd heard correctly.

"I wanted to be sure," Rhodes persisted. "I didn't want to say a word before."

"What the hell are you talking about?" Deal glanced at Kaia, who gave him a who-knows look in return. A certain degree of conspiracy in that look, as well, something that sent a jolt through him. A feeling as dangerous as anything he'd picked up from Rhodes and his thugs. *Kaia can be trusted? Trusted to do what?*

"Rhodes *is* my real name, but I haven't used it for a long time," the man before him said. He passed his hand in front of his face in an odd gesture. "And what you're looking at isn't me, either."

"You could have fooled me," Deal said evenly.

Not very long ago at all, he had been on his way to the store for a couple of scoops of ice cream, he thought. Spend an hour's time with his earnest-to-a-fault daughter. Say hello to his wife, who sometimes seemed as elusive as the otherworldly man standing in front of him. At the end of it all, go home, tumble into bed, and get ready for a hard day's work. Whose life had that been, anyway? In what dimension did such simple actions take place?

"I'm Richard Rhodes," the man said once more, as if it should mean something.

Deal stared at him, his expression blank. "I'm sorry," he said. "You'll have to try me again."

"Richard Rhodes," the man repeated, his tone that of the aggrieved minor celebrity trying to get past the maître d's stand at Joe's Stone Crab. "We went to school together."

Deal, who noted the emphasis on *school,* could only shake his head. "I'm sorry . . ."

"Gullickson Preparatory," Rhodes insisted. "In Miami. Freshman year."

Maybe it was the Scotch, Deal thought. Yes, he had attended the private school Rhodes mentioned, forced there by his mother, who feared he'd never crack a book without a headmaster brandishing a cane. But it was barely midterm before his father had become convinced that Deal's football prowess would be better served at one of the city's public school powerhouses. Deal barely remembered his time at Gullickson; certainly the name Richard Rhodes meant nothing.

"You played football," Rhodes said, as if it mattered.

"And you were a geek in the band. You've had it in for me ever since."

The man smiled thinly. "I played tennis, number-one singles. I also had a driver's license and a little British convertible that my father had sent over on a boat. I didn't envy you in the slightest."

"I'm glad to hear it," Deal said, searching his memory, trying fruitlessly to conjure up a picture of a sandy-haired kid in tennis whites vaulting into the seat of a sports car, roaring off with a fourteen-year-old version of Kaia.

Kaia, meantime, shifted on the arm of the nearby couch, stretching her arms high to yawn. Deal knew enough to keep his eyes on her face. She gave him a smile. Deal stared back. Somehow it was difficult to think of this woman as ever having been fourteen.

"We weren't friends, but our fathers were," Rhodes continued.

Deal turned back to him. The man seemed obsessed, to say the least. But there *was* that snapshot, wasn't there? Deal's father and mother, carefree as a couple from a jazz-age novel, arm in arm with the dashing young man on that very dock outside. "My father had a lot of friends. He didn't talk to me about all of them," he said, finally.

"Fathers and sons," the man before him said. There was a certain sadness in the way he shook his head, and for an instant, Deal felt a connection to this unknowable man, his grip white-knuckled to the edge of his desk as if it were keeping him from flying off the planet. "My father's name was Grant. Grant Rhodes. They called him Lucky, occasionally. After that old Cary Grant film."

Deal allowed himself a nod of recognition. He'd seen the movie on late-night television, long ago: an urbane gambling ship owner gets a conscience, aids the war effort against the Nazis. A black-and-white picture, in every way . . .

Then it came to him with a jolt—the note scrawled across the back of the photograph from his father's files: Quicksilver Cay. A lifetime ago. "The bastards got *Lucky.*" Of course. "Lucky" with a capital L.

Lucky Rhodes. Though he could not register the details, the name itself seemed to fit. Perfect for another of the endless cast of Runyonesque characters that moved through his father's life. Deal could conjure up the sound of the name rolling off his father's tongue, the emphasis on the irony of a name and a destination rolled up into one, already the suggestion of a tale to come. If the details of Lucky Rhodes's story remained vague, it was probably because Deal had listened to it with half an ear or less: "Met one hell of a crook in the islands over the weekend, son. We drank into the wee hours, ended up at his mansion on the bay . . ." Et cetera, et cetera.

There had been a million stories like it, or so it had seemed: a million similar plots spun out at cocktail hour, over dinner, during after dinner drinks, and late into the night. Politicians, Miami Beach celebrities, visiting dignitaries, visiting firemen—all were grist for Barton Deal's mill. Even the smallest of Deal's own exploits became the stuff of drama: "Let me tell you what happened Friday night on the playing field, ladies and gentlemen. You wouldn't know it to look at this boy right here, but he's a powerhouse . . ."

And Deal would twist away from his father's grip, away from whatever overheated rendition of a touchdown pass thrown, a home-run ball hit Garrulous, life-of-the-party, larger-than-life Barton Deal. As vigorous, as rough and ready, as impossible to miss as they come. If Grant Rhodes had been the alter ego of urbane Cary Grant, then Barton Deal had been John Huston incarnate.

"Your father saved my father's life, in fact," Rhodes was saying. "He helped him escape from Miami at a very difficult time—"

"Escape?" Deal said, shaking his head. "Your father was *from* Miami?"

Rhodes glanced at Kaia before he answered. *Something apologetic there,* Deal thought. "You see all this," Rhodes said, waving his arm at their surroundings. "You hear of private schools and my father's association with important people . . . and yet you wonder why you haven't heard of him."

"Grant Rhodes," Deal repeated, still searching his memory bank. *Lucky* Rhodes? But nothing came.

"My father was a gambler, a professional," Rhodes said. "He operated what once were called supper clubs. The food wasn't bad, and there were bands and dance floors. But they were casinos, first and foremost."

"The China Clipper?" Deal asked. "That was your old man's place?" It was a fabled establishment from Miami's past, a private club that had come into being during Prohibition and which had lingered on well past the repeal of the Volstead Act. Local officials had been willing to turn a blind eye to certain hijinks as long as tourism was served and the right palms stayed greased. The China Clipper, located well up the Intracoastal Waterway north of the 79th Street Causeway, the very fringes of Miami civilization at the time, had been torn down sometime after the Second World War, well before Deal's time, but he'd heard plenty of stories. He was the son of Barton Deal, after all.

"The China Clipper, the White Lotus, Blue Lagoon." Rhodes shrugged. "There were several along the coast, in fact, from Palm Beach southward to Miami. He even had a steamship refitted as a club and anchored just outside the twelve-mile limit for a time, the *Polynesia*. There wasn't anything on board that you couldn't get at one of the mainland spots, but my father was a romantic at heart. Something in the concept appealed to him."

"A romantic mobster?" Deal asked.

"He wasn't a mobster," Rhodes said. "Not in the way you mean it, anyway. When it came to business, he was a lone wolf. It's the quality that led him into trouble, ultimately."

Deal nodded. "It usually does."

"I believe that's one of the things that drew your father and mine together," Rhodes said.

"Nobody ever called Barton Deal a team player," Deal said.

Rhodes nodded. Deal noticed that the man was back to staring at him intently. "I meant what I said earlier, Mr. Deal. It may not feel that way to you, but you *are* my guest. You're free to leave at any time."

Deal considered the words, unable to stop a sidelong glance at Kaia, who had slid down, tucking herself into a corner of the plush sofa. "As in right now?" he asked.

"I'd advise waiting for morning," Rhodes said. "The reef out there can be tricky."

"Your man found his way in well enough," Deal said.

"He was operating under a great sense of urgency."

"Maybe I feel the same way about getting back."

Rhodes gave him a sympathetic look and leaned forward. "The truth is that Basil reports a bit of a problem with the screws on the boat." His regret sounded sincere. "I'm afraid we'll have to wait for better light to take a look at things."

Deal nodded. "Why am I not surprised?" He glanced around the room again. "What if I just make a couple of phone calls, then, put everybody's mind at ease back home—"

"If a phone were available . . ." Rhodes said. He trailed off, opening his hands in a gesture of helplessness.

"You don't have a telephone?" Deal asked, his voice rising.

"I do apologize," Rhodes said, shaking his head. "Circumstances dictate the utmost caution. But perhaps the delay will give us some time to get to know each other . . ."

"You think we're going to buddy up, Rhodes? Dig out the Gullickson yearbook? It just doesn't work that way."

Rhodes nodded as if he'd expected as much, but he didn't respond. Instead, he pushed himself away from his desk and crossed over to the bar. He picked up a glass, inspected it in the light, polished it against his sleeve. He poked about the clutch of bottles, seemed to find what he'd been looking for.

"From Haiti," he said, showing the bottle to Deal. Rum, it looked like. A label resembling aged parchment. "My father made a fortune smuggling this brand into the States. But that's hardly a crime to condemn a man for, is it?" He poured some of the amber-colored liquid into the glass, his drink neat as well. Deal found himself wondering who the ice had been put out for.

"Look, Rhodes. I don't care if your old man was a bootlegger, and I sure don't care if he ran a floating crap game with a few call girls on the side. I just want to know why you brought me here."

"Of course you do." Rhodes nodded. He saluted Kaia with his glass and sipped at the rum. "As a man whose father had his own image problems, I'm sure you'll understand—"

"You want to talk about *your* father, that's fine," Deal cut in. "Leave my old man out of it."

Rhodes glanced at him, saw Deal's hands gripping the arms of the overstuffed chair. His gaze flickered toward the darkened doorway, as if he might be calculating how long it would take Frank or Basil to make it inside. *Too long,* Deal was thinking. *Way too long.*

"Yes," Kaia said, rising from her place on the couch. "Remember your manners, Richard." The way she moved toward the bar might have seemed casual, but Deal noted she had placed herself squarely between him and Rhodes.

"Can I freshen you up?" she asked, already pouring Scotch into his glass.

"You want to know why I asked you here," Rhodes said. "I'll have to tell you the story."

"Ice, wasn't it?" Kaia was saying. She opened her hand—a magician's flourish—and Deal heard the faint clink of tiny cubes against crystal.

He stared at her, wondering where the ice had come from.

"Don't be too surprised," said Rhodes, amused. "She's quite the trickster, Mr. Deal."

"I don't doubt it," Deal said, pulling his gaze away from her. Usually it was the man who performed the magic, wasn't it? The woman was just there to look at. Here was a different package altogether, or so it seemed.

"You were going to tell me a story," he said to Rhodes.

"Your father and mine." Rhodes nodded. He gestured toward the dock with his glass. "We have some time."

"This is yours, then," Kaia said, handing the drink his way.

Deal glanced up at her. He'd had women hand him drinks before. He was a grown up after all. But the look she gave him—that he'd rarely seen. It was over in an instant, her hand withdrawn, the glass heavy as lead in his, but *Still,* Deal thought. *Still . . .*

"Of course, if you're done in . . ." Rhodes was saying.

Not a bad way of putting it, Deal thought, but he had a sip of the smoky Scotch anyway. From the corner of his eye, he saw Kaia tuck herself into the cushions of the willing couch. He tilted his glass toward Rhodes. "Go for it," Deal said.

And Rhodes did.

thirty-one

"You done good on the Eclipse," the man in the dark blue suit said, tossing the briefcase onto Barton Deal's desk.

Barton Deal nodded, though he didn't like the tone of the compliment. The "Eclipse," Anthony Gargano's pet name for the hotel, was finished now, doing land-office business on Miami Beach as the Eden Parc. Enough business that the trustees of the Teamsters Fund, which bankrolled the project, were satisfied at least, despite numerous cost overruns and despite the fact that Anthony Gargano had been convicted on several counts of bank fraud and tax evasion and now sat in a federal prison in rural Illinois.

"What's that?" Barton Deal asked, pointing at the briefcase.

The man in the suit, whose name was Sandro Alessio, shrugged, glancing down at the briefcase as if he'd never seen it before. "What's what?" he said.

"For God's sake," Deal said. "You think this place is bugged?"

It was Friday, Deal's secretary had gone to lunch early, and the two of them were alone in DealCo's spanking new downtown offices, a gleaming glass-and-steel building that sat between the Everglades Hotel and the *Miami News* building, an incongruous structure done up to resemble the ancient Tower of Seville. Flush with his success from the Gargano contract, Barton Deal had secured a prime corner space in the new building. Out one window he could gaze at a reminder of all that the princes of Europe had accomplished; out the other, he could see a gigantic electrified billboard where a neon terrier tugged the bottom of a little girl's bathing suit down over her butt, thousands and thousands of times a day.

In either direction he could see the vast blue stretches of Biscayne Bay as backdrop to it all, a seemingly endless stretch of untroubled water where sailboats zigged and zagged, fishermen fished, and bathers bathed, all of them protected by Coppertone. *The good life, South Florida style,* Barton Deal thought, watching a flock of gulls soar by, even though there were getting to be more and more types like the looming Alessio to be encountered here.

He reached for the briefcase and pulled it toward him. If there was a bomb inside, then the man who'd delivered it was a kamikaze. Alessio didn't look like a kamikaze, though. He looked like two hundred and forty pounds of Italian mobster wrapped in a five-hundred-dollar suit, which is exactly what he was.

Barton Deal unsnapped the briefcase and raised the top. Stacks and stacks of well-worn bills bundled up inside. He looked at Alessio again. "What *is* this?"

"Maybe it's your draw," Alessio said.

Deal shook his head. "The hotel's built. I've already been paid."

Alessio shrugged. "Maybe it's a bonus. Most guys, they don't get so worked up when somebody gives them money."

"Why would Anthony Gargano send me a bonus? He's in prison."

"Who said anything about Ducks? That asshole's finished." Alessio was staring over Barton Deal's shoulder now, in the direction of the Coppertone billboard. The look on his face suggested he saw something alluring there.

Deal stared at the stacks of bills before him, trying to calculate how much it was. All twenties across the top, he noted, but it could easily be ones on the lower layers, or clipped-up construction paper for that matter. He'd seen some interesting things in the time he'd spent around Gargano and his pals.

He was also thinking about the fact that his office *was* bugged, and that if he wanted, there was a little button under his desk that he could nudge with his toe, start up a hidden tape recorder, all of it installed by a certain government agency that had also proclaimed its satisfaction with how Deal's association with Anthony Gargano had gone. Enough satisfaction that they were willing to overlook some of the profits Deal had made, so long as he was willing to continue to cooperate.

Something was keeping Barton Deal from nudging the button at his knee, though. For one thing, he had a healthy distaste for the position his own government had forced him into. For another thing, a person drops a hundred thousand dollars on your desk, whole new emotions are born. No need to rush into anything, was there—another lesson hanging around Gargano had taught him.

"Did you say something?" Alessio asked. He was still staring out the window in the direction of the billboard.

"Not me," Barton Deal said.

"You got to sit here all the fucking day, stare at that thing? It'd drive me fucking nuts," the guy said, his narcoleptic gaze still out there.

Crazy in what way? Deal wondered. "You get used to it," is what he said, glancing over his shoulder.

"Yeah," Alessio, his tone indicating anything but agreement. "Why I came down," he said, "I'm consolidating some operations in the light of Ducks's unfortunate outcome with the law."

"You're taking over the rackets in South Florida?" Deal had already heard that Alessio, a former Gargano underling, was mounting a bid to assume control of the mob's operations on the Beach, but it never hurt to confirm a rumor.

Alessio waved his hand as if there were gnats in front of his face. "I thought maybe you could help out with a problem."

He sat down in one of the chairs that had been delivered to the office that very morning. Rosewood and black leather, the latest thing from Scandinavia, the clerk at Robinson's Office Supply had assured him. Two hundred and seventy-five dollars apiece, but Barton Deal had liked the way they looked, especially with the clerk perched on the edge of one, her legs crossed, the view all the way to paradise, playing like she was going to take dictation for him.

Right now the chair was creaking ominously under Alessio's weight, but *What the hell,* Deal thought. He cut his glance back at the briefcase. He'd left off his calculations, but there seemed to be enough there to cover a chair.

"What kind of a problem?" Deal asked. He could turn on the recorder any time he wanted to, he told himself.

"Not really a *problem*," Alessio said, shifting around as if he couldn't get comfortable. "More of a loose end, if you catch my drift."

Barton Deal shrugged. The less he said, the better. Another lesson he'd learned.

"Something you'd be in a position to help us with."

Deal shook his head. "If it's about the hotel—"

"Forget the hotel, okay?" Alessio said. "Fucking hotel's built, it's over and done with. The goddamned ocean swallowed it tomorrow, nobody'd give a crap."

Except for maybe the folks inside, Deal thought. "Why don't you tell me what it is?" he said.

Alessio glared at him. "That's what I'm getting to, okay?"

If it wasn't okay, Deal knew what he could do about it. He nodded to Alessio, which was about the only acceptable response.

Alessio looked back at him like he was thinking maybe he'd made a mistake. Deal stayed cool, staring back. They were impressed by that, he'd found, a civilian who didn't look away. They might have thought he was crazy, but it was a kind of crazy that had earned him some respect.

"We've been getting into some things down here," Alessio said, shrugging. "The books, the hookers, like that."

Barton Deal nodded again. Bookmaking, prostitution, loan-sharking, the once-freewheeling craps and card games that moved around town . . . a few years ago all of it had been mostly freelance and homegrown. But as more and more of Gargano's associates had made their way to wintertime Miami Beach for a little respite from the weather and the stacking of the bodies in Detroit, and Chicago, and New York, they'd found time on their hands. Enough time to look around and realize that there were vast, untapped opportunities here in paradise, that in fact business and pleasure could be combined. They had been running all things illicit in Cuba, after all. Why not install the franchise in Miami as well?

None of these considerations applied to Barton Deal, however. He was a building contractor. A contractor who had proved willing to work with a rather questionable clientele, no question of it. But his direct association with the rackets themselves was nil.

"Everybody's gone along for the most part," Alessio was saying. He gave a shrug that suggested what had happened to any of the local talent who'd taken exception to being muscled out. "But there's a certain individual wants to be a pain in the ass."

"This is someone I know?"

Alessio nodded. "He's a pal of yours, used to run the Lotus freaking Blossom up in Palm Beach."

Deal stared back. "The White Lotus?"

"Whatever kind of Lotus."

Deal shook his head. "Are you talking about Grant Rhodes? He closed that club years ago."

Alessio raised an eyebrow to indicate the smallest amount of tolerance for Barton Deal's naïveté. "He still runs that boat out of Lauderdale."

"The *Polynesia*? It's a party ship—"

"It's a floating casino is what it is," Alessio said, sounding more like an aggrieved Broward County commissioner than a racketeer.

"Well, maybe there's a crap game every once in a while, but Lucky only goes out on weekends, and then it's only during the season . . ."

Alessio started out of the chair at that, but his bulk had complicated things. The rosewood arms slid only so far down his ample hips and refused to go further. Barton Deal found himself staring across his desk at a gangster caught in a crouch, one who looked like he was being buggered by a Scandinavian office chair. He also knew that if he laughed, he could die. Was it time to switch on that recorder, maybe catch one great guffaw followed by a gunshot?

Instead he stared back evenly at Alessio, who reached with studied calm to grasp the chair arms, then peel the thing off his backside. "You make enough money," the guy said. "Why don't you buy yourself some fucking chairs that fit?"

Deal nodded. Had Shakespeare himself been there to deliver any other response, he would have taken a bullet between the eyes.

Free of the chair now, Alessio leaned across Barton Deal's desk and pushed the lid of the briefcase down with a thick forefinger. The case closed with a snap. Alessio peered into Deal's eyes as intently as any ophthalmologist. *Now* he was supposed to say something, Deal understood.

"You want me to talk to Lucky," he said to the guy. He'd known Grant Rhodes for years, from the time he'd been old enough to talk his way into the China Clipper, the most flamboyant of Rhodes's fabled clubs. Barton

Deal with the Dead

Deal, the son of a Coral Gables real estate salesman and a pillar of the Presbyterian Church, had found the urbane, world-traveled Rhodes and his velvet-frocked pleasure palaces fascinating, a veritable mirror of a so-phisticated world that he knew existed but had only glimpsed in films and on the pages of the magazines his mother subscribed to. More astonishing, he'd discovered that Rhodes was scarcely ten years older than himself.

It wasn't long before a bond had formed between the two men, Rhodes taken by Barton Deal's brashness and expansive personality, and apparently willing to play the role of the older brother Barton Deal had always longed for. By the time Barton Deal was into his twenties, the two were friends, Rhodes willing to run a tab for Barton that never seemed to come due, Barton Deal always to be counted on to bring an ever-growing entourage along when he visited the Clipper, the White Lotus, and later, the floating *Polynesia* that he and Alessio had just discussed.

Maybe he'd never gotten out of South Florida, Barton Deal thought, staring across his desk at the dour mobster in front of him, but his asso-ciation with Lucky Rhodes had been the next best thing. Lucky was a gambler and a former rumrunner, and there were ladies of questionable reputation who were to be found on the premises of his establishments, all of which made him a criminal by some lights, Deal supposed. But compared to the cretin standing in front of him at the moment, Grant Rhodes seemed a living saint.

"I'll talk to him," Barton Deal continued. He'd explain things to Rhodes, who was more or less retired anyway, a guy with all the money he'd ever need, and better things to take up his time, including a son the age of his own Johnny-boy. The *Polynesia* was more a hobby than anything else, time to put the damned ship in mothballs if it meant that much to the likes of the guy in front of him. You *can* fight city hall, Barton Deal thought, but progress was another matter.

"Forget a bunch of talk," Alessio said, cutting into his thoughts. He reached into his coat pocket and pulled out a pistol. *Mark of a good tailor,* was the first thought that crossed Barton Deal's mind. Even on an oaf, a place had been found to disguise a handgun's bulk.

He was also wondering, if he *were* about to die, why hadn't he started that recorder? At least it'd be on record, the way he had gone down.

"Or you can talk to him all you want," Alessio was saying. He clapped the pistol down on top of the briefcase. "But when you're finished talking, you take this and blow his ass away."

Barton Deal glanced at the pistol, then up at the guy in front of him. "You're kidding, right?"

Alessio moved his chin from side to side, very slowly. One cycle: right, left, back to center again.

"Lucky Rhodes is a friend of mine."

"So what? How many friends you think I whacked?"

Barton Deal stared at Alessio for a moment, deciding that it was a question best not pursued. "Why would you want *me* to do this?"

"People tried to talk to this guy. He don't want to listen."

"I know *why* you want to kill him. I'm asking why *me*. I'm not a killer."

Alessio stared at Barton Deal as if he were simpleminded. "That's the whole point. Guy's not stupid. He packs heat, and he's always got his boys around. But you're his friend."

Which brought them full circle, didn't it? Barton Deal closed his eyes and pinched the bridge of his nose. "Look, I couldn't do it," he told Alessio. "I wouldn't have the nerve."

Alessio waved his hand. "You'd be surprised how easy it is."

Deal paused. It was clear that to Alessio they might as well be arguing about who was going to take out the garbage. "Did Gargano authorize this?" he asked.

The question brought color to Alessio's cheeks. "Fuck Tony Gargano. That needle-dick goombah is right where he belongs. I'm the one who *authorizes* now, you understand?"

Barton Deal looked into Alessio's eyes and nodded to show that he understood. "Suppose I just picked up this gun and shot you instead?" he said.

It got something of a grudging smile from Alessio. "You could try. But even if you got lucky, there'd be blood and brains and dirty money all over your office. People running up and down the hallways, cops in here asking a bunch of embarrassing questions." He shook his head, as if he'd come to a certain conclusion. "I don't think so, Mr. Deal."

"Then what makes you think I'll kill Lucky Rhodes?"

"Because if you don't, someone is liable to kill *you*," the guy said. "But first they'd probably shoot your old lady, and after that, they just might put a bullet in that kid you're so proud of. Maybe two or three bullets." He said it all matter-of-factly, the way he might have talked about clipping a hangnail.

Barton Deal held his anger in check, remembering not to look away. "That's all I have to do? Kill Lucky Rhodes?"

Alessio shrugged. "You want me to look around for some other jobs, I will." Bring up irony to this guy, Deal thought, he'd assume you were talking about some kind of metalwork.

"So that's what all this money is for?"

"Look at it any way you want to," Alessio said.

"You put a suitcase full of money on my desk, you ask me to kill Lucky Rhodes, how I am supposed to look at it?"

"You as stupid as you sound?" the guy said. "Just do what you gotta do, everything'll be square."

"I'm glad to hear it," Barton Deal said.

"One of my guys'll go along just to make sure everything goes okay."

Deal nodded. "Why am I not surprised?"

"He'll meet you at the Lauderdale marina, eight o'clock tonight," Alessio continued.

"Tonight?"

Alessio waved a hand. It was not a matter for debate.

"How am I supposed to explain one of your gorillas to Lucky?"

Alessio stared at him. "You say he's a mark. You done that for your pal before, haven't you?"

Barton Deal felt a twinge, but he kept it to himself. "It won't make any difference. If your guy's packing, he'll never get off the dock."

"*You're* carrying the gun, asshole. My guy's just going along to make sure. You talk to him, he'll tell you how it's going to go."

Barton Deal stared back at him. Of course. He was simply being used as the cover, the stalking horse. If Barton Deal went along, could be cowed into killing his own friend, then fine. But there would be a goon there in any case, to make sure. Deal sighed inwardly. There didn't seem much more to say.

"Don't look so glum," Alessio said, gesturing at the briefcase. "You think people throw all this money at you 'cause you're a nice guy?"

"I always liked to think so," Deal said.

"Well, welcome to the real world, dickhead," Alessio said. He started for the door, then turned back. He reached into his pants pocket and moved to slap whatever it was down on Deal's desk. "I almost forgot," Alessio said. "You're gonna need these."

Deal stared down at the six shells that jiggled like jumping beans on the polished surface before him. Thirty-two caliber, maybe. Maybe thirty-eights. He wasn't much of an expert. He glanced over at the pistol for a moment, then up at Sandro Alessio.

Alessio grinned, but there wasn't much approaching humor there. "Aren't you glad you didn't try it?" he said.

Barton Deal said nothing.

And then the big guy was gone.

"Welcome, Barton," the voice came over the intercom. A little scratchy with what sounded like electrical interference, and the sound quality terrible on the speaker bolted to the ship's bulkhead, but it was undeniably Lucky Rhodes's voice on the other end. Comforting as a jazz station disc jockey, and always happy to hear of the arrival of an old friend. "And tell me whom you've brought along."

Deal turned to the man standing beside him at the top of the gangway, feeling the gentle roll of the ship under his feet. He'd met the guy half an hour ago at the Lauderdale Marina docks. An inch or two taller than himself, thin but wiry, he'd stepped out of the shadows of an oleander hedge a half dozen yards from where Barton Deal had parked his new Chrysler, had introduced himself as Sandro Alessio's friend.

The guy made a decent appearance for a killer, Barton Deal thought: wore his dark hair slicked back, kept his mustache pencil-thin, had found himself a decent suit. Maybe Alessio had his own tailor make up some cheaper knock-offs for his henchmen. Deal leaned close to the speaker and pressed the intercom button under the watchful eye of two big men in white dinner jackets who guarded the way toward the foredeck. Party lights glittered along the rigging lines up there, and the strains of Cole Porterish dance music drifted out over the gentle swells accompanied by the chatter of unseen guests: *Just one more night of joy among the lotus eaters,* Deal thought, and wished that's all it had to be.

"This is my cousin Mel, from Cleveland," Barton Deal spoke into the intercom.

About certain things, Alessio had been correct. "My cousin Mel from Cleveland" was a phrase that he and Lucky had settled on long ago. It stood for something like, "I am bringing you a pigeon who is so loaded he can hardly fly."

Nor did Barton Deal really mind setting such marks up for a fleecing. After all, they were the types who were bound and determined to get rid of their money anyway. Why not let Lucky relieve them of the burden? At least they'd be well entertained in the process, and there was no chance that they'd be slipped a Mickey, rolled, and dumped in an alley somewhere to wake up the next morning with a knot on the back of the head and nothing to show for it but the vague memory of a pretty girl's smile. No. If a mark was intent on a screwing, then that's what he got at one of Lucky Rhodes's clubs, and he could get it in every imaginable way.

On this evening, most of the passengers had already boarded the *Polynesia* in Palm Beach. Because the sheriff of Broward County was running against a reformer bent on cleaning out the scoundrels from the bailiwick, the ship would not make port in Fort Lauderdale until after the elections. Barton Deal and "Mel" had been ferried out to the *Polynesia* aboard a gleaming wooden water taxi—all gloss-lacquered and gleaming brass—an accouterment that Lucky had brought in all the way from Venice. Just getting in the damned thing made you feel otherworldly, Barton Deal thought, though he hadn't asked if his traveling companion felt the same way.

There had been a couple of girls to jump leggily onto the boat just as they were about to depart—one redhead, one blonde, both wearing upswept hair, sequined dresses, and smiles that promised the world. Barton Deal had accepted a dollop of champagne in a flute from the water taxi captain, as had the two women, but "Mel" had declined. It was left to Deal to entertain the girls during the short run out to the *Polynesia*. Despite all the distracting thoughts in his mind, he'd done his best to oblige.

The girls had clambered up the gangway ahead of them—*The view, the view,* Barton Deal thought—and had presumably already passed the checkpoint to join the party on the foredeck. Too bad he wouldn't be partying tonight.

"Well, you and Mel come on down," Lucky Rhodes's voice came over the speaker. "We're about to set sail. I'm eager to meet your cousin."

That was Lucky for you, Barton Deal thought, watching as the two gatekeepers moved to pat Mel down. They were quick but thorough: "Mel" with his hands above his head like a man being robbed at gunpoint, one of Lucky's men working his hands above the belt, the other working deftly below.

"That's fine, sir," said one of the men as he straightened up. Mel gave him a grudging nod.

"You're okay, Mr. Deal," the guard said, waving him along without a search.

The two of them followed after the second guard, who moved a short way along the rail toward the foredeck, then stopped and turned to motion them through a bulkhead door.

"Mind your step," the big guard said, ushering them through.

"Guy's a faggot," Mel said to Barton Deal as they moved down the plush carpeted passage ahead of the guard. "Had his hands all over my prick back there."

"Maybe he thought it was a little gun," Deal said.

Mel shot him a dark look.

"Or maybe he thought you were just happy to see him," Deal added.

"Fuck you," Mel said. "You got the piece, right?"

"I have it," Deal said. He remembered the feel of the heavy weapon as he'd holstered it. Handle a gun out on the target range, it's just a piece of machinery. Hold one you might have to shoot someone with, it's got blood and guts of its own.

"Just keep thinking how it's going to go."

Barton Deal nodded, leading the way around a turn in the passage. *Helpful hints from your local assassin,* he thought, wondering how he'd gotten himself into this, anyway. He'd introduce his "cousin," they'd spend the evening playing on the DealCo tab. When the ship reached port back in Palm Beach, they'd go see Lucky again to settle up.

While Rhodes's men were occupied with securing the evening's take and escorting the main body of the passengers off the boat, that's when it would happen. And though getting down to Rhodes's cabin from topside was complicated, going the other way was a piece of cake. They'd be off the ship with the rest of the crowd before anyone discovered the body. That was the plan, at least.

Something caught his eye as he rounded the turn, something that stopped him short. "Take a look at that," Deal said, pointing as the wiry guy made his way up beside him.

The passage had opened up here, the dim orange-ish light cast by the wall sconces behind them replaced by a shimmering blue-green glow that filled the hallway like a ghostly liquid. The guy stopped, his seen-everything expression unsettled for a moment.

There were a series of thick glass windows lining one side of the passageway that stretched off in front of them, offering a view into the depths of what might have seemed a swimming pool at first. Deal had been in a bar in Honolulu with a similar setup once—he and his wife had sipped mai tais and watched big-busted girls made up like mermaids swirling around in some kind of underwater ballet.

But this was no swimming tank, or at least there were no mermaids frolicking inside. Instead there were fish: schools of little teal-and-fuchsia ones whirling around like neon smoke, some medium-sized snapper and jack in there as well, but those fish, too, were moving especially fast whenever the shadows of the two featured creatures swept across the deep.

For it was two massive hammerhead sharks who were the showpiece, the big gray things swirling endlessly around the made-up reefs and phony shipwreck set in the midst of it all: hammerheads gliding here, hammerheads swooping there, up to the top, and down again, around and around the confines of an artificial sea. From where Barton Deal stood, you could see all the way across the huge tank to the windows on the opposite side: he had a murky view of a cocktail lounge, or a ballroom maybe, where men and women in suits and evening gowns milled about, and danced, or held drinks and watched the fishies, too.

"Fucking A," the wiry man said.

"I had a malamute with eyes like that once," Barton Deal said, caught by the rhythms of the sharks' endless dance. "But his were on the front of his head."

"What do they *feed* those things?" the wiry guy said, his studied cynicism evaporating for the moment.

"Meat," said the guy in the white dinner jacket who'd caught up to them. "Lots of it."

"Fucking A," the wiry man repeated. And then the three of them moved on.

"It's all right, Andrew," Grant Rhodes said, dismissing the man who'd escorted them down the labyrinthine passageways. "These gentlemen are friends of mine."

Andrew gave his boss an uncertain look, but turned to go out the way they'd come. Barton Deal felt a twinge: maybe it was the weight of the pistol beneath his dinner jacket, he thought, or maybe he was sad to see Andrew go.

"Quite a setup you have here," said the wiry man to Grant Rhodes.

The three of them stood in front of a one-way glass that offered a soundless view into a room where a tall, rail-thin man in a tuxedo dealt a hand of chemin de fer. On the other side of the felt-covered table sat two couples—the men steely-haired, titan-of-industry types in black tie, their companions more reserved, evening-gowned versions of the women who'd been on the water taxi, everyone intent on the game.

One of the men made an almost imperceptible gesture toward the cadaverous dealer, and another card was offered up on a paddle by an assistant. It seemed like a glimpse into another dimension, Barton Deal thought: fortunes might be won or lost, but somehow, real trouble would not dare intrude. Rhodes pressed a button then, and a heavy wooden panel closed over the glass.

"Happy to have you aboard," Rhodes replied. He was in tux shirt and tie, his jacket draped over the back of his desk chair. "Those folks shouldn't be playing until we've cleared the twelve-mile limit, but"—he shrugged—"we're among friends, aren't we?"

When they'd been buzzed through the thick bulkhead door into his office, he'd been in his desk chair on an intercom phone with what sounded like a pit boss. The moment he'd seen Barton Deal enter, however, he ended the conversation and was up and around to greet the two of them, a broad smile crossing his avuncular features, as if their arrival was something he'd awaited for years.

Deal with the Dead

They could have been camel drivers just made it across the Sahara bearing gifts untold, knights returned home with the Grail itself. Nor did it have anything to do with Cousin Mel's feathers about to be plucked, Barton Deal thought. If men were going to lose their money, time had shown they'd mind it less losing to Lucky Rhodes. With his reassuring arm around your shoulders, whatever got inserted elsewhere simply hurt less somehow.

"Baccarat appeal to you, does it, Mel?" Rhodes asked, gesturing at the shrouded window.

"Bones is more my game," the wiry man said.

"Then you've come to the right place," Rhodes said. He turned to Barton Deal. "Hasn't he, Bart?"

Deal nodded, trying to imagine how things would change with men like Sandro Alessio and his goons in charge. A customer has a complaint, he files it full fathoms five, no need to take off his concrete overshoes.

"I hadn't seen the aquarium, Lucky," Deal said, turning toward the door. "It's a touch. A very definite touch."

"You have to amuse yourself," Rhodes said, shrugging as a smile crossed his guileless features. A man with an unwavering gaze, but a way of leaning back from a conversation as if to encourage your every word. "Isn't that the point of life?" he said.

The expression on the wiry man's face suggested he'd never considered the issue.

"I'd say it was," Barton Deal spoke up.

"Must be a lot a trouble to keep it going," the wiry man said.

Rhodes nodded. "Most things you care about are troublesome," he said.

Try getting your reptilian brain around that one, Barton Deal thought, glancing at his companion.

"Did you show Mel the craps tables on your way down?" Rhodes asked.

"We were in too much of a hurry," Deal said.

Rhodes smiled. "No need to hurry, we've got the whole evening in front of us."

The smile of the perfect host, Barton Deal thought. Every detail attended to, the night laid out like a buffet banked with endlessly replenishable delights. Lucky Rhodes, who'd been everywhere and seen everything—more, in fact than Barton Deal could imagine. *Time to get this over with,* he thought. They would do this now.

"Actually, we don't have the whole evening," Barton Deal said.

Rhodes turned to him, good-natured puzzlement on his features. "What's that you say, Barton?"

Deal shrugged, scarcely glancing at the wiry man beside him. There was no going back now. "The fact is we came down here to kill you. Me and my good buddy, 'Mel.'"

Grant Rhodes began to laugh. "Oh, that's a good one—"

"I'm serious, Lucky—"

Rhodes held up his hand, trying to stifle his guffaws. "Stop it, Bart—"

"What the fuck," the wiry man said, his features contorting.

"See, I'm packing the gun," Deal said, pulling back the lapel of his dinner jacket to show the bulky shoulder holster. "Fuzz-nuts here came along to make sure everything proceeds as planned."

"I'll tell you, Barty-boy—" Grant Rhodes's eyes were leaking tears of laughter now.

"You stupid bastard," the wiry man said. He raised his arm and brought it down in a flourish. There was a snapping sound and Barton Deal saw it: a tiny pearl-handled derringer had somehow appeared in the man's hand.

"You *do* have a teeny little gun," Barton Deal said.

"And you are a fucking dead man," Mel said, swinging his gun hand toward Deal.

Deal ducked, his hand going for the pistol at his shoulder. He was likely to be late, he thought. He might have expected a knife, a garrote, maybe some serious brass knuckles, but a derringer on a sling holster had been a bit of a surprise.

He was on his way toward the corner of Rhodes's desk when the explosion sounded behind him, accompanied by a stinging sensation in his arm. The sound was stunning in the close confines, snuffing out Deal's hearing as abruptly as if a powerful pair of hands had slammed against his ears.

"Mel" was stumbling backward across the room, a stitching of red dots across his forehead, a vacant expression upon his sour face. There was a second explosion—felt more than heard by Deal's numbed ears—and he watched a blossom of red erupt silently on Mel's chest. The impact took the man off his feet, driving him against the opposite wall. He hit hard and slid downward, trailing blood all the way.

Deal, on the floor now, glanced up at Lucky. Lucky's mouth appeared to moving, but whatever he was saying was lost, as if he were speaking from behind a thick glass wall. Deal sensed movement and turned to see Andrew stepping smartly through the bulkhead door, the stubby-barreled shotgun he'd used on Mel still smoking.

Andrew checked to be sure that Mel was no threat, then turned and gestured toward the doorway. In moments, the office seemed full of people. Two steely haired men were working to sling Mel's body inside what looked like an oversized duffel bag—the two "titans of industry" who'd posed as baccarat players, Deal realized, the whole lot of them shills, even as one of the gowned and bejeweled women who'd been in the room bent over him, concern etched on her dark contessa's features.

There was a high-pitched ringing in Barton Deal's ears now, which somehow seemed a good thing. ". . . your arm," he heard the woman who had bent over him say. He glanced down at his shoulder and saw a spot of blood the size of a silver dollar.

"Nothing to worry about," he told the woman, though he couldn't hear his own voice quite yet. He mustered a smile for her and tried to push himself into a sitting position. He was still smiling goofily at her when the pain surged up from his wounded shoulder and he passed out like a drunk in her arms.

thirty-two

"QUITE A STORY," JOHN Deal said when Rhodes finally paused. "What's it have to do with me?"

"I'm getting to that," Rhodes told him. He splashed more Scotch into his glass and held up the bottle for Deal, who shook his head. "But there are a few things I'd like to show you, first."

Deal shrugged.

Rhodes rose from his desk and moved toward the doorway. "I'll just be a moment," he said, then disappeared down the dark hallway.

Deal glanced over at the couch where Kaia had dozed off. Her head was tilted back, her mouth opened ever so slightly, as if she'd been about to say something when her lights went out. The pose might have seemed vaguely comic on someone else, he thought. Kaia Jesperson was composed and lovely, even in her sleep.

He turned away from her, thinking back on the conclusion of Rhodes's tale: His father had come to on a couch in Lucky's office, Rhodes had explained, his hearing more or less back to normal, the cadaverous guy—a former corpsman on Guadalcanal, as it turned out—finishing a bandage where a pellet from Andrew's shotgun had winged Barton. "Andrew felt like hell about it," was the word from Lucky.

The ship's office had been put back in order, Mel's body gone, the long bloody trail the wiry man had left erased from the opposite wall, as though everything Barton Deal had witnessed had been only a troubling nightmare. The *Polynesia* was steaming back to port in Palm Beach—the result of engine problems, or so the passengers had been told.

Lucky's captain on the water taxi had spotted the piece under Barton Deal's coat right away, had radioed ahead with word. It had been Rhodes's decision to let things play out. Lucky Rhodes's instincts had served him well in a lifetime as a gambler—and they had not failed him in this instance either. No way he'd been able to accept that Barton Deal meant him harm. No way on earth.

John Deal thought about that more than anything as he waited for Rhodes's return: the trust that Lucky Rhodes had apparently had in his own father. Was there anyone that he himself could trust so completely? Janice, he guessed, when she was Janice, anyway. And Vernon Driscoll, whom he doubted about as much as he might have his own right arm.

Driscoll would step in front of a train on his account, no question. And that meant something, didn't it? Meant you mattered in some elemental way. And if you had no one in whom to place such trust, what did *that* imply?

Deal glanced at Kaia again. Something told him Rhodes had no such person of the likes his story had suggested. No Janice, no Barton Deal. Just Frank and Basil and Kaia Jesperson, all of them who seemed accidental moons in their temporary orbits.

"Have a look at these." It was Rhodes's voice. Deal glanced up from his reverie to find the man returned to the room with a sheaf of news clippings in his hand, clips that had been placed in protective plastic holders, but so old they had nonetheless yellowed with age:

"Flamboyant Casino Owner Dies in Freak Accident," read the headline of the first story Rhodes handed over. The piece was from the *Fort Lauderdale News,* led by an overheated account of the gruesome discovery made aboard the *Polynesia* on that fateful night. Officers from the Palm Beach County Sheriff's Department had been called aboard the ship by shaken employees who had made the discovery: what little remained of Grant Rhodes after he'd apparently fallen into the shark tank he maintained aboard his notorious floating pleasure palace. No mention in the story, of course, as to just how many palms had been greased to make sure Mel's remains had been identified as those of Lucky Rhodes.

Deal glanced up at Rhodes, who smiled as if to approve of his father's ingenuity. He took the first clip back from Deal and handed over another.

This clipping from the *Miami Herald,* Deal saw, dated a week or so later, concerned the puzzling death of an as-yet-unidentified white male who had apparently tried to dive from the balcony of an unoccupied upper story suite at the Eden Parc Hotel into the swimming pool far below. The man, nude and presumed intoxicated, had landed headfirst on the flagstone decking, which was complicating the process of identification.

"Let me guess," Deal said to Rhodes. "Sandro Alessio."

Rhodes nodded. "It's a family newspaper," he said. "They didn't go into the oddity of why certain of his lower body parts had been found lodged in his throat."

Deal stared at Rhodes. "More of your old man's work?"

"Hardly," Rhodes said. "But picture this: Two days after the events on board the *Polynesia,* Anthony Gargano, convicted felon, sits in a cell perhaps larger and at least as well-appointed as this library, whiling away an afternoon working on the evolving appeal of his case, when a package arrives, special delivery, from Miami. Inside he finds a spool of audio tape with a note that suggests Mr. Gargano might like the style of music contained therein. It takes an hour or two, and considerable effort on the part of certain federal prison employees, but before the close of business on that day, a reel-to-reel tape recorder somehow makes its way into Gargano's cell. Which is when Anthony Gargano gets to hear in no uncertain terms of the feelings his trusted lieutenant Sandro Alessio holds for his incarcerated boss."

"You're saying my old man sent that tape?"

"What does it matter who sent it?" Rhodes said. "The fact is, it had to be sent. The lives of decent men were at stake."

"So you say," Deal replied.

"You know I'm right," Rhodes countered.

"So the books are wiped clean, your old man makes a graceful exit out of Miami because he knows there's a hundred more Alessios where the first one came from. He tidies things up and comes down here to live out his days in peace."

Rhodes shook his head. "You paint such a pretty picture . . ."

"Well, I'm happy for him. And I'm happy for you," Deal plunged on, thrusting the second clip back at Rhodes. "Your old man works on his gin and tonic and his tan the rest of his life, you go to private school, get a sports car for every A on your report card, what could be prettier than that? You still haven't gotten to the point where I come in."

"You've *always* been in it," Rhodes blurted, his jaw thrust, his practiced gentleman's air gone hard.

Deal paused. "What are you talking about?"

Rhodes was working to calm himself. He glanced at the couch, where Kaia Jesperson had come awake. She pushed herself up from the soft cushions, wondering what was coming.

"My father lived less than a month after he returned to this house," Rhodes said. "He was found washed up on the rocks beneath the dock you walked upon."

Despite himself, Deal glanced out the darkened door of the study the way they'd come.

"He was drowned," Rhodes said. "It had been intended to look like an accident—one arranged by Gargano or one of his associates—but whoever did it wasn't very careful. There was a chunk of his scalp torn away, and all his fingernails were broken from where he'd tried to claw his way back into the boat."

Deal started to say something, but Rhodes was going on.

"He had a skiff he liked to take out, to flats-fish with a guide. On that morning, someone pushed him out of that boat, then held him under," Rhodes said, his gaze gone elsewhere now. "Obviously, it hadn't been an easy task."

"I'm sorry," Deal said when Rhodes paused. He turned away, trying to conjure up the face of the man he'd seen in the snapshot with his parents—that visage of contentment and ease, now transformed to a wild-eyed mask, great explosions of air bursting up through the spangled water as "Lucky" Rhodes lunged and lunged again for the railing of his boat, his hair knotted in the fist of an expressionless thug.

And another picture had come conjuring itself out of the past, this one of his own father, seated at the desk in the office of the house on South Miami Avenue, lining up the proper chambers of his .38, pressing the cold steel pistol tip to the flesh of his palate, then dialing home for good.

"I found a picture," Deal said finally, turning back to him. "In some of my father's things. Taken on the dock down there, I think. My parents. It must have been your father they were standing with."

"This one?" Rhodes said. He reached for one of the wooden frames turned away from them on the desk, swiveling it around so that it faced them. Deal stared stupidly at the photograph encased there: an eight-by-ten, faded with time but the subject perfectly clear. It was a replica of the snapshot he'd found in his father's hidden câche: his mother, his father, and Rhodes's father standing on a dock beneath a mansion and a glittering Caribbean sky—a frozen moment on a perfect day in paradise.

Deal tried to make sense of all the thoughts that rushed through his mind. Rhodes's father had found this place, his mother and father had come to visit . . . then the elder Rhodes had been murdered. Was that what it was? Perhaps Barton Deal had been followed by the men who wanted Rhodes's father dead . . . or perhaps the son's suspicions were even darker than that. Above all, where did Talbot Sams figure in all of this?

"Are you suggesting that my father had something to do with your father's death?" Deal asked, looking up from the photograph.

Rhodes laughed, a short, barking sound so unexpected it seemed more like a cry in the quiet room. "The thought's never crossed my mind," he said.

"Then what . . . ?" Deal shook his head, still holding the photograph before him.

"This photograph was taken years before his death," Rhodes said. "My father bought this place in 1946 from a German on his way to Brazil. The man was in a great hurry, I've been told. There wasn't much haggling over price."

Rhodes took the framed photograph from Deal and placed it back on the darkly polished desktop as he continued. "Your parents came here often in the early days, that's another thing I've learned. If I ever met them, I don't recall. I would have been very young." He took a deep breath and glanced at Kaia, who seemed as intent as Deal on this tale.

"But I owe your father a great debt of gratitude, that's the plain truth of it," Rhodes continued. His expression suggested that Deal would understand.

Deal stared back at him, feeling his head starting to throb again. It was late, and he was exhausted. He'd fought a pair of thugs, been knocked cold and ferried across the Straits of Florida to some off-the-map island in the Bahamas, where he'd awakened and been assured he wasn't kidnapped. He'd learned his father had been friends with the gangster father of the man who claimed not to have kidnapped him, and now it seemed that all this man wanted to do was make friends.

"You brought me all this way to say thanks?" Deal said. "Why not just send me a note? Or we could have hooked up at the next Gullickson Prep reunion, that's probably rolling around any day now: 'Hey, Deal, let me buy you a beer.'"

"I don't think they'll be inviting me to Gullickson's any time soon," Rhodes said.

"Yeah? You're behind in your alumni dues?"

"It's a bit more than that, I'd say." Rhodes shrugged. "About fifty million more."

Deal stopped. Gullickson Prep. Fifty million dollars. He looked more closely at the man standing in front of him. A lot of good work on that face, all right, but the shape was still vaguely the same, and if the smarmy George-Hamilton–like features had been chiseled into something a bit more rugged, the overearnest stare was still the same. All those headlines. The white-collar take of the century. Of course.

"Halliday," Deal said at last. "You're Michael Halliday." Rhodes/Halliday gave him a nod of recognition. "The Prep School Flimflam Man."

"I never liked the ring of that," Rhodes said. "Far too tacky for the complexity of what went on."

"You brought all your rich buddies into a bond-trading Ponzi scheme, then flew the coop." Deal paused, then glanced at Kaia, who seemed amused by it all.

"Vastly oversimplified by the press, I assure you," Rhodes said. "And if my clients hadn't been such greedy bastards to begin with, they'd have never lost a dime. Stupidity doesn't respect a bank account, that much I can tell you."

"You're an innocent man, is that your story?"

"I took risks, bent certain regulations, as was expected of me. What do you think the unhappy client will say when the luck runs dry?"

Deal shook his head. They could go on like this forever, he realized. And something else had occurred to him. "You're also supposed to be dead." He'd read the accounts: Notorious bond trader over the side of a yacht in the Mediterranean. Eyewitness accounts. Good riddance to a bad actor.

"Drowned, in fact," Rhodes said, nodding. He paused, glancing out the open doorway himself. "You might appreciate the poetry of that."

Deal was still examining the man's features. "Whoever you went to did good work," he said, "but I don't think a little plastic surgery's going to get you back into any good restaurants in Miami."

"I have no interest in going back to Miami," Rhodes assured him.

"Then what's all this with Aramcor and the free-trade port?"

Rhodes shook his head. "Call me an unwilling partner on the project," he said. "As soon as I can liquidate my interest, that will happen. But when I saw you had bid for a piece of the action, it gave me much easier access to the information I needed."

"We're going to get to the bottom line here, Rhodes—or Halliday, or whatever you want me to call you. I just know we are."

"After all you've heard, you surely understand the need for careful explanation," Rhodes said.

"I'm up to my ears in it," Deal said. "And I still don't know what you want from me."

"I want the money," Rhodes said. "*My* money."

Deal stared at him blankly. "That's probably what all those doctors and lawyers and judges said when you skipped town."

"That money's long gone," Rhodes said dismissively. "Others I did business with saw to that. I'm talking about money that belongs to me."

"And this is money you think *I* have? I'm sorry, Rhodes. You must have banged your head on your way back to life."

"I'm certain that you have it," Rhodes said, disregarding the last. He reached into his pocket, then came out with his hand in a fist. He made a tossing motion toward Deal, as if ridding himself of something vile. As his fingers uncurled, something silver flashed in the dim light of the study.

Deal leaned back instinctively and threw up his own hand to ward off whatever it was—knife, dagger, tiny weapon from the miniature martial arts parade . . .

The glittering thing slapped against his palm and his hand closed around it in reflex. He knew what it was now, didn't have to look, didn't have to check in his pocket to see what might be gone. *The key,* he told himself. The goddamned key.

"I only want what's mine," Rhodes was saying. Deal noticed that Kaia Jesperson had swung her slender legs to the floor and now leaned forward, listening intently.

Her pajama top had loosened, presenting him with views of flesh vee'd by black silk that only made the moment that much more difficult to comprehend. He had opened his mouth to say something, though he wasn't sure what it was going to be. What happened next made the issue moot.

thirty-three

THE WINDOW BEHIND THE couch exploded in a shower of fragments, at the same instant that the arm of the sofa, where Kaia had been resting moments before, erupted in a flurry of stuffing. The slug, flattened as it ripped through the heavy frame of the sofa, bit into Rhodes's desk, blasting the photo of Deal and his parents into smithereens. The three of them were still staring at one another in shock as the echo of the shot rolled across the grounds outside.

"Get down," Deal cried, diving toward the couch. He caught Kaia Jesperson by the shoulders and took her to the tiled floor as another shot came through the shattered window, this one blasting a gouge of plaster from the opposite wall.

"The lights," Deal called as he twisted around looking for Rhodes. Feather stuffing and plaster dust swirled in the air of the study, a surreal tropical snowstorm.

Rhodes, who was on his hands and knees behind the corner of the desk, yanked at the dangling lamp cord. The thing flew off the desktop, its glass shade splintering. There was a bluish pop as the bulb blew apart, and in the next moment the room was in darkness.

Another shot sounded outside, this one striking the outer wall of the house. Large-caliber slugs, Deal reasoned, as the sound of impact reverberated through the room. Hollow points that would pierce a body cleanly, come out the backside transformed to the size of a plate, pushing everything it met right out of the way.

"You all right?" he asked Kaia.

"For the moment," she said. If she was trembling, he couldn't tell it. "Rhodes?"

"All right," the hurried reply.

There was a fourth shot from outside and a section of books exploded into confetti on the shelf above them. Another shot sounded then, this from a different weapon. Another and another, and then a sharp cry.

"That's Frank," Rhodes called. He was starting up from behind the desk when a fusillade of fire blew through the window, tearing the bookshelves to shreds.

"Maybe not," Rhodes cried, diving back to the floor beside them.

There were more cries from what seemed to be the front of the house. Small-arms fire there, booming in the hallway, and the crashing of glass. More shouts and cries, then the sound of heavy footsteps in the hallway.

"Boss?" The unmistakable sound of Basil's deep voice.

"We're here," Rhodes called. "Keep your head down."

Basil came through the doorway in a duck walk, his bulky form outlined in the moonlight that drifted through the shattered window. "Three of them at the front. I took them out, I'm pretty sure."

"Is Frank in the back?"

"Out there somewhere." Basil nodded, glancing toward the window.

Several smaller-caliber shots erupted on the grounds once again, followed by a longer period of silence this time. "That's him," Basil pronounced. "That takes care of our sniper."

"Don't be too sure," Deal said.

"We've got to move," Rhodes said. "No telling how many there are."

"Those fucking Turks," Basil growled.

"Turks?" Deal asked.

"Follow me," Rhodes called. He was already scrambling back around the desk. "Lend a hand, Basil."

The big man followed after his boss, leaving Deal and Kaia to scramble in their wake.

"Watch the glass," Deal said.

"If that's the worst thing that happens . . ." she muttered, scooting past him.

Deal found himself nodding, though he knew she couldn't see him.

He heard a grunt from around the big desk, the sound of stone grinding on stone, the creak of unoiled hinges. There was a deep *thunk* as something fell back, and Deal felt a gust of dank air sweep over him.

By the time he made it around the desk, scattering glass shards heedlessly with his palms, he'd understood. Basil crouched above the port that had opened in the library floor, his fingers curled under the heavy lid. Rhodes had already disappeared into the passage, and Basil was assisting Kaia as she backed down the dark steps.

"Get a move on," Basil said to Deal. Something heavy was battering at the front door of the house now. Shrieks of wood, more shattering glass.

Deal struggled over the upturned lid and ducked through the passage where Kaia had disappeared just as the front door gave way with a crash. He found himself staggering backward down a narrow, rough-hewn stairwell, moving by touch alone, clawing at the sides of the passage to keep from pitching over. He heard the passageway door slam closed above him, and suddenly the clamor from the front of the house was silent, just the sound of a bolt sliding home, followed by the scuffing sounds of Basil's footsteps above him and the harsh rasping of the big man's breath.

"Keep moving," Basil called. "I don't want to trip over your ass."

"Just take it easy," Deal said.

"Here!" He heard Kaia's voice out of the darkness in front of him, felt her hand at his chest take a fistful of shirt.

He was at the bottom of the steps, he realized, and felt her pulling him along down a gently sloping passageway. He stumbled momentarily, threw up his hands, felt warm flesh beneath her flapping pajamas.

"Richard's gone ahead," she told him as he steadied himself. "The passage leads to the docks. Hurry now."

She was off then, and Deal followed wordlessly, his fingers tracing the damp contours of the passage to keep himself from falling, urged on by the steady panting of Basil at his back. Though the flow of air had lessened, there was still a steady breeze that suggested Kaia was right.

The passage was cut through the same soft coral as that underlying the Terrell estate, he realized, as fragments fell away beneath his touch, and sandy grime drifted down into his hair.

Billions and billions of sea creatures had laid down their lives to save his: that's what Deal found himself thinking as he scurried along. Running for his life, and musing on the wonders of oolite.

"Careful." He heard Kaia from up ahead, felt her hand at his shoulder. "We're near the entrance, now."

"Let me past," Basil said quietly. "I'm the one with a gun."

Deal was in no position to argue. He stepped aside, pressing his back against the rough wall of the passageway as Basil pushed his way on by.

Deal's eyes had adjusted to near cave-fish level by now. He saw Kaia beside him, her pajamas reknotted firmly, and beyond her the vague glow that filtered in through the opening to the passage, a cleft in the rock shrouded by hanging ferns and tendrils of underbrush.

Rhodes stood just inside the mouth of the passage, where the shadows kept him hidden. Deal crept quietly up to join him along with Basil, Kaia just behind. Rhodes turned, his eyes widening as if to question the quality of the silence outside: the slightest lapping of waves at the reef-protected shore, the rustle of the breeze through the fronds, the distant pulse of tree frogs and insects from the land above.

"Could be they're all up at the house," Basil said quietly.

Rhodes nodded. "Only one way to find out," he said, edging toward the entrance to the passage.

"Is that our only weapon?" Deal asked, nodding at the automatic pistol that Basil had slung by a strap at his shoulder.

Rhodes turned his hand over without comment, displaying a small-caliber pistol in his palm. Deal nodded. He was left with his hands, then, and he supposed there was some appropriateness in that. He'd made a life using his hands. Might as well try and save it with them.

Basil had his pistol ready as he pushed quietly through the fronds. He hesitated, surveying the shoreline near the dock, then finally motioned to Rhodes. "Nobody on the dock," he said. "Not that I can see, anyway."

"We'll try to make it to the boat," Rhodes said to Deal and Kaia. "If there's shooting, take cover here."

Deal nodded, sticking close on Rhodes's steps as they moved out over the rocky shore. He turned to offer a hand to Kaia, but she was moving nimbly, even though her feet were bare.

Basil moved quickly across the rocky shingle of beach to a set of steps carved into the incline leading to the dark finger of dock. He glanced out over the deserted planks to his left, then back in the other direction, toward the house.

Deal heard the thudding of footsteps across the darkened swath of lawn then, and saw the big man tense, raising his weapon to fire. "Get down," Deal whispered, spinning toward Kaia. She dropped into a crouch near the embankment.

Rhodes came up toward the embankment with his pistol braced, flanking Basil by a dozen yards or so. Deal stared out into the darkness, wondering what he was supposed to do. Throw a few rocks? Call out assurances to the men with the guns?

As it turned out, he was able to manage something. The fact that he hadn't moved for cover yet gave him an angle on the man running toward them that the others didn't have. "Don't shoot," he cried as he saw who it was.

Rhodes glanced back at him in puzzlement, but Basil never wavered. He had his weapon homed in on the direction of the sounds, ready to fire.

"It's your brother," Deal called, lunging for Basil's arm. "It's Frank."

Basil jerked his arm away from Deal's grasp. "You better hope it is," he growled.

Another moment or two and the familiar silhouette was outlined against the starlit sky, clear enough for Basil's reassurance. "Well, god-damn," he said. He glanced at Deal, then stood up to call, "It's us, little brother!"

Frank went sprawling for cover, his gun hand braced in reflex.

"Cut the shit," Basil called again.

"Sonofabitch," Frank said, scrambling to his knees.

They were all up the embankment then, joining him at the place where the dock spliced onto land.

"I thought I was history—" Frank began.

"You still could be," Basil observed.

"What's going on up there?" Rhodes cut in.

Frank shook his head. "They're tearing through the house. I'm not sure how many, six or eight of them. I saw a couple lying by the front door."

"Babescu's men?" Rhodes asked.

Frank nodded. "There's a boat put in by the caretaker's place, the next cove around. Thirty-footer maybe, like one of those cutters the Bahamian cops use. Can't be that many left, whoever they are."

"You got the one with the rifle, that was shooting into the house?" Basil asked.

Frank nodded. "Sonofabitch sitting in a tree," he said. "Shot him right up his ass."

Basil grunted something that sounded like approval. Rhodes's attention was still on the distant house. "They'll be down here soon enough," he said. "As soon as they realize we're gone."

Basil looked at his boss. "You want to wait, see if we can take them?"

Frank shook his head. "We're a little short on firepower."

Rhodes glanced at Kaia, then back at Basil. "We have the faster boat, don't we?"

"They got a Bahamian police cutter?" Basil shrugged. "If we can beat them to the open water, we ought to be all right."

"Then we're out of here," Rhodes said. And in the next moment they were all pounding down the dock.

Deal stood near the rear of the boat, listening with mixed emotions as the big engines of the Cigarette kicked into life. Plenty of power there, all right . . . but a roar like that would carry easily back to the house, no matter what was going on inside. He glanced toward the front of the cockpit of the boat, past Basil, who was working intently at the controls, to where Kaia stood at the opposite rail. Rhodes was beside her, his arm around her shoulders, saying something in her ear. Whatever it was, Deal hoped it was reassuring. He could use a bit of reassuring himself.

Frank, meantime, had untied the last of the lines and jumped down into the cockpit even as Basil was swinging them away from the dock. "You trying to leave me, big brother?" Frank called as he hit the deck and rolled.

"You want to hang around till you see the whites of their eyes?" Basil gunned the engines then, making conversation all but impossible as they hurtled down a moonlit channel marked by stone breakwaters on either side.

Less than a hundred yards out, the breakwaters fell away behind them, and Basil cut the engines abruptly. "What's wrong?" Kaia called from her place at the rail They were still making headway, but compared to that initial burst of speed, they might as well have been crawling.

"The reefs," Deal told her as he made his way forward. "We'll have to pick our way out to deep water from here." He didn't know how far it was, nor how tricky this particular set of shallows might be, but the grim possibilities were many: they could shear off their props on a rocky outcrop, run aground on a sandbar where they'd be sitting ducks, or simply tear out the bottom of the boat and sink.

Over the rumbling near-idle of the Cigarette, came a distant echo of other engines, these of a slightly higher pitch.

"Fucking Turks," Basil muttered, glancing over his shoulder.

"We can't use the spotlight to check the reefs," Rhodes said. "They'll home right in on us."

"You have a hand-held?" Deal asked the big man behind the wheel.

Basil glanced at him. "You're the 'red-right-returning' guy, right?"

"Come on, Basil," Deal said as the sound of the distant engines grew. "We don't have a lot of time."

Basil rummaged inside a compartment on the console and came up with a rubber-coated marine flashlight. Deal reached for it and snapped it on. Nothing you'd want to mount a search-and-rescue mission with, he thought, but it would be a hell of a lot harder to spot at a distance. In any case, it would have to do.

Deal kicked off his leather-soled shoes, then pulled himself up over the low windshield onto the glossy foredeck of the slow-moving Cigarette. He made his way out to the prow in a hurried duckwalk and flattened himself on the deck, dangling his chin over as far as he dared. When he was steadied, he snapped on the light and angled the beam down toward the water.

Directly in front of them, the water held a satisfying dark-green cast. Ditto to the left. On the right, however, the color was trending toward a silty white. He made a frantic motion with his left hand and felt Basil swing the boat around accordingly. It would work, he thought. He could get them out to deep water this way, given enough time.

But time was the very problem, wasn't it? He craned his neck and glanced back to see the running lights of the cutter as it rounded the shoulder of the cove that had separated them only moments before. The engine noise of the cutter had redoubled suddenly, and he made out the beam of a powerful searchlight sweeping the waters close to the dock. Another minute or two and they'd make the dock channel, a couple more after that and the cutter would be on their heels.

It was hopeless, he thought, glancing out toward the darkness of the open sea. They'd never make it that far without being overtaken.

"Better get back here," Basil shouted. "I'm just going to open her up, we'll have to pray we don't hit anything."

Another hopeless prospect, Deal thought. It would be like drag-racing across a mine field.

"Wait," he called back, sweeping the water frantically with his light. That underwater ridge line was still trailing along their starboard side. Here and there he caught glints of jagged outcroppings, glinting in the beam of the flashlight like giant fangs.

He switched off the light and scrambled back over the deck to the windshield. "How much water does this thing draw?"

Basil shrugged. "Couple feet maybe, a little more if the screws are all the way torqued."

"And the cutter'll draw three, three and a half?"

"I suppose. Hard to know for sure."

Deal nodded, glancing back at the prow of the Cigarette. That was the way boats of this class achieved their speed on plane: nose high up in front, tail digging down behind, till hardly anything was dragging water but the stern and the screws. "Let's get everybody out here on the prow," he said. "The weight will help keep the nose down. Even if it makes an inch of difference, it'll help. You keep us going as fast as you can without planing."

"I can do that," Basil said. "But I don't know what good it's gonna do."

He cast a glance backward. The cutter had reached the dock channel now. The scream of its suddenly revving engines cut clearly across the quarter-mile of water separating the two craft.

"They're just gonna follow us wherever we go," he added.

"That's what I'm counting on," Deal said. "Let them come. When I give you the signal, make a hard right, take us right over the reef line we've been skirting."

Basil gave him a dubious look. "You want to take us *into* the shallows?"

"And I want you to switch on the running lights, the searchlight, everything," Deal continued. "Let's make sure they see us."

"Why don't we just shoot ourselves right now and be done with it?" Basil said.

"Do as he says," Rhodes cut in. "I see where he's going with this."

"Man—" Basil said, but he wasn't used to arguing with his boss.

Deal switched his glance back to the cutter. Their pursuers had come out of the dock channel now and had throttled back slightly. "Come on, Basil. Hit the lights, let them see us. Everybody else out here with me."

As Basil flipped switches on the console illuminating the running lights, Kaia came over the windshield, followed by Rhodes and Frank. "Find a cleat and hang on," Deal called to the others.

"Put the searchlight at about two o'clock starboard," Deal called to Basil. "Get our speed up as much as you can."

"I hope you know what you're doing," Basil called, but he snapped on the powerful beam. In the next moment, Deal felt the Cigarette's engines surge, and they were moving rapidly forward.

He heard the answering roar of the cutter's engine and saw the beam of their pursuers' searchlight sweep over them. There was a rattle of automatic gunfire in the distance, and Deal knew that it was only a matter of time until the bullets found their mark.

"Can you go any faster?" he called to Basil.

"It's your funeral," Basil called, notching the throttle higher.

The cutter was closing in now, its engines stoked flat-out, no need for caution with the Cigarette showing the way, lit up like a careening birthday cake. There was another burst of fire, and the windshield of the Cigarette exploded in fragments. Deal saw men rushing to the forward rail of the cutter, bracing automatic weapons as they ran.

"Now," he cried to Basil. "Hard to the right. Everybody hang on!"

Basil swung the wheel and the Cigarette cut toward the milky line of the reef. Deal felt his weight shift toward the port side behind him, but he held fast to one of the cleats anchored in the foredeck, ignoring the pain as the metal points dug into his hand.

"I'm falling," Kaia cried, grasping wildly for Rhodes's hand as she slid backward over the smooth fiberglass surface.

Deal reached out with his free hand and caught a fistful of her pajamas. Even as he steadied her, there came an ominous grinding sound beneath them, the sound of the Cigarette's hull scraping one of those treacherous outcroppings.

The cutter was looming ever closer: now seventy-five yards . . . now fifty . . .

Another burst of gunfire ripped a line of fiberglass a foot from Deal's shoulder.

"He's going to ram us," Basil called. He drew his pistol from his belt and squeezed off several rounds toward the looming cutter. One of the gunmen went down, but the others fired undeterred.

The pilot *was* willing to ram them, Deal saw. Would send his much heavier boat right through the middle of theirs if he could, blast them to smithereens . . .

. . . forty yards, thirty—a steady rattle of gunfire from the prow of the cutter now. Maybe Basil *was* right, it was his funeral, and theirs as well . . .

. . . Basil and Frank both emptying their weapons at the speeding boat behind them . . .

. . . and suddenly there was a terrible, rending crash that sent the gunmen at the prow of the cutter sprawling, the bottom of the cutter torn open on the reef, twisting crazily on its side, teetering, ready to flip . . .

. . . when the explosion came, a blast that obliterated the cutter in a boiling ball of flame, sending shards of ruined boat and God knows what raining down upon the Cigarette.

"Cut the engines," Deal cried to Basil then, and that is what the big man did.

thirty-four

Strange how nearly being pulverized into shark food could alter your sense of loyalties, Deal thought, as the Cigarette cleared the last of the reefs and Basil shoved forward on the throttles of the powerful twin engines. The boat rose up almost immediately in the water like a big cat that had taken notice of something interesting on the gloomy horizon. There was a moment's hesitation, then the craft began to hurtle across the waters at a breathless speed.

So much for the difficulty with the screws, Deal thought. And so much for all the troublesome nighttime navigation. And wasn't he glad that it had been just so much bullshit.

He glanced back toward the island they'd left, now little more than a low and ragged silhouette ranged against the moonless sky. A glow had sprung up in the middle of the cay, however, a glow that grew even faster than the Cigarette's ability to carry them away. At first, Deal wasn't sure where the light was coming from, but eventually he understood.

"The bastards," Kaia Jesperson said beside him. She'd come up from the cabin of the Cigarette, her pajamas traded for a T-shirt and shorts she'd found below, her feet in a pair of Top-Siders that seemed a size or two too big. Someone else might have looked faintly absurd, he thought, studying her in the glow from the running lights.

"They've torched it," Deal said, joining her backward gaze. He thought of ancient books curling up, centuries-old furniture flaming into cinders, photos and paintings and vats of smuggler's hooch, all of it transforming into featureless atoms that would drift back down to the sea as soot.

He glanced at Rhodes, who stood at the opposite corner of the open deck, bracing himself against the pounding of the wave tops, his gaze steadfast on the darkness that lay ahead. *Not a thing out that way to see,* Deal thought. And supposed that was the very point.

"All he wanted was a life," Kaia said, shaking her head sadly.

Deal glanced at her. They could virtually shout a conversation here and have none of it be audible a few feet away. The throb of the engines, the roar of wind and spray—what she'd just said had already been flung halfway back to Quicksilver Cay.

"You think it's that easy, just dial the clock back, ask for 'do-overs'?"

She looked up. "That's how you see it, Mr. Deal? Things are cast in stone, just grin and bear it?"

Deal hesitated. What was he supposed to say—you don't like the way things are going in life, just press a button, change the channel? "I believe in consequences," he told her. "You do certain things, they never go away."

"And you?" she asked. "You've got nothing to live down? Nothing you'd want to take back?"

He stared at her for a moment. "I didn't say that."

She was watching him carefully. "Things you've done that wake you up at night, you wish they were only dreams?"

Her standard deadpan stare came with it, but there was something in her eyes, he thought. "You sound like the expert," he said.

She gave him a humorless smile. "Oh, I'm expert, all right," she said. Her gaze held his for another moment. And then she went to join Rhodes at the front of the cockpit.

"You've got that key?" It was Rhodes's voice at his shoulder.

Deal had been at the back of the boat, staring out into the gray mist that had rolled into the cove where they'd anchored. The sound of the dinghy motor was nearly lost already, Frank on his way to shore to fetch a car and make whatever other arrangements Rhodes deemed necessary, Deal supposed.

Basil leaned against the control panel, his arms folded, idly watching the two of them through the predawn haze. "Maybe I lost it," Deal said, staring back at Rhodes. "Or maybe I threw it overboard."

Rhodes gave him a tolerant smile. "I'd like it back, if you don't mind."

Deal heard the whine of the electric pump as the toilet flushed below. "Excuse me," he said to Rhodes. He turned away, unzipped, relieved himself over the transom. When he'd finished, he turned back to Rhodes, zipping up. "You took that key from me in the first place. What do you mean, you want it back?"

Rhodes stared at him, puzzled. "I don't know what you're talking about."

"For chrissakes," Deal said, thrusting his hand into his pocket. "*This* is what I'm talking about—" He stopped then, feeling the expression freeze on his face. He brought out his hand, opened it.

Both of them stared down: two very similar keys lay in the palm of Deal's hand. The one he'd retrieved from his father's stash, the other that Rhodes had tossed at him just as the shooting broke out the night before, or so it seemed. Deal cupped his palm and jiggled it so that the two keys fell together with a tiny clink. Point to point, ridge to ridge, valley to chiseled valley. A perfect match.

Deal looked up into Rhodes's eyes. Rhodes looked back, with equal surprise.

"You want to tell me what this goes to?" Deal asked, handing over one of the keys.

"Only if you'll tell me where it is," said Rhodes.

Deal stared back, still speechless. Finally, Rhodes began to explain.

thirty-five

IT WAS WELL AFTER midnight when Barton Deal heard the familiar rumble of boat engines from somewhere out on Biscayne Bay. Duke, the old chocolate lab who lay on the dock at his side, picked his head up and stared out intently into the brine-laden darkness. For the hour or more they'd been waiting, the dog had steadfastly ignored any number of signals that might have set a hunting animal on point: the nocturnal splashings of mullet and shallows feeders working the pilings beneath them, the rustlings of invisible raccoon and possum prowling shoreside behind them, the almost inaudible wheelings and swoops of owls in the dark air above. There'd been one sharp cry as a wood rat was taken aloft in a set of unseen talons from somewhere close by, but the dog had taken his cue from his master. Nothing was really important except for the matter that had brought them out here tonight.

"That's her," Barton Deal said. He rubbed absently at the nearly healed wound in his shoulder, then bent to give the dog a reassuring pat as he pushed himself out of the webbed lawn chair. "That's *Miss Priss,* all right."

He glanced back at the big stone-and-wood house behind him, its peaked roof and jutting gables vaguely backlit by the glow of the mile-distant Miami lights, but he needn't have bothered. It was only the two of them on the property this weekend. His wife and young son were off on a "gallivant," as Barton Deal liked to call her forays around the state of Florida.

The two of them had set out on Friday in the Chrysler he'd just bought, headed up to Cypress Gardens to watch the water-ski show, where a whole pyramid of young men and women had apparently learned to whiz across the surface of a lake as one. Barton Deal knew his wife liked water-ski shows, and though he wasn't so sure about young Johnny-boy, he was sure they'd have a grand time together. The two of them always did. If nothing else, she'd spoil the boy to death.

The boat's engines were growing louder, their character unmistakable. He could identify that sound as surely as he might come awake in the middle of the night and know the character of the woman breathing at his side. His life had depended on both, after all, and on more than one occasion. The dog was up, too, extending one of its back legs and then the next, in a quivering, anticipatory stretch.

"Just take it easy," Barton Deal said. "There's nothing in this for you."

The dog glanced up as if it understood.

Though the boat's running lights had likely been burning when she was further out toward the shipping lanes, they were extinguished now, and Deal knew she was being brought in through the shallows by feel. If he'd had any less confidence in the men who'd taken her, he might have worried. In this case, he'd given over his trust long ago.

He saw the boat's hooded searchlight snap on momentarily, pulsing their prearranged code. Barton Deal brought up the heavy-duty flashlight he had clipped to his belt and punched out the answer. They might have used radio to go back and forth, but it was safer this way.

He heard a whine from deep in the dog's throat and heard the click of his nails as he danced on the concrete. "Simmer down," Deal told the dog, and the sounds subsided. Deal turned and folded up the lawn chair, leaning it against a piling.

By the time he could make out the boat's shadow drifting up out of the darkness, the engines had died away. The *Miss Miami Priss,* a forty-five-foot Bayliner with a flying bridge and a broad rear deck, was moving free now, sliding sideways toward the dock, her rails low in the water. He put out a foot as the bow closed to the pier and felt—or presumed that he felt—the great weight of the cargo she was carrying.

The shadow of a man had hopped from the stern to the dock, moving like an inky cartoon silhouette to tie off a line back there, while another—

a bulky man with Oriental features—came up from the darkness like gathering mist to hand the bow rope to Barton Deal.

"Any trouble?" Deal said to the man who'd handed him the line.

"Nothing we weren't prepared for, Barton," said a third man, who held back from the others, standing by the shrouded crate that dominated the deck behind the cockpit. He was tall and thin and stood with nonchalance, as if he just happened to find himself on board, as if none of this were out of the ordinary at all.

"That's good," Barton Deal said.

"Everything all right on your end?" the man said as he took Barton Deal's hand and stepped up onto the dock. He moved easily, athletically, and Deal knew his friend hadn't needed the boost. He'd only taken the hand because it had been offered. That was the kind of man he was.

"How's the arm?"

Deal glanced at his shoulder and nodded his head. His arm was fine.

The dog came up between them, his tail erect, his legs moving stiff as a jackbooted soldier's. "He's a friend, Duke," said Barton Deal, and the dog danced a grudging step back.

"Your winch up to the task?" Barton Deal's friend said, glancing up at the davit arms that arced out over the dockside like miniature cranes.

"Those davits can raise anything she can carry," Barton Deal said.

His elegant friend nodded and gestured to the two men he'd brought. The pair moved quickly to release the davit lines and fasten them under the shrouded cargo.

"What did you bring to move it inside with?" his friend asked as the men did their work. "A forklift?"

"Didn't think we'd need the noise," Barton Deal said. He gestured toward the end of the dock, where a kind of pallet truck was parked, a device with a vague resemblance to the carts that grocers use to move crates of produce from loading docks inside for stocking. Only this particular pallet truck was three or four times the normal size, with big balloon tires and heavy flooring—a hand truck big enough to haul the *Miss Miami Priss* herself, or so it seemed.

"The things you know about, Barton," said his friend, as if such knowledge mattered. "What do you use *that* for?"

Barton Deal shrugged. "Last time it was the air-cooling unit for an office building, where we couldn't get a big enough Hyster in." He gestured at the shrouded cargo on the back of the boat beside them. The two men had secured the lines. While one had climbed back on the dock, the other stood at the davit winch to steady the load, awaiting his orders. "But air conditioning's not what you've got there, is it?"

His friend gave a little smile by way of answer.

"Well, come on now, bring it up," Barton Deal said. "I'd like to get some sleep tonight."

His friend nodded, then turned to gesture to the man by the winch. The man bent his broad back to the task and began to crank. At first, the buoyancy of *Miss Priss* gave aid to the process, but finally the heavy pallet had lifted from her decks. The davits groaned with the load but—true to Barton Deal's word—held fast. A few minutes more and the cargo had been eased atop the big hand cart. In moments, the two men were on their way up the gently inclined path toward the house, one towing, the other pushing from behind.

It cost them a half hour of sweaty maneuvering and a healthy gouge along one of the stairwell walls, but with Barton Deal working the brake on the hand cart, and with the aid of the two strong backs his friend had brought along, the load had finally been guided down the hastily built ramp and into the cellar. Barton Deal had knocked the ramp together out of two-by-eights taken from the site of a Burdine's warehouse his firm was building in a new industrial park out by the airport, and the muscles in his forearm still ached from the unaccustomed work. It had been a few years since he'd done much carpentry himself.

"You don't see many basements in South Florida," Barton Deal said. He was standing with his friend, watching as the two helpers levered their load into the recess he'd prepared along one of the coral-rock walls. "Water table's too high most places."

"You don't see many of those, either," his friend said pointing at the object that his men had deposited.

Deal nodded. The cellar was dimly illuminated by one bare lightbulb that dangled from the cobwebbed rafters. The dog sat at their heels on the damp floor, still whining occasionally, as if the presence of the massive strongbox disturbed him. It was black, trimmed in gold leaf, the height of a refrigerator and nearly twice as wide, a seam down its middle with matching brass handles on either side. Along both sides of the box were ragged metal edges, bubbled and discolored where a welder's torch had recently worked.

"I thought we'd never get the bastard cut out."

Deal glanced up. It wasn't like his friend to curse. *But under the circumstances,* he thought . . . under the circumstances, it might be understood. The two helpers were hoisting the heavy shelving that would hide the recess and its contents back into place now.

After he'd finished with the ramp, Barton Deal had spent his afternoon rigging the shelves so they would swivel out and back, a false wall of a kind, like something you'd see in a boy's adventure film, though he suspected all the trouble wasn't really necessary. His wife, deathly frightened by anything that crept, crawled, or slithered, hadn't set foot in the cellar the entire time they'd lived in the house. And his nine-year-old son showed no proclivity for cavelike places either, spending every spare moment piloting his little Jon boat about the sparkling bay.

He'd managed to surround himself with some people of laudable instinct, Barton Deal told himself as the shelves he'd fashioned fell into place. He snapped off the cellar light and followed the others up the ramp. At least there was that much to be proud of.

"I'll be in touch soon," his friend said. They were back at dockside now, the engines of the *Priss* burbling. The dog lay on the dock where it had kept vigil earlier, its broad head sunk on its paws as if all matters important had been concluded.

Barton Deal nodded and reached out his hand. He saw the glint of silver, felt something strike his palm. He put the key into his pocket without looking at it.

"You want to tell me what *that* is?" Barton Deal asked, pointing at the dark bundle that remained on the deck of the *Priss.* It might have been baggage, or wrapped-up welder's equipment, but Barton Deal knew it wasn't. He'd noticed the bundle after the strongbox had been raised, had been thinking about it all the while.

His friend hesitated. "Perhaps it's better that you don't know," he said.

Barton Deal thought about it. "That's my boat," he said.

His friend nodded. "He was *my* man."

As if it explained everything, Barton Deal thought.

"He meant to kill us all, take everything for himself," his friend continued. "If it hadn't been for Julian . . ." He gestured toward the impassive Oriental man at the wheel. "It ends here, Barton," his friend said. "Don't worry."

"I'm not worried," Barton Deal said. *Though there might have been a time,* he thought. Back when the town he'd grown up in was a sleepy outpost on the edge of the continent and crime consisted of stealing grapefruit off a neighbor's tree, or selling the same underwater lot to idiot Northerners half a dozen times in a day. How complex his life had since become, he thought.

He felt the weight of the key in his pocket. "How much is in there, anyway?"

His friend shrugged as if it hardly mattered. "Everything I have." He gave Deal a look. "There's plenty there for both of us, you know."

Deal nodded. "Your money's safe, here," he said. "As long as you need me to keep it."

"A week or two, just until I'm settled in the islands, until I'm sure everything's going to be safe," his friend said.

"How about your son?" Barton Deal asked.

"He'll be safe in boarding school," Rhodes said. "I've seen to it." The man reached into his pocket and handed Deal an envelope.

"What's this?"

"Keep it handy," Rhodes said. "Just in case something should happen."

Barton Deal stared at the envelope, then tucked it into his back pocket. There was a pause and then the two moved to share a brief embrace.

"We'll see your boat gets back," his friend said as they stepped apart.

"I know you will," Barton Deal said.

His friend raised his hand to say goodbye. Barton Deal did the same. Then the man stepped easily aboard the boat and was gone.

thirty-six

Off the Miami Coastline
The Present Day

"THERE IS MUCH I may never know, but one thing is certain," Rhodes said to Deal as he wound down his tale. "My father never got the chance to come back for his money." He held his key up in the gray morning light. "My guess is that what's left is resting in a deposit box somewhere. And though I have a key, it won't do me any good. I'm wagering your father's name is on that box and that you're the only one who can get it open now."

John Deal was shaking his head as Rhodes finished the story. All pieced together from a few facts, some scraps of memory, and a whole lot of conjecture, or so Deal was telling himself. The two of them stood side by side at the rear of the boat, staring out into the dissipating mists. After a moment, he turned to the man beside him.

"What you're telling me, my old man took *care* of you."

Rhodes shrugged. "I don't think he thought of it that way. I never saw him, not once. The money changed hands several times before it reached me. My father set it up that way, to keep me safe."

"Why wouldn't he have put everything in a bank account somewhere, or tell my old man to do it that way? The money could have gone out automatically."

"And bring the IRS baying like hounds? The kind of business my father conducted involved great quantities of cash and a limited amount of bookkeeping, Mr. Deal. If he had lived longer, he might have developed a more creative accounting procedure."

Deal thought about it. "Yeah, you seem to have gotten pretty good at that."

"I don't see the purpose of insult," Rhodes replied mildly.

Deal looked away, still shaking his head. "So the way it turns out, I'm hitching rides to school back then, carrying hod on construction sites because my old man thinks it'll be good for me, and you're tooling around in sports cars—"

"Your father was simply fulfilling an obligation. He had no way of knowing how the money was spent—"

"Jesus Christ, Rhodes," Deal said, whirling back on him. "Don't you get it? It's like I had some brother, some evil twin the family never told me about. He screwed up, they gave him cashmere coats and sent him to Europe, I got to stay home and work in the shop."

"Your father never even knew the name I was using," Rhodes said. "He simply did what he'd promised to do. All those years."

Deal released a breath then, one it seemed he'd been holding for most of his life. He'd spent the best part of the last decade trying to rebuild what his old man had pissed away, trying to live down a legacy of shame that rose as high in his mind as the downtown bank towers he might have taken pride in, and now he was to supposed to accept a conman as a virtual brother?

"My old man died broke," he said, at last. "My guess is that if there was cash anywhere at hand, he'd have spent it. Yours or anybody else's."

"That may be so," Rhodes replied. "But those payments reached me just like clockwork, every quarter on the quarter, year after year after year. As nearly as I've been able to discover, they stopped precisely when he died."

Deal stared at him for a moment. "Everything else aside, Rhodes, aren't you a little old to be chasing after a trust fund?"

Rhodes dropped his gaze for a moment. "I'll grant you that, Mr. Deal. I will indeed." In the next moment, he was staring brightly at Deal again, apparently recovered. "But it's *my* money we're talking about, isn't it?"

Deal laughed, but there wasn't any humor in it. "What makes you think I haven't spent it?"

Rhodes gave him a rueful look. "I thought about that possibility, of course, but as I said before, I've had a good long look at your balance sheets. If you've made anything to speak of these past few years, I'd like to know where you've put it."

Deal felt heat rising at the back of his neck. He heard footsteps on the deck behind him and saw that Kaia Jesperson had come to join them on deck. She'd tied her hair back in a knot, had scrubbed the makeup from her face. You might take her for a teenager if you didn't know better, he thought.

"Let's say you're right, Rhodes. Let's say there's a pot of money resting behind a door these keys will open. Even so. What makes you think I'd be willing to help you find it?"

Rhodes stared back as if the question were outlandish. "Because, Mr. Deal"—he glanced at Kaia, then back again, something like a smile on his face—"*you* are an honest man."

thirty-seven

"Not a bad life you lead down here," Russell Straight said to Driscoll. Straight had his gaze on the retreating backside of their waitress, an image that reminded the world why Spandex shorts had been invented.

They'd pulled over for coffee at an outdoor café in Coconut Grove, the place just coming to life as the sun struggled up behind a thick morning fog and a screen of banyan trees on the far side of the street. There was a crowd of birds hidden somewhere in all the foliage, screeching loud enough to make Russell raise his voice.

Driscoll could smell salt and seaweed on the desultory breeze that filtered toward them through the thick, tendril-trailing trees. Biscayne Bay was just a couple hundred yards from where they sat—there would be people already out on its glassy surface, frolicking on sailboats and sailboards, others in motor-driven stinkpots headed for the distant reefs and mangrove shallows to fish and dive. Straight was right, he supposed: There were just a whole panoply of pleasures having to do with sun and water and balmy temperatures around here, including the sight of a well-built young woman in tight shorts.

"Beats the shit out of Wheeling . . ." Driscoll said, shifting his bulk uneasily in the canvas director's chair they used at the curbside tables, "most of the time." He would have been more comfortable indoors, hunkered on a solidly anchored stool in front of a counter, kitchen odors and burping coffee makers and the clanking of pans instead of all this pleasantness, but there was a maintenance crew cleaning and waxing the floors inside. Paradise it would have to be, then, though the surroundings seemed incongruous with the mission at hand.

"So what's next?" Russell Straight asked, staring at him across his steaming coffee cup.

"I'm thinking," Driscoll said, though he hadn't been thinking at all, not the way Straight would take it, anyway. They'd spent a fruitless night searching for Deal, had caught a few hours' sleep in the car, waiting outside the DealCo offices off Old Cutler. "I can drop you off anytime, you know."

Straight shook his head. "Long as you're on the case, then count me in."

"Up to you," Driscoll said, giving his all-purpose shrug. "We can go back by Janice's condo, try to find someone who saw something."

He didn't think there was much point in it, of course. Janice's porch opened out directly into the thickly landscaped grounds. A person could hop over the rail and in a few short steps reach the canal that led out to open water. You could tie off a boat and load—or unload—just about anything, carry it in or out of one of the apartments without ever being seen by a soul. It was one of the reasons why a certain brand of tenant liked living on the property, Driscoll understood. There was probably as much drug traffic flowing through secluded dockside condos like these as there was through the Port of Miami.

The neighbors he'd talked to last night—who gave the distinct appearance of having smoked a couple of bales themselves—had neither heard nor seen anything, at least nothing corresponding even vaguely to events in the real world. Driscoll had no reason to think he'd have any more luck today.

The waitress was back now, setting down a plate in front of Straight that bore three eggs, a slice of ham, some bacon strips, a short stack of pancakes, and a pie-shaped chunk of shredded hash-browns. "You want a side of beef with that?" Driscoll asked. He'd been feeling guilty about asking for cream cheese along with his bagel.

Straight glanced at him. "I got a certain metabolism," he said.

Driscoll nodded. "So does a rhinoceros."

"You need to exercise more," Russell said, pouring syrup over all the items on his plate.

"You got me there," Driscoll said. He scooped all of the cream cheese out of its little dish, smashed it on a single half of his bagel. He'd see how that went. He could always ask for more.

He nibbled at his bagel, watching Straight down an egg in a bite, chase it with half of a pancake. Straight swallowed, then paused, his fork held over the plate. "I got something on my face?"

Driscoll shook his head.

"Chewing with my mouth open?"

Driscoll shook his head again.

"Then what are you staring at?"

Driscoll gave him a shrug. "I was just wondering what makes you tick."

Straight shook his head. "You gonna keep on with that suspicious cop stuff till you die, drop right in the harness. Like that old fart we went to see at the bank yesterday."

Driscoll glanced up at him. "Who's we?"

"Deal and me."

Driscoll thought about it. He'd always found it useful to ponder any information that came as a surprise. "You went to the bank with Deal? For what?"

"Don't go getting any ideas," Straight said.

"What kind of ideas should I get?" Driscoll pushed his bagel aside with the back of his hand. The squawking in the trees had ratcheted up a notch, it seemed. The way it used to get at his in-laws' house, Marie and all her aunts and cousins crammed into the same kitchen, everybody talking at once, the noise would drive you clean out of the house.

"Like he withdrew a bunch of money, somebody would want to take it from him."

Driscoll folded his hands patiently in front of him. "No, Russell. If you took a bunch of money from Deal, I don't think you'd still be hanging around. But why don't you tell me what happened at the bank?"

"He went down to find out about this key he found," Straight said. "A safety-deposit key, he said."

Driscoll nodded. "And which bank was this?"

Straight shrugged. "It doesn't matter. The guy said it wasn't from their bank."

"This is the old guy you mentioned earlier?"

"You do it just like a cop," Straight said. "Come up with a question for every answer."

"I know, Russell," Driscoll said patiently. "The old guy—a bank officer, I'm guessing—he looked at this key and said it didn't come from his bank."

"He wasn't even supposed to say that much," Straight said. "The woman who went and got him was pissed off he gave any information away—"

Driscoll held up his hand as if he were halting traffic. "Let's drop back here. Why was Deal so interested in this key to begin with?"

Straight shrugged. "I think it had something to do with his old man."

"And why would you think that?"

"Because he found it in an envelope, a bunch of stuff that belonged to his old man, hidden away in some of the office files."

Driscoll reached to pinch the bridge of his nose with his fingers. "Let me make sure I'm following, Russell. Deal found an envelope that his father had put somewhere, and inside it was this key?"

"Yeah," Russell Straight said.

"And where did this happen, exactly?"

"I already said. Back at the DealCo office."

"And where is this envelope?"

Russell Straight shrugged. "I don't know. Maybe he put it back in the files. All he had when we went to the bank was that key."

"Well," Driscoll said. "I think we have solved the problem of what to do next." He was already pushing himself up from the table, looking around for their waitress.

"Hey," Russell Straight was saying, piece of toast halfway to his mouth. "I'm not finished."

But Driscoll was already moving toward his car.

thirty-eight

"I THOUGHT WE WERE going to the bank," Russell said. He was staring suspiciously across the climbing elevator car at Driscoll.

"We most definitely are," Driscoll said, holding his arm up to show his wristwatch, "but the bank isn't open yet."

"We could have finished breakfast, then."

"I miscalculated," Driscoll said. "If it makes you feel better, I'll buy you a big lunch." He was watching the numbers jump across the elevator panel. The higher the floor, the more important the office, in this building, anyway.

"But what are we doing *here*?"

Driscoll glanced at him. "You worried I'm going to turn you in or something? Relax, Russell. You're not a federal case. Yet."

Russell nodded, but he wasn't agreeing with anything. "That's another thing about a cop," he said.

"Tell me."

"Thinking things are funny when they're not. A crack like that is a form of abuse, it really is. Psychological. A kind of police brutality."

"You should go to college, Russell. A mind is a terrible thing to waste."

"I graduated from college," Russell said. "Me and Leon both. Hard-Knocks College. Knocksville, U.S.A."

Driscoll nodded soberly. "You're not as funny as I am," he noted. The elevator doors were sliding open now, and he moved out. He didn't care if Russell Straight followed him or not, but he sensed the man's footsteps in his wake.

They were high enough up in the building that the linoleum in the hallways had turned to carpeting, and no indoor-outdoor crap with a pattern meant to disguise coffee stains, either. This was carpet that cushioned your steps, the kind meant to remind you—if you were to tread upon it every day—that you were somebody now. And the walls themselves were different, as well. Instead of gray-green finished concrete, there was wooden paneling halfway up, then some tasteful dark-blue linen wallpaper the rest of the way to the stuccoed ceiling. Every half-dozen steps there was a brass sconce set that threw the light out in a golden glob, just so.

Thank God it wasn't his ex-wife trailing along with him, Driscoll thought. He'd have to hear about a remodeling plan for his apartment the next several years of his life.

Driscoll passed three doors that didn't interest him, found the one he was looking for at the end of the hall: "United States Attorney" was the legend formed in raised brass letters, "Chief of the Criminal Division" in slightly smaller letters, just below.

They'd been screened and had picked up visitor's tags in the lobby below—but he still had to announce himself through an intercom mounted in the wall. There was a camera mounted somewhere as well, he knew, though he didn't spend any time looking for it. When the buzzer sounded, he turned the knob and Russell Straight followed him into the office.

A spacious anteroom with comfortable chairs and an array of magazines, and an opaque window with sliding panels set high up on the opposite wall. Just like an upscale doctor's office, Driscoll thought, though in these quarters, you couldn't take a pill for what ailed you. He was on his way to rap on the glass when a door beside it swung open.

"Mr. Driscoll?" the male receptionist asked. "Come this way."

As Driscoll started forward, the receptionist planted himself in Russell Straight's path. Driscoll hesitated, then stopped, annoyed by the officious prick's manner. "He's my assistant," he said, the words more or less a surprise to his own ears.

The receptionist stopped. "You'll have to wait," he said. He turned and went back into the inner chambers, leaving them in the anteroom.

"Assistant, huh?" Russell said as the door clicked shut. "What's the pay?"

Driscoll didn't smile. "How's jack-shit sound?"

"About what I'd expect," Russell said mildly.

In a few moments, the door opened again and the young guy reappeared, a look of true annoyance on his face. "Follow me," he said grudgingly. Which they did.

"Nice view," Driscoll said, gazing down through the still-gauzy sky at the vast sprawl that was Miami: an endless grid of streets and low-slung buildings, stitched through by drainage canals and dotted here and there by shallow lakes that had once been quarries. Where they got the rocks to build all the buildings and pave the roads, he thought. Fill the holes with water, and an ugly thing gets pretty, how it all works out. In the distance was the bay, with all those sailboats and other conveyances he'd been imagining earlier, all the tiny pleasure craft etching wake lines across the mirrored image of the sky. Nothing to do out there but have fun.

"I'm glad you like it," the man behind the desk said. He didn't bother to look out himself. His expression suggested that scenery bored him.

"Sit up here, keep an eye on the whole damned town," Driscoll said. "Something goes wrong, you can just push a button, have it taken care of."

The man glanced at an appointment book that lay open by his telephone. "I'm talking to you as a favor," the guy said. "I don't have a lot of time."

Driscoll nodded. The guy wore a good suit, had a neat haircut. Trim, with a handball player's build, a touch of steel at the temples. Bucking for a kick upstairs, all the way to Washington, Driscoll supposed. He had the proper look about him, anyway. The nameplate on his desk said his name was Scott Thomas. No one he'd ever heard of, but then he'd been out of the loop awhile.

"People probably get that wrong all the time," Driscoll said, gesturing at the nameplate.

"Excuse me?" Thomas said.

"Your name," Driscoll said. "Thomas Scott, Scott Thomas. Nobody ever called me Driscoll Vernon, that much I can tell you." Driscoll sensed Russell Straight shifting uneasily at his side. *Let him learn a few things,* Driscoll thought.

"Driscoll Vernon," the guy behind the desk said without missing a beat. "Now what did you come here for?"

"Talbot Sams," Driscoll said. "There's one for you."

Thomas stared at him without expression. "This is someone I should know?"

"I was hoping," Driscoll said.

"Then abandon hope," Thomas said.

Driscoll was unfazed. "He confronted a client of mine, identified himself as a special agent in charge of an undercover task force operating in Miami. He wanted my client's cooperation in providing information having to do with the free-trade port project."

"There is no such task force," Thomas said.

"If there was one, would you admit it to me?"

"Divulge the existence of an undercover operation? What do you think?"

Driscoll shrugged. "How about this guy Sams? Does he work for you?"

"I've never heard the name," Thomas said.

"Maybe this is an operation directed out of Washington," Driscoll said.

"If one were, I'd be aware of it," Thomas said.

"Maybe they don't want you to be aware of it."

The man gave him a tolerant smile. "There's not much I don't know about."

"I'll bet," Driscoll said. "But there's a lot of guys working for Justice down here. Maybe you could check your computer, see if one of them goes by the name of Sams."

Thomas glanced at the thin LCD monitor on the credenza behind him. There was a screen saver displayed there, an endlessly repeating three-sixty panorama of a desert landscape. "I can give you the number of someone to speak to in Washington," Thomas said. He laced his fingers together, set his hands down on the desk to indicate the matter was closed.

"Is that the 'one-eight-hundred-eat-shit' number?" Driscoll asked.

"I'm sorry I can't help you," Thomas said. He was smiling pleasantly.

"So am I," Driscoll said. "How long since you left Albuquerque, anyway?"

Thomas glanced at the screen saver. "Not bad, Driscoll. The man who asked me to see you claimed you weren't unintelligent."

"Less than a year, I'd guess," Driscoll said. "Pretty soon the nostalgia starts to fade. Before long, you'll have palm trees and flamingoes on there. Or else guys with fast boats and big guns."

"I've been here six months," Thomas told him. "It was the Phoenix office, actually."

"Phoenix, Albuquerque . . ." Driscoll said, shrugging. "All that beach, not a drop of ocean."

Thomas managed the briefest of smiles. "It has indeed been a pleasure, Mr. Driscoll—"

"So what's the big push these days, Thomas? Illegal immigration? There'd be plenty of that in Arizona. You must have bagged wetbacks by the thousands for them to bring you all the way down to South Florida."

"Trying to impress me won't do any good," Thomas said. "There's not a job opening anywhere in the division."

"Okay, Mr. Thomas, we're done," Driscoll said, placing his business card down on the desk with a snap. "But you should know that this Sams guy not only threatened my client, he assaulted me as well, and made threats on my life. If I held a position within the government, and such information were brought to my attention, I'd want to look into it."

Thomas glanced at the card as if he'd noticed a smear on the polished mahogany surface. "Oh, indeed we would," Thomas said.

"You have a sudden rush of memory about this Sams guy, give me a call," Driscoll said. "It'd be better for you if I found out that way. Otherwise, it could get embarrassing."

Thomas looked almost amused. "Is that some kind of a threat?"

Driscoll shook his head. "I'd call it more of a promise," he said. And motioned for Russell Straight to follow him out.

thirty-nine

"You pissed *that* guy off pretty good," Russell Straight observed. They were back in Driscoll's Ford now, pulling out of a spot in front of the Federal Building reserved for the U.S. Marshal. Driscoll slipped a printed pass off his dashboard and handed it over to Russell.

"Put that in the glove compartment, will you? Try not to bend it."

Russell examined the pass, then shook his head. He opened the glove compartment and glanced inside. "What else you got in here? Dolphins tickets, maybe?"

"Who cares about the Dolphins, with Marino gone?" Driscoll said. "Just put that thing away."

Russell did as he was told. "So, is that the secret to being a good private eye? Be sure and piss everybody off?"

Driscoll gave him a look. "Guy wasn't going to tell me anything, no matter what, okay?"

"Then why'd we go there?"

"Because *that* is the secret to being a good private eye, Russell. You make every call, you knock on every door. You never know when you're going to get lucky."

Russell thought about it. "Sort of like hitting on women, then."

Driscoll sighed. "I suppose so."

"But you'd have to have the right kind of personality."

"Is that supposed to mean something?"

"I'm just saying," Russell replied.

"The guy's on notice, and I'm on tape," Driscoll said. "If he wants to, he can let somebody else down the food chain know it's okay to let it slip to Driscoll what he wants to know. All sorts of things can happen."

Russell nodded uncertainly, then turned to stare out the window as they passed through the downtown shopping district. The sidewalks were starting to crowd with a motley assortment of pedestrians. Office workers in their power suits, roly-poly *señoras* with their netted shopping *bolsas,* Nordic-looking tourists in shorts and T-shirts and leather sandals. Most of the signs in the shop windows were printed in languages other than English, and not all Spanish either. Chinese, French, German, even a couple Driscoll couldn't be sure of. It was like being in Casablanca, he thought, with a few professional sports franchises thrown in.

He saw the sign for the bank looming up ahead and glanced behind him, cutting the Ford in front of a delivery van. No blast of horns, no gunshots in their wake. Maybe Miami *was* mellowing out, Driscoll nodded.

He eased into the entrance of the adjoining parking garage, cranked down his window to take the ticket that scrolled from the entrance stanchion with a buzz. Russell Straight gave Driscoll a look as he tucked the ticket into his shirt pocket.

"Don't you have some kind of a freebie for this place, too?"

Driscoll raised an eyebrow as he swung into a space marked "Bank." "Yeah," he said, pointing at the sign. "They call it validation. Something they came up with just for private detectives."

"You *are* a funny dude," Straight said, and followed him out of the car.

"I'm afraid Ms. Acevedo isn't in today," the receptionist told them. "She's attending a training session in Orlando."

What could they train you for in Orlando, Driscoll wanted to ask, outside of how to wear your Mickey and Minnie ears? But he kept the question to himself.

"What about the old guy?" Russell asked. "The one who worked here since forever?"

The young receptionist cut her glance at Russell. Maroon silk blouse and a gray wool skirt that offered a plentiful view of her slender legs. Glistening black hair and a look that wouldn't be out of place on the cover of a magazine that discussed a dozen ways to enjoy sex without dinging your nails.

A flaming YUCA, Driscoll thought—a young upwardly mobile *cubana*—being hassled in her place of business by a black guy she didn't know, didn't owe a thing. He was waiting for her to cut him dead, maybe even go for the letter opener on her desk or a can of mace in her purse, when she did something that astonished him.

She smiled. She'd run her gaze over Russell's physique and honey-colored features, and had actually smiled.

"You must mean Mr. Nieman," she said, her gaze holding Russell's.

Driscoll did a double take, wondering if she'd mistaken Russell for a *compadre,* but he knew it wasn't possible. A moment of harmony between a Cuban and a black in Miami? Things were changing indeed.

"He was old." Russell shrugged. "Kind of stooped-over."

"He's such a sweet man," the receptionist said, nodding. Her gaze seemed to question whether Russell Straight might be sweet himself.

"Could we talk to this Nieman?" Driscoll cut in.

She turned, her businesslike demeanor regathering itself. "I'm afraid Mr. Nieman's not in today, either."

"He went to bank school, too?" Russell asked.

She turned. "Of course not. He's not really involved in the day-to-day of the bank any longer. It's a shame. He really loves it here. Even though they don't give him much to do, he hasn't missed a day of work since I started."

Russell nodded. "Maybe you could give us his phone number, then," he said. "We just wanted to ask him a couple of questions."

"I'm sorry," she said, and the tone of her voice suggested she *was* sorry. "I can't give out that information."

Russell nodded sympathetically. "Suppose *you* were to give him a call, see if he'd be willing to talk to us."

Driscoll glanced at Russell, who ignored him. *A man doing his own thing,* Driscoll thought. *And not so badly, either.*

"I guess that would be all right," the receptionist said. She swiveled her computer monitor to make sure they couldn't see the display, then punched some buttons on her keyboard. She scanned the readout, found what she was looking for, then picked up the phone and dialed, her eyes still on Russell.

"I'm sorry," she said, after a moment. She gave Russell a look that seemed more pouty than dismayed. "He's not answering."

She placed the phone back in its cradle. "If you want to leave your number, I'll have Mr. Nieman call you. And Ms. Acevedo, if you want—"

"Sure," Driscoll said, handing over one of his cards.

She scanned it quickly, then looked up at Russell. "And you are . . . ?"

"My name's Russell. Russell Straight." He nodded at Driscoll. "I'm his partner."

Driscoll opened his mouth to say something, but decided to let it go. "Do you have a card?"

"Not with me," Russell Straight said.

"I want to thank you for your help, Ms. . . . ?" Driscoll said.

"Ruiz," she said. She turned to Russell. "Carolina Ruiz." She was extending a business card between two of her perfectly manicured fingers.

Russell glanced at Driscoll then took the card with a nod. He seemed to be fighting a smile all the way out to the bank's lobby.

"You forgot to get your parking ticket stamped," he said to Driscoll.

"I'll spring for it," Driscoll said, not bothering to look at him.

"I suppose if I'd pissed her off, she'd have given me the guy's number right away?" Russell said mildly. He held open one of the swinging doors that led out to the entryway where the building's elevators were stationed.

Driscoll didn't say anything. He waited for an elderly woman with a cat under her arm to come through the open door, then made a beeline toward a bank of phones in the outer lobby.

He dropped some coins, punched in a number, and stood waiting, ignoring Russell's quizzical expression. "Osvaldo?" he said, when the connection was made. "Yeah, it's Vernon. Uh-huh. Well, you need better lighting in that parking lot, that's one thing. Right. I'll tell you about it later. Meantime, how about you run this number on the reverse directory?"

He recited the ten digits, then tucked the phone under his chin and dug a pad and pen out of his coat pocket. He leaned back against the marble-clad wall as he waited, staring in a noncommittal way at Russell.

After a moment, Osvaldo's voice was buzzing in the receiver again, and Driscoll turned to write down something on his pad.

"Sure," he said, as he finished up. "Go ahead and run the name, see what you can turn up. I'll get back in a while." Then he hung up.

He glanced at the notes he'd made, then looked up at Russell. "Klaus Nieman? Seventeen twenty-nine South Bayside Avenue? That sound right to you?"

"We didn't get into first names," Russell said. "How'd you get the phone number, anyway?" Then his expression shifted as it dawned on him. "You watched her dial, didn't you? Damn!"

Driscoll gave him a look he'd used on a number of his dimmer suspects during his days on the squad. "Rocket science, Russell. This business is nothing less."

Russell nodded, hurrying after Driscoll, who had already turned toward the parking garage. "Don't you want to call him yourself?"

"Didn't you hear the lady inside?" Driscoll called over his shoulder. "The man's not answering. We're just going to drop by, make sure everything's all right."

forty

IT WAS SHORTLY AFTER nine when Deal heard the whine of the dinghy motor approaching the anchored Cigarette. The fog had burned away somewhat, enough to turn the atmosphere around them from lead to a milky shroud, but Deal still couldn't see more than twenty yards into the stuff.

Some time before, Rhodes had gone below with an offhanded wave, a cellular phone tucked at his chin. There'd been a series of muffled conversations, that much he could make out, but Deal hadn't been able to distinguish any specifics beyond a random yes or no.

Basil, meanwhile, had kept his station near the controls, his arms folded, his gaze hooded but steady. *Patient as a gangster Buddha,* Deal thought. Kaia Jesperson had remained on the deck as well. She was sitting in a padded seat that ran across the transom, her legs drawn up under her, staring quietly, intently, out into the swirling mists as if she might be reading runes there. If she noted the distant whine of the dinghy's motor, she gave no sign of it.

As a matter of fact, Deal thought, maybe he'd been wrong. The sound of the motor seemed to have died away now, replaced by an unearthly quiet: nothing out there moving apparently, not a thing going on. Pale air and milky sea joined into one indistinguishable prospect, as if time had stopped and the earth were gearing up for another go even as he watched.

And that's how *he* felt, he realized. As if he were reconstituting himself on the very edge of an unknown continent, trying to find the right jumping-off point for an unknown life ahead. Given all the things Rhodes—or Halliday—had told him, why should he feel otherwise?

In one way, he supposed, he was in the very position that Talbot Sams had urged or wished upon him just a few days ago: get next to this target of a federal manhunt, deliver proof that Michael Halliday, notorious felon and fugitive from justice, was still alive. And though their discussion had not reached that point, he'd been surely meant to assist in the apprehension of the man.

Sams could hardly have anticipated how well it would work out, Deal thought, casting his gaze at Basil's glowering presence. Developments so convenient, in fact, that they made any present thoughts of cooperation seem largely theoretical, even if Deal were so inclined. In one respect, he had turned up precisely where he was supposed to be.

But beyond his own resentment at Sams and his methods, there was the matter of why the government agent had not shared everything he knew about Rhodes/Halliday at the outset. Could it be possible that Sams was unaware of the connection between Barton Deal and Lucky Rhodes? It seemed unlikely, but then again, all that had gone between the two men had taken place so many years ago—even Deal himself had lived a lifetime unaware.

Yet if Sams *were* aware of it, why keep quiet? Did he worry that some strange genetic predisposition existed that would make Deal automatically sympathetic to any member of the Rhodes criminal clan? Did he think that Deal might, in fact, recognize Richard Rhodes as some long-lost prodigal?

If Sams had read his Bible stories properly, Deal thought, there was nothing to worry about on that score. The brother who stayed home, who played the game by the rules, felt no compelling need to take up the cause of his wayward counterpart. Things just didn't work that way. Or maybe Talbot Sams had skipped Sunday school.

No, there was simply no way that Sams could have anticipated what Richard Rhodes would have to tell him, Deal had concluded. Nor that Deal, instead of delivering Rhodes up to justice, would be on the verge of leading him to a fabled pot of gold.

And yet if it was there, that is exactly what he intended to do. Whatever the truth was, he would hand over the money to Rhodes, break the last link to the lowlives and suspect action that his father had ever forged. As far as the issue of crime and punishment went, that was Talbot Sams's job, not John Deal's. *Let Rhodes run, let Sams chase,* Deal thought, none of this was his concern, though gazing at Kaia Jesperson certainly had its appeal.

She turned then, as if she were well aware of Deal's gaze, giving him something of a smile. "I was just thinking about the lotus-eaters," she said. "That it might have been a lot like this on their little island."

"They had Cigarette boats and guns?"

"Surrounded by this fog," she said, undeterred. "The sense of being anywhere and nowhere at once. The incredible feel of this air . . ." She trailed off.

Deal thought about it briefly. He was used to such balminess, this time of year anyway, the temperature often holding at that perfect balance point where bracing gave way to comfort. Is that what it was, he wondered, the thing that had brought everyone stampeding into Florida never to go home again—the hustlers and the pioneers, the pirates and the aging and the refugees and all the just-plain-folks? The lotus-eaters' temperature, stay here with us forever?

"I read the story in college," he said to her at last, "so maybe my memory's fading. I still don't remember the part about hanging out with conmen and their bodyguards."

She lifted her eyebrows. "That seems harsh, after all you've heard."

He shrugged. "Why should I believe it?"

She fixed him with her expressionless stare. "Who could make up such stories?"

"That's probably what all those people Rhodes fleeced were saying to themselves. 'He seemed like such a nice young man' and all that."

"Perhaps he is."

Deal shook his head, thinking about appearances. Looking at Kaia, for instance, someone might find *her* the picture of innocence. "How'd you come to be part of all this?" he asked her.

She gave him a speculative look, then seemed to make a decision. "I met Richard in Turkey," she said, glancing at Basil. If the big man was interested in the conversation, he didn't show it. His chin had lowered to his chest, and his eyes had closed. It was the sort of pose that invited some foolish move, Deal thought. He was this close to solid land. He could bide his time.

"There was a man who owed me money," she continued, "but he wasn't willing to pay. Richard was kind enough to offer me passage back to the States."

Deal nodded. "And now you're finally here."

"So it would seem," she said.

He glanced in the direction of shore. "Is this where you get off, then?"

She shrugged. "Richard's in love," she said, as if she were discussing a medical condition.

"How about you?" he asked.

She gave him a thoughtful look. "That's a rather personal question."

He shrugged. "I'm just making conversation."

"You don't seem the type."

He thought about it. "You're right," he said. "I'm not."

"But you *are* interested."

He stared at her. "You're an interesting person." It was true, he thought. He'd met his share of attractive women, had found himself attracted, in turn, in passing at least. Especially since all the trouble had arisen between himself and Janice. It was normal, he'd always assured himself. But it had been a long time since he'd felt an unaccountable tug like this. And it was more than her physical attributes, though those were not to be discounted. Something about that juxtaposition of apparent innocence with an underlying wisdom, goodness side by side with evil. Who wouldn't be intrigued? he wondered.

"I think I've never been in love, actually," she said.

He gave her a skeptical look. The sound of the dinghy motor was back, much closer this time. Perhaps the boat had been in a cove, the engine noise screened by the ever-present mangroves.

Kaia ran a hand through her thick hair, gave it a toss. She glanced in the direction of the sound. "Perhaps there was the illusion of it once or twice, when I was a schoolgirl," she said.

"That seems like a waste," he heard himself say.

"I haven't wasted anything," she said, pursing her perfect lips. "But *in love,* that's a different matter."

Deal nodded. The door to the cabin opened then and Rhodes appeared, his cell phone tucked away. He glanced at Deal then at Kaia. If he'd heard anything of their conversation, his expression didn't reflect it.

Basil was back to full-alert, his eyes dutifully on his boss. "That's Frank?" Rhodes asked, nodding in the direction of the approaching motor.

"It better be," said Basil.

"We're on our way, then," he said

He turned to Deal. "Let me make something perfectly clear, Mr. Deal. You are free to go. Say the word, I'll have you set on shore, you can proceed as you wish."

Deal stared back. "You don't think I'd go straight to the police?"

Rhodes shrugged. "And tell them you've been consorting with a dead man?"

Deal thought that one over. Another shadowy figure inviting him to cry wolf. First Sams, now Rhodes.

The damnable part was its truth. Ordinary cops would probably react just as Rhodes assumed they would. What proof did he have of Rhodes/ Halliday's existence? A bump on the head? If anything, that might argue the other way. As for Talbot Sams, *he* might find the news intriguing, but Deal had already thought that one through. There would be no helping Talbot Sams. Given the choice between Sams and Rhodes, there was simply no contest.

"What's to keep me from going after the money myself?"

Rhodes shook his head. "That's one thing I'm *not* worried about."

"If I'm as straight as you seem to think I am, maybe I'd just hand it over to the cops."

Rhodes considered it, then met Deal's gaze full on. "It's a matter of honor, Mr. Deal. I've been straightforward with you—"

"This once in your life?"

Rhodes paused. "My father was a gambler, but he wasn't a cheat." Rhodes stared at him defiantly. "I carried on his practice . . . and his methods as well. My clients demanded certain things from me, then complained when they suffered reversals. It's the modern way. No one feels they deserve a setback. There's no such thing as bad luck. There's no ill in a privileged life that can't be cured with an orchestrated wave of accusations, followed by a stiff lawsuit."

Which may have accounted for the zeal of the Gullickson Prep crowd, Deal thought, but not for that of Talbot Sams. Sams, the representative of law and order. The public servant, bent on chiseling another notch in his moral gun, so intent on serving justice, he'd commit any moral outrage to get the job done.

What a position to find himself in, Deal thought, glancing off into the mists. He could see the vague shadow of the approaching dinghy now, and considered again the option that Rhodes had presented him with. Step into the little boat, have himself ferried by Frank back to shore, go on his merry way. Call Janice, reassure her he was all right, worry about everything else later.

He wondered briefly what his own father would have done in the situation, but he didn't ponder long. Unlike Rhodes, he had no such source of moral authority, ambiguous as it might seem to others, upon which to lean. If Rhodes was to be believed, his father had been an honorable man. He might have been murdered by criminals, but in Rhodes's mind, at least, he was always there to point the way, to posit what was right from wrong.

And Deal might have had the same. He'd heard all the legendary stories about Barton Deal, had seen the man in action close up. And there had been a time when there was nothing more important than to carry on—in whatever pale fashion of his own—his father's awesome legacy.

But the suicide had changed all that. Proven the rumors and the whispers and the accusations true. Even if he hadn't done all the things that business partners and rivals and bank examiners had alleged, he hadn't stayed around to fight. And while Deal could never forgive Talbot Sams for his part—placing Barton Deal in the middle, in the position where no man, no saint could have resisted the temptations placed before him— still, it had been his father's decision to make.

And it was not that Deal lacked compassion. His heart ached when he thought how lonely, how bereft of hope, his father must have been when he pulled that trigger. But one thing was certain: that action had taken away his father forever, at least in the way he would have welcomed his memory now.

What would you have done, old man? That was the eternal question. One to which there would never be an answer.

"Are you all right?"

It was Kaia Jesperson's voice, bringing Deal back. He blinked as if surprised to find himself standing on the deck of a mist-shrouded boat in a cove on the ragged South Florida coast. Her expression was concerned, and he wondered for a moment how long he'd been silent. But Rhodes stared back at him without alarm, as if he knew something of the enormity and number of the thoughts that had been streaming through his mind.

The dinghy emerged from the fog. Frank used a boat hook to draw the smaller craft near. Deal felt the tug and the shudder of water beneath his feet, felt the nudge as the two boats met.

"So what do you think, Mr. Deal?" Richard Rhodes asked.

Deal looked at him. "I want to give you your money back," he said. A decision. One he'd made all by himself, no ghost of Barton Deal hovering over his shoulder. He knew there was no other way.

forty-one

"YOU SURE THIS IS the right place?" Russell Straight asked, as Driscoll pulled the big boat of a Ford up to the curb.

"You're looking at the numbers, aren't you?" Driscoll said.

Russell checked the slip that Driscoll had handed him, then again at the listing gate stone that bore the address. He nodded, but Driscoll was already getting out.

There were a matching pair of gate stones, actually, pillars constructed of white-painted brick and set across from each other at the mouth of a grown-over limestone drive that led back from the street, a broad boulevard where the overhang of the massive banyans and ficus turned the already overcast day into near-dusk.

It had been a grand neighborhood once, that much was clear, an area of broad, deep lots, many with spacious back lawns that ran down to the bay. The area lay only a mile or so south of the business center, and many movers and shakers of earlier eras had been able to step out of their downtown offices and find themselves in Shangri-la before they'd got their ties undone.

And there were still impressive homes scattered about, some two-story colonials with massive columns lining their façades, others carrying a Mediterranean stamp: barrel-tiled roofs of many gables, broad, high-arched windows with wavering panes, rough plaster finish tendriled with ivy and other unidentifiable vines. Like many homes in the neighborhood, however—checkered here and there by high-rises and chain-linked lots where other condos were on their way—the glory days of this place lay well in the past.

Its once-red clay roof tiles—the sort that had been molded over the thighs of Cuban craftsmen—were blackened now with mildew, and tree shoots had taken root in the gutters. Some tiles had slipped away altogether, and Driscoll could easily imagine a pastiche of water stains on every upper-floor ceiling.

Weeds sprouted in the drive, and burrowing tree roots had sent the gate stones leaning crazily away from each other. The yard needed cutting, the trees pruning, the crumbling plaster façade a re-do, along with a coat of paint. As for the infrastructure, he didn't even want to think about it: plumbing, electrical, structural . . . it would give Johnny Deal and all the artisans he could round up a couple of years of headaches to put this humpty back together again.

Driscoll wondered briefly about Klaus Nieman, the man they were going to see, thought about what the vibrant young receptionist back at the bank had said. Once Nieman had been a mover and shaker, too. Now his useful days were long gone. Just a pleasant creaking codger, moldering away inside his moldering house, one faltering fingerhold left on the planet.

Old man, old house, Driscoll thought with a sigh. He pursed his lips. A position he was headed toward himself, and not so far along, now, was it? Maybe Neiman had already croaked, in fact, lying in his bed behind the blank eye of one of those upper-story windows there, like Miss Emily in that Faulkner story he'd never gotten out of his mind: *So long, comrades, the hell with the whole frigging mess.*

"This don't look a whole lot different from Georgia, right here," Russell was saying as he gazed about.

Driscoll roused himself from his reverie. "I'll take your word for it," he replied, then led the way to the house.

Surprisingly enough, the doorbell worked, its deep four-noted chime echoing mightily behind a solid-looking teak entry door. Driscoll waited for the echoes to die away, then rang again.

"Maybe he went to the doctor," Russell said.

Driscoll nodded. "Or maybe he took the day off to go deep-sea diving.

Why don't you go peek in the garage, see if there's a car, or a horse and buggy still inside."

Russell glanced at him, evidently not sure how much he liked taking orders. Driscoll was about to go have a look for himself when he heard the unmistakable sounds of footsteps from inside the house. "Never mind," he said to Russell. "We're in luck."

Driscoll heard a faint rasping sound as the cover on the other side of the door's peephole was moved aside. You couldn't be too careful in Miami, Driscoll nodded. He and Russell could be crackheads, after all, home invaders, Cuban commandos ready to strike at the doorstep. After a moment came the clacking of deadbolts sliding open—first one, then two.

He was fishing in the breast pocket of his coat for one of his business cards when the door finally swung inward, loosing a wave of housebound air that suggested they were the first guests since Prohibition. It swept over them like a living presence: hints of mold and mildew, musty drapes, rugs that hadn't been vacuumed since Eisenhower, cabbage cooked in another decade, a cat box in every room. Driscoll, his eyes stinging with the blast, held his mouth open, ready to introduce himself and his assistant-for-the-day, when he stopped short.

"Some luck," he heard Russell Straight muttering at his ear.

"Gentlemen," came the voice from the doorway before them. "What a pleasant surprise. Come right inside."

Driscoll hadn't gotten a good look at the man the first time he'd met him, for it had been dark and there had been quite a few things on his mind. But the voice, he'd never forget. That same false unctuousness, a tone so phony it would have Dale Carnegie throwing up on his shoes.

Driscoll, of course, no longer wanted to go inside this house. In fact, he wanted to forget everything about Klaus Nieman and Russell's chance mention of a visit to the bank with Deal.

He wanted to go back to a not-so-long-ago moment in time, sitting in the sunshine at the nice little Grove restaurant with the birds chirping and the smell of the sea in the air and him gazing at the cute winking behind of a waitress so young she couldn't pronounce the date of his birth.

If he couldn't go back that far, then how about another path not taken: He could have gone directly from the office of the Chief Dickhead in

Charge of Justice to one of his sources at DEA or Customs and stayed right on the trail of Talbot Sams.

But he hadn't, had he? Instead, he'd followed his instincts, which—he'd have to admit—were not so shabby when it came right down to it. After all, he thought, he'd found his man. The proof was right before his watering eyes.

"Do come in," Talbot Sams repeated, as if he were welcoming them aboard the pleasure barge of the doges.

And because Sams had a pistol trained upon the both of them, that is exactly what they did.

forty-two

"THIS IS WHERE YOU grew up?" Kaia Jesperson said, her gaze steady toward the house as Basil brought the Cigarette slowly across the shallows toward the dock. The fog had lifted finally, but the day was still deeply overcast, the air still, as if the world had not quite made up its mind where to go.

Deal felt himself nod an answer to Kaia. He wasn't quite sure he could speak. The feelings that had gripped him the moment he caught sight of the house from out on the bay still held him fast—it seemed as if a chunk of two-by-four had lodged somewhere in his throat.

The trees on the grounds were bigger and far more ragged, the place itself somehow smaller, but the vista he'd beheld so often had somehow superimposed itself on reality: He was a boy again, putting about these very flats in the dinghy his old man had given him the day he'd turned eight, and he had just glanced up across the sun-spangled water to wonder if it might be time for lunch, the suspicion that his mother might be up on that broad lawn calling—that mental vista was somehow unchanged.

And he'd been right not to come back these many years, he thought, fighting off the pangs that welled inside him. Look what could happen. He'd been properly heedful of this curse.

"We're about to run out of water," Frank called back toward his brother. The more lithe of the two, he'd been sent out to the prow of the boat, where he crouched like some living hood ornament, peering down to check the channel's steadily diminishing depth.

"When's the last time a boat docked here, do you suppose?" Rhodes had turned to gaze at Deal as well.

Deal shook his head again. "A long time," he said at last.

"You're sure that it's occupied?" Rhodes asked, doubtful. They were close enough now to see the flapping shreds of an awning that had once shielded a broad rear patio.

Fine green canvas it had been once, Deal thought. The very best. Anything less would have been unthinkable for Casa Deal.

Deal shrugged. "The property manager says so. As long as the taxes are paid, the insurance kept current, I try to stay out of it."

Kaia glanced at him. "You haven't been back since your father's death?"

He turned to her. "Once," he said. "The day my mother died of a heart attack."

Kaia's eyes narrowed, and her lips parted as if she might be about to say something, but no words came.

Go ahead, Deal wanted to say, *go ahead and ask. Why haven't you sold it? What the hell are you doing, keeping your hooks into this crumbling shrine to misery? A place you can't even go to. A place you can't let go.*

Of course there was no sane answer. But he would have understood if she had wanted to ask.

"We're churning mud," Basil said. He had his hands on the wheel, was staring over his shoulder toward the rear of the boat. A bright plume of silt trailed in the shallows behind them.

"Can you get us in?" Rhodes asked, nodding toward the nearby dock.

Basil shrugged and glanced into the shallows. "If not, you can just about walk from here."

The big man turned then and called out to Frank, still poised in his wary sprinter's stance, "Careful you don't fall off." Basil turned the nose to port. The stern of the craft swung around behind them then, steadying as Basil worked the wheel. They were pointed back out to sea now, the engines cut, drifting silently in perfect parallel toward the dock.

Frank reached to catch one of the listing pilings, and Deal heard a groan as the line went tight. He stepped as if by instinct onto the weathered dock, an aft line in his hand. There were still a few cleats screwed to the curled planks, but he wasn't going to trust them. He tied the line he held to another of the twisted pilings, then turned to offer Kaia a hand up as Rhodes and Basil gathered their things. "Watch your step," he cautioned her.

She came up easily, passing close to him, and he caught that hint of jasmine and lemon as she stood near him in the still, thick air. He felt her eyes on him, that same stare, as if she were wondering just how long he might bear up.

And that is when it struck him, an insight that held him motionless for a moment. She might know *him*, but she herself was unknowable. The impossible, unknowable woman. It was the essence of her appeal. You might encounter her, but you would never *have* her. Just like Daisy and the poor sap who chased hopelessly after her.

Deal had read the novel exactly once—a long-ago English class plunk in the middle of the Gainesville piney woods, most of his classmates asleep or stupefied by football—but he had never gotten it out of his mind. He thought of that electric scene—Gatsby pulling out drawer after drawer of expensive shirts, flinging them through the close air of his bedroom like a knight shaking out his colors, crazed to prove himself to this woman—and he was sure now that Rhodes had done something of the same. Kaia stood only inches away, after all, and Deal sensed everything it was her mission in life to send.

He wanted to go to Rhodes, take him by the shoulders, explain how impossible was his task. Deal himself had fallen in love, lived out his version of the story with essentially the same woman. He'd taken it for a college boy's crush, so many years ago. But here he was still, after a lifetime, trying to have his Janice, his prospects about the same.

Armed with such knowledge, he might have said something grand to Rhodes or Kaia, he supposed; but even if he'd found the right words, what good would it have done? You might try and write the story, he thought, but most of the time the story writes you. He sighed inwardly and turned to Kaia.

"Pick a line of nails," he said to her, and she stared back as if he'd lost his mind.

He was pointing down at the planks between their feet. The dock had been laid with eight-foot boards. Every sixteen inches was a line of nail heads where the planks were fixed to the underlying joists. The nail heads rose slightly from the weathered wood, running off like like-minded ant trails toward the shore. "Walk right along any one of them."

She stared at him, still shaking her head. "Why?"

"Because it's strongest there," he said.

She nodded finally, and turned to do as she was told. He watched her walk: *And who wouldn't,* he thought. But if anyone thought he'd gained the slightest advantage over her, then woe it would be to him.

Basil and Rhodes had stepped up from the boat by then, and soon they all were trooping along nail-lines toward the shore.

"Nobody's answering," Frank said, shaking his head as he came back from the front of the house. Basil had already rattled each of the French doors that ran along the back of the place, to no avail.

"I'll guess *that* is the cellar entrance," Rhodes said after a moment, pointing at something off the side of the patio.

Deal followed his gesture and nodded. The big wooden hatchway Rhodes pointed to was set in a shallow alcove, angling down from the rear of the house like the entrance to the storm cellar in Dorothy's Kansas home. It was a sight you might expect in the Midwest, all right, but an odd sight down here indeed.

Deal motioned for Rhodes to wait, then took the coral path that led to the doors and reached to test the latch. He was only mildly surprised when he found the main door groaning up at his touch. All things were beginning to seem destined to him now.

Dank air rose from the carved pit below. On the second carved step down, a toad the size of a salad plate sat blinking, stunned by the sudden light. Deal had never liked the cellar, and the toad was a reminder why. What was an unaccountable source of pride for his father—"Hell, there's not half a dozen of these in all Miami, son"—was an equally distasteful place for Deal. He gravitated to the outdoors, the light, the water, the air—the sense of freedom it all gave. What would a basement do, besides give you a case of the creeps?

He reached to swing the companion door up, and the toad was past him in a three-foot leap. *A bufo,* he thought. Another unwelcome guest come to South Florida only to thrive, and nobody get any funny ideas: There were poisonous sacs on the back of the things, enough there to kill an unwary house pet, toxic enough to have a person stupid enough to pick one up happy to settle for warts instead.

"Goddamn," Basil said, watching the thing bound off into the overgrown shrubbery.

"There's a frog and then some," his brother said.

The skies had turned to an evil gray now, and Deal felt a raindrop splatter icily on the back of his neck. He glanced at Kaia and Rhodes, then moved on down the steps. Grit-laden and mossy, streaked with mineral deposits, they seemed as though they hadn't been traveled in a century. There was another entrance, off the kitchen pantry, but Deal had always avoided that as well. Over his father's objections, they'd gone to the Biltmore Hotel to ride out any hurricane threats, his mother as adamant about the matter as he.

He tried the knob of the door at the bottom. He felt the latch give, then pushed. The door opened a few inches, then hung up the moment it fell free of its crooked frame. Chilling raindrops were whacking down around them now, and a breeze had picked up off the water.

"I'll get it," Basil said, elbowing impatiently past him. He leaned his burly shoulder into the frame and shoved. There was a grinding noise and the door gave another foot before it lodged again. It was raining full-out now, and the others were crowding down the steps toward shelter.

"See if there's a switch," Rhodes called to Basil as the big man pushed his way inside, fumbling with the flashlight he had clipped to his belt.

But there *was* a light already on in there, Deal realized as he stumbled inside on Basil's heels: an odd blue sliver of flame, floating like a huge, disembodied pilot light in the cellar darkness ahead. Deal heard the loud hissing sound, caught the smell of gas, and sensed something terribly wrong.

He had turned to shout a warning to the others: "Go back—"

But the rain outside had turned to a roar, and no one was paying attention. Frank's frame had already crashed into him, and he saw the silhouettes of Rhodes and Kaia as they hurried through the opening just behind.

Basil's light snapped on for a moment, illuminating a patch of grimy concrete flooring. Deal saw a pair of legs splayed out on the floor, legs clad in a pair of dated double-knit trousers—only one person he knew wore such things—and an equally familiar pair of black brogans with the toes pointed up at the ceiling.

He heard a heavy thud, like the sound of a melon being slammed to the ground, heard Basil groan, and saw the flashlight beam tumbling free.

"What the fuck—?" Frank said, charging on even as Deal ran backward, trying to push Kaia and Rhodes toward safety.

There was another gut-wrenching thud and the sound of a second body falling . . . then a grinding noise as the cellar door slammed shut. Deal felt a moment of panic, all the bad scenes from all the lousy movies running through his head at once:

"Don't go down in the cellar," the audience cries as one, and still the dumb-asses do it. That's what he was thinking as he groped in the darkness for Kaia and Rhodes, and that's when the lights came on.

forty-three

"GOD LOVES A PARTY," Talbot Sams said, smiling out over his pistol at them.

The bare bulb that dangled from the ceiling still jittered on its cord, sending shadows flittering about the room even though no one moved a muscle. Basil lay on his stomach, his head twisted to the side, his jaw opened at an odd angle. There was a thin trickle of blood inching out from the spot where his forehead met the concrete. His upturned eye stared blankly at the cobwebbed floor joists above.

Frank lay not far from his brother, face down, the back of his skull oddly flattened. His arms stretched back at his sides, his fingers twitching like worms writhing up toward light. Tasker stood above him, an aluminum baseball bat in one hand. He nudged Frank's shoulder with the toe of his shoe. There was a shuddering gasp, and Frank's shoulders drew up for an awful moment, then collapsed. After that, even his fingers were quiet.

What had happened to the Wheatleys wasn't the worst part of the scene before them, though. Deal realized now that the blue flame he'd seen belonged to a still-hissing acetylene torch, its tip hanging down from a wheeled cart not far from where Sams stood. He also saw that the trousers and brogans he'd had a glimpse of did in fact belong to Vernon Driscoll: His friend sat on the floor a few feet away, unmoving, his legs splayed out in front of him, his arms tied behind a rusting steel floor support. There was a purple knot on his cheek and his head lolled quietly to one side. Only the fact that they'd bothered to gag him with a strip of duct tape across his mouth gave Deal hope that he was still alive.

In the far corner of the basement, Russell Straight lay on his side, trussed with duct tape like a silvered mummy, his hands and heels joined behind him in a knot of tape. He had been gagged as well, yet he was still conscious. Deal could make out the frantic blinking of his eyes, as if Russell might be trying to send some coded message out his way.

Tasker noticed Deal's gaze. "There's two strikes right here," he said, waving his bat vaguely at the fallen Wheatley brothers. "Maybe you'd like to be number three."

"Be quiet, Tasker," Sams said mildly. "Turn around, the three of you, lean forward, hands up against the wall. Feet back and spread apart. No foolishness, now, or I'll give Mr. T. his head."

Deal turned, and saw that Kaia and Rhodes had obeyed as well. Kaia's face was set in a mask, her gaze stony. Rhodes, on the other hand, sent Deal a scathing glance.

"If you're responsible for this—" he hissed through his teeth at Deal.

"Are you crazy—" Deal began, then from the corner of his eye caught a glimpse of something moving: It was Tasker striding forward, using both hands to piston the end of the bat, striking Deal just above his kidney. His legs went numb with the force of the blow, and he was on the floor before he realized fully what had happened.

He was gasping for breath, fighting the pain that held him rigid while Tasker's hands roamed his body, searching for weapons. By the time Sams's man was through, feeling was beginning to return to Deal's legs, first a tingling at the tips of his toes, then a fire that flew to every nerve ending. Maybe that meant he would still be able to walk.

He blinked, managing to lift his chin off the grimy floor. Tasker stood behind Kaia now. He kicked her feet further apart, then ran his hand up the insides of her thighs, the front of her shirt, pausing as the mood struck him. Kaia stared at the wall, expressionless, as if she could see through stone. You can *encounter* her, Deal thought, sure. Not even Tasker could get beyond that point.

In a few moments, Tasker had moved on to Rhodes, pausing as he found something in the man's jacket pocket. "Bad boy, Mr. Rhodes," Tasker said, coming out with a pistol in his hand. He leaned close, the tip of the pistol jammed hard against the flesh in front of Rhodes's ear. "I think I'm going to use this," he said. "First on her, and then on you."

"Get away from there, Tasker," Talbot Sams called. "On your feet, Mr. Deal. Your hands on the wall above your head, where I can see them."

Deal managed to make it to his hands and knees, steadying himself for a moment before he rose. As he leaned into the wall, an awful burning awoke in the small of his back. He'd taken such hits in his linebacking days. He could remember how it felt to be pissing blood.

He resisted the urge until it lessened, then looked over his shoulder at Sams. Someone else over there in the dim reaches of the basement, a tall man, an old man, tied to a support post in a standing position. He was upright but motionless, his chin resting on his chest.

"You remember Mr. Nieman, don't you?" Sams said, lifting the man's head by his white shock of hair.

What Deal saw sent his stomach tumbling. The stoop-shouldered bank officer he'd met only yesterday, though it seemed an eternity had passed. Good-natured, out of the loop Nieman. Not a clue about anything.

Where Nieman's pale blue eyes had been were vacant, blackened sockets. Deal gaped at the hissing torch, then back at Sams, who let Neiman's head fall back limply on his chest.

"We'd managed to work up to the location of the safe, Mr. Deal." Sams turned and gestured toward a distant wall of the cellar. The feeble light of the bulb barely reached that corner, but Deal was able to make it out: a section of shelving jammed with paint cans, grimy jars, cast-off kitchen appliances—all the detritus of a household life—had been swung out from the wall, revealing the massive strongbox that rested in a niche behind. The ship's safe that Rhodes had described, Deal realized. He'd known it would be here somewhere. He wondered if he would have ever found it himself.

"We were working on where we might find the key when you arrived," Sams said. "Foolish of Mr. Nieman to resist, really. We'll cut it open if we have to," he added, nodding again at the idling torch. Deal stared at the strongbox again: Where he might have expected a combination dial to be was a silver lockplate and keyhole instead. So much for safety deposit boxes, then.

"Klaus . . . ?" Deal heard Rhodes mutter at his side.

"Stay right there!" Tasker barked.

Deal turned to see that Rhodes had pushed himself away from the wall and was moving toward Nieman's limp form. Tasker took one pivoting step, bringing the end of the bat around in a vicious arc. Rhodes, his gaze still frozen on Nieman, never saw it coming. The blow took him in the stomach, dropping him in an instant. He was writhing at Deal's feet, clutching at his gut, painful strangling sounds rising from his throat.

Deal started away from the wall. "Please," Tasker said, bringing his pistol up. "Do me the favor."

"Back in place, Mr. Deal," came Sams's unctuous voice.

Two pistols trained on him now, Deal registered. Grudgingly he resumed the position.

"They're old chums, you see," Sams explained, glancing down at Rhodes's writhing form. "Klaus Neiman worked for Mr. Rhodes's father in various capacities. He served as a kind of guardian for the boy after his father's demise. Quite loyal, it would seem. Though there's been no contact for many years, not since Rhodes—or Halliday, as he was known—fled the country. Once I discovered who Nieman was, I've kept close watch."

Deal's mind was running snatches of Rhodes's stories helter-skelter, as if a series of movie projectors had snapped on simultaneously: a tall, cadaverous man who'd dealt chemin de fer and wielded a welder's torch himself, who had bandaged his father's wounded shoulder, who'd greeted him and Russell inside the offices of a private bank . . .

Meantime, Rhodes still struggled at Deal's feet. Bleary-eyed and gasping, he lifted his chin off the seeping floor, an expression of loathing directed at Sams.

"You're scum—" he managed before Tasker stepped forward to place his foot on top of Rhodes's head, pressing it back firmly to the concrete.

"Look who's talking," Tasker said.

"Bastards," Kaia Jesperson muttered. The expression on her face chilled even Deal.

"Perhaps the girl can help us with the keys," Sams said, gesturing at the hissing acetylene torch. "Bring her over, won't you, Tasker? We'll let her twist tongues with our pet snake here."

"Fuck you, Sams," Deal said. Let him and Tasker shoot. He was beyond caring. "Here's your goddamned key." He jammed his hand into his pocket, then flung the thing across the room. At the same moment, he saw Rhodes's hand shoot out, the fingers uncoil.

Two glints of silver, two dull clinking sounds, twin chunks of stamped-out metal tumbling across the scarred flooring to rest at the feet of Talbot Sams. Sams smiled at Tasker, who'd stepped back warily, his pistol at the ready.

Sams turned back to Deal. "A surfeit of riches," he said. "Very noble of you both."

"He'll kill us anyway," muttered Kaia Jesperson.

"Of course I will," said Sams. "But it will be far less painful now."

"Who are you, Sams?" Deal said. "You're no agent—"

"Oh, indeed I was," Sams cut in. "How else do you think I'd have come upon this felon's trail?"

"He's a thief," Rhodes said, trying to raise himself to a sitting position. His face was pale. He coughed and his lips were suddenly spattered with blood. "He'd come to make a practice of stealing from the targets of his investigations. When it was discovered, the Department drummed him out."

"Sticks and stones—" Sams shrugged, shooting a glance at Rhodes. "Mr. Pot-Calling-the-Kettle-Black here had more than two hundred million dollars with him when he fled the country. I just missed laying hands on it a couple of times, and I've spent a long time looking for it since."

He glanced down at Rhodes with what might have passed for fondness. "When he was reported dead, I thought the money might be gone for good. But when Ferol Babescu was murdered, it struck me. For that much money, perhaps even the dead had learned to walk again."

Deal shook his head, staring at the distant wall where the safe rested like a dumb and featureless god. Slowly, it had begun to dawn on him.

"You've known about my father and Lucky Rhodes all along—"

Sams turned to him, a look of bemusement on his features. "Of course I knew. It was something I stumbled upon during our original investigation of Halliday. When I finally realized who Halliday's father actually was, I knew where he must have hidden his ill-gotten gains."

Deal stared back, his mind racing. "You think Halliday—" He broke off, glancing down at the man sitting dazedly between them. Rhodes/Halliday wiped at his mouth, then stared in apparent confusion at the blood smeared across the back of his hand.

"—you think Rhodes stashed his money with my father before he fled the country?" Deal continued, shaking his head.

"You're wrong, Sams," Rhodes managed. His voice sounded thick. "That money's gone. Gone forever."

Sams smiled patiently. "Is it, now?" he said. He bent carefully to the concrete floor and picked up the two keys. "Well, we're about to find out."

He glanced at Tasker as he straightened, flashing the pair of keys. "Keep an eye on them, Tasker . . ."

He had turned then, on his way for the waiting safe, when there was a scuffling of footsteps on the stairs leading down from the pantry, and Sams abruptly stopped.

forty-four

"FEDERAL AGENTS!" DEAL HEARD a voice from the shadowy stairwell. "Stay where you are."

Tasker, shielded from the man on the steps by the support posts, raised his hand to fire.

"Look out," Deal cried, but he was too late.

The report of Tasker's pistol echoed deafeningly off the stone walls surrounding them. The agent who'd asked everyone to freeze, a thin man with an acne-scarred face, took Tasker's shot in the shoulder. Though the agent had managed to squeeze off a round of his own, his aim was wide. He'd spun halfway around when Sams fired, the shot taking away the side of the man's face.

There was the sound of another set of footsteps retreating up the stairs, and Tasker hesitated only a moment before he ran in pursuit, ducking into the stairwell, squeezing off a burst. There was a muffled groan and the sound from above of another body falling.

Deal made his own move then, lunging over the groggy Rhodes toward Talbot Sams, who spun about, trying to raise his pistol into position. Deal kicked at Sams's arm, catching him in the fleshy tissue just above the elbow. Sams cried out and his pistol clattered off into the dark reaches of the cellar. The man went over backward with the blow, tumbling hard against the tanks of the portable welding setup.

The hose uncoiled as the tanks went over, lashing at Sams with its blue head of flame. Deal was scrambling after him, trying to get a grip on a leg, an arm . . .

. . . when he felt a searing pain trace across his chest, and smelled what he realized was his own charring flesh. He stumbled back, slapping at the streak of fire that ran across his chest, feeling his feet go out from under him as he stumbled over Rhodes.

Sams was closing in now, the acetylene torch in his hand. He lunged down at Deal with his face twisted in rage, ready to finish the job. Deal tried to turn away, but Sams's knee dropped to his chest, pinning him. Sams spun a control knob and the flame shot out the length of a knife blade, the cool blue tongue transformed to orange. He brought the torch down toward Deal's face, the flame close enough to singe his flesh.

"Let's make you up like Mr. Nieman, shall we?" Sams gloated. He thrust the torch toward Deal's eyes . . .

. . . then suddenly something interposed, turning the hissing flame back upon itself.

Sams swung his gaze up in astonishment. Kaia Jesperson stood there, her bare hand outthrust, blocking the flame from Deal's face . . .

. . . Deal caught his breath, waiting for her scream of pain, the stench and crackle of charring flesh, but inexplicably, there was none of that.

Impossible, but still it had happened, Deal thought. Kaia's expression was neutral, her steady gaze seeming to reach Sams's soul.

Sams had pulled the torch back. His mouth worked oddly, as if he might be trying to form some question, but he never got the chance to ask it. In the next instant, Deal twisted out from under the stunned man's knee and came off the ground, swinging as he had never swung before.

His fist caught Sams's cheek with a force that numbed his arm to the shoulder. The man staggered sideways, the torch sliding from his grasp. Deal followed with another blow that took Sams above the heart and sent him over on his back, where he lay unmoving, his eyes blinking vaguely.

Deal found himself closing in reflexively, thinking he could do it, aim one kick to the side of Sams's lolling skull, cave in that exposed temple, snuff out one scourge of life with perfect justification . . .

. . . when he heard a shot behind him and glanced to see that Russell Straight was on his feet and grappling with Tasker, holding the hench-man's gunhand upward in both of his own. Russell was still wrapped in tape, tatters of the gray stuff flying from his limbs, but he had worked himself free—likely what he'd been trying to signal earlier, it flashed through Deal's mind—*I've got myself loose, just hang on.*

Meantime, the two men staggered about in a parody of a drunken dance, Tasker's gun erupting again, and then a third time. The hammer fell a fourth time, but this on an empty chamber.

Russell released his hold on Tasker's gunhand, and launched a punch that moved so quickly it was a blur. There was a sharp crack at Tasker's jaw, and he groaned, falling backward under a rain of punches that came with mechanical precision from Russell's fists, snapping Tasker's head first one way, then another.

Deal was turning back toward Sams when he caught sight of Kaia. For a moment, the world seemed to stop. She was in a sitting position now, slumped with her back against the rain-leaking wall, a dark stain spread out at her shoulder . . . one of the rounds from Tasker's pistol had struck home, he realized.

"Kaia?" he called, dropping to his knees in front of her. Her eyes flickered, fighting to focus.

She seemed to find him then. "I'm all right," she managed, her voice faint.

His hand went quickly to her wrist, turned her hand over gingerly to inspect her palm. He saw a patch of reddened flesh and a blister the size of a half-dollar, but nothing compared to the damage he expected.

He shook his head. "That torch . . . how . . . ?"

She looked at him with the barest of smiles. "A mistake about the blister," she said woozily. "I do hot coals pretty well. I'm a little out of practice with blowtorches . . ."

"Kaia—?" he began, the questions piling up faster than he could comprehend. And Rhodes's words echoing above it all: *She's quite the trickster, Mr. Deal.*

"Some day I'll explain it to you," she began. She might have said more when her expression changed abruptly. She lifted her hand weakly, pointed over Deal's shoulder. "He's getting away—"

Deal whirled in time to see Talbot Sams staggering across the littered cellar floor and up the pantry stairwell. Deal brushed Kaia's cheek with his hand as he rose in pursuit, spinning toward the stairs, clambering over the bodies of the fallen agents. He came through the pantry in a rush, his arms braced for a blow, but there was no one there, and no one in the wreck of a kitchen, either.

Dishes, he saw, towers of them stacked high in the sink, caked with moldering food, and newspapers piled crazily on the kitchen table. On his way out of the pantry, he leaped over a clutch of fallen brooms and mops—and what had those been used for in the last half-century?—then careened through the dimly lit dining room toward the front of the house.

He tried the entry door next, but found the deadbolt still in place. Sams had not escaped that way, then. He spun around to face the French doors arrayed opposite the great room, offering a spacious view out to the rear. It was still raining outside, the sky darkly overcast, but there was plenty enough light to see.

The doors were still closed, the grounds deserted. The man was somewhere in the house, Deal told himself. Still somewhere in this house.

He cut his glance toward the oak staircase leading to the second story, but it was blank, nothing moving there but dust balls, lolling in the drafty air. Deal turned and began moving across the broad living room, past the yawning fireplace—*"Never buy a house without a fireplace, son . . . especially in the tropics."*

"You're right, old man," Deal answered. Maybe he said it in his mind, maybe he was mumbling aloud as he moved.

For it had come to him with unshakable clarity now, and his mind was elsewhere—ten years elsewhere in fact, all the pieces of the puzzle falling into place even as this chaos unfolded about him. He could see the scene playing out as surely as if it had happened before his eyes:

Michael Halliday fled, two hundred million dollars missing, and Talbot Sams comes calling, come to see Barton Deal one last time. Oh, yes, Deal thought. He knew now what had happened.

Deal glanced through an archway into the closed-in porch they called the Florida room then. His mother had kept her sewing table in there, also an easy chair and a lamp for reading, a few potted cacti in another corner. Nothing in there now, of course, nothing but more stacked and yellowing newspapers and an umbrella stand lying on its side.

Only one more room on the bottom floor, he thought, staring across the living room to the half-opened door of his father's study. And it was fitting that room should be the last to check. Deal hadn't been in it since the night he'd found his father, head flung back over his desk chair—what there was left of a head, anyway.

He eased quietly across the dark and dusty floorboards, replaying the words he'd found in his mother's diary a few weeks after she'd died, words laid carefully in a spidery blue hand:

Doctor G. says the sight could have been worse, that when they close their mouths around the barrel, everything explodes. Johnny was spared that much at least. At least Barton had that much decency, not to suck on his gun.

But decency hadn't had anything to do with it. It hadn't happened that way at all. But what it had cost them all these years to think so.

Deal moved on across the silent floorboards to the archway of the study and paused to stare through the partly opened door. No broad and gleaming desk inside there any longer, of course. No tufted-leather swivel chair. No old man to smile a welcome for his Johnny-boy.

Just a few fanned-out paperbacks on the shelves where leather-bound classics had once been housed, cheek by jowl with his father's humidors, his pipe racks and geegaws, including a stuffed gray fox he'd hit with his car one night, coming drunk out of the parking lot of the Biltmore Hotel, another grand party in his wake. Barton Deal had taken the fox to be stuffed, then kept it as a joke. *That was the kind of a man he was,* Deal thought. *Who the hell else would have done such a thing?*

Deal stepped into the room then, his eyes registering the empty gloominess ahead of him, some other set of senses telling him what was rushing at him from behind. He ducked and rolled, feeling the baseball bat glance off his shoulder as he fell. There was pain, of course, but nothing to compare with what would have come if he hadn't been moving with the blow.

Deal rolled on, came on his feet, then ducked a mighty two-handed roundhouse that Talbot Sams aimed at his head. Instead of retreating, Deal stepped into Sams's charge. He drove his one good fist into the man's stomach, hard enough to lift him off his feet.

Then, as Sams doubled over, Deal drove his elbow down against the man's skull, just above the ear. Sams fell to his knees, and the bat skittered wildly across the floor.

Sams started to scramble for it, but Deal kicked his hands out from under him and the big man's cheek bounced off the bare floor. Sams was on his back now, staring vaguely up at Deal, both of them gasping with exertion.

"It was you, Sams. You did it." Deal felt himself listing dizzily to one side, his shoulder throbbing, his arm dangling like a limb that had gone into endless sleep. "It wasn't suicide. You killed him. You thought he had the money."

Sams stared up at him, gathering his strength, his lips moving soundlessly at first, until the words began to come. "He *did* have it. I just couldn't find it and I couldn't make him tell me. But I did finally, didn't I? It's down there right now. All of it."

He fell back, staring up at the ceiling, moistening his lips with his tongue. His expression suggested he might be talking as much to himself as to Deal. "For the longest time, I thought you'd taken it. But you live like a church mouse. All these years. I knew you didn't have it."

Deal stared down at Sams, shaking his head. Even though he was hearing the words, his mind had difficulty accepting them. "You ruined his life, and then you killed him. For money. For a fucking pile of money—"

For a moment, Deal was lost in his dismay, taken over by the enormity, by the senselessness of it. All these lives. All this waste . . .

It was all the distraction that Sams needed. He ducked toward something strapped at his ankle and rolled over, making a sweeping motion with his hand. Deal staggered back as the blade that had appeared in Sams's hand swept an inch from his midsection.

Sams was up now, still panting, but his eyes had regained their porcine focus. He smiled. "You're out of business, Mr. Deal. And it's about time, I'd say."

He made his rush then, and Deal let him come, twisting away at the last instant. Only a delaying tactic, sure, but what else did he have but time?

He shoved Sams hard as he went by, using the arm that still obeyed. Sams hit the wall with a force that seemed to shake the room. He hesitated, then spun about.

There was an odd expression on his face, a look that suggested he'd forgotten something important. After a moment, his eyes regained their focus, and he glanced down at himself. Deal's eyes followed. Both of them stared now at the bone handle of the knife that protruded from Sams's stomach.

Sams raised his hand to the knife handle, and for a moment, it seemed as if he intended to pull the blade free and come after Deal once more.

Deal took an unsteady sideways step, then bent and grasped the fallen bat in his one good hand. He willed his other hand onto the handle as well. He staggered back, wavering, trying to measure his swing. Talbot Sams's bloated face wavered before him like a pumpkin, like a piñata, like a curve that would hang until the end of time.

Deal drew back, ready to swing. And that is when Sams went down.

For a few moments, Deal stared at the dead man lying at his feet. He wavered ready to collapse himself, wondering what the roaring in his ears might be. Then it came to him. Boat engines, he realized, the throaty roar of a departing Cigarette.

He staggered slowly from the study and across the dark boards of what had once been his family's living room, the legendary gathering place where anyone who'd been anyone had come to tip a glass with Barton Deal. Past the Florida room and fireplace, through dining room and kitchen, pantry door and pantry, and down the gore-slimed stairs.

What he found did not especially surprise him:

Driscoll groaning now behind his duct tape gag, and Russell Straight on his hands and knees, groggy, trying to figure out what might have hit him.

Klaus Neiman still hung limply where he had died, and on the bloody floor between the bodies of Frank and Basil Wheatley lay the good Mr. Tasker, his arms splayed at his sides, one dark puckered dot placed squarely in the middle of his forehead.

The safe door was hanging open, and its contents, whatever they had been, were gone. Gone too were Rhodes and Kaia Jesperson.

Of course, thought Deal, staggering on across the cellar. *As it was surely meant to be.* Russell Straight had made his way to Driscoll now, was working the big ex-cop free of his gag and bonds.

He made his way to the cellar's outdoor entrance and up the short flight of stairs. The sound of the engines was gone, the view of the bay blanked out by the advancing squall.

Deal lifted his face to the pelting rain. *So many people gone, old man. When are you coming back?*

forty-five

IT WAS A BALMY spring night, a perfect night for baseball. The University of Miami, perennial private school power in the city, was hosting its crosstown rival, Florida International, the upstart public institution. Lots of players on both sides whose names ended in *a* or *o* or *z,* Deal noted, scanning the program. Local bragging rights on the line. A big crowd, one side of the stands calling out good-natured insults as the two teams got ready to take the field, the other side chanting back. He'd got the passes unbidden in the mail, from one of the new building-supply wholesale houses that had sprung up to service the burgeoning port project.

And why not accept the tickets? Deal had thought. He'd been working hard. The date fell on one of the nights he had with his daughter, the game was always spirited, the stadium easily reached from Janice's Coconut Grove condo. Why not?

"Is there going to be a fight?" Isabel glanced up, concern on her earnest features as the chants and catcalls grew in volume. *Hurricanes blow! F-I-Who?*

Deal stared at her a moment before he answered, his thoughts kicked back an eon, or so it seemed. *Is there going to be a fight?* Kaia Jesperson standing in the doorway of Rhodes's study, that noncommittal, green-eyed gaze on his.

"No, sweetheart," he told his daughter. "They're just teasing, that's all."

She nodded, but the expression on her face told him she wasn't fully convinced. Deal put his arm around her narrow shoulders and hugged her close. She snuggled in, willing to be convinced in that way.

Deal smiled down at her, but as the Miami pitcher trotted to the mound to begin his warm-up, and the crowd noise grew even louder, he found his thoughts drifting again. Months now since it had happened. No word from Kaia, none from Rhodes. Nor had he expected any.

"How'd you get here, Mr. Deal? Who else was with you?" The harsh questions of Scott Thomas, the Department of Justice official who'd shown up with a squadron of backup in time to accomplish absolutely nothing, except tag the bodies.

He'd come by boat, Deal had explained. With the Wheatley brothers, who'd been killed by Tasker. Tasker himself had been killed by a shot from Talbot Sams's pistol. You might want to call it "friendly fire."

Then where was the boat that had brought them? As to that, Deal had said, he had no idea. He'd heard the engines as the Cigarette departed, but he'd been too busy with Sams to have a look. Perhaps an accomplice of Talbot Sams had seen what was happening and fled. In any case, Deal had no idea what had happened to the Cigarette, and that much of it, at least, was true.

Had he known, Scott Thomas demanded, that Klaus Nieman, a man with long-buried ties to gambling interests in Miami, had been his tenant? Deal had not, and his property agent was quick to explain why Deal hadn't known.

And what had been in that hidden safe? the agent had wanted to know. There had been nothing in the safe, Deal told the man. Take a flying look for yourself.

There'd been some bluster about charges of obstructing justice, even the threat of implicating Deal in the death of Talbot Sams, former Department of Justice investigator. But Sams had long been a target of a manhunt undertaken by his own agency, and despite all the cajoling and the threats, nothing had come of it.

Two crooked former agents had died after killing a bank officer and two competing thugs during the commission of a crime, and Russell Straight—returned to Georgia to work out the terms of a parole violation—and Vernon Driscoll—recovering slowly from the effects of a brutal beating—had backed Deal's story, first to last. Enough bodies on hand for the end of a Shakespeare play, in Vernon Driscoll's words. Case closed, or as good as closed.

Deal caught sight of his old friend then, making his way carefully up the stairwell toward their seats, balancing a cardboard drink-carrier in one hand, an unfamiliar device in the other. "Why is Uncle Vernon using a cane, Daddy?" Isabel asked. "Did he get old?"

Sure, Deal almost said, *everybody does.* As he also thought about sharing with his daughter the ancient riddle: *What creature begins life on four legs, then moves to two, and ends on three?* But he decided against it, savoring the crack of the ball in the catcher's mitt below. It was too promising a night for talk of tragedy.

"He got hurt, Isabel," Deal told her. "But he's a lot better. He'll be getting rid of the cane pretty soon."

Driscoll gave them a weary smile when he collapsed into the chair beside them. "Why didn't you ask for seats on the bottom row," he said.

"They're freebies," Deal told him. "Sorry about the climb."

"It's all right," Driscoll said. He pulled his drink out and passed the holder down. "I'm losing weight this way." He held up his cane and smiled.

"You forgot the popcorn, Uncle Vernon," Isabel cried, as the drink container came her way.

"Doggone it—" Driscoll said, starting up.

"Sit still," Deal said, "one large popcorn, coming up."

He was across the aisle to the steps and downstairs quickly, but not before he heard the umpire's mythic call. He caught sight of the Miami pitcher's first delivery and heard the sharp report of an aluminum bat in response. First pitch, first swing, a clean single to left, and a fresh round of chanting from above as he ducked into the tunnel that led toward the refreshment stands.

He saw someone coming toward him from the opposite direction—a tardy fan rushing to see what the fuss was about, he thought at first. But then he caught sight of the odd profile, the balding dome, the frizzed-out hair at the temples, the bulbous nose and the flapping, oversized shoes.

A clown, he realized, just part of the evening's festivities. Deal was about to hurry past him when a white-gloved hand caught him at the shoulder.

"You win," the clown called in a loony voice. He held up an envelope in his other hand.

"That's okay," Deal said. He'd won his share of bogus "prizes." "Give it to somebody else—"

"Oh, no," the clown said. "You're the one." He reached forward and tucked the envelope in Deal's shirt pocket, then hurried on down the tunnel toward the brightly lit field.

Deal watched the clown disappear into the brightness at the other end, fingering the envelope in his shirt pocket. He'd won a "free" cell phone that would cost him about $10 a minute to use, he suspected. Or maybe a vacation to Disney World if he'd just sit through a couple days' pitch for a time-share sale. He shook his head and hurried on toward the concessions.

While a young woman wearing what he hoped was a temporary U of M tattoo on her cheek went to scoop his popcorn, Deal opened the envelope to have a look. There was a folded notecard inside, heavy cream-colored stock with no identifying markings. He opened the card and found handwriting there, a neat flowing script in what looked to be a feminine hand.

"Sir?"

Deal glanced up from what he'd been reading. The young woman with the tattooed cheek was standing there, a tub of popcorn outthrust. "That's three dollars," she said, nodding over his shoulder where a young couple waited their turn. "I gotta take care of these people."

"I'm sorry," Deal said, handing over some bills in a daze.

He tucked the envelope back into his shirt pocket and took up the popcorn, hurrying back toward the tunnel.

"That's too much," the attendant was calling after him, but Deal had his mind on more important things.

Deal had found no clown anywhere in the stadium, of course, and he knew better than to check with anyone in charge. He'd delivered the popcorn to Isabel and sat with his arm around her, chatting idly with Driscoll, answering his daughter's every question about the arcane rules of baseball until she'd finally fallen asleep and he'd borne her off toward home.

The score was tied at the time, and since they'd come in separate cars, Driscoll decided he would stay to see how things turned out. If he'd noticed Deal's distracted state, he'd been good enough to let it go. They were neighbors, after all. There would be plenty of time to talk.

Deal had delivered Isabel home to Mrs. Suarez's care, then left, with assurances that he'd be back soon. He piloted the Hog down 8th Street to Douglas Road, then south all the way to the Grove. He threaded through the back streets, dodging the late-night traffic as best he could, making his way onto Main Highway and finally to Old Cutler Road.

He'd moved most of his day-to-day operations to a portable he'd leased on the site of the International Free Trade port project, but there would always be the Old Cutler offices, so long as there was a DealCo, anyway. He'd also gotten rid of the management firm that had handled the leasing of his family's home and had applied for the permits to begin restoration. It would take a fortune that he didn't have, he thought, and none of it could bring his old man back, of course, but it was a process he could start on at least.

He swung off Old Cutler, down the secluded lane, the Hog wallowing through the ruts and potholes. Not much rain recently, but when the moon was right, the tides sometimes flooded the road in its lower spots. Something else to be taken care of, he thought. One day when there was time.

He made it to the parking area of the office without incident, the headlights of the Hog sweeping across an empty lot. He'd expected as much, but what was to keep him from hoping against hope?

He parked, killed the Hog's engine, got out, and stood in the cool wash of moonlight, listening. Nothing but the ceaseless tree frogs, the occasional whine of a rare cool-weather mosquito, the ticking of the Hog's manifold under the hood. *Florida*, he thought. *The essence of it, right here.*

He went up the wooden steps, found the door locked, just as he'd left it a week or so before. He used moonlight to find his key, opened the door, flipped the light switch, saw that there was no one behind his desk, no one behind his door, no one for company, in fact, but ghosts.

He stared at the file cabinet in the corner, still dented and listing, its contents long since replaced, as haphazardly as they had ever been. He thought about pulling the card the clown had delivered from his pocket again, thought about checking things just to be sure, but he didn't. He had memorized the words the moment he'd read them.

He walked to the cabinet, put his hand on the drawer that the note had designated, and hesitated once again. There could be a bomb rigged up inside, he supposed—pull the handle, send yourself to kingdom come? He could have told Driscoll about everything, could have brought his friend along.

But something had told him he might follow those instructions safely, and they had stipulated that he come alone. He saw no reason not to obey.

He snapped the drawer's little button switch with his thumb and gave the handle a jerk. The drawer rolled open easily on its guides. No blast of fire. No explosion. Just a soft thunking sound when the mechanism achieved its reach.

Deal stared down at what had been carefully stacked there for him and wondered if this was the moment when Thomas Scott or Scotty Thomas—or whatever the hell his name was—would burst through the door with his shield and gun upraised . . . but that didn't happen, either.

It was only Deal there in the office, with all those upturned images— the faces of long-dead statesmen and presidents—laid out in stacks before him. He stood there, reading and rereading the note in his mind. *The very least we could do,* she had closed, no further elaboration.

He'd noted the scent of jasmine and lemon the moment he'd opened the envelope. He might have reached for his pocket, checked the note again, but he didn't have to. He recalled the scent clearly. As he could visualize the hand that wrote it, the hand that had somehow turned back fire and in that way saved his life.

No need for any assistance, now, John Deal. He stood alone in the office and conjured up the ghosts.